PROMISED SPLENDOR

Against her will Glenna felt her breasts swell at his touch, their peaks full and erect as his mouth swooped down to sample once more the silken warmth of her flesh. Then he left her briefly and when he returned there was no longer a barrier of clothing between them. Then he parted her legs and slid smoothly in place in the cradle of her thighs. The moment Kane's hardness touched her, she arched against him, seeking, accepting, whatever he wanted to give her. Liquid fire coursed through her as he buried himself deeper between her thighs.

"I won't cheat you, Glenna," he rasped. "I promise you'll find only pleasure in my arms."

Other *Leisure Books* by Connie Mason:

ICE & RAPTURE
BRAVE LAND, BRAVE LOVE
WILD LAND, WILD LOVE
BOLD LAND, BOLD LOVE
TEMPT THE DEVIL
FOR HONOR'S SAKE
BEYOND THE HORIZON
TENDER FURY
CARESS AND CONQUER
MY LADY VIXEN
DESERT ECSTASY
WILD IS MY HEART

Promised Splendor

Connie Mason

LEISURE BOOKS NEW YORK CITY

To my mother—my biggest fan
and
To my sister Lee—for her courage

A LEISURE BOOK®

June 1999

Published by

Dorchester Publishing Co., Inc.
276 Fifth Avenue
New York, NY 10001

ISBN 0-8439-4608-3

Printed in the United States of America.

PROMISED SPLENDOR

1

Great clouds of choking dust skipped across the plains and billowed through the open windows clogging Glenna's dry throat and settling uncomfortably on her fair skin and sadly begrimed clothing. She coughed twice, then sneezed, glancing sheepishly at her fellow passengers only to discover that they were experiencing the same distress as the westbound locomotive spewed dust and ashes indiscriminately over everyone and everything.

Since the Kansas Pacific met with the Union Pacific and Central Pacific in 1870 travel west was made much easier. When Glenna left Colorado in 1868 the citizens of Denver, angry over the railroad's decision to bypass Denver in favor of Cheyenne, were attempting to build a spur between the two cities. Against all odds they succeeded only to have the Kansas Pacific reach their city shortly afterwards.

Glenna sighed wearily, glancing at the three other women with whom she shared the cramped seating arrangement. A woman named Sal sat next to her and directly opposite were Sal's two traveling companions, Pearl and Candy. Sal caught Glenna's eye and flashed a friendly smile.

"A mite warm, ain't it, honey?" she sighed, fanning herself vigorously with the brim of her useless little hat. "I'd give my soul for a bath." Glenna nodded in silent agreement, as did the two other women.

Though Sal, Pearl and Candy weren't the sort Glenna would normally choose as companions, they had certainly helped pass the long, weary days and nights since she had first boarded the train in St. Louis. Their speech was anything but refined and their manner of dress much too loud and suggestive for Glenna's tastes, whose own gray serge paled in comparison to the ruffled pastels of the other three ladies.

"I hope this is the last train ride I'll be taking for a long time," Glenna contended, plucking the damp bodice of her dress away from her clammy skin, wishing she had the nerve to unfasten the top buttons to allow the breeze to fan her heated flesh. "Do you plan on staying in Denver or are you just visiting?" she continued, envying Sal and her companions their low necklines and partially bared shoulders.

Pearl and Candy, both dark-haired beauties with snapping brown eyes, tittered behind their hands but were silenced by a sharp reprimand from blond, blue-eyed Sal, the oldest by a few years and clearly the spokesman of the group.

"From what we hear, Denver is growing by leaps and bounds," Sal explained confidentially, "and money pouring into town from the gold and silver mines that abound in the area. If things work out to our liking we'll stay."

"Do you have relatives in Denver?"

Both Pearl and Candy flashed Glenna incredulous looks, but were again warned by a single glance from Sal. "No, but we have a promise of . . . jobs. There is a lot of money to be had in a boomtown like Denver and we intend to stake a claim to a share of it."

"I suppose," replied Glenna doubtfully. It was difficult to imagine these three frivolous women finding suitable employment in a rugged town like Denver, a city still on the outer fringes of civilization despite the gold bonanza and railroad. Little did Glenna dream that in just twenty years hence Denver would escalate from just under 5000 to over 106,000 souls.

Glenna O'Neill had left Denver four years earlier at the age of sixteen to attend a finishing school in St. Louis. Against her wishes, she was quick to add when questioned. A rough-and-tumble mining camp was no place for a growing girl, her father, Paddy O'Neill, had declared when he first noticed the unwanted attention his young daughter was creating among the miners and drifters flooding the area. Until the day he heard a miner making salacious comments about the budding beauty of his daughter, Glenna was still his little girl; a barefoot, flame-haired pixie with a touch of the auld sod in her emerald green eyes.

But when Paddy was forced to take a hard look at Glenna he saw not only those endearing features he loved but a pleasantly rounded, petite figure on the brink of womanhood; a beauty unmatched by any save her dear departed mother.

After the first gold strike in Colorado in 1859 Paddy O'Neill was one of the 150,000 brave souls who ventured forth in search of riches and fame, grubstaked by a childhood friend from Ireland who immigrated to America some years before Paddy and became a successful banker. To this day they remained fast friends though Paddy's loan had long since been paid in full.

Paddy settled first at Placer Camp, a community of miners that straddled Cherry Creek, Auraria on the southwest and St. Charles on the northeast. St.

Charles, on the western reaches of Kansas Territory, was renamed Denver City for James W. Denver, then governor of the territory. In 1860 Auraria and Denver consolidated and in 1861 became the federal capitol.

When gold grew scarce in Placer Camp Paddy again appealed to his friend for a grubstake and filed a claim about twenty miles west of Denver on the south-fork of Clear Creek, in the foothills of the Rockies. It was there, at Golden Promise, so named by Paddy, that he panned his first significant find in 1865. It was also at Golden Promise that Glenna's mother, Colleen, died in childbed along with the tiny boy she carried nearly to term, leaving a thirteen-year-old Glenna motherless in a man's world.

By then Paddy had gained sufficient wealth to build a snug cabin of sawed lumber and several small outbuildings. He also constructed an elaborate sluice and rocker, hiring two or more men to operate the contraption consisting of a flat wooden trough built on a slant with a shallow hopper at the high end and wooden strips or riffles nailed across the trough.

Even now Glenna could picture in her mind's eye her father shoveling creekbed gravel and sand into the hopper whose wire mesh covering screened out stones and pebbles. Then he would douse the sand that went through the screen continuously with water, washing it down and out the trough. Heavier gold was caught behind the riffles and Glenna recalled vividly the thrill she experienced when she watched her father scrape out the gold that remained behind.

But no matter how many nuggets or flakes Paddy O'Neill panned out of Clear Creek, he searched continually and tirelessly for the mother lode and greater wealth. The mother lode, Glenna knew, was the source of the gold her father panned from Clear Creek. So far the elusive riches had remained concealed from Paddy's eyes.

Once Paddy made up his mind about his daughter's future, he acted decisively and swiftly, startling Glenna with his haste. Within weeks of her sixteenth birthdav she was packed off to Miss Murdoch's Boarding School For Genteel Young Ladies in St. Louis. What a change it made in her life!

Overnight she went from a wild tomboy, indulged by her father, to a sedate young lady with much to learn in order to satisfy the standards set forth by stern-faced Miss Murdoch and enforced by her equally staid staff of teachers. For four long, frustrating years Glenna longed to return to her father and his Golden Promise, but Paddy was adamant that his only child have every advantage. So as long as Paddy and Golden Promise prospered, Glenna remained with Miss Murdoch.

"Is your father meeting you in Denver?" Sal queried, picking up the lagging conversation that had ground to a halt while Glenna's thoughts roamed.

Startled by the question, Glenna flushed, then admitted somewhat sheepishly, "No, he doesn't even know I'm coming home. I . . . just decided I'd had enough of St. Louis and school. Besides, I haven't heard from Da in weeks. My allowance failed to arrive when it should have and I'm worried about him. I scraped up what money I had and left Miss Murdoch's behind. For good, I hope."

Sal smiled indulgently. "Was it that bad? Miss Murdoch's, I mean."

"Worse," grimaced Glenna distastefully. "I know Da expected me to stay another year and possibly find a rich husband, but I've had enough. And I don't need a husband. I'm sick of the big city, tired of playing the lady and languishing behind closed doors unable to move about freely without prying eyes following my every move. It might have been all right for a sixteen year old but I'm fully grown now and perfectly capable of taking care of myself. It's time Da learned I am no longer a child!" Her voice grew defiant and for a moment she forgot her audience was three women apparently as independent as she wished to be herself.

"Hey, you don't have to convince me," laughed Sal, winking broadly at her two companions who rolled their eyes in commiseration.

"How will you get out to your father's claim?" asked Pearl who had already learned about Paddy O'Neill and his Golden Promise as the train chugged its way westward.

"I'll rent a horse at the livery. Old Pete is a friend of the family and he'll trust me until Da can pay him."

"Twenty miles is a long way, won't you be afraid to travel alone?" asked a wide-eyed Candy.

"I know the trail like the back of my hand," boasted Glenna. "I could travel it blindfolded."

"Just the same—" said Candy, thinking more of wild animals, both human and otherwise.

"It's a shame your allowance didn't arrive so you could travel first class," Sal sighed wistfully as one of the more affluent passengers strutted down the aisle, lording it over those whose means forbade them from venturing into the higher domain but allowed those in first class to roam at will.

Glenna agreed but did not say so for fear of hurting Sal's feelings, a woman who had been nothing but kind to her. Surreptitiously she glanced around at her fellow passengers and wrinkled her nose distastefully. Behind her a man, his wife and two young children under the age of five were battling the dust and ashes by constantly waving soiled handkerchiefs before their faces. Across the aisle a grossly fat man sprawled over two seats snoring loudly while other passengers, all sizes, ages and shapes, sought comfort on the hard upholstered seats.

While those in first class had the luxury of seats

that made up into berths at night, second-class passengers were often crowded into seats and forced to sleep sitting up or crouched into uncomfortable position. Had Glenna's allowance arrived in time she would now be sitting in relative comfort rather than suffering the endless trip under less than desirable conditions. But if Sal, Pearl and Candy could endure then so could she, although the stench of unwashed bodies, her own included, was beginning to make her nauseous.

One thing that both first- and second-class passengers had in common was the need to leave the train en masse for meals. And all too often the fare at each frequent stop consisted of fried eggs, fried potatoes and fried steak, hardly food fit for a delicate palate. It got so that Glenna would rather skip a meal or two than venture forth at a stop and wolf down an unpalatable meal in the ten minutes or so allotted. More food was left congealing on plates than was consumed by harried passengers, it seemed, encouraging Glenna to leave the train only when hunger pangs grew too severe to be ignored or nature called.

To Glenna the succession of towns stretched endlessly, like links in a chain with no beginning or end. St. Louis, Kansas City, Topeka, Dodge City, all these stops along with hundreds more whose names she couldn't remember; towns no more than a grouping of run-down shacks. But soon she would see Denver—and Da. Would he be angry with her for leaving school? She hoped not. But it didn't matter. She'd already made up her mind. She'd had enough of Miss Murdoch and the cold, dreary walls that had imprisoned her for four long years.

Tilting her head against the back of her seat Glenna closed her eyes and dozed fitfully, unaware of the large herd of buffalo grazing on the plains outside the window, or of the town that lay just ahead. Not even the tall, dark man who strode down the aisle from first class with all the grace of a lithe animal, balancing his well-honed body on the balls of his feet and long supple legs, captured her attention. But Sal noticed; so did Pearl and Candy who nudged each other and preened coquettishly for the benefit of the handsome stranger.

Kane Morgan strolled the aisles in a loose-limbed gait, yet nothing escaped his line of vision, whether signs of imminent danger or a beautiful woman. Boredom drove him from his first-class section to where those less fortunate were forced to travel, and he was slightly disgusted with himself for using the discomfort of others in order to dispel his boredom.

Kane was on his way to Denver from his home in Philadelphia. And all because of a letter written to his father. A letter that made little sense. And because that letter had reached his home a scant two weeks after the death of his father from a stroke, he was now on his way west. Not that he minded, actually. The change of scenery would be welcome.

Some weeks ago a letter had arrived for Patrick Morgan from his friend and one-time partner in a mining venture in Colorado. From the gist of the letter his father's friend had made some kind of discovery and needed help—whether financial or otherwise was not specified. It was too important to trust to a letter.

Being the younger son and less involved in the banking institution founded by their father than his brother, James, Kane elected to travel to Denver in answer to the plea from his father's boyhood friend from the old country. He hoped his business wouldn't take too long, for his fiancée, Ellen Fairchild, was already planning their wedding.

Twenty-eight-year-old Kane Alexander Morgan was a man of strong emotions. Restless, a wanderer at heart, it was a mystery how Ellen Fairchild managed to wring a proposal out of him. It was also a mystery to

Kane, should the truth be known, for he held no strong feelings for the rather haughty and pale Miss Fairchild whose cool beauty evoked no passion in his loins.

It was an advantageous match, one which his parents and brother had advocated, and somehow he found himself trapped into an engagement he cared little about. But if he had to marry one day it might as well be to Ellen, a woman he had known since they were children. For years everyone assumed they would marry and their engagement came as no surprise.

When Kane went off to fight in the war between the North and the South in 1862 he had been a wild, reckless youth of eighteen, but he had learned a lot in ten years. He had also grown up, though a streak of recklessness remained in him still. Nor did he lose his restlessness or zest for life.

Outside the moving train a herd of buffalo grazed peacefully along the track, oblivious to the clatter of the rails and roaring of the engine. Kane paused a moment to watch and saw that other passengers were doing the same, some pointing and gesturing at the size of the huge shaggy animals. Turning away, his eyes fell on four ladies seated together, somehow looking lovely despite the combination of dust and wind working against them.

At nearly the same moment Pearl spied Kane and nudged her companions furiously, preening and making eyes at the handsomest man she'd seen in ages. Well over six feet tall, broad of shoulder and slim of hip, Kane Morgan's rugged features defied convention. Though not classicially handsome, he immediately drew one's attention, exuding power, authority and pure animal magnetism.

Piercing gray eyes with the ability to smolder with passion or turn cold with fury dominated his face. He had a wide, sensual mouth whose lips tended to turn up with humor and a straight nose that fit his features perfectly. Coal-black hair worn longer than was the current fashion curled in tendrils at the nape of his neck. Ridiculously long lashes veiled his expression as Kane casually studied the three gaudily dressed women as well as the fourth who appeared to be sleeping, his wide experience intuitively identifying them as whores. Probably on their way west to the goldfields, Kane surmised rightly, to ply their trade and probably earn far more than many of their customers.

But it wasn't the three preening butterflies who attracted Kane's attention, rather it was their flame-haired companion who slept so peacefully through all the din taking place around her that drew Kane's probing gaze. Her perfect features and unblemished complexion, though lightly speckled with tiny freckles as well as fine grains of dust, were flawless and far superior to her sisters-in-trade. Though the other three women were no slouches in the beauty department, they nevertheless seemed coarse and unrefined next to their sleeping companion.

Kane briefly wondered at the drabness of the sleeping woman's dress, but somehow it detracted little from her natural beauty and seemed appropriate. He wished she would wake up so he could see the color of her eyes. It was as if God were listening to him for he got his wish when some of the passengers began shooting out the windows at the buffalo, awakening Glenna with a start.

Green! determined Kane, smiling. Just as I thought, eyes as green as the grass in spring. Taking a vacant seat nearby that faced the green-eyed girl, Kane studied all four women intently, hoping to discover if all were of the same profession or if the green-eyed beauty was merely forced to share a seat with the trio.

"What happened?" asked Glenna, startled by the shooting going on around her. "Is it Indians? Or train robbers?" Either one was a distinct possibility in this day and age, Glenna knew.

"Neither," laughed Sal indulgently. "Just a few bored passengers shooting at buffalo." Seeing the fear lingering in Glenna's face she impulsively settled an arm around the younger girl and squeezed. "It's all right, honey, relax."

Sal's friendly gesture banished any doubts Kane might have harbored concerning Glenna and whether or not she was of the same ilk as the other three women. Although she seemed to be cut from a different cloth it was obvious from their casual intimacy that she was traveling with them and that she shared their ancient profession. The green-eyed girl seemed less like a whore than any woman he had ever seen, but as Kane well knew, looks were often deceiving.

Pearl and Candy were too busy glancing coquettishly over their shoulders at Kane to pay much heed to the buffalo hunters leaning out the windows. Pearl's dark eyes narrowed jealously when she saw the direction of Kane's gaze, which lingered hungrily on Glenna.

She poked her seat companion in the ribs and whispered in Candy's shell-like ear loud enough for Sal and Glenna to hear. "Don't look now but that gorgeous hunk of man is staring at us." She nodded her head in Kane's direction.

Against her will Glenna shifted her gaze from the window and found herself lost in smoky depths the color and consistency of smoldering ash. Kane tipped his hat at a rakish angle, acknowledging her rude stare, the corners of his wide mouth tilting upwards in amusement. Annoyed by his outrageous behavior, Glenna assumed a haughty look and turned away. But not before carefully noting his striking features and powerful build.

In that instant Kane came to a decision. Uncoiling his long frame he eased from his seat and started down the aisle toward the four women. His sudden movement caught Glenna's eye, and unconsciously she compared him to a sleek animal with no extra flesh, just sinew and muscle, his movements catlike, quick and fluid.

"Good afternoon, ladies," smiled Kane, tipping his hat courteously as he came abreast of his prey. "I hope the shooting isn't annoying you."

"No more than anything else on this God-awful trip," declared Pearl, rolling her eyes to give emphasis to her words. "But then I don't imagine you know what I'm talking about, you traveling in first class and all."

"Pearl!" scolded Sal, turning her eyes to Kane in open appraisal. "I'm afraid Pearl isn't much of a traveler, Mr. . . . er . . . Mr.—"

"The name is Kane, Kane . . . Alexander," Kane supplied, unwilling to divulge his last name to a group of whores until he knew more about the situation in which he was placing himself.

"I'm Sal, and these other ladies are Pearl, Candy and Glenna." When she pointed out Glenna, Kane couldn't help but notice she was much more beautiful up close than from a distance.

"Where are you ladies bound?" he asked, looking directly at Glenna who chose to ignore his pointed question.

"Denver," Pearl was quick to supply, hoping to capture the man's attention for herself. "How far are you going, Mr. Alexander . . . Kane?" She batted her long lashes coyly, ignoring Candy who was beginning to seethe over Pearl's attempt to monopolize Kane's attention.

"What a coincidence," Kane exclaimed. "I'm getting off in Denver myself. Are you visiting, or—?"

"We're working girls, Mr. Alexander," explained Sal candidly, not realizing that inadvertently her words included Glenna, thus identifying her as one of them. Perhaps we'll see you one day in . . . our . . . er . . .

place of business," she continued suggestively.

"Perhaps," Kane hedged, looking at Glenna for confirmation of Sal's invitation.

If the truth be known, Glenna was paying little heed to the conversation taking place around her. From the moment the strange man impaled her with his heated gaze she became like a flustered schoolgirl. Though twenty years old she had had little contact with men since the age of sixteen when her father had sent her away. Miss Murdoch felt dutybound to act the watch-dog and protect the innocence of her young wards. For four years Glenna was afforded little opportunity to meet men, especially a man as fascinating as Kane Alexander.

Her mind refused to acknowledge that his eyes seemed to linger on her rather than on her vivacious seatmates. She was far too busy taking in the almost impossible breadth of his shoulders, slim hips and long muscular legs to dispute or approve any of the words falling about her deaf ears. She heard his deep, rumbling voice, bubbling with suppressed humor and little else.

Had she been aware of Sal's careless words that included her, she would have been mortified. But strange as it may seem, Glenna, in some ways still naive in the ways of the world, had no idea she had been associating with three "fallen women"—the term for whores she had been taught to use by the prudish Miss Murdoch—and even less idea that Kane assumed her to be one of the sisterhood.

2

Reluctantly Glenna stirred herself to join the exodus to the depot restaurant to partake of the questionable fare being offered. Since she had declined the noon meal she thought it prudent to put something in her stomach no matter how indigestible. Thank God there was only one more night to get through before Denver, Glenna thought, sighing gratefully.

"Are you joining us?" Sal asked as she and her companions moved into the aisle. Kane had already returned to his own seat and the three women had talked of nothing else since.

"Yes," replied Glenna, shaking the pervasive dust from her thoroughly wrinkled skirt. "But we'd better hurry if we intend to get through a meal before the train leaves."

As it turned out the noise, bustle and smell of the depot restaurant did little to spark Glenna's appetite and in the end she turned back towards the train rather than join those hardy souls jostling for a seat at the three-sided counter that resembled a square with one side open. It certainly wouldn't hurt her to go hungry a while longer and far preferable to suffering nausea or stomach upset the rest of the night. Kane must have had the same idea for they nearly collided trying to enter the same car at the same time.

"Aren't you hungry, Glenna?" Kane asked as he stepped aside courteously to allow her to enter first.

"If I was I quickly lost my appetite, Mr. Alexander," Glenna remarked dryly. "What about you? Surely you haven't eaten already."

"I would say this depot restaurant is about as bad as any I've seen, and I've seen plenty in my day," Kane grimaced. When they reached Glenna's seat Kane did not wait for an invitation, but joined her. "I have a better idea."

"What kind of an idea, Mr. Alexander?" asked Glenna warily.

"I still have some fruit left that I brought aboard for just such an occasion. And some tinned delicacies. Would you care to join me?"

Fresh fruit! It sounded wonderful. Why not? thought Glenna. "If you're sure you have enough then I'll be happy to join you, Mr. Alexander."

"More than enough. But only if you call me Kane."

"Kane it is," sparkled Glenna, dazzling him with the brilliance of her smile.

Kane left and returned a few minutes later bearing a basket filled with apples, pears and an assortment of tinned food. "It pays to come prepared," he quipped, setting out their feast on the empty seat opposite them.

As they ate, Glenna lost some of her shyness and began responding warmly to Kane's friendly overtures. "Do you mind if I ask you a personal question?" Kane asked when they had eaten their fill.

"I guess not," shrugged Glenna, "my life certainly holds no mysteries."

"I don't imagine it does," remarked Kane dryly. "You seem awfully young to be doing this sort of thing."

"I'm twenty, Mr. . . Kane," bristled Glenna, assuming he meant traveling alone without a chaperone. "I was but sixteen the first time and survived. Pearl, Candy and Sal were probably even younger than I their first time."

"That's a rather candid answer, Glenna. Do you enjoy it?" His obvious amazement puzzled her.

"It's not bad once you get used to it," she explained blandly. "But you should know better than I. Obviously you do it often enough." As before she assumed he was still talking about traveling by rail and her response sent him into peals of laughter, bringing tears to his eyes.

"I always enjoy it," he quipped, by now thoroughly enchanted as well as entertained by Glenna and her honesty. "Sometimes more than others. But as long as we're being truthful, do you really enjoy being a w—"

Glenna never heard Kane's last words for they were completely drowned out by the train whistle signaling a general exodus from the depot restaurant. But when Glenna would have asked him to repeat himself, she was forestalled by the appearance of Sal, Pearl and Candy returning to their seats, still chewing and somewhat out of breath.

"Well!" fumed Pearl, thoroughly disgruntled at finding Kane and Glenna alone and obviously enjoying themselves. "Had I but known there was better fare to be had right here I would have remained aboard with Glenna." She eyed the remains of their repast then glared at Glenna spitefully.

Pearl's blatant jealously flustered Glenna and she wondered if they considered her "fast" for sharing a meal with a stranger. Certainly Miss Murdoch would be horrified and Glenna suppressed a giggle at the thought.

"It was remiss of me not to invite all four of you to share what was left in my basket," apologized Kane smoothly when he realized he was the cause of dissension among the women. "Please forgive me."

"Well, if you put it that way," Pearl allowed grudgingly, obviously not at all pleased, "you're forgiven. You're much too handsome to stay mad at anyway."

"Would you like to step out on the platform with me, Glenna?" Kane asked once all the girls were seated comfortably. "The breeze might prove welcome as it has grown quite close in here."

Once the passengers had filed in and taken their seats the air indeed had grown fetid with the clutch of unwashed bodies crammed into the confined area. But Glenna thought it prudent to refuse. She wanted nothing to jeopardize her reputation or her friendship with Pearl and Candy who were glaring daggers at her.

"Thank you, Kane, but I'm quite comfortable right here," demurred Glenna primly.

"I'd love to go!" interjected Pearl, tripping over Candy and Sal in her haste to reach the aisle where Kane stood waiting.

Kane stole a lazy, mocking glance at Glenna but immediately stifled his disappointment as he gallantly offered Pearl his arm. "Then let us be off," he said gaily.

After wending their way through several cars Kane and Pearl finally arrived at the caboose and stepped out onto the narrow platform surrounded by a waist-high iron railing. Pearl clutched Kane's arm to steady herself and swayed deliberately against the hard wall of his chest, making certain her soft breasts pressed intimately against him.

Kane suppressed an amused smile at her clumsy attempt at seduction. Did she think him a callow youth to fall for her whore's tricks? For the time being he decided to play along, at least until he obtained the information he sought.

"How long will you be in Denver, Kane?" Pearl asked in a voice suggesting future pleasure should he linger in the boomtown.

"I'm not sure," hedged Kane. "Where will I find you should I desire female companionship?"

Pleased with herself for attracting an intriguing man like Kane, Pearl smiled broadly. Not only did Kane appear to be wellborn, but his bearing suggested money as well. All kinds of things were possible with Kane as a client and Pearl intended to make certain she was the one to whom he came for his pleasure.

"We will be working at the Red Garter for the time being," she revealed. "But as soon as we earn enough we plan on recruiting more girls and opening our own place. We're going to make it the best bawdy house in Denver. Will you come to see me at the Red Garter, Kane? I promise you won't be disappointed with what I can do for you."

"I'm sure I won't," grinned Kane, "and I promise to drop by your place of business at my earliest opportunity. Will Glenna be working there too?"

"Glenna?" frowned Pearl, disgruntled. "Why? Do you think she'd be any better than me?"

"Just curious," shrugged Kane carelessly. "Have you known her long? What is her last name?"

"Not long," allowed Pearl. "If you're so curious about her why don't you ask Glenna yourself? Most of us prefer not to use lastnames. That way our families might never learn how we earn our living. Take me, for instance. I ran away at fifteen with a no-good drifter who promised me the world and gave me to another man when he tired of me. Eventually I ended up in a whorehouse in St. Louis. It would kill my parents to know how I ended up."

"I'm sorry," murmured Kane, truly feeling remorse at what Pearl had been dealt by fate.

"Don't be," laughed Pearl harshly. "I've a far better life now than I would ever have had if I remained at home. By now I would be married to some farmer and have a passle of kids hanging on my skirt, old before my time and nothing but a drudge to a demanding husband."

"I always wondered if whores enjoyed their work," mused Kane thoughtfully.

"Well this one does," answered Pearl, tossing her dark head haughtily.

"And Glenna? Does she also enjoy her work?"

"I told you," snapped Pearl, becoming annoyed with Kane's obsession with Glenna, "you'll have to ask her. I make it a point never to pry." Pearl knew she wasn't being truthful with Kane where Glenna was concerned but it irked her to be with a man whose thoughts were on another woman. Any fool could see that Glenna was no whore. All Kane had to do was open his eyes.

Duly chastised, Kane dropped the subject. He couldn't explain why the flame-haired Glenna intrigued him, but intrigue him she did. Pearl would have been astounded to learn that all her seductive wiles made little or no impression on Kane while Glenna's aloof airs drew him like a bee to honey. She looked so innocent, yet the lush curves of her rounded body promised untold delights. Little did Pearl know that the concealing gray serge worn by Glenna was infinitely more seductive than the gaudy, revealing clothing worn by Pearl and her companions. Either Glenna was more experienced in her subtle approach to seduction or as innocent as she seemed, Kane decided. And given her profession the former seemed more likely. Whichever it was, Kane intended to discover the truth for himself.

* * *

"Kane promised he'd come to visit me," crowed Pearl importantly, "just as soon as we're settled in. I don't know when I've seen a more attractive man."

"You certainly monopolized him," said Candy sullenly.

"Girls," chided Sal. "There will be plenty of men where we're going so there's no need to fight over one man. Besides, he seemed mighty interested in Glenna." As usual her shrewd eyes missed nothing and she genuinely liked the younger girl. She and Kane would make a perfect couple.

"Interested in me!" shot back Glenna. "I think you misread his intentions, Sal. Why would Kane waste his time on a drab like me with women as beautiful as you three around?"

"You truly are an innocent, aren't you, honey?" Sal said, shaking her head in disbelief.

Glenna smiled uncertainly, wondering if she had just been handed a compliment or an insult.

3

At the depot Glenna parted company with her traveling companions without giving a thought to asking where they would be staying, so anxious was she to reach Golden Promise and her father. Nor did she notice Kane hurrying off about his own business as she gathered up her bags and asked the stationmaster to keep an eye on them until her father could collect them.

Never had Glenna been so glad to see a place in her life as she was to see Denver. The city had grown by leaps and bounds during her four-year absence. From the crush of people scurrying about their business it wasn't difficult to imagine the city growing to the tremendous size of 5000 people which it now boasted. Many new buildings had been erected as well as long wooden boardwalks lining either side of the street, now muddied by spring rains. The city stretched as far as the eye could see, sprawling outward from the newly designated capitol.

Glenna wrinkled her nose at her own stench as she considered taking a room at the hotel, bathing and eating a decent meal before heading out to Golden Promise. But the slimness of her purse reminded her that what little coin she had left would not stretch so far. Besides, it was still early and if she left immediately she could reach the claim by nightfall. Well, perhaps she had enough money for a meal, Glenna amended as her stomach set up a clamor that couldn't be ignored.

The bulk of her baggage safely stowed in the station, Glenna swiftly made her way to the livery carrying a carpetbag containing a change of clothes and a few essentials. The sharp odor of horses and leather assailed her nostrils when she entered the familiar building she remembered so well from her childhood. She wondered if old Pete was still in charge and if he had changed any in four years.

"Can I help you, Miss?" A grizzled elderly man emerged from the deep shadows and hobbled toward Glenna. She smiled warmly when she recognized Pete's weathered features. Though he had earned a few more wrinkles these past four years and his scraggly beard was more unkempt than she remembered, Pete remained basically unchanged from the cantankerous old man who had run the livery stable for years, even before she and Da had moved east.

"Pete, don't you remember me?" Glenna asked. "Have I changed so much?"

Squinting his eyes in concentration, Pete's brow suddenly cleared and he flashed a wide, toothless grin. "Why, if it ain't Paddy O'Neill's girl, Glenna. The marshal's been expectin' to hear from you. My, ain't you turned into a real beauty. Paddy would have been right proud if he could see you now."

Pete's choice of words puzzled Glenna and she was about to ask him to explain when she spied a brown and white spotted mare in one of the stalls that she'd recognize anywhere. She had ridden Belle often enough as a child, and Da sometimes hitched her to the supply wagon when a trip to Denver was necessary. She walked to the stall and gently rubbed the mare's nose, murmuring softly to her. Belle snorted in recognition.

"Is Da in town, Pete? I'd know Belle anywhere."

A look of total bewilderment crossed Pete's craggy features. "You ain't heard?" he asked hesitantly. "You didn't get the marshal's letter? He tried sending a telegram but the doggone Injuns cut the line atwixt here and Topeka so he writ ya instead."

"The marshal wrote me a letter?" An invisible shroud of foreboding suddenly wrapped cold arms around Glenna. "Is something wrong with Da? Is he sick?"

"You sure you never got the marshal's letter?" Pete questioned sharply.

"Positive!" Glenna insisted, nearly shouting from frustration. "I probably had already left St. Louis by the time the letter arrived. I . . . I just decided to leave on my own. Now will you tell me what is going on?"

"You'd best see Marshal Bartow, Miss Glenna. He can tell you better than me," Pete said evasively, looking decidedly uncomfortable.

Whirling on her heel Glenna took off on the run, her long hair billowing behind her like a red banner. A few minutes later she burst into the marshal's office slamming the door behind her. Hands on hips she blew in like a full-fledged hurricane and faced the marshal defiantly.

"What's happened to my father, Marshal Bartow?" she demanded breathlessly. "If he's sick tell me where he is and I'll go to him immediately."

"Sit down, Glenna." Having been marshal for over fifteen years Bartow knew nearly every man, woman and child in the boomtown. Keeping order was a full-time job and more often than not a thankless one. It was times like this he wished he had embraced another occupation.

"Just tell me where Da is, Marshal, and I'll not bother you further."

"Didn't you get my letter?"

"No, I must have already left St. Louis before it arrived. Why did you write me? Was Da unable to do so himself?"

"Glenna, this would be much easier if you would sit down," Marshal Bartow sighed, motioning toward a chair.

Glenna sighed resignedly then plopped down into the straight-backed chair, tapping her foot impatiently. "All right, Marshal, I'm seated. Now please tell me about my father."

"It happened about two weeks ago, Glenna. Your father came into town for supplies and took a room at the Denver Arms. No one knows what really happened during the time he was in town, but evidently he started out for the claim the next morning and never made it. He was found on the outskirts of the city, shot in the head. If it's any consolation, he died instantly."

Horror-stricken, Glenna gasped, then shot out of the chair like a rocket in flight. "No! What are you saying! Da dead? Oh, my God! Da! Da!" Try as she might, Glenna was not strong enough to hold back the sobs threatening to inundate her frail body. Tears of anguish streamed freely down her grimy cheeks while Marshal Bartow allowed her time to vent her grief.

After a time the heartrending cries stilled and Glenna slowly began to assimilate all the marshal had told her. Nothing made sense. What had the marshal said? Her father had been shot? Ambushed and killed? By whom? And why?

"Why would anyone do such a thing?" asked Glenna tearfully. "He had no enemies. Everyone liked him."

"I don't know, Glenna. Paddy couldn't have had much on him to steal. There was talk that his claim was played out, finished. These days he barely panned enough to keep you in that fancy school in St. Louis. The last couple times he came into town he seemed preoccupied, almost as if something was on his mind. Ask Pete at the livery if you don't believe me. Everyone knows he's been searching for the mother lode for years but never found it. It's a mystery why anyone would kill him. If it was robbery nothing was touched in the wagon."

"There had to be a reason, Marshal," said Glenna emphatically. "Were there no clues? Nothing?"

"No, Glenna, nothing. Paddy was pretty close-mouthed as you well know. I'm sorry, my dear, you're just going to have to accept that we may never find the killer or killers."

"I won't accept that, Marshal! You'd better find the murderers!" Glenna declared hotly, "Because if you don't, I will!"

"Are you certain you know of no one who might harbor a grudge against your father?"

"No, Marshal. I haven't a clue. You're the law and it's your duty to see that Da's murderer is brought to justice for his crime. I won't rest easy until you find the person or persons responsible. What do you intend to do about it?"

"I haven't given up on this, Glenna, but you have to understand this is a lawless territory inhabited by the dregs of society lured by the promise of wealth. Anyone could have killed him."

"Then you'll continue the investigation?"

"Yes," Bartow promised sincerely. "But I don't want you interfering, do you understand, Glenna?"

"I understand. As long as you do your duty I'll stay out of it."

"Listen, Glenna, your father's killer thinks he's gotten away clean," explained Marshal Bartow. "Let him continue to think that way while I quietly begin investigating Paddy's movements that day. Someone must have seen something out of the ordinary. He was in town several times before he was killed, waiting for an answer to a telegram he sent, I understand. Do you have any idea who he might have contacted, or why? Was he in touch with you, perhaps?"

"No, Marshal, I'm sorry. I haven't heard from Da in ages and I began to worry when weeks passed with no word from him. Then when my monthly allowance failed to arrive I felt in my bones something was wrong. Poor Da," she moaned as if in pain. "If only I had been here I might have prevented this."

"There is no way you could know your father would be killed, nor could you have prevented it. You might have been a victim yourself. Until we find the killer you'd best stay in town at the hotel where I can keep an eye on you."

Glenna drew herself up to her full five feet, three inches and declared, "I now own Golden Promise and I'll not be frightened off from what's mine!"

"Be reasonable, Glenna. A deserted mining camp is no place for a woman alone. The area abounds with drifters and ne'er-do-wells looking for easy pickings."

"What happened to the two men my father hired?"

"Gone. Left shortly after your father was killed. Who was to pay them if they remained?"

"I would have seen to it. Is it true? Is the Golden Promise really done for?"

"It appears that way. I arranged to have Paddy buried beneath that big aspen on the hill overlooking his claim. While I was out there I searched the cabin and outbuildings and found nothing of value; not a sign of either dust, flakes or nuggets anywhere. I suspect the rumor is true and the claim is next to worthless."

Glenna was quiet a long time, her face sad. "Poor Da, he never realized his dream. He died before he found the mother lode. And he was so certain it was there."

Marshal Bartow, a soft-hearted man though he tried hard to conceal it behind a gruff manner, patted Glenna awkwardly. "Come along, Glenna, I'll see to your bags and settle you at the hotel."

"I'm going out to the claim, Marshal," Glenna declared stubbornly. "I have no money to stay elsewhere. All I have is Golden Promise and I'll work it myself if I have to."

"Doesn't Paddy have a partner somewhere back east? Surely he'll help out when he hears about your father. He might even come out here and see to your welfare."

"Patrick Morgan is a good friend of Da's but he no longer has an interest in Golden Promise. Da bought out his share a long time ago, although as far as I know they kept in touch. Mr. Morgan gave Da a grubstake when no one else would help him. But he's an old man now, older even than Da. He's been a good friend to my father for as long as I can remember. I'll certainly write to him but I'll accept no handouts. I'm perfectly capable of making my own way."

Marshal Bartow looked skeptical but had no wish to further antagonize Glenna at a time when she needed it least. She already had more heartache than she could handle. But he intended to contact Patrick Morgan himself to apprise him of Glenna's dire straits. If he was such a good friend to Paddy, he would want to see Paddy's daughter safe and well-cared for.

"Where does this Patrick Morgan live?"

"In Philadelphia. He's a banker. But I've never seen him."

"Glenna, in all conscience I can't let you go out to your claim alone. You can stay with me and my wife for the time being. Then after we hear from Mr. Morgan we'll know more about what to do."

"Thank you, Marshal, that's kind of you, but I'm afraid I must decline your offer. I . . . want to visit Da's grave and look over the claim. Maybe he left me a message . . . or something. If the wagon is still at the livery stable I'll just drive it out there."

The lawman grunted in exasperation. "I'm not your guardian so I can't legally stop you, Glenna, but I strongly advise against it. Do you have any relatives I could notify?"

"Not in this country, Marshal Bartow, but I appreciate your concern. I'll be back in a few days to see if you've made any progress in finding Da's killer."

"Good luck, young lady. I'll do my utmost to find the man responsible and bring him to justice."

Old Pete couldn't believe his ears when Glenna informed him she was taking Belle and leaving for Golden Promise immediately. "You must be loco, Miss Glenna," he protested vigorously. "It ain't fittin' for you to go galavantin' over them hills by yourself let alone live in that remote area with no one to protect you."

"I'll manage," Glenna declared belligerently. "Da taught me how to shoot when I was twelve. Is the wagon here? If it is would you hitch Belle up, please?"

"The wagon is out back. The marshal returned it to town after Paddy's body was found."

"Good," nodded Glenna. "Now I can collect my bags at the station and take them with me. How long will it take, Pete?"

"I don't move as fast as I use to, Miss Glenna, give me fifteen minutes or so."

Just then Glenna's stomach growled loudly, reminding her that she'd had nothing substantial to eat since the day before. Pete must have heard it too.

"Why don't you hop over to the hotel and eat. When you come back I'll have everything ready for you. I'll even go and pick up your bags for you while you're eating."

Glenna thought of the all too few coins remaining

in her purse but decided to follow Pete's advice anyway. Hard telling what she'd find in the way of supplies once she reached the cabin. The shock of her father's senseless death still held her in a kind of limbo. She expected tomorrow, after everything had time to sink in, she would feel much worse. How could she go on without Da to love and protect her? It wasn't fair that he should have been taken from her before she'd had a chance to tell him goodbye, or let him know how much he meant to her.

Kane Morgan tried to keep track of Glenna once he left the train but soon lost her in the crush of people milling about the depot either meeting loved ones or seeing them off. Finally he gave up. At least he knew exactly where to find her once he located Paddy O'Neill and learned the reason behind his urgent summons. When he engaged a room at Denver's finest hotel, The Palace, he questioned the desk clerk and discovered that the Red Garter was a gambling hall of some renown located on the main street. Some of the most beautiful girls in the territory were employed by the owner, Judd Martin, and the rooms above the saloon were put to good use by those lovely ladies.

Somehow Kane couldn't picture Glenna entertaining men in those rooms. She just didn't seem the type. For some obscure reason he wanted to be the only one to sample those delectable charms; the only man with the right to strip those demure clothes she wore from her supple form.

What was the matter with him? he wondered absently. Why should a whore capture his imagination to the extent that he was eager to forget his obligations for a romp in bed with the little red-haired witch? She knew her business, he'd give her that much. She knew exactly what she was about by concealing her lush curves from neck to ankle and acting the lady. She had him panting over her like an untried boy.

After enjoying a refreshing bath and good meal, Kane decided to rent a horse and ride out to Golden Promise immediately. Already in possession of the directions, he rented the best horse in Pete's livery stable, purchased supplies necessary for the trip, strapped his Colt revolver to his slim hips, shoved his new Winchester model 73 in his saddle holster and left Denver. Only two hours behind Glenna driving the wagon, his thoughts were consumed by a flame-haired little tart he'd give his right arm to bed.

4

Old Belle knew the trail by heart and Glenna dozed off and on seated on her high perch, the reins held loosely in her hands. Not much had changed in the four years since she had left the teeming city. The forest was still dense, the foothills steep and winding, the Rockies rising against the blue of the sky lofty and capped with snow.

As dusk approached Glenna had forgotten just how dark and desolate it could be beneath the tall aspens and pines whose shadows appeared as menacing sentinels guarding the path. Then suddenly blackness descended like an encompassing shroud; there was not even a moon to light her way, and Glenna knew a moment's panic. She had counted on some natural light from above to guide her, but nothing seemed to be going right since stepping off the train.

The winding, rock-strewn path was dangerous enough in full daylight but treacherous by night. To urge poor Belle on would be both foolhardy and dangerous, not only for the animal but for herself as well. The logical alternative was to stop somewhere, pass the night sleeping beneath the wagon and start out again at first light. Ever practical, Glenna began searching for a likely place to spend the night. The sound of bubbling water drew her attention and she urged Belle off the trail through a break in the trees and soon came to a level grassy place beside a lazy stream. Halting Belle, she worked swiftly to unhitch her and secured her to a nearby tree to graze on the sparse blanket of green beneath her feet.

Rummaging around in the bed of the wagon, Glenna blessed her father for keeping a box of emergency supplies on hand whenever he ventured from his claim. One never knew what kind of danger one would encounter and Paddy was a firm believer that it was best to be prepared at all times for come what may. Pete had not touched a thing in the wagon so Da's belongings were just as he had left them, intact inside the waterproof box in the wagonbed.

Glenna found a box of matches and after gathering kindling and dead wood laying nearby, quickly built a fire and set a pot to boiling for coffee. She also took out a tin of beans and a piece of hardtack which would serve well enough to satisfy her hunger. But before she ate a more urgent need assailed Glenna. The gurgling water sounded too inviting to be ignored. A much-needed bath would feel heavenly and Glenna wasted no time in disrobing and entering the clear stream, catching her breath as the icy water lapped about her knees.

Only waist deep, Glenna sat on the sandy bottom and quickly lathered herself with the soap taken from her bag along with a clean chemise which she left on the bank. Next she tackled her hair, feeling the dirt and grime rinse away with the suds. Shivering from cold, Glenna quickly finished her bath and waded to shore, drying herself with a blanket from her father's box of supplies and donning the clean chemise. Then she wrapped herself in the blanket and knelt beside the fire to dry her hair, helping herself to the pot of coffee which by now sent out a delicious aroma wafting through the trees.

A twig snapped nearby and Glenna jerked to attention, the hair at the back of her neck standing upright. "Who's there?" she called out, swallowing the lump of fear forming in her throat. The profound sounds of silence met her straining ears. Belle whickered softly and Glenna came to her feet, shifting her eyes in all directions. Nothing but thick darkness was visible beyond the ring of light generated by the campfire.

Slowly Glenna began edging toward the wagon where her father's old pepperbox lay amid the sundry supplies, praying the gun was loaded and ready to fire. But she never made it as three men burst from the concealing thicket, their bearded faces and rough clothes identifying them as prospectors down on their luck or drifters searching for easy prey.

Glenna screamed, her heart beating furiously. What did these men want? Why hadn't she listened to the marshal and waited till morning to reach Golden Promise?

"Well, well, ain't you a sight for sore eyes, pretty lady," cackled one of the bearded men as he slowly approached the quaking girl, motioning his companions to spread out, effectively blocking any escape Glenna might have taken.

Gulping back her fear Glenna decided to brazen it out and stand her ground, hoping her show of courage would catch them off guard. "Who are you and what do you want?" she demanded to know, lifting her chin defiantly.

"We're just fellow travelers like yourself," replied the spokesman. "I'm Wiley Wilson, that's Jimbo on your right and Lem to your left. Your fire looks mighty invitin' and that coffee smells downright good."

Pulling her blanket tighter about her shivering form Glenna wished she had had the foresight to put on a dress after her bath.

"Where's yer man?" Jimbo asked, casting his gaze about cautiously.

"He's . . . hunting for our supper," Glenna lied, thinking quickly. "He should be back at any time. You're welcome to a cup of coffee before you go if you don't mind sharing the cup."

"Ha!" laughed Wiley derisively. "There ain't no man! We been watchin' you for some time and there's no sign of a man or anyone else."

"That's not true!" shot back Glenna. "You'd be wise to leave before he returns."

"Sure, pretty lady, we'll leave, won't we boys? Right after we help ourselves to more than a cup of coffee."

"I . . . I don't have much to offer in the way of food," Glenna replied, pretending ignorance.

Hoots of laughter met her words. "We'll take whatever you have to offer, pretty lady," snickered Lem lewdly.

By now all three men surrounded Glenna in a tight circle, the light from the campfire clearly illuminating their dirty, bearded faces, leering grins and ragged clothing reeking of stale sweat and filth. Panic, stark and profound, crumbled Glenna's courage as she frantically searched for an avenue of escape, realizing instinctively that she was at their mercy.

"Let's see what's under that blanket," Wiley exclaimed, reaching out a grimy paw and jerking the rough covering from between Glenna's numb fingers. An appreciative groan escaped from the throats of all three men as light from the flickering flames enticingly outlined Glenna's slim form beneath the thin lawn shift, her glowing shoulders pearly as the purest alabaster.

"My Gawd!" breathed Jimbo reverently. "Ain't

she somethin'." One hamlike hand reached out tentively to touch the satiny flesh bared to his lustful gaze.

"Keep away from me!" shrieked Glenna, backing away until she came in painful contact with the wagon at her back. Mesmerized by the flash of graceful limbs moving beneath her meager garment, the men did not advance, but watched from a distance of five or six feet.

Making contact with the wagon reminded Glenna of her father's pepperbox resting just inches behind her. Exploding into motion, Glenna whirled, grasped the gun from the open box with both hands and turned, waving it in the direction of the three men menacing her, startling them from their frozen stances.

"The bitch has a gun!" warned Lem, eyeing Glenna warily.

"That old relic?" scoffed Wiley disparagingly. "She couldn't hit the broad side of a barn with that."

"Try me!" Glenna declared, feeling decidedly braver with a weapon in her hands, though she wished it was Da's Spencer rifle she held instead. "I'm a good shot and will gladly prove it if you don't turn around and leave. Right now!" she ordered when no one moved.

"What do you think, Wiley?" asked Jimbo, unwilling to put Glenna's threat to the test.

"I think she's bluffin'," contended Wiley. "Besides, I'm hankerin' fer a little of what she's got lots of. It's been a long time since I laid a woman, let alone one as young and tender as this red-haired hellion. I say we rush her. What do you say, boys?"

Jimbo licked his lips, then nodded. "Count me in, Wiley." Lem grinned lewdly, quickly adding his own agreement.

"Stay where you are!" warned Glenna, her arms growing numb with the weight of the gun. Vaguely she wondered if she could kill a man if forced to and decided she could, knowing what they intended to do to her.

At Wiley's silent command, he and his two companions burst into action, reaching Glenna at the exact same moment her finger squeezed the trigger. Only Wiley reached her first and her shot went wild as he grasped her hands, aiming them skyward. Sobbing in frustration she struggled fruitlessly in Wiley's strong arms, kicking and scratching like an animal snared in a trap. Lem and Jimbo joined in the foray and soon rendered Glenna helpless but hardly subdued.

"Shit!" cried Jimbo, clutching the fleshy part of his upper arm where Glenna's sharp teeth sank in. "The bitch bit me!" She was rewarded with a blow to her face that knocked her nearly senseless.

Rendered groggy from the blow, Glenna felt the air kiss her skin as her chemise was ripped from her upper body. Rough hands grasped soft flesh as her breasts were mauled and pummeled repeatedly by three pairs of eager hands. Then she felt the ground beneath her back, tiny stones and gravel pitting her soft skin.

"Spread her legs, Jimbo," Wiley grunted as he knelt at her feet. "You keep her from bucking me off, Lem." The men moved to obey, their eyes glued to the gleam of tender flesh bared to their gaze.

"I ain't never seen nothin' so sweet," Wiley declared, raising the hem of her shift. "Her hair is as red down there as it is on her head."

Unbuttoning his pants and grasping his swollen member, Wiley prepared to launch his assault upon Glenna's resisting body, unaware of a pair of steely eyes, dark with rage, watching from a short distance away.

Kane was lost. Somewhere along the trail he had made a wrong turn and ended up wandering about in the woods in total darkness as night settled around him.

Cursing his luck, he had almost decided to camp for the night in the first wide spot he came to. It was his own stupidity, he thought furiously, for allowing a red-haired whore to consume his thoughts so completely. Women had never occupied an important place in his life, not even Ellen, his fiancée. He enjoyed them for the pleasure they gave him; loved them as the moment dictated, then promptly forgot them.

Why then did Glenna's bewitching face and form continue to plague him, filling his mind until it refused to function properly? Perhaps he should have taken the time to bed the little witch; to sate his body with her until she no longer teased his senses. Kane laughed wryly, wondering how many men were doing exactly what he wished to do with her this very night. He made a silent vow to visit the Red Garter the moment he returned to Denver and fully possess her in order to rid himself of this terrible itch he had for her.

Suddenly a shot reverberated through the stillness of the black, moonless night, bouncing off the nearby hills to the valley below. It took a full minute for Kane to react as he listened carefully to determine the source of the disturbance, his finely honed body tensing, his senses warning of danger. Nothing but silence followed the single shot and Kane kneed his mount in the direction he thought the shot had originated. Reflexively he removed his Winchester from the saddle holster, laying it across his thighs as he urged his horse to the left, listening for the slightest sound.

Carefully picking his way through the concealment of the trees, Kane suddenly became aware of a flickering light and immediately headed in that direction. When he was close to hear voices, he dismounted, tethered his horse and stealthily approached on foot, his rifle firmly in hand. When the high-pitched scream of a woman in distress caused the hackles to raise on the back of his neck, Kane knew his decision to remain concealed had been a wise one.

As Kane moved closer he recognized a campsite of sorts. A campfire glowed dimly and the smell of coffee filled the air. Shifting his gaze he saw the outline of three men near a wagon, their attention focused on something lying at their feet. Judging from the scream he heard only moments before he intuitively knew the prone form to be that of a woman. And he gathered from the men's lewd comments and actions, she was about to be assaulted.

Kane raged inwardly. No woman deserved to be treated in such a vile manner no matter what the circumstances! The sound and sight of the woman's struggles tugged at Kane's soft heart and the knowledge that he was outnumbered bothered him not at all. What did disturb him was shooting three unsuspecting men in the back. It went against his nature.

The whole of Kane's life had been governed by his love of adventure, tempered by justice, chivalry and his sense of fairness. Thus it was that Kane stepped lightly into the clearing and called out to the three men bending over the wildly resisting woman.

Glenna knew she was about to be raped and prayed she would pass out before the final degradation. Even death would be preferable to what these depraved monsters planned for her. She felt Wiley slobbering at her bared breasts and cringed as an obscene hardness probed the juncture of her thighs, knowing her fervent prayers would not be answered. Concentrating mightily on placing herself on a level above physical pain and degradation, Glenna did not hear the harsh voice challenge her three tormentors as Kane slipped out of the darkness looking much like an avenging angel with a gun.

"Step away from the woman," Kane ordered in a voice brooking no agrument.

"What!" exclaimed Wiley, his member instantly wilting against Glenna's leg.

Jimbo did not wait to find out what it was the intruder wanted as he acted instinctively and true to form, rising from his crouching position, gun in hand. Sensing the man's intent, Kane automatically pumped the Winchester and squeezed off a shot, the ball finding its mark in Jimbo's right hand. A movement to the left caught his eye as Lem drew, his shot barely missing Kane's head. Almost at the same instant Kane pumped and fired, his aim sure and true as Lem fell dead.

Screeching and cursing, Jimbo dropped to one knee, grasped his fallen weapon with his left hand and squeezed off a shot at Kane, hoping Kane's attention had been distracted by Lem long enough to keep him occupied. But Kane was too experienced in hand-to-hand combat to let his guard down for long. More by instinct than sight Kane sensed his danger and whirled, his rifle barking in response. Kane, his reflexes honed to a fine degree, was faster than Jimbo, his shot hitting Jimbo squarely, sending his opponent's shot wild. It was obvious from the amount of blood spurting from the wound in Jimbo's chest that if he wasn't already dead he soon would be. Satisfied that both men no longer posed a threat, Kane turned his sights on Wiley.

"Whoa, stranger," whined Wiley, holding his hands out beseechingly. "I ain't got no argument with you. Hell, I'm willin' to share if you are. Besides, she ain't nothin' but a whore else she wouldn't be travelin' out here alone. And there ain't a whore alive what's worth dying over."

"Even a whore deserves better than what you and your friends planned for her," Kane barked harshly. "But I don't usually go around shooting a man in cold blood. Your friends would be alive now if they hadn't drawn on me. Now move," he prodded, motioning with his Winchester.

"What are you going to do with me?" asked Wiley, his voice cracking with fear.

"I'm giving you a chance to get out of here alive. Just turn around, drop your holster and keep moving."

"You wouldn't take a man's protection away from him, would you?" complained Wiley. "No telling what I might meet up with out here in the wilderness."

"Just shut up and do as I say," warned Kane, risking a glance at the near naked woman who had finally risen to a crouching position. Her face was in the shadows and he could see little of her features.

But Wiley had noticed the direction of Kane's glance and laughed nastily. "Ha! I shoulda known you wanted the woman fer yourself. Well, yer welcome to her. I'll git, but I ain't givin' up my gun. Out here a man's damn near naked without a weapon. You can shoot me in the back if you want but I ain't givin' up my gun," he repeated. So saying he turned on his heel and disappeared into the darkness. He gambled and won. Kane could not shoot him in the back.

Kane waited a good five minutes before allowing himself to relax. He felt certain the man wouldn't return, especially since his two companions were now dead and could not help him. Obviously the man was a coward and wouldn't return unless the odds were in his favor, Kane decided with a sneer. Once again he glanced at the silent woman kneeling in the shadow of the wagon and was filled with compassion for her.

"Are you all right, miss? Did they . . . did they hurt you?"

"N-no," came the whispery reply. "You arrived in time."

"If you'll be all right for a few minutes I'll get rid of these . . . er . . . bodies." Then he spotted the blanket Glenna had used to cover herself, swooping down to retrieve it. "Here," he said, tossing it in Glenna's direction. "Cover yourself." Concern turned his voice gruff.

He longed to go to her, to comfort her as his chivalrous nature demanded, but instinctively knew she needed a few minutes to pull herself together. He also needed the time to drag the dead bodies from sight and bring his horse closer to camp.

"I'll . . . be fine," croaked Glenna, her voice barely recognizable. "Thank you."

Even in her fright Glenna knew the man who had stumbled upon her camp and handily dispatched her tormentors. Kane Alexander! What was he doing out here so far from Denver? Over and over she thanked God for his timely intervention no matter what had brought him to her.

When he first appeared she feared for his life, the thought of his demise affecting her in a strange way. Could he survive such overwhelming odds, pitted against three armed men bent on rape and mayhem? she wondered bleakly. Then Jimbo made his move, proving to be no more than an annoyance to Kane as he efficiently cut his odds. Glenna held her breath when Lem drew, wanting to scream out a warning, but her voice failed. In the end it wasn't necessary for Kane quickly dispatched Lem to an ignominious death. She was sorry to see Wiley escape so easily but could understand Kane's unwillingness to shoot a man in the back.

Rising to her feet and pulling the blanket about her ruined shift, Glenna watched Kane drag both bodies into the woods, realizing that he had not yet recognized her. After a long interval he returned leading his horse which he tethered near Belle, and turned to face Glenna who had made her way to the fire and was sipping a cup of strong coffee.

Kane spent more time than necessary getting rid of the dead men. Having no implement at hand with which to dig a grave, he did the next best thing. Dragging the bodies into a narrow ravine he then scouted around in the dark until he found several rocks small enough to handle. These he rolled into place above the bodies, protecting them after a fashion from wild animals. Then he led his horse back to camp. At long last Kane turned to face the woman he had just rescued, and gasped in shock as recognition took his breath away.

Flickering light from the campfire danced upon the burnished head of the woman seated upon the ground staring pensively into the dying flames. The same glorious creature who had filled his thoughts all day rose to her feet the moment she became aware of Kane's gasp of astonishment. Her perfect features floated before his startled eyes; full lips slightly parted, green eyes shimmering with unshed tears, hair like the sunset, all red and gold curling about her pale face and tumbling in damp tendrils reaching nearly to her waist. She was breathtaking and Kane did what he should have done the moment danger no longer existed. He held out his arms, softly calling her name.

Her name was warm on his tongue and was all Glenna needed to free her from her frozen limbo as she flung herself into his welcoming embrace. It was like finding a safe port in a storm, Glenna realized with a start as she relaxed and allowed his comfort to surround her.

"Kane, thank God!" she sobbed, dampening the front of his shirt.

"What are you doing out here alone?" he asked, his voice harsh with disapproval. "Why aren't you at the Red Garter with the other women?"

"The Red Garter?" Glenna asked dumbly. Wasn't that a saloon? What did it have to do with her? She was about to ask when he forestalled her by scooping her up in his arms and sitting down on a nearby stump, settling her cosily on his lap.

"Tell me what happened, Glenna," Kane asked, resisting the urge to plant a kiss on her red lips. "Who were those men and what were you doing here with them?"

"I wasn't with them!" bit out Glenna indignantly. "I left Denver alone and when it got too dark to continue I camped here for the night. Those men—they wanted to—they tried to—oh, God, Kane, I don't want to talk about it."

She began to sob softly and Kane soon forgot his questions as he soothed and patted the warm body nestled so comfortably in his arms. He wanted to ask why she was traveling alone, where she was going and why she had left her three companions at the Red Garter to charge foolishly into a pontentially dangerous situation. But Kane realized Glenna had just about reached the end of her endurance and wisely decided to wait until morning to question her further. Right now he was content to sit back and enjoy Glenna's softness curled so trustingly against him.

Then suddenly the sky opened up and it began to rain. Kane had expected it all evening so was not too surprised, just annoyed that it couldn't have held off till the morrow. "Damn!" he cursed, searching the perimeter of the campsite for possible shelter. His eyes fell upon the wagon and he rose abruptly, setting Glenna on her feet.

Half asleep and swaying on her feet, Glenna asked fearfully, "What is it, Kane?"

"Nothing, Glenna, don't be afraid. I won't let anything happen to you. It's raining and we need to find shelter."

"Oh," breathed Glenna, relieved.

"Are there any more blankets in your wagon?" Glenna shook her head. "I have one strapped to my saddle. I'll get it. In the meantime crawl beneath the wagon before you get soaked, I'll join you shortly."

Glenna did as she was told, already feeling chilled from the cold rain which was growing heavier by the minute. Huddling beneath the wagon wrapped in the meager covering, Glenna shivered, glad for Kane's warmth as he slid in beside her, dragging his saddlebag behind him.

"It's pretty cramped under here," he grinned apologetically, "but it's better than sleeping in the rain. Use my saddle bag as a pillow and try to get some rest. We'll talk in the morning."

Gratefully Glenna nodded and squirmed into a comfortable position, pulling the saddlebag beneath her head. But with the rain came a raw wind and try though she might she could not control the shivers racing along her spine.

Kane lay down beside her, painfully aware of every gentle curve and valley of her softly yielding body. His heart hammered wildly against his ribs and his loins ached as he vividly recalled the desire she aroused in him from the first moment he set eyes on her. He felt her body tremble with cold and moved closer in order to share his own body heat. His action served only to bring forth another round of trembling as she made to withdraw.

"Glenna," chided Kane, exasperated, "I'm only trying to keep you warm. Now be a good girl and lie still. I know you had a harrowing experience but I won't hurt you."

"I know, Kane, and I'm sorry. I'm not afraid of you, truly."

"Good," he sighed, reaching out and settling her deeper into the curve of his body.

Automatically he reached over to secure the blanket closer about her and his fingers brushed against naked skin, causing an ever-spreading quiver of pure pleasure to throb through Glenna, warming her chilled flesh as nothing else could.

A staccato burst of raindrops hit the wagonbed above them. The wind keened. Being close to Kane was like nothing she had ever experienced before. Excitement shivered over her skin, cascading through her veins, and Glenna raised her eyes to see Kane staring at her curiously. She parted her lips to speak.

In that instant something strange happened to Kane. The urge to kiss those sweetly parted red lips grew so strong that he threw caution to the wind and covered her mouth with his, languidly exploring the generous outline with his tongue before boldly plunging inside. Glenna's token resistance melted as Kane's kiss deepened and his tongue met and meshed with hers. She whimpered softly in denial when his lips left hers to move downward, sliding along one cheek to nibble at the sensitive hollow of her throat, continuing as he boldy parted the blanket covering her bare breasts.

"My God, I can't stop myself, Glenna," groaned Kane as if in pain, staring at the creamy perfection of her breasts.

His words finally released Glenna's frozen senses as she realized what was happening. She hadn't escaped rape by three men just to be seduced by Kane Alexander! she raged inwardly.

"Kane, no!" she cried, reacting instantly by pushing frantically against the hard wall of his chest.

"Why not?" Kane murmured convincingly. "I want you and I can pay. I'm not like those other men. I told you I won't hurt you. I want to make love to you."

"Pay? I don't know what you're talking about, Kane. Stop, please!"

"Glenna, don't play coy with me. I wanted you the first time I set eyes on you and I still do. I planned on visiting you at the Red Garter the moment my business allowed."

"The Red Garter?" Why did Kane keep talking about the Red Garter? Glenna wondered curiously. Then magically all thought deserted her as Kane's lips found her breasts, teasing them to stiff, aching peaks, then soothing them in the heated depths of his mouth. Glenna moaned, carried away by the tide of newly awakened passion, her mind whirling, sensation upon sensation mounting until she was consumed by delicious lassitude.

One hand slipped between her thighs and Glenna groaned mindlessly as long fingers parted tender flesh and probed gently in an intimate caress. It seemed as if he knew just how to touch her, and where, to give her the most pleasure, but that still did not make what he was doing right. Glenna called on all her willpower to give voice to her protest but found her words effectively stifled when Kane's mouth seized hers once again in a kiss that sent her senses reeling and her resolve fleeing.

Against her will Glenna felt her breasts swell at his touch, their peaks full and erect as his mouth swooped down to sample once more the silken warmth of her flesh. Then he left her briefly and when he returned there was no longer a barrier of clothing between them, her torn shift having already been disposed of. When he parted her legs and slid smoothly in place in the cradle of her thighs, it seemed nothing like the obscene act Wiley had tried to impose upon her. The moment Kane's hardness touched her, she arched against him, seeking, accepting, whatever he wanted to give her. Liquid fire coursed through her as he buried himself deeper between her thighs.

Sensing her surrender, Kane's excitement escalated. He was barely able to restrain his desire to plunge into her soft sheath and ride her to completion. No matter what she was she deserved better. For some obscure reason Kane wanted to give her more pleasure than she had ever known with any other man.

"I won't cheat you, Glenna," he rasped, entering her gently. "I promise you'll find only pleasure in my arms."

The moment Kane felt soft flesh tightly sheath him, his control snapped and he paused no longer at the silken portals, but sought to enter eagerly, hardly expecting the cry of pain wrenched from Glenna's throat. No! It couldn't be! he told himself, pushing forward once more. A barrier blocked his passage and Kane drew back, staring into Glenna's pain-glazed features. But then the urgency of the moment won out over his good sense and he drew back, expertly opening the barrier to his pleasure in one downward stroke, causing Glenna to scream in agony, struggling to fling off Kane's considerable weight.

"Lie still, love," Kane whispered tenderly. "The pain will soon go away and then there will be nothing but exquisite pleasure." His amazement at finding her a virgin had nearly undone him but his passion ruled him and he quickly shed any feelings of guilt. His one consuming desire was to possess fully the woman writhing beneath him.

Slowly the feeling of fullness replaced the pain and once Glenna relaxed Kane began a subtle movement inside her. In a short time Glenna felt a tingling begin at the juncture of her thighs, spiraling upward to encompass every part of her body. The sensation grew, magnified, until a pounding began in her head and she gasped in delight, causing Kane to increase his tempo. Ecstasy thundered through her veins as he moved with easy precision, drawing her slowly into the vortex of rapture. He slid full and deep inside her, his emotions flaming to even higher peaks as small groans of pleasure escaped her lips.

And then rapture exploded with a savage cry of sheer delight that broke through the darkness to float on the wind. His own release imminent, Kane's passion took flight, her name wrenched from the back of his throat as he crumbled into a million pieces, joining Glenna in her journey to the stars. Never had a woman so completely dominated his senses as did the glorious redhead whose virginity he had just stolen!

5

Slowly coming back to earth cradled in each other's arms, the yearnings of their flesh temporarily sated, their lips touched again in the warm afterglow of their lovemaking. Then the magic of the moment was destroyed when Kane asked harshly, "Just who in the hell are you really? Why did you lead me to believe you were a whore?"

"What!" exclaimed Glenna, the real world suddenly intruding upon her dreams. "What ever made you think a thing like that? Certainly not me!" she bristled indignantly.

"No words were needed. Your choice of traveling companions labeled you where mere words failed," Kane remarked wryly.

"My traveling companions? You mean Sal, Pearl and Candy are—?" Kane nodded. "My God! I had no idea! They were friendly and their company helped take the edge off boredom. Sal, especially, was very kind. I was merely their seat companion."

"Glenna, are you truly that innocent? It seems

impossible in this day and age. Where have you been hiding these past years?"

"In a finishing school," Glenna complained bitterly. "Protected by an overzealous Miss Murdoch. After four years I decided I'd had enough and left."

"Glenna, I'm sorry. I should never have listened to Pearl."

"Pearl? She told you I was a . . . whore? Why would she do that when I had no idea she was one?"

"Jealousy, I guess," shrugged Kane. "She probably resented my interest in you and decided to get even by hinting that you were a whore just like she was."

"But why, Kane? Why did you think I was like them when my dress and manner suggested just the opposite?"

"Perhaps it was something you said or something I wanted to believe. I told you I wanted you. Thinking you were a whore made everything simple. And our conversation on the train—well—I assumed we were talking about the same thing. Obviously I was wrong. Dead wrong.

"I'm sorry, Glenna, not for making love to you, but for believing you were something you're not. I didn't mean to take unfair advantage of you. I thought I was bedding an experienced whore. I never expected to find an innocent virgin."

Glenna was silent for long time, her mind a turmoil of indecision. Was she sorry it happened? No, she decided emphatically. If there was any blame she must share it with Kane.

"I'm not sorry either, Kane. Truth to tell I offered little resistance. From the way you dispatched those drifters you could have been a hired gun, but it mattered little. You were gentle and . . . and I have no regrets. Even if you disappeared tomorrow I'd feel the same."

Kane flushed guiltily, for though he wouldn't

disappear on the morrow he would surely return to Philadelphia in the near future to marry Ellen. Somehow that thought was not comforting. Not after knowing Glenna. But did he really know her? He sought to remedy that immediately.

"Where is your family, Glenna? How could they allow you to travel alone? And what in the hell are you doing in the middle of nowhere at night?"

Glenna sighed, wondering where to begin. Finally she said, "I told you before that I left school. No one knew I was coming home."

"Home? Where exactly is home? Surely not here in this wilderness."

"Home is my father's claim, Golden Promise. I hoped to reach it before nightfall. But old Belle has slowed down in four years and no amount of prodding could hurry her steps."

Kane's mouth dropped open in astonishment as he raised up on one elbow to stare into Glenna's emerald eyes. "Oh, no!" he groaned aloud, slapping his forehead in dismay. He had just seduced the daughter of his father's old friend, Paddy O'Neill! The man he had traveled hundreds of miles to see. "You're Paddy O'Neill's daughter!" It was more of an accusation than a question and Glenna's brow furrowed in puzzlement.

"You know my father?"

"Not personally. You see, my father and yours have been friends for years. My father gave Paddy his grubstake years ago."

"Your father is Patrick Morgan? But your name is Alexander," Glenna said, by now thoroughly confused.

"Kane Alexander Morgan," Kane revealed sheepishly. "I don't always use my last name. Especially going into a situation I know nothing about."

"What situation?"

"Paddy wrote to my father several weeks ago asking for help. He didn't explain other than to say it was urgent and secret."

"So your father sent you here to find out what Da wanted," Glenna mused thoughtfully.

"Not exactly," Kane hedged. "My father died some weeks back and I felt compelled by virtue of our fathers' long friendship to come out here and offer my help to Paddy. Do you know why he wrote my father?"

Glenna shook her bright head. "I'm sorry. I have no idea. Da was not the best of correspondents. And I'm sorry about your father."

"I guess we'll just have to wait for Paddy to explain."

Now it was Glenna's turn to express astonishment. "You mean you don't know? You haven't heard? Surely someone in town must have told you."

"Told me what?" pressed Kane.

"About Da. He's dead. It happened over two weeks ago. I . . . I just learned about it myself."

Kane's eyes turned tender as he gazed at the young woman with sympathy, for she was too young to be left without a protector. Then to became a victim of near rape so soon after learning about her father . . . It's a wonder she held up so well under the pressure. He suffered a pang of remorse at the thought that he had added to her distress by mistaking her for a whore and taking her virginity.

"What did Paddy die of? I had no idea he was sick. Or was it an accident?"

"Da was murdered!" spat Glenna, her voice cracking with emotion. "He was bushwhacked and killed just outside of town. So far the marshal has come up with no suspects and no clues to point out the killer."

"My God, Glenna, I'm sorry! If only I knew what his call for help was all about, or had gotten here sooner."

"I thought the same thing, Kane. I should have

returned home long before now. In my heart I knew something was wrong."

"Do you have any idea what might have been troubling him?" questioned Kane, seizing on Glenna's words.

"No, not really. I know only what the marshal told me."

"Which is?" prompted Kane.

"That Da was having financial problems. It seemed his claim played out and his dream of finding the mother lode was never realized. For some unexplained reason Da was killed and why is a mystery to me. Oh, Kane, it's all so confusing."

"Well, Miss Glenna O'Neill, it looks as if we're sort of partners now. For my father's sake I intend to stay until Paddy's murder is solved. I owe you that much."

"Thank you, Kane, for both myself and my father. I'm sure he would rest easier knowing someone cared enough to find his killer."

They were silent a long time, Glenna thinking about her father and Kane about the woman resting in his arms. What he told Glenna was true. He was sorry he had seduced her and found her a virgin but not sorry he had made love to her. He knew he should tell her about Ellen and his coming marriage but somehow the time wasn't right. How could he tell a woman with whom he had just made the most extraordinary love that he was about to wed another? A woman to whom he had never made love and had no desire to.

Finally Kane said, "Get some sleep, Glenna. Tomorrow is another day and I'm here to help you. I won't desert you. I'll remain until all this is resolved." Was he promising something he couldn't deliver? Kane wondered fretfully as Glenna burrowed deeper into his arms, sighed once then promptly went to sleep. Only time would tell.

* * *

Widening streams of sunlight parted watery gray clouds forecasting a glorious day as Glenna stretched awake, wincing at the unaccustomed twinges of discomfort originating from the secret place between her thighs. She smiled in remembrance, wondering why she felt no remorse at giving herself without reservation to a man she knew nothing about. For when Kane made love to her she had no idea he was the son of her father's friend.

Glancing about she saw that Kane had already risen and was busily tending the fire and seeing to both his horse and Belle. It gave her a chance to study him at leisure without him knowing.

Bare to the waist he was slim-hipped and lanky but moved with the feline grace of a mountain cat. Tight pants fitted firm buttocks and long thighs like a second skin. The gunbelt strapped low around his hips served to emphasize his manliness.

His shoulders were broad, as was his chest, but not so broad that they detracted from his overall leanness. He didn't merely walk, he sauntered. His swaggering hips and rolling gait brought a flush to her cheeks for they suggested a talent not limited to merely walking. As she studied him she wished he would use that talent on her once more.

Abruptly Kane turned. Amusement splashed through his smoky-gray eyes. "Do you see anything you like?" he asked with a twinkle.

Glenna had the grace to blush. Standing there without a shirt he resembled a bronze god, strong and awesomely handsome. "I . . . I didn't mean to stare," she stammered. "How . . . did you know?"

"I always know when a beautiful woman is looking at me." His words triggered an emotion she couldn't define. It flashed across her face and shimmered off her like waves off the arid prairie in summertime.

"Kane," she whispered, hot desire spiraling through her.

Kane read the invitation in her eyes and voice but fought the urge to take her. Lord knows he wanted her but he wanted to be sure she came to him this time of her own free will. He had no wish to take unfair advantage of Glenna's helplessness again. Before he made love to her it had to be with her full knowledge and consent.

Kane knelt before her, his eyes tender, feeling emotions he had never felt before. "Are you sure, Glenna?"

"Positive, Kane," she replied, licking her lips in avid anticipation.

"Say it, love. Tell me what you want."

"I want you to make love to me," she replied without the slightest hesitation. "I need you, now."

My God! she thought wickedly. Was this the demure schoolgirl, Glenna O'Neill, speaking? Overnight Kane Morgan had wrought a complete change in her. Was she any better than Sal? Or Pearl? Or Candy? Of course, she promptly answered. I want Kane because of the way I feel, not for money. Then all logic fled as Kane, grinning devilishly, quickly shed his pants and joined her beneath the wagon.

Needing no further encouragement, his body already hard and throbbing, Kane found Glenna ready also and he entered her eagerly, his masculine body descending to make them one. Then he was a warm, demanding flame within her, feeding a fire that raged out of control.

This is much better than last night, Glenna thought dreamily, her hands tunneling through crisp black waves at the nape of Kane's neck. Her straying thoughts were shattered as Kane teased her mouth with soft kisses, nibbling gently, touching their sweetness with his tongue. And then the feeling began deep in the pit of her stomach. Kane sensed it and abruptly tenderness and care yielded to hard, fierce passion as he effortlessly brought them both to climax.

They reached Golden Promise shortly after high noon. The moment Glenna climbed down from the wagon seat her eyes unconsciously sought the stately aspen standing on the hill rising above them. "Da lies there beneath that tree," she murmured as a pang of sadness wrenched at her heart. Without giving a thought to Kane she started toward the hill and her father's final resting place.

"Glenna! Where are you going?" Kane called to her departing back.

"Marshal Bartow said Da was buried up there," she replied, pointing toward the top of the hill. "I need to visit with him, Kane."

"Wait, I'll go with you, love."

"No! I . . . I want to be alone, Kane. You understand, don't you?"

Kane nodded and watched as her lithe form moved effortlessly up the hill, picking her way carefully around rocks, boulders and loose gravel.

After they had made love again this morning his spirits soared; he felt as if he could spend the rest of his life waking up each morning with Glenna in his arms. What in the hell was the matter with him? he wondered. He'd made love to plenty of women, more than he could count. What made Glenna so special? If only he had met her before. Before he succumbed to his family's wishes and asked Ellen to marry him.

Surely he hadn't fallen in love with Glenna, he mused thoughtfully. Love played no part in his enjoyment of women. He wanted nothing to do with love, for to love someone was to give up a part of yourself, and that Kane was unwilling to do. After a lengthy time spent in mental combat, Kane decided to enjoy each day as it came. If Glenna still wanted him, he would gladly oblige, but he could offer her no promises. One day soon he must return to Philadelphia to marry Ellen whether he wanted to or not. If he weren't such a coward he would tell Glenna about Ellen and his wedding plans. But selfishly he kept that information to himself. For the short time they had together he wanted nothing to interfere with their enjoyment of one another. It was wrong of him, he knew, but he couldn't help himself.

Glenna found the cabin she and Da had occupied for many years little changed. The curtains she had made before she left still hung at the windows. Her small bedroom, hardly more than an alcove, was just as she left it. It appeared clean and well-cared for, as did the rest of the cabin consisting of a combination dining/living room, a kitchen and a second bedroom which belonged to her father. It was larger and better equipped than most prospectors' cabins because Paddy wanted to make it a home for his only child.

"You may as well sleep in the cabin, Kane, and make use of Da's old room," Glenna offered as Kane carried in her bags.

"Are you sure, Glenna? I could make do with a pallet in one of the sheds."

"I'm sure, Kane. In fact, I'd feel much safer with you sleeping in the cabin."

And easier for us to be together, he speculated happily. A slow smile hung on the corners of his mouth as he anticipated long rapturous nights teaching Glenna the various methods of love. Not once did he consider that he might be using Glenna for his own pleasure for he fully intended to give her as much pleasure as he received.

"Glenna, what in the hell are you doing?" Kane

had just returned to the cabin from an inspection of the sluice and rocker to find Glenna literally tearing the cabin upside down. Drawers were thrown open, clothes strewn about the room and bedding piled in a heap on the floor.

"I'm looking for a letter, or note, or any kind of message from Da," Glenna wailed desperately. "But there's nothing, Kane. Not even the tiniest amount of dust or flakes to show for years of backbreaking labor. Did you find anything outside?"

"Just tools and such in both sheds. Did you stop at the bank first to see if Paddy left anything there on deposit for you? Surely he's taken something out of the creekbed in the last months."

"I didn't think of it," Glenna admitted sheepishly. "I just wanted to get out here as quickly as possible and say my goodbyes to Da."

"As you can see, Glenna, there's nothing out here for you. A week or two should be ample time to work the stream and determine if there might be anything of worth trickling down from the hills. Perhaps the marshal is right and it's time to give up Golden Promise."

"Leave Golden Promise!" gasped Glenna. "Never! Where would I go? This is the only home I've ever known. It's Da's dream. Given time, I know he'd have found the mother lode."

"Glenna, be reasonable. You're a woman alone. There's no way you could work this claim on your own."

"I'll hire help. There has to be a way. What about you, Kane? Won't you help me?"

"I can stay but a short time, Glenna. Maybe long enough to find your father's killer, but my home is in Philadelphia. I have . . . obligations there. My stay here was never meant to be permanent."

"You mean you won't stay! Not even after . . .

after—" Her voice faltered and she sought to conceal her hurt.

"The first time we made love, Glenna, it was entirely my fault. I seduced you. But this morning it was what you wanted. You remember I asked you if you were sure. Don't try playing upon my sympathy in order to get me to stay and work this worthless claim. Sooner or later my responsibilities will force me to return. It's best you know that from the beginning."

"Responsibilities be damned!" Glenna ground out reproachfully. "Leave now if you must. I don't need you, or any man." Her pointed chin jutted out defiantly and Kane, exasperated as he was, felt the sudden urge to grasp her in his arms and kiss her sweetly parted lips; she looked so adorable when aroused by anger. But of course he didn't for fear she'd fly into a rage.

"It's true I came to you willingly," Glenna countered hotly, "but you can be damn certain it won't happen again!"

"Whether you believe it or not, love, you need me right now. I owe it to both our fathers to see that justice is done."

"And when you leave? What of me? And Golden Promise?"

"Forget the claim, Glenna. If it was of any worth I'd gladly help you out. But no matter what, I won't leave you destitute. Were my father alive he would settle a sum on you to keep you in comfort until you marry. I can do no less. Or better yet," he amended in a sudden burst of enthusiasm, "I'll take you back east with me. You can live with my mother. She'd be glad for the company and see that you are properly launched into society."

"The hell with society! And I don't need a keeper. I've had one for the past four years. Nor do I want your charity. I can make my own way, you'll see!"

Green eyes snapping, red hair flying, Kane thought

she'd never looked more beautiful. Though it would be a severe test for his willpower he would honor her wishes. He would place a tight rein on his urges and not bed her unless he was invited. Dear God! Give him strength.

Over the next few days Kane carefully examined all aspects of the claim. He had studied mining extensively, partly because of his father's interest in it and partly out of curiosity, and he decided that Paddy had chosen his site well. At this point the creek had lost most of its carrying power, widening to a placid stream, its current diminished. As the stream bent to the left a gravel bar protruded, creating a natural obstacle for the stream to deposit its treasure. All around them rose the foothills from which the gold had washed down from the lodes exposed from ages of being left unprotected to weather and erosion.

The mother lode could be anywhere in those foothills, and if Paddy hadn't found it in years of searching he and Glenna hadn't a chance in hell of finding it in a few days or weeks, Kane concluded.

Glenna toiled tirelessly beside Kane, working the sluice and cradle-like wooden rocker until the blisters rose like warts on the palms of her hands and her back and shoulders were one massive pain. After ten days with nothing but a token show of color, Kane was ready to call it quits. But Glenna stubbornly refused to give up.

"Face it, Glenna," Kane pointed out. "Golden Promise has given up its last treasures. There's nothing out here for you. I'll give you a day or two to gather up anything of value and then we'll leave. It's time I called on the marshal anyway."

"I'm not leaving, Kane. I'll pan my hand if I have to, but I know there's still gold washing down from the mother lode. If only I knew why Da wrote for help.

What kind of help did he need? Why didn't he leave a message for me?"

"I'm afraid that's something we'll never know, Glenna. You just have to accept it. This claim isn't your entire life. Find a man you can love, get married, have a family."

I've already found a man I can love, Glenna mouthed silently. But he has no room in his life for me. It hurt, but it wasn't the end of the world. Golden Promise was all she had and she intended to keep it. One day she'd learn Da's secret, and until she did she'd stay put no matter what Kane said.

"Do what you have to do, Kane," Glenna retorted stubbornly. "Go back to town, go back to Philadelphia. I'm not your concern."

"I need to talk to the marshal, Glenna, to find out if he's found your father's killer. I'm afraid I can only stay in Denver another week or two and I intend to see Paddy's death avenged. You've no choice but to return to town with me, I won't leave you out here alone."

The argument ended there and Kane assumed he had won until after supper that night when Glenna presented him with a long list of supplies for him to purchase in town.

"Mr. Howard at the general store will give me credit," she said sweetly.

"Dammit, Glenna! How many times do I have to tell you! You're the most stubborn woman I know! You can't stay out here alone."

"I'll be fine, Kane, truly. You'll only be gone a day or two anyway."

"But what about when I return to Philadelphia? What then?"

"I'll hire someone to help me. Give them a share of the claim, maybe. I'll get by somehow."

"There are times I'd like to wring your beautiful neck, Glenna," Kane sighed, recognizing defeat.

Sleep escaped Glenna. She and Kane had parted at bedtime, each going to their own room. If Kane gave her a long, searching look when she bid him goodnight she chose to ignore it. Why should she be used to slake his passion when she was nothing more to him than a warm body? Granted, he held some feelings for her, but not enough to keep him from returning to Philadelphia and those responsibilities he spoke of so often. Yet Glenna could not deny she wanted him, recalling the magic of their coming together with vivid clarity.

Restless, yearning for something she had no right to, Glenna left her bed and walked to the window. The moon slipped from behind a bank of feathery clouds and washed the earth with its silvery glow. A gentle breeze stroked cool fingers over her heated flesh. Driven by an insatiable need she refused to define, Glenna left her room, walked through the door and into the night.

Moonlight dusted the trees and hills with silver and sent a pale shimmer of light dancing upon the water flowing past the shadowy forms of sluice and rocker. Clad only in a voluminous white nightgown, Glenna strolled aimlessly along the bank of the creek, wandering upstream until the cabin was but faintly visible in the distance. Only then did she stop, staring pensively into the water sparkling like a million diamonds beneath the surface. To Glenna it appeared almost as if a chunk of the moon had broken off and lay at the bottom of a pothole in the middle of the shallow stream.

It took several minutes of intense concentration before Glenna realized what she was looking at. Like a bolt of lightning the magnitude of her discovery nearly jolted her off her feet. Without a doubt in her mind Glenna knew she was looking at a piece of rock called float; large pieces of quartz or rock broken off from the lode and washed into the streambed by natural occurrences such as rock slides or earthquakes. All she and Kane would have to do to find the mother lode was work their way upstream panning as they went.

Had her father already discovered other pieces of float and finally located the mother lode he had spent years searching for? Did he write Patrick Morgan for help because he needed big capital to develop and mine his lode? Glenna knew that once the lode was found miners had to be hired, machinery bought to drill deep tunnels and an ore-crushing stomping mill must be built.

Mindless of her surroundings Glenna flung off her nightgown and waded into the icy stream. The gentle current lapped about her knees and she reached midstream with no mishap. Kneeling, she scooped up a piece of float about the size of her fist and held it up to the moonlight to assure herself she hadn't been mistaken. To her delight pale veins of yellow shimmered from the blue-gray chunk of rock. Shrieking from pure joy Glenna waded out of the water, float grasped tightly in her fist, and raced toward the cabin calling out Kane's name every step of the way.

Kane reared out of a sound sleep into total confusion. Still in a stupor he heard Glenna screaming out his name at the top of her lungs and he reacted instinctively, long years of training coming to his aid. Jumping into his pants and snatching up his Winchester, he stumbled through the darkened cabin cursing loudly when he banged his shin against a chair in passing.

He came out of the door at a run, certain that Glenna had been attacked by wild animals when she answered a call of nature in the middle of the night, only to be stopped dead in his tracks by an ethereal, fairy creature standing completely nude beneath the revealing light of the moon. Bathed in silver and gold, taut breasts peaking deliciously, every supple line of her body clearly defined, the gold statue was holding her arms out to him. The fiery brand of bright red hair on her head and between her thighs lighted his way like a beacon and Kane moved forward as if in a trance, one from which he never wanted to awaken.

The suddenly the dream disintegrated as the golden goddess screeched his name, flinging out words, forcing him to concentrate.

"Kane, I've found float! The claim isn't played out like everyone thought! Look! It's gold! Do you know what that means? It's from the mother lode, Kane, I know it is."

"Glenna, what are you doing out here without your clothes? And what in the hell are you babbling about? You just scared ten years off my life."

"Look at this, Kane!" Glenna thrilled breathlessly as she held out the piece of float for Kane's inspection. "I found it upstream in a natural pothole. See the streaks of gold? I'm sure there's more where this came from. Do you know what this means, Kane?" Words spilled from her tongue without control.

Kane took the bluish rock from Glenna's hand, examining it as best he could beneath the moonlight. "Well, what do you think?" she asked impatiently.

Kane bent her an inscrutable look, a lopsided grin hanging on the corner of his mouth. "I think you'd better get inside and put on some clothes before you catch your death. You're sopping wet."

"Damn you, Kane!" Glenna snapped, exasperated. "You know what I mean. Those yellow veins in the rock are gold. There's no reason to abandon the claim now."

"Glenna, one piece of float doesn't mean a thing. True, somewhere up there lies the mother lode, but that's a vast area and you may never find it."

"I'll find it," declared Glenna with grim determination. "With or without your help."

Turning on her heel she presented her delectable

backside as she walked away. "Where are you going?"

"Back to where I found the float. There's bound to be more where this came from."

"Oh, no, you're not," Kane retorted, bounding after her. "You're going to bed, preferably mine."

"What!" Any protest she might have voiced was cut off when she found herself lifted off her feet and transported back to the cabin in a pair of strong arms. She was suddenly, painfully aware of the hard, muscular promise of his body against hers and the fire of response was kindled in her instantly despite her earlier resolve to resist Kane.

Damn! she chafed inwardly. Why did he have to be so handsome? There should have been a law against stacking so much strength, charm and good looks in one virile package.

Sensing capitulation, Kane emitted a hoarse growl and carried her straight to his bed, tumbling across the mattress beside her. Suddenly she was nothing but response and instinct in his arms as he reached out and pulled her beneath him, lowering his head to kiss her fiercely, tasting, drawing deeply, ravaging her with his loving attack.

The muscles of Glenna's thighs quivered as she felt the treacherous weakness desire brought on as it raced through her. She protested weakly when he drew away long enough to remove his pants, then he was lowering himself slowly, the hard shaft of his passion moving against her moistness. Her lips separated in a low gasp, her heavy lids dropped. He entered her, plunging deeply, his own joy soaring as her arms clamped tightly around him, drawing him deeper. And as ecstasy burst within her Glenna knew why she had been created. All these years she had been biding her time, waiting for Kane Morgan!

6

To Glenna's chagrin Kane was gone when she awoke the following morning. A note weighted down by the piece of float rested in the middle of the kitchen table. She read his words thinking of all that had passed between them the previous night.

> Dear Glenna,
> I didn't have the heart to wake you and I wanted to get an early start. After your find last night I knew I couldn't talk you into leaving so I'll try to return as soon as possible. You know why I must go into town, we already discussed it. I know how excited you are about the float but I don't think it changes a thing. We'll talk about it when I return. Keep the Spencer handy at all times, you mean a lot to me.

Glenna read and reread the note, wanting to squeeze more into it than there was. Kane didn't say he loved her, or that he wouldn't return eventually to

Philadelphia. The only thing positive she gathered from his words was that he cared for her. He probably cared for his . . . his . . . horse—or dog. But that wasn't love. She'd do well to forget her own feelings and concentrate on finding the lode now that she knew it existed. She didn't need a man, especially one who didn't need her.

The gloom of dusk had settled around him when Kane rode into town. He had gotten an early start and made good time. So good, in fact, that he was able to take a leisurely bath before going down to the dining room for supper. If the clerk at the Palace wondered where he had been these past ten days he didn't mention it, even though Kane knew it was on the tip of the man's tongue. After all, he had paid his rent for a month in advance.

The entire twenty-mile trip between Golden Promise and Denver was one of reflection for Kane. The image of Glenna standing like a nude, gilded goddess in the moonlight was imprinted forever upon his brain. If he lived to be one hundred he would always remember her that way. How could he casually turn his back on her when it came time to leave? Kane wondered distractedly. In the few days he had known Glenna she had come to mean a great deal to him, more than a mere affair of passion, more even than he cared to admit. But whatever they had together must be forgotten, set aside, once he left Denver to marry Ellen. A passion such as theirs was too hot to last anyway, Kane consoled himself regretfully. But Glenna was not like all the other women he had known and loved briefly, torridly, then promptly forgotten, he decided emphatically, recalling the previous night and their spontaneous coming together. Glenna was like no woman he had ever met nor was likely to meet again.

With several hours to kill after supper Kane

decided to visit the Red Garter, having heard so much about it from Pearl. It was only a short distance from the Palace Hotel and, deciding the walk would do him good after a long day in the saddle, he made his way toward the largest saloon of its kind in Denver, its hundreds of lights blazing a welcome as he entered through the swinging doors.

Raising his eyebrows in astonishment Kane was unprepared for such grandeur. The foyer floor was laid in black and white tiles and hanging from the ceiling was a large cut-crystal chandelier. The far wall was completely mirrored, making the main room appear much larger than it was. Rich upholstered red velvet chairs sat around black lacquered tables and red velvet draped the long windows. A tall archway led to the gaming room and on the other side of the foyer Kane caught a glimpse of a platform-like stage and ornate piano. The opulence of the surroundings lent a whole new meaning to the word saloon.

It was obvious this was no cheap gambling hall hastily erected to serve miners and rough prospectors. The Red Garter was a special establishment erected for the sole purpose of catering to the needs and desires of that new breed of men called gold or silver barons who went through their newfound riches as quickly as they made them. Denver teemed with such men.

Kane sauntered into the gaming room, spotted an empty seat at the blackjack table and joined the half-dozen or so men trying their luck. He promptly lost the first game, then surprised himself by winning three in a row. His luck held and he won two more before taking his chips and ambling over to the roulette table. He had just placed his bet when a sultry voice whispered in his ear, "It's about time you showed up, handsome."

A frown carved deep lines in his forehead as he turned to greet Pearl, recalling how she had purposely led him to believe Glenna was a lady of pleasure.

"Hello, Pearl," he greeted sourly.

"My, but you're glum tonight," she teased, pressing her generous curves against him suggestively. "I know a cure for that. How about it, Kane? My room is at the top of the stairs." She motioned toward a carpeted staircase leading from the room to an upper floor.

Eyeing Pearl distastefully, Kane had to admit she looked stunning. Dressed daringly in a green satin gown that brazenly displayed her charms; shining black hair coiled expertly atop her head, Pearl could entice any man she desired. But strangely enough, Kane wasn't interested.

"Not now, Pearl," he said, his voice quietly emphatic. "I'm on a winning streak and don't want to push my luck by stopping now."

Full red lips pursed into a pout, Pearl was determined not to be ignored. "Come on, honey, the first one's free," she whispered huskily, pulling on his arm coaxingly. "I'll be your luck."

Kane fumed inwardly, aware of the loud guffaws and lusty advice taking place around him and intended for his benefit. Thanks to Pearl's sexual advances and his own reluctance, he had suddenly become the center of unwanted attention. Giving Pearl an exasperated look he rose and motioned her toward the stairs, gray eyes glued on the seductive sway of her hips as she glided across the floor. She led him up the stairs and directly to her room.

The minute the door closed behind them Pearl launched herself into Kane's arms, but was surprised to find her advances thwarted when Kane caught and held her at bay. "What's the matter, honey?" she asked caressingly. "Do you want me to take off my clothes first? I won't disappoint you, Kane."

"I'm sure you won't, Pearl, because you'll not have the chance. I didn't come up here for that."

"What in the hell did you come for? Certainly not to talk."

Kane laughed humorlessly, his lip curled contemptuously. "That's exactly why I'm here."

Pearl shrugged impatiently. "Well then talk so we can get down to business. Where have you been all this time?"

"My comings and goings are not important. What is important is your reason for lying to me about Glenna."

"Glenna? Glenna O'Neill? What has she got to do with us?"

"Why did you lead me to believe she was a whore and would be working here at the Red Garter?"

Pearl shifted uncomfortably, looking decidedly guilty. "What does it matter? That prim miss couldn't satisfy you like I could. She's probably still a virgin and would faint if you so much as took off your shirt."

Amusement splashed through Kane's gray eyes and his lips twitched into a wry grin. If Pearl only knew, he thought, delicious memories of Glenna caught in the throes of ecstasy flashing through his brain. "It makes no difference what Glenna is or does, Pearl, you still had no right to lie to me."

"Who told you the truth?" Pearl asked, eyes narrowed suspiciously. "Everyone could tell you wanted the virtuous little chit. Is that it, Kane? Are you angry because she wouldn't let you bed her?"

"So help me, Pearl, if you ever spread lies about Glenna again I'll personally see you punished. Do I make myself clear?"

"Perfectly," ground out Pearl sullenly. Disgusted, Kane turned to leave. "Wait!" Pearl cried out. "Don't leave, Kane. We're not finished."

"I'm finished," Kane declared emphatically. "If you'll excuse me I have a date at the roulette table." Then he was gone, leaving a fuming Pearl in his wake.

* * *

The next morning bright and early Kane called on Marshal Bartow. He introduced himself and the marshal immediately recognized the name.

"I didn't expect you so soon," he said to a confused Kane.

"You were expecting me?" puzzled Kane.

"Actually, I expected a much older man. And I thought you might write or wire in response to my telegram, not come in person."

"I think it was my father you tried to contact, Marshal, not me," Kane informed him. "My father, Patrick Morgan, is dead, but I've come in his stead in response to a plea for help from Paddy O'Neill."

"Then you already know about Paddy." Relief softened the marshal's craggy features. "Have you seen Glenna?"

Kane nodded. "I've been out to Golden Promise, looking over the claim. Glenna tells me Paddy was killed. Have you caught the man responsible?"

"I've come up against a blank wall, Morgan," Bartow admitted frankly.

"Are you going to do something about it?" Kane challenged. "I promised Glenna I'd stick around until her father's killer is brought to justice."

"It's not that simple, Morgan," explained the marshal. "I'm conducting an investigation but so far have come up empty-handed. I'll tell you exactly what I've learned thus far."

Kane settled back, concentrating on the marshal's words.

"Paddy drove his wagon to town the day before his death intending to buy supplies; a list was found on his body. He checked into the Denver Arms, took his evening meal in the dining room and later showed up at the Red Garter.

"He met a man there, a stranger, obviously,

because no one seemed to know him. The last time Paddy was seen alive was when he walked out of the saloon. From all accounts Paddy and the stranger parted company on good terms. The man's name is Eric Carter. The next day Paddy was found dead not far from the city."

"Is this Eric Carter still in town, Marshal?"

"He was as of yesterday," Bartow replied. "He came in here asking directions to Paddy's claim. I questioned him at length but he seemed to know nothing of what happened after he and Paddy parted. He even expressed sorrow over Paddy's death."

"Where is he staying, Marshal?" Kane asked, rising to leave. "I'd like to talk to him personally. It seems strange that he should ask about Golden Promise."

"He's at the Denver Arms. Wait, Morgan," the marshal called out as Kane headed toward the door. "There's something you should know first. I didn't find out till yesterday myself."

Kane froze, all his senses flashing a warning. "What is it I should know, Marshal?"

"Before he died Paddy sold his claim to Eric Carter. For $5000."

"What! Impossible. According to Glenna Paddy would never sell Golden Promise."

"After speaking with Mr. Carter, I'm inclined to believe he did. He had taken nothing of value from the claim in months and he needed the money to keep his daughter in that fancy school back east."

"I find it difficult to believe Paddy would have sold his claim without finding the mother lode."

"Didn't you say Paddy wrote your father for help?"

"Yes, but—"

"Mr. Morgan, I found it hard to swallow myself but Eric Carter produced a bill of sale and deed, all legally signed by Paddy and properly filed by Carter. I can't accuse a man of murder with no proof. The desk clerk claims Paddy saw no one after he retired for the night and that Carter didn't sleep in his room that night. When questioned, Carter admitted he spent the night with a woman from the Red Garter and it checked out. My hands are tied where Carter is concerned."

A hopeless gloom settled over Kane. Poor Glenna. How could she bear yet another tragedy in her young life? "What's the woman's name, Marshal? The one Carter spent the night with?"

"Her name was Conchita, a cute little Mex whore. But you'll learn nothing from her. The poor girl was killed in an accident a week or so back. A runaway carriage."

"Christ!" exploded Kane. "Is there no end to this?"

"If it makes you feel any better, I went over to the Red Garter and learned that Carter was there that night and seen going upstairs with Conchita. So his story checks out."

"It's too pat, Marshal," scoffed Kane derisively. "In fact, it stinks. Are you blind? Obviously the man ambushed Paddy and stole his deed! Then he killed Conchita before anyone could check his alibi. Do your duty, Marshal, or I will take the law into my own hands."

"Simmer down, Morgan, I'm not as stupid as you seem to think. I'm not completely convinced of Carter's innocence and I haven't dropped the investigation, not by a long shot. I don't want Carter to think I'm suspicious of him. I want him to go about his business. If he's guilty of murder he'll make a mistake, and when he does I'll be waiting. I have to admit, though, that the man doesn't look or act like a cold-blooded killer. It's just possible that Paddy was set upon and robbed by drifters. He didn't bank the $5000 Carter claimed he paid Paddy in gold and the money wasn't on Paddy's body."

"That's because he never gave Paddy $5000," Kane barked.

"Perhaps," admitted Bartow. "But that has to be proved."

"Let me help, Marshal, I can—"

"Keep out of it, Morgan. I'll handle this in my own way."

Kane seethed inwardly, furious that he wouldn't be allowed a hand in trapping Paddy's killer. "In the meantime, what about Glenna? She's lost her home, her inheritance, everything. How in the hell do you think she's going to live?"

"That's where I hoped your father might help. She needs a guardian. Take her back east with you, Morgan, until I get all this straightened out. It could be dangerous for her to remain."

"Ha!" snorted Kane derisively. "You know Glenna as well or better than I do. You know damn well she won't leave Denver. She's determined to see her father's killer brought to justice. That little lady has a mind of her own and no amount of coaxing will change it."

Marshal Bartow slanted Kane an assessing look, weighing his next words carefully. "You can charm her into it, Morgan, you seem the type. Hell, you could even marry her!"

Kane grinned, thinking of how complicated his life would be married to Glenna. It sure as hell would't be dull! "It's not a bad idea, Marshal, but I'm already engaged. In fact, if I don't hurry home for my wedding I'll have the whole damn Morgan clan breathing down my neck."

"Too bad, it sounded like a good idea. You did say you stayed out at the claim with Glenna, didn't you?" Bartow asked slyly.

Kane flushed, suddenly flustered. "I . . . er . . . it's not what you think, Marshal. I feel a certain responsibility toward Glenna and that's as far as it goes."

"Oh, yes, I forgot. You're engaged," Bartow commented dryly. "What do you intend doing now?"

"I'm going to send a telegram, pick up a few supplies and talk to Carter before I head back to the claim. I want to tell Glenna about Eric Carter before he shows up at Golden Promise and drops his bombshell."

"You may be too late," muttered Bartow. "I got the impression he was going to go out there first thing this morning. Said he hadn't claimed his property yet because he had some loose ends to tie up in Silver City first. He didn't even know Glenna had returned from school until I told him. He promised he'd give her all the time she needed to pack up and leave."

"My God, Marshal, and you let him go!" cried Kane, jumping up in alarm. "The man may be a killer and Glenna is out there alone! What were you thinking of?"

"Calm down, Morgan. Carter won't hurt the girl. He's too smart for that. He'd hang for certain if Glenna was harmed, for he'd be the first person I'd bring in."

"I've got to get out there, Marshal. He's already got an hour or two on me."

"Morgan, don't interfere," warned Bartow as Kane prepared a hasty departure. "If Carter is our man I'll see that justice is done. Don't do anything foolish."

Giving the marshal an openly defiant look, Kane sailed through the door.

Although Kane itched to mount his horse and rush immediately back to Glenna, there was one pressing duty left to perform. It was imperative he send a telegram to Ellen and also one to his mother explaining in as few words as possible his reasons for postponing his wedding by a few weeks. He knew it was bound to cause a lot of anger and resentment on Ellen's part, but there was no help for it. Under no circumstances would he leave Glenna now when she needed him most. Had he known the consequences wrought by his telegrams he might never have sent them.

Glenna rummaged around in her father's trunk until she found a pair of trousers that fit reasonably well and an old plaid shirt. Rolling up both sleeves to the elbows and both legs to the knees, Glenna prepared to return to the spot where she had found the piece of float the night before. Perhaps the find wasn't important to Kane but to her it meant everything. It even helped explain Da's call for help. It was evident to Glenna that he had finally found the mother lode and needed money to buy mining equipment; it was too big an operation to finance on his own. So once again he had turned to his old friend for help and advice.

Only a wealthy man like Patrick Morgan had the means to grubstake such a venture. Damn Kane! she seethed in impotent rage. Why couldn't he see the importance of her find? He'd damn well better listen to her when he returned. If not she'd trace the float and find the mother lode herself despite his pessimism.

Searching in the supply shack Glenna found the gold pan she was looking for. Four inches deep, ten inches across the bottom and fifteen inches across the top, Glenna knew exactly how it was used. Pan in one hand, shovel in the other, she headed upstream, wading into the middle of the stream where she had found the piece of float the night before. Placing a shovelful of streambed sand in the pan, she submerged it in the water and spun it slowly in a circular motion to wash out sand and silt over the top, knowing that the heavier gold would remain on the bottom.

She labored tirelessly all day, working her way further upstream, gaining nothing but huge blisters on her palms and tips of her fingers for her efforts. At dusk her toes began to shrivel and she was considering calling it a day when she abruptly came upon another piece of float. Blue-gray in color like the first, it was smaller, but the sparkle of gold unmistakable.

Now there was no doubt in Glenna's mind that her father had been killed because he had found the mother lode and his secret had been discovered. But as it turned out Da was killed for nothing because the claim belonged to her. It just didn't make sense. If claim jumpers had killed Paddy they would have already been out here working the claim. Where were they?

After eating a frugal supper put together from her meager supplies, Glenna retired, wishing Kane were there to share her thoughts, her hopes—and most of all, her bed. Oh, she knew she would never have more of him than she had now, but she intended for this time together to last a lifetime.

The next day Glenna found a piece of gold-bearing quartz and was ecstatic, renewing her efforts with a vengeance though her arms ached and her blisters developed blisters. By late afternoon exhaustion claimed her frail body and reluctantly she trudged back to the cabin with her find, carefully concealing it with the other two pieces on the bottom of her trunk, shoving it out of sight under the bed.

Glenna was just finishing supper when the sound of a lone horsemen alerted her to the fact that she was soon to have company. Uttering a cry of joy she was on the verge of flinging open the door to welcome Kane back when she recalled his words cautioning her to keep the Spencer nearby at all times.

Taking up the rifle where it rested in the corner she made sure it was loaded then cautiously opened the door. About the only thing she could tell from a distance was that her visitor was a man. Nearly as tall and broad as Kane, he rode as if he were a part of his mount, relaxed yet ready for anything. But within minutes Glenna knew it wasn't Kane. His longish blond hair waving in the wind was a far cry from Kane's raven locks. Holding the Spencer tightly, Glenna waited until the man reached the cabin, dismounted and stood before her.

"Miss O'Neill?" he asked courteously. Glenna nodded warily. "I realize you don't know me but I knew your father."

His words somewhat reassuring, Glenna allowed herself to relax, but not so much as to release her grip on the Spencer.

"You're a friend of my father's? What's your name?"

"Forgive me for not introducing myself sooner. It's Carter, Eric Carter."

"I don't recall ever hearing your name before," returned Glenna suspiciously.

"You wouldn't know me, Miss O'Neill, I'm from Silver City. I met your father shortly before he . . . died."

"Do you know anything about my father's death?" asked Glenna hopefully. "Is that why you're here?"

"Miss O'Neill, I'd give anything if I could change things, but I can't," Carter revealed, a hint of pity in his steady blue eyes. "The truth of the matter is I met Paddy O'Neill briefly two weeks before he was killed and again the night before. At that time I negotiated a business transaction with him."

"What kind of transaction, Mr. Carter?" All Glenna's instincts told her she was about to hear something she wouldn't like.

"Your father sold his claim to me the night before his . . . death." Carter knew there was no easy way to tell her so he took a deep breath and blurted it right out.

A cry of dismay was wrenched from Glenna's

throat. "You lie! Da would never sell Golden Promise. It was his dream."

"I have a bill of sale, Miss O'Neill, and the deed to the claim. All legally signed and recorded. I'm sorry. At the time of the sale I had no idea Paddy had a daughter. I only learned about you after . . . after—"

"After you killed him!" Glenna supplied, aiming the Spencer at a thoroughly shocked Carter. "You killed Da and stole the deed," she accused hotly. "He'd never sell the claim willingly."

"Not true, Miss O'Neill," denied Carter, eyeing the muzzle of the Spencer warily. "You'd recognize your father's handwriting, wouldn't you?" Glenna nodded. "Here, take a look at this." He reached in his pocket.

"Pull it out nice and easy, mister," growled Glenna menacingly. "One false move and you're dead."

Carefully removing a folded piece of paper from his coat pocket, Carter gingerly handed it to Glenna. She read it through, slanted Carter an inscrutable look then read it again. "It says here you paid $5000 for the claim. What happened to the money? The marshal said nothing of value was found on Da's body."

"That I can't tell you, Miss O'Neill. I left Denver the next morning same as your father. To go to Silver City. I had some loose ends to see to before I could begin working my claim. But you do recognize your father's handwriting, don't you?"

"Yes," Glenna admitted slowly, "but you could have gotten it at gun point. The only way Da would sell Golden Promise was by force."

"Do I look like a man who would hold a gun to a man's head and force him to do something he refused to do? Do I look like a killer?"

Wavering, Glenna forced herself to take a good long look at Eric Carter. His clear blue eyes bore not a hint of guile, nor did he act like a man capable of cold-blooded murder. She had no idea what a killer looked like but Glenna's senses were fairly accurate when she judged him devoid of the killer instinct.

Eric Carter was a gambler; a man who lived by his wits and the turn of a card, but he was no killer. Riding a tide of incredible luck in Silver City, Carter grew bored and decided to try his hand at some other venture. Leaving the bulk of his winnings in a bank in Silver City he came to Denver and met up with Paddy O'Neill. In the course of their conversation Paddy offered to sell him Golden Promise. Carter jumped at the chance and arranged a meeting two weeks hence, at which time he would have the asking price of $5000 cash.

Carter returned to Silver City, cleared out his bank account and concluded the deal, receiving the deed and bill of sale in return. Immediately the next morning he left again for Silver City and this time remained for two weeks while he tried to persuade his mistress into accompanying him to Denver. In the end Carter returned alone for the woman refused. Being the mistress of a successful gambler was one thing but it was quite another being a miner's woman. Even before Carter left she had found another lover. This one a rich silver baron whose newly acquired fortune was slowly being depleted by Carter's former mistress.

Although Glenna recognized a glimmer of truth in what Eric Carter said, she still wasn't totally convinced. With the Spencer aimed at his chest, she considered all the reasons why her father might have sold his claim. But all she could think of was how much Da loved and believed in Golden Promise. After a long interval she could come up with no situation under which her father would willingly part with his claim. That left Eric Carter guilty of murder despite his vehement denial, despite the fact that he neither looked nor acted like a killer.

"No matter what you say, Mr. Carter, I know you killed Da," Glenna accused irrationally. "Otherwise there's no logical explanation. And if the marshal won't do anything about it I will." She cocked the rifle and Carter paled as he looked death in the face.

Acting out of desperation and pure instinct, Carter dropped to the ground as Glenna's shot whizzed harmlessly past his prone form. Then he lunged for Glenna's legs before she could cock and aim again.

Glenna hit the dirt with a thud, the Spencer flying from her hand as she found herself pinned to the ground beneath Carter's hard body. "I don't want to hurt you, Miss O'Neill, but I refuse to stand idly by while you take potshots at me. Once and for all, I didn't kill Paddy O'Neill. I'm a gambler, not a killer. I'll let you up only if you promise to behave yourself. You can take all the time you need to pack and leave but nothing you can do or say will stop me from working my claim."

Glenna's chin jutted out determinedly, eyes flashing green fire, and suddenly Carter realized what an incredibly beautiful woman she was. So lovely in fact that he was almost tempted to ask her to stay on as his mistress. Almost, but not quite. This one would not hesitate to do him in once his back was turned.

"Well, Miss O'Neill . . . Glenna?" he asked, testing her name on his lips. "Do I have your word you'll behave yourself?"

Glenna was prepared to tell him to go to hell when suddenly she felt the crushing weight of Carter's body leave her. Like a rampaging bull Kane tore into the man he assumed meant Glenna bodily harm. He was nearly to the claimsite when he heard the shot and spurred his mount into breakneck speed. He died a thousand deaths imagining all kinds of terrible things. Why, Glenna could already be wounded, or worse yet, dead at the hands of the same man who killed her father. For in Kane's prejudiced eyes Eric Carter was already tried and convicted of Paddy O'Neill's murder.

When he spied the two bodies grappling on the ground red dots of rage exploded in his brain and he tore into Carter with an enraged bellow. "You bastard! What have you done to her?" he roared, fists flying furiously.

"Who in the hell are you?" Carter panted, trying his best to defend himself and failing miserably.

Finally Glenna found her voice. "Kane, wait, don't kill him!" While she grappled with Carter a strange thing happened. The sincerity of his words finally sank in and gave her second thoughts.

"Tell me one good reason why I shouldn't kill this son-of-a-bitch!" Kane exclaimed. "He killed your father and tried just now to do you in."

"No, Kane, you got it wrong. I just tried to kill Carter. But now I'm not so sure I was right. Maybe he didn't kill Da. Maybe he is telling the truth."

Looking eternally grateful, Carter said, "Thank you, Miss O'Neill. I was definitely telling the truth when I said I did not kill Paddy O'Neill."

"Now try and convince me!" Kane growled tersely. "You'll find I'm not so gullible."

"Who in the hell are you anyway?" Carter repeated, picking himself off the ground. "Whoever you are you sure pack a wallop."

"I'm Kane Morgan, a friend of the O'Neill family. Now tell me why I shouldn't rid the world of a killer?"

Carter cast a nervous glance at Kane's Winchester, cleared his throat and began again the tale of how he met Paddy and bought the claim. When he finished Kane stared at him relentlessly, dark brows drawn together in a frown. Everything he said could have happened except that too many gaps remained unexplained. Like what happened to the $5000 Paddy was paid for his claim. And the reason Paddy sold it in the first place. Yet what if Carter was telling the truth?

Rarely a creature of impulse, Kane wisely decided to accept Carter's story for the time being. At least until the marshal completed his investigation. And since Glenna would now be forced to return to town, he, of course, would accompany her and be on hand to prod the marshal into action.

"You're not completely exonerated in my eyes, Carter," Kane warned accusingly, "but for now you hold all the cards. Just keep in mind that Marshal Bartow and I will be watching you closely from now on."

"Watch all you want, Morgan, but you'll find nothing to link me with O'Neill's murder. I'm a gambler from Silver City, nothing more, nothing less."

Both men stood glaring at one another, neither willing to give an inch until Glenna interrupted the tense moment by saying, "Kane, I . . . I believe Mr. Carter, at least until someone proves otherwise."

Kane could sense her distress at being forced from the only home she'd ever known and had no wish to add further to it by forcing the issue with Carter. Besides, the marshal would have his hide if he tried to prevent Carter from possessing something that was legally his. Beneath his breath he cursed Paddy for being so secretive and dying without a clue as to why he sold the Golden Promise.

7

Sadness settled over Glenna like a heavy mantle as she packed her meager belongings. With fondness she recalled all those years spent in the snug cabin with Da and Mama before she died. Golden Promise was an integral part of her life and leaving it now, perhaps for good, was tearing her apart.

Kane was of little help in assuaging her pain as he helped her pack the few mementos collected over her short span of years. "Do you have any money, Glenna?" he asked with concern.

Her green eyes awash with unshed tears, Glenna shook her head. "Not unless Da left something for me in the bank."

"There's nothing in the bank, honey, the marshal already checked when he learned Paddy had the $5000 from the sale of the claim on him the night before his death."

Glenna shrugged, caring little about money when her heart was breaking. What could Da have been thinking of to sell Golden Promise? That one consuming thought occupied her mind as she automatically folded and packed. Suddenly she came upon the float she had hidden in the bottom of her trunk.

"I still have the float I found, Kane," she said, excitement coloring her words. "I found two more sizable pieces while you were gone. Surely they're worth something."

"Glenna, honey, I think for the time being you should keep quiet about your find. Otherwise you're liable to start a stampede out here."

"Then I'm penniless, Kane. What am I supposed to do?"

"Don't worry, I'll take care of you," he murmured, his discerning eye taking in her disheveled appearance. Until that moment so much had happened so fast that he failed to notice her unorthodox clothes. The snug trousers hugged her neat little rear like a second skin. Long legs, bare from the knees down, had acquired a golden hue from exposure to the sun these past two days. The plaid shirt covering her torso did little to conceal her nipples straining against the material worn thin from years of use.

Desire churned through him, turning his eyes smoky-gray and causing his loins to contract painfully. To look at her was to want her. But Glenna was too distraught to notice the light kindling in his eyes.

Kane's words succeeded only in rousing her ire. He said he would take care of her, not that he would marry her. Did he think she would content herself with being a kept woman? Hadn't Kane already told her he felt no remorse for taking her virginity? At least not enough to offer marriage. Obviously he was not willing to alter his lifestyle for the daughter of a miner. A woman far beneath his own station in life despite the fact that Da and his father were friends.

"I can take care of myself, Kane," Glenna insisted

belligerently. "I'm perfectly capable of finding a job and supporting myself without your help."

Kane sighed, realizing he had said something to anger Glenna but admiring greatly her spunk and strength. Though she had no inkling of his plans, Kane had every intention of taking Glenna back to Philadelphia with him. He cared far too much for her to leave her on her own in a rugged town like Denver.

She would make a wonderful mistress, he thought wistfully, though he knew in his heart Glenna would never conform to being any man's mistress. If only . . . but it was too late, Ellen was the woman he had proposed to and eventually would marry.

The trip to Denver proved uneventful. Kane had spent the night in the storage shed with Carter in order to keep an eye on him as well as preserve Glenna's reputation, although he yearned to be in her bed. It had been days since he last obtained rapture in her arms.

The next morning Kane had loaded Glenna's trunks in the wagon and they left Golden Promise, perhaps for the last time, Glenna thought grimly as she watched over her shoulder until they rounded a curve and the cabin was lost from sight. Eric Carter lent them the wagon instructing them to leave it at the livery for him to pick up when he came to town later to hire miners to work his claim.

They arrived in Denver at dusk. Kane drove straight to the Palace Hotel.

"Kane, I can't stay here," Glenna protested. "It's far too expensive. Take me to the Denver Arms. It was good enough for Da and it's good enough for me."

"I said I'd take care of you, love," repeated Kane patiently. "I have the means to keep you anywhere I please and it pleases me to have you nearby."

"I'll bet," snorted Glenna derisively. Her voice

took on a brittle quality Kane had never heard before. "Kane, I won't be a kept woman. I can and will take care of myself."

"Humor me," Kane cajoled. "In view of our fathers' long friendship you can't refuse. My father would want it no other way. Stay here at least until you find a job and are earning enough to support yourself." Which will never happen, thought Kane smugly. He knew it was selfish of him to want Glenna when he had no right to her but he couldn't help himself. The feelings she evoked in him both confused and puzzled him, but no matter what, he just couldn't let her go so easily.

Too tired to protest, Glenna acquiesced, agreeing to remain at the Palace only if he allowed her to pay him back when she got a job. Her first request was for a bath. Then after a meal taken in her room she went immediately to bed, too distraught to interpret the gleam in Kane's eyes when he came by later to bid her goodnight. If he hoped to be invited to spend the night he was sadly disappointed, for Glenna was too exhausted and shocked by the turn of events these past few days to even consider such a request.

Feeling far from ready for sleep, Kane decided on a sudden whim to pay a visit to the Red Garter. His luck had been so fantastic the last time he gambled there he hoped for a repeat performance. He was running out of cash, and though he intended to wire his bank for more he realized it would take too long to arrive for what he had in mind.

Sal spotted Kane the moment he walked through the door. She was sitting with Judd Martin, the owner of the saloon and as of two days ago his new mistress, replacing a woman named Conchita who had recently been killed in an accident.

"Excuse me, Judd, honey, while I go say hello to an old friend," Sal said, breaking out into a grin at the sight of Kane.

Judd scowled darkly, his handsome bronzed face etched with deep lines of jealousy. But before he could voice a protest Sal was already up and hurrying to greet Kane.

A suspicious man by nature, especially when things failed to go his way, sometimes ruthless, often cruel, Judd Martin was a man accustomed to instant obedience. Whether bullying a defenseless woman or hiring goons to kill an enemy, Martin appeared to be a man without scruples. Smooth as slick cream on the outside, tough as nails inside, he was devilishly handsome with rusty-colored hair and pale blue eyes that could turn cold as ice when provoked. And he was provoked now. He fumed in silent rage seeing his mistress run off to meet another man. Until he tired of Sal she was his exclusively. No other man dared set his sights on her. There were plenty of other trollops around for that purpose.

But being new in town Sal wasn't aware of Judd's bent toward jealousy as well as cruelty. She was oblivious to everything but her pleasure at seeing a friend again. And despite their brief acquaintance she considered Kane a friend.

"It's good to see you, Kane," Sal greeted with an exuberance that was part of her nature. "Pearl told me you were here a couple of weeks ago but I must have been . . . er . . . busy. Where have you been keeping yourself?"

"Here and there," Kane smiled evasively. Of all three women he liked Sal the best. "Thought I'd drop in for a little action."

Sal laughed throatily. "You've come to the right place. Should I find Pearl? Or maybe you'd prefer Candy. Unless you see someone else you fancy. Sorry I can't offer myself but I belong to Judd Martin now."

"That's not the kind of action I had in mind, Sal," winked Kane outrageously. "Thought I'd try the gambling tables tonight."

"Sure, honey," replied Sal agreeably, taking his arm and leading him toward the gambling room.

Suddenly a tall, lean form blocked their path. Judd Martin, a cheroot trailing black smoke about his thin features, appeared anything but friendly as he glared menacingly at the man monopolizing his current mistress.

"Who's your friend, Sal?"

"Judd," exclaimed Sal, failing to interpret the warning in Martin's grim expression. "This is Kane Alexander, I met him on the train."

"It's Kane Alexander Morgan," Kane corrected, finding it no longer necessary to conceal his real name.

"Morgan?" Sal frowned. "But—"

"I'm sorry, Sal, I don't always use my full name. Sometimes I find it expedient not to."

Shrugging philosophically, Sal said, "Any name you want to use is fine with me, honey." Then she turned to Judd. "This is Judd Martin, Kane. He owns the Red Garter."

Kane held out his hand in a friendly manner only to have it ignored by Martin. "Sal is my woman," he ground out from between clenched teeth.

Kane's dark brows met in the center of his forehead and his gray eyes went murky. "I wasn't trying to cut in, Martin, I came here to gamble. Now if you'll excuse me I see an empty place at the roulette table." Glancing apologetically at Sal he made a hasty departure, muttering darkly under his breath. Lord knows he hadn't come here to make trouble, and tangling with a man like Judd Martin could lead to big trouble. Not that he was afraid of trouble, it's just that he had more important things on his mind right now.

Sal rounded on Judd the moment Kane was out of hearing. "See here, Judd, you don't own me! I was merely greeting a friend."

The flash of his hand gave scant warning as Judd recoiled and struck out, one large hand connecting with Sal's cheek before backhanding her on the other on its return trip. Her cry of pain alerted Kane and he whirled in time to see Judd prepare to strike Sal yet one more time. But before his hand connected with tender flesh, Kane's fleet steps carried him back to the couple and Judd found his wrist trapped between steely fingers.

"I wouldn't do that if I were you, Martin," Kane warned ominously. "If you insist on striking someone, pick on one your own size."

Standing eye to eye the two men glared at one another, each aware that an enemy had been made for life. Judd was the first to break contact, twisting from Kane's grasp. "Don't meddle in my affairs, Morgan," he hissed. "I don't know who you are but no one intrudes in my business and lives to tell of it."

"Are you threatening me?"

"What do you think?"

"I think you're a coward who beats women."

Martin's eyes blazed dangerously as he made a mental note to find out all about Kane Morgan. Sal saw what was happening and urged Kane to move on, her voice pleading.

"Please, Kane, don't cause trouble. I'm sure Judd will calm down once he realizes there is nothing going on between us. Go on to your gambling, I'm not hurt, really."

Kane wavered, looking from Judd to Sal, deciding after all that he had no business interfering with a man and his mistress. "You win, Martin," he muttered. "If Sal is satisfied with her treatment who am I to interfere?" Then abruptly he turned on his heel, oblivious to the sudden quiet that had descended upon the room and the dozens of pairs of eyes staring at him with awe. It took a brave man to stand up to Judd Martin, and few lived to boast of it.

* * *

Glenna slept late the next morning so she had no idea Kane had called on Marshal Bartow after he wolfed down a hasty breakfast. Bartow was not too happy to see him, especially after he had already heard this morning about Kane's run-in with Judd Martin.

"You sure have a way of stirring up trouble, Morgan," he said sourly.

"If you're talking about Martin, I don't like the bastard."

"He's the wrong man to tangle with," Bartow warned. "I've never been able to pin anything on him but he employs a whole passle of men to do his dirty work. He has acquired several mines through devious methods and is one of the richest men in the territory. I'd be wary of him if I were you."

"I can handle Martin if and when the times arises," Kane shrugged carelessly. "But right now he's not the problem. It's Eric Carter I'm concerned about."

"I assume he told Glenna about the claim. How did she take it?"

"Just like you'd expect," Kane said grimly. "I'm worried about her. Too much has happened to her in too short a time. She's got more guts than I gave her credit for." His blatant admiration was not lost on Marshal Bartow who smiled a secret smile.

"Is she staying at the Denver Arms?"

"No, the Palace. I . . . I'll see to her care until . . . other arrangements can be made." Bartow nodded, the corners of his mouth twitching suspiciously. For a man about to be married Kane appeared to have an uncommon interest in Miss Glenna O'Neill.

"The reason I came by, Marshal, is that I'm planning on leaving for Silver City tomorrow. I intend to learn all I can about Eric Carter. Though he appears to be exactly what he says, I'd feel better knowing more about him."

"Have you already spoken with him? Does Glenna feel the same way about him that you do?"

"At first she wanted to kill him, and almost did, but somehow he managed to convince her he was in no way involved in Paddy's death. I'm not so gullible."

"All right, Morgan, go to Silver City if you must, and report to me when you return. In the meantime I'll continue the investigation here. But don't get your hopes up. I've been a lawman a long time and learned the obvious suspect isn't always the guilty one."

"I shouldn't be gone more than a week or so," Kane told Glenna over a table laden with food.

"I think you're wasting your time, Kane," declared Glenna with a sigh. "I'd give anything to find my father's killer but I think it's futile to go to Silver City. I can't see Eric Carter in the role of murderer. What troubles me most is his reason for buying a claim that has produced nothing in months, if we are to believe the rumors. No, Kane," Glenna repeated with an air of finality, "only a gambler would take that kind of risk. I'm convinced Eric Carter knows nothing about mining."

After supper Kane saw Glenna to her room, but instead of bidding her goodnight he followed her inside and closed the door firmly behind him. All evening he had thought of little else but having Glenna alone, undressing her slowly and thrusting deep inside her moist warmth, taking them both to glorious heights of rapture. So much time had elasped since he last made love to her he fought desperately to contain his ardor as he faced her.

"I don't want to leave you tonight, Glenna," he whispered huskily, his eyes dark with desire. "I want to make love to you."

He advanced slowly, drawing her inexorably into a web of passion. When his arms surrounded her and pressed her close she could feel his aroused maleness against her, firm and powerful.

Damn! Glenna silently raged, not only was he the handsomest man she'd ever met but also the most appealing. He possessed a casual wit and gentleness that contrasted with his sometimes steely manner. And yes, damn him, she wanted him. Even if it was for a short time only. Perhaps she could convince him in the time they had left together that she would make him a perfect wife.

Her defenses all but destroyed by the love she already bore this man, they came together in an explosive, wild rapture, clothes flying in all directions. Dear God, how she wanted this man! "Love me, Kane," she implored in breathless gasps. "Please love me."

Elation surged through Kane as he swept her up in his arms. "Glenna, love, you drive me wild. I'll never get enough of you."

Tenderly he placed her in the middle of the bed, following close behind. His tongue slid over her hungrily as he sought release from the torment she constantly stirred in him, and her soft sigh of surrender lured him deeper into ecstasy. Drunk with the taste of her satiny skin he moved his mouth to hers for a demanding kiss. Sweet and throbbing languor suffused them as they pressed heated bodies closer, exploring each other with exquisite care until their blood pulsed with the delight and mystery of it.

His hand dipping between her thighs, she felt warm and wet to him, and he burrowed between her legs, the pleasure so intense when he entered those silken portals that she cried out again and again. He moved with lazy precision, stroking, savoring, drawing her slowly to the edge of ecstasy.

Glenna felt herself drowning in a sea of emotion. Every part of him assaulted her, the spicy scent he wore, the taste of him and his thrusting tongue and the rough strength of his body. All the while he labored lovingly over her he kissed and stroked and licked at her nipples until they were pebble-hard and stinging electric thrills ran over her. And then the white-hot flame became too violent to contain as Glenna exploded in violent rapture.

"I love you, Kane!" she cried out mindlessly. But Kane was far beyond hearing as his own moment came upon him and he galloped to the highest peak, collapsing finally in a panting heap of quivering flesh.

"I never knew anything could be so wonderful, Kane," Glenna murmured, her heart beating frantically against her ribcage. "If only—"

"If only what, love?" Kane asked lazily, brushing a stray tendril of glorious hair from her flushed face.

"If only it could always be like this."

"Glenna, I swear it will always be this good between us," Kane promised in a moment of weakness. Immediately he regretted his words. He had no right to promise her anything. God, what a predicament! What could he tell her? He opened his mouth to speak, "Glenna—"

"No, Kane," Glenna said, placing a finger to seal his lips. "Don't make promises you can't keep. I ask only one thing of you. Don't fight what's happening between us. I know you're not thinking in terms of marriage and I'm not pressing for a commitment. Just don't close your mind to me."

If Glenna only knew, Kane groaned inwardly. Actually marriage was very much on his mind. His marriage to Ellen. If there was any way possible he would fight to keep Glenna in his life. If only he could please his family as well as himself. Though Ellen might become his wife, Glenna would be the woman of his heart, and his pleasure.

Lacking a better answer, Kane whispered, "You're mine, Glenna, I'll never let you go."

Interpreting his words to suit her mood, Glenna burrowed deeper into his arms, begging him with her eyes, hands and lips to make love to her again.

Though Kane had been gone only two days, already restlessness and boredom became Glenna's constant companions. She missed him beyond reason. No longer was there a doubt in her mind that she loved him—hopelessly and irrevocably. She'd loved him from the first moment she set eyes on him aboard the train when just the sight of him sent her blood racing through her body.

Thinking to assuage her terrible longing, Glenna took a few of the coins Kane had left her and went shopping. He had won them gambling, she knew, but had accepted them with the understanding that one day she would pay him back. Thus it was she found herself in the general store fingering a fine length of satin she had no business looking at let alone buying.

"Glenna! How nice to see you again."

Glenna whirled around, surprised to see Sal standing beside her. "Sal!" she exclaimed, somewhat embarrassed. Since Kane had told her the truth about Sal and her companions she no longer felt comfortable with them. Perceptively, Sal sensed Glenna's feelings and made to withdraw.

"It's all right, honey," Sal said softly. "I understand if you don't want to talk to me. I knew you'd learn about us sooner or later." She turned to retrace her steps.

"Sal, wait!" called out Glenna. Who was she to condemn Sal for living the life she wanted when she,

Glenna, was no longer the innocent she had been several weeks ago? "Don't go. Tell me how you've been. Come with me to the hotel and join me for a cup of coffee."

Sal hung back. "I . . . I think it best if we keep our friendship private," she suggested. "For your sake, honey,"

"I don't care what people think," retorted Glenna defiantly. "Are you going to join me or not?"

Giving way reluctantly, Sal nodded her head and they soon found themselves renewing their friendship over a cup of coffee in the dining room of the Palace Hotel beneath the disapproving eyes of several upstanding citizens.

"I heard about your father, Glenna, and I'm sorry," Sal said sincerely. "Do you know who did it?"

"No, not a clue. How did you know?"

"Honey, I work at the Red Garter. There are no secrets in a place like that."

"Did you also hear Da sold his claim to a man named Eric Carter just before he died?"

Sal nodded, her face revealing the pity she felt for the younger woman. "How are you supporting yourself, Glenna? I suppose you have the money your father got for selling his claim."

"The money wasn't found on his body," Glenna revealed bitterly. "He panned nothing of value for months and left me little in the way of worldly goods."

"How are you living? You are staying here at the Palace, aren't you?" Her sharp eyes took in the grandeur of the place.

"You remember Kane Alexander, don't you?" Her expression guarded, Sal nodded. "His name is really Kane Alexander Morgan. His father and mine were old friends. Kane came to Denver in response to a plea from Da but he arrived too late. Anyway, Kane is . . . well . . he's loaned me the money to live on until I find a job." Her flushed face spoke volumes which an astute

Sal picked up on immediately.

Morgan? thought Sal in a burst of insight. Kane and Glenna. No wonder he wanted nothing to do with Pearl. "So Kane is a friend of the family." Sal's words brought a bright flush to Glenna's face, revealing far more than she was willing to divulge.

"He seemed awfully interested in you on the train," Sal continued blithely. "And that was before he knew who you were. He's quite a man. I see him now and again at the saloon."

Glenna looked up sharply. She knew Kane gambled at various times at the Red Garter but did he go there for other recreation as well? she wondered bleakly. Had he found his way into Pearl's bed. Or Sal's? All these thoughts must have been conveyed to Sal by the changing expressions flitting across Glenna's mobile features for Sal interpreted them correctly and saved Glenna the embarrassment of asking those questions himself.

"When I said Kane came in to gamble, I meant just that. He doesn't take any of the girls upstairs, though Pearl has tried repeatedly to entice him. He's faithful to you, honey."

Sal's words brought streaks of crimson crawling up Glenna's neck. How had she guessed Glenna yearned to ask the very question? Did Sal also suspect that she and Kane were lovers? "How . . . how did you know?"

"It's obvious," laughed Sal delightedly. "One look at your face and anyone interested would guess you love Kane Morgan. Does he love you? He must if he's being faithful to you. You are lovers, aren't you?"

"Sal! How can you ask such a thing?" Shocked, Glenna glanced around furtively to see if anyone had overheard Sal's outrageous remark. Thankfully, no one but the two of them were left in the dining room at this hour.

"I wasn't born yesterday, honey. Kane Morgan is a

damn hard man to resist. And once he sets his sights on something or someone he usually gets it. Obviously he wanted you, even from the first. It's nothing to be ashamed of. You're the kind of girl a man marries once he takes her innocence. Has he proposed yet?"

"No, and I'm not sure he will," Glenna replied candidly. "He doesn't love me, not like I love him. Oh, he cares for me to some extent and," blushing profusely, "enjoys me. He feels more responsibility for me because of the friendship enjoyed by our fathers, which goes back a long way. I'm hoping to change all that."

"I'm sure you're wrong about Kane, honey," Sal contended, patting her hand consolingly. "If anyone can change that rascal's mind you can."

Glenna smiled gratefully, then tactfully changed the subject. "What about you, Sal? How have you been really? Do you . . . enjoy your work?"

"It's a job," shrugged Sal philosophically. "The pay is good but the hours are long."

"Sal, there are other jobs, you know?"

"Not for me, honey. It's too late to change now. But don't pity me," she said brightly, almost too brightly. "My luck has changed. I'm Judd Martin's mistress. Having only one man to please is strictly pleasure."

"Judd Martin?"

"He owns the Red Garter."

"I'm glad you're happy, Sal. What about Pearl and Candy?"

"Pearl is doing all right. She has worked up a respectable following and is quite popular. Candy is as empty-headed as ever but most men find her endearing. She'll do fine. I figure Judd will tire of me one day and when he does the three of us will have enough saved up by then to start our own . . . business."

"I wish you luck," Glenna said sincerely.

"And I you," returned Sal. Suddenly she glanced at the small timepiece pinned to her lapel. "Oh, my, look at the time! I have to run."

"Let's do this again," Glenna suggested innocently. "The only people I know in town are a few old friends of Da's like Marshal Bartow and Pete at the livery. Living as I did on the claim pretty well isolated me, preventing me from forming friendships with people my own age."

Sal's soft blue eyes grew misty, moved greatly by Glenna's generous offer of friendship. She shook her head doubtfully. "I appreciate it, honey, but I don't think it's wise. From now on if we happen to meet in the streets pretend you don't know me. I'm not the kind of person for you to associate with."

"I won't do that, Sal. I don't care what people think."

"Kane's a lucky man, Glenna, you're one woman in a million. I hope he has the good sense to hang on to you. But enough of this chitchat. Judd will come looking for me if I don't show up soon." Both women rose and walked together into the lobby, so engrossed in their conversation neither noticed the tall, elegantly dressed and coiffed blond standing before the desk surrounded by a mound of luggage. She and the clerk appeared engaged in vigorous conversation.

The harassed clerk spied Glenna as she and Sal were saying their last goodbyes and eagerly called out to her. "Oh, Miss O'Neill, would you come here a moment please?"

Puzzled, Glenna nodded and approached the desk, Sal stopping a short distance away but within hearing range. She cared little for the looks of the haughty blond and decided to stick around should Glenna need her assistance.

"Can I help you with something, Mr. Wilton?" Glenna asked courteously.

Flashing Glenna an apologetic look, Wilton said, "I hope so, Miss O'Neill. This is Miss Fairchild," he nodded toward the blond woman who stood appraising her through strange yellow eyes that reminded Glenna of a cat. Glenna acknowledged the woman with a bright smile.

"Miss Fairchild is looking for Mr. Morgan. I know he left a few days ago but he hasn't given up his room. I thought—you being such good friends and all—you might know where he's gone."

"I sent him a telegram," complained the woman in a reedy voice, "and expected to be met. Now I find he's not even here."

"Indians must have cut the lines again, Miss Fairchild," the clerk explained. "But perhaps Miss O'Neill knows when Mr. Morgan will return."

"This is just like Kane," pouted the blond accusingly. She glared at Glenna. "I suppose you're Paddy O'Neill's daughter. It's your fault Kane couldn't make it home in time for our wedding."

"Your wedding!" gasped Glenna in total shock.

"Yes, our wedding. Didn't Kane tell you? I'm his fiancée, Ellen Fairchild. We were to be married in a few days but Kane sent me a stupid telegram postponing the ceremony until his return. He said something about staying until he found someone to take the responsibility of Paddy's daughter off his hands." Those weren't the exact words but after seeing Glenna, Ellen decided it wouldn't hurt to embellish a little. Or in this case, a lot.

"I . . . I didn't know," Glenna stuttered, dismay followed by hurt marching across her face. "Did Kane ask you to come to Denver? Had he known of your arrival I'm certain he wouldn't have gone to Silver City."

"Silver City! Once we're married he'll have to cure himself of his wanderlust. That's why I came to Denver.

Nothing or no one," she emphasized, "is going to stop this wedding. It's what both our families want and what I want."

"Miss Fairchild," Glenna said, sensing the woman's animosity, "Kane should be back in a few days. I'm . . . I'm sure he will be glad to see you. Meanwhile, I suggest you take a room and wait for his return."

"I suppose there's nothing else to be done. Are you certain this is the best hotel the town has to offer?" she addressed the clerk.

"Oh, yes, Miss Fairchild, I'm sure you'll be well pleased with our accommodations."

"Are you staying here, Miss O'Neill?" Ellen asked.

"Yes, I am. And please call me Glenna."

Ellen glanced about, taking in the rich decor with a jaundiced eye, then sniffed delicately. "Your father must have left you well off if you can afford to stay here. And of course you must call me Ellen."

Glenna chafed at the jibe, wanting nothing more than to escape from the intimidating woman Kane was to marry.

Refusing to be goaded by Ellen's snide remarks, Glenna shrugged carelessly. "I'll leave you to get settled, Ellen. I hope you enjoy your stay." She turned abruptly to escape those probing cat-eyes and spied Sal standing nearby, her expression one of pity. Unwilling to be stripped of her pride before another woman, Glenna rushed past her friend and up the stairs to the sanctuary of her room.

8

Hard on the heels of tears came anger. It hurt, hurt terribly, to think that Kane had played her for a fool. How coulld she be gullible enough to think he cared? Oh, he cared all right, for his own needs and pleasures. She was nothing to Kane but a warm, willing body used to slake his lust while he waited to marry another woman. How could she have been so foolish? What made her think a man like Kane could love her in the first place?

The knowledge that Kane had a fiancée changed everything. What had happened between them now seemed sordid and dirty instead of wonderful and right. If there was one thing she had learned from the experience it was that things weren't always what they seemed. Had Kane told her he had a fiancée she would never have allowed him to make love to her that first time. Or would she? Would she willingly give up the rapture she found in his arms because another woman had prior claim to him? She doubted it. Besides, it was too late to step backwards and find out. But she was damn certain of one thing, she would not play the fool again.

Pacing back and forth Glenna made many decisions that night. The first was to move from the Palace into less expensive lodgings. To her way of thinking she was no better now than a kept woman, and that she couldn't endure. Her first priority was finding a job, which she intended to do first thing in the morning. By scrimping and saving she'd soon pay Kane back for all the money he'd given her. She didn't need his charity, or anything else, for that matter. Da had instilled in her a sense of one's self and she'd be damned if she'd allow an oversexed egotist to ruin her life!

The next morning Glenna donned her most attractive dress, a light-green muslin sprigged with yellow spring flowers, and made her way to the dining room. After a sleepless night of calling Kane every vile name she could think of, she felt exhausted and ill-equipped to deal with the harsh realities of life in a world where no one cared about her. Once Kane was married he would promptly forget about Paddy O'Neill and his daughter.

Choking down a piece of buttered toast Glenna was suddenly aware of a frantic conversation taking place between one of the waitresses and the headwaiter. They were standing so close Glenna heard every word being spoken.

"Are you certain, Carol, that you have no idea if Lila is coming back to work?" the headwaiter asked of the nervous girl.

"N-no, Mr. Lawton. She told me she intended to elope with her boyfriend today," Carol explained, wringing his hands.

"She had no business leaving me shorthanded like this. What is this world coming to when young people treat their responsibilities so lightly?" Lawton digressed, throwing up his hands in disgust.

It took Glenna all of ten seconds to react. "Mr. Lawton," she said, catching the man's attention. Carol welcomed the opportunity to slip away unnoticed as the headwaiter turned toward Glenna.

"Can I help you, Miss O'Neill?" By now Glenna was well-known to all the hotel staff, carefully noted as a person special to Kane Morgan, a man whose influence and wealth was quite impressive once it was learned exactly who he was. The Morgan name, a prestigious one in the world of finance, was recognized even as far west as Denver and beyond.

"I couldn't help overhearing your conversation," Glenna said, "and perhaps I can help you."

Lawton looked embarrassed. "It's nothing for you to worry over, Miss O'Neill."

Glenna smiled her most charming smile, and drew a deep, steadying breath. "I'd like to apply for the job just vacated by the girl who eloped."

"You would—" From the way young Kane Morgan watched over the girl Lawton doubted Glenna need worry about a job, or anything else. "Miss O'Neill, I'm rather busy this morning. As you can see I'm shorthanded." His brusque tone was mildly reproving and Glenna flushed, but was far from intimidated.

"I don't mean to be a nuisance, Mr. Lawton, it's just that I truly need a job. I'm strong and willing to work hard. Won't you please consider me?"

"But Mr. Morgan—"

"What I do is of no concern to Kane Morgan," Glenna bit out furiously. "I need a job to support myself and if you won't hire me I'll apply elsewhere."

Convinced by the sincere quality in Glenna's voice, Lawton peered at her through new eyes. She was beautiful, personable and well-spoken. She would definitely be an asset to the Palace Hotel. "If you're serious about wanting to work, Miss O'Neill, we certainly can use a young woman like you. When can you start?"

"Do you mean it, Mr. Lawton? Do I really have the job?" Glenna could hardly contain her excitement. She had been prepared to trudge the streets of Denver in search of work for days, if necessary, only to have a suitable job literally fall in her lap.

"Will tomorrow be too soon?" she asked when Lawton nodded in answer to her question. "I need to find other lodgings first. What . . . what does the job pay?"

"I'll have to speak with the manager but I'm certain your wages will be the same as Carol's. Ten dollars a week and meals. You will work six days a week and your hours will begin at seven in the morning and end at seven at night. Is that agreeable?"

"Perfectly," Glenna nodded. The hours were a bit long but as meals were included she had no reason for complaint.

"If you prove satisfactory your wages will be increased by two dollars at the end of six months. Oh, yes," Lawton added, "your uniform will be supplied, for which your pay will be docked one dollar a week. Of course you may keep all your tips."

Tips! Glenna had nearly forgotten about that. Why, in a place like this they could really mount up in a week. All things considered she was well-pleased. "I'll be here bright and early tomorrow morning. And thank you, Mr. Lawton, you won't be sorry."

Although Glenna inquired about the cheapest room the Denver Arms had to offer, inflation and the times rendered it above her modest means. Undaunted, she tried two boardinghouses, but soon learned that they were inhabited almost exclusively by rough miners and prospectors. Most young women her age were either married or sheltered by their families.

As a last resort she called on Pete at the livery stable in hopes he might know of a good family willing to take in a woman boarder.

"Why, Miss Glenna, it's glad I am to see you. I heard that your daddy sold his claim and I swear I don't know what he was thinking of. The last time I saw him he was heading out of town and seemed happy as a lark. Said something right puzzlin', though. Said he never thought a promise could take on a new meaning."

"Do you know what he meant, Pete?" Glenna queried, as perplexed as the old man.

"Nope. Not an inkling."

Glenna sighed dejectedly. "What I came for, Pete, is to ask if you know of a good family who might be interested in taking in a boarder. The Palace is far too grand for me although I've just taken a job in the dining room as waitress."

Pete scratched his head, deep in thought. "I don't have much truck with families, Miss Glenna. The menfolk is who I usually deal with," he finally said. "But I did hear tell that Widow Jones over on Main Street is lookin' for a female lodger. She's havin' a hard time findin' one 'cause she's feared to take in the type of person usually lookin' for lodging, her being alone and all. She's just a wee thing but she's got more spunk than most women. Except you, Miss Glenna. I admire the way you've held up under all the tragedy that's been heaped on you."

"Da wouldn't like it if I caved in now. For his sake I have to be strong. I intend to see his killer brought to justice."

"What about this Morgan fella? Heard tell he's here to see that the marshal does his job."

"Kane wants the same thing I do," Glenna agreed. "Our fathers were friends. But his time in Denver is limited. He has . . . responsibilities at home." She turned to leave. "Thanks, Pete. You've been a great help. I'll call on Mrs. Jones immediately."

Kate Jones proved to be a robust little woman with gray hair wearing rimless glasses perched atop a pert nose. Merry blackberry eyes surveyed Glenna from tip to toe, apparently liking what she saw as a smile split her pleasant features. Having stated her business in precise, friendly terms, Glenna waited for the tiny, plump woman to finish her perusal, allowing herself a glimmer of hope that the room wasn't already taken or beyond her meager means.

"So you're Paddy O'Neill's daughter," she finally said, inviting her inside the small but comfortable home.

"Did you know my father?" Glenna asked, surprised. "I . . . I don't remember you."

"You wouldn't," Kate Jones said. "My husband and I came to Denver about four years ago. Richard's claim lay not far from Paddy's on Clear Creek. We became friends. My Richard was killed a year ago in a landslide. Paddy helped me sell the claim so I could buy this small house. To supplement my meager savings I rent the upstairs bedroom."

"Is it still available?" Glenna asked hopefully, praying it was and within her means.

"It is," Kate nodded. "I'm afraid to rent it to just anyone. The last renter was the schoolteacher but the city just built her a cottage near the school."

"I am in desperate need of lodgings, Mrs. Jones. Would you consider me as a renter?"

"I would, my dear. You are just what I'm looking for."

"How . . . how much is it?"

"Eight dollars a week including meals."

Glenna's heart sank. Eight dollars! She only made ten, nine after the deduction for her uniform. "What would it be without meals? My job at the Palace includes meals."

"Without meals?" She calculated swiftly in her head then said, "Six dollars should suffice, Miss O'Neill. Will you be able to manage that?"

"Oh, yes, Mrs. Jones," said Glenna enthusiastically. That would still allow her three dollars a week plus tips for incidentals and a little left over to repay Kane his debt. "When can I move in?"

"Immediately, if you'd like. There's a separate entrance around to the back so you can come and go as you please. Would you like to see it?"

"Yes, please," agreed Glenna, beaming. "Although I'm sure it will suit me just fine."

Kate Jones led Glenna to an inside staircase guarded by a closed door at the top. "I usually keep the door locked, Miss O'Neill. That way we both can preserve our privacy. I had the outside entrance built when I found it necessary to take in a boarder. One can't be too careful these days."

"I understand, Mrs. Jones, and please call me Glenna."

"Then you must call me Kate. Paddy talked of you so much I feel I already know you."

To Glenna's delight the room proved to be large, cheerful and nicely furnished. Besides the big bed covered by a beautiful handmade quilt, the room boasted a comfortable chair, desk, wardrobe and dresser. A nightstand occupied the space beside the bed and several lamps were scattered about the pleasant room. A small stove sat in a corner to provide warmth as well as to heat bath water. It was more than adequate and Glenna expressed her pleasure.

"There's a pump out back," Kate pointed out, "where you can draw your water. There's also a brass tub behind the screen. You can heat the water on the stove." Glenna saw a pile of wood neatly stacked beside the stove.

"Thank you, Kate, I'm sure I'll be very happy

here," smiled Glenna appreciatively. "I'll have my trunk brought over today."

"Here is your key, my dear. Please don't hesitate to call on me should you desire company or need help. It's not easy being all alone in the world. Take it from one who knows."

By evening Glenna was settled into her new home. Pete was happy to transport her trunk to Kate's house and even lugged it up the stairs for her. Kate had invited her for supper and after a delightful meal and congenial conversation, Glenna retired early and slept deeply, dreams of Kane creating a new layer of pain to wrap around her heart. The thought that Kane might have performed the same wild, uninhibited enchantment upon Ellen ripped her into a million pieces. The right to experience his special brand of love was no longer hers; he belonged to another.

Kane stepped off the train and hurried his steps to the Palace Hotel despite his weariness. He'd spent a hectic week in Silver City learning everything there was to know about Eric Carter. He'd talked to countless acquaintances and even his ex-mistress. During his return trip to Denver he had sorted it all out in his mind and was anxious to impart all his findings to Glenna.

Glenna! God, how he'd missed her. Unbidden the little red-haired chit had crept into his life and bewitched him. Though the feeling felt foreign to him, his heart was filled with the sight and essence of her. He had finally come to the inevitable conclusion that he and Glenna belonged together, and Ellen be damned!

Kane barely spared the time to deposit his bag in his own room before hurrying to Glenna's. He knocked once then burst inside, all the color draining from his face at the intimate scene he had so rudely interrupted. A man and woman were in bed engaging in strenuous sex! Both participants were panting and moaning loudly, throwing Kane into confusion. At the first sign of intrusion the burly-chested man reared up from the bed stark naked, quickly shielding the woman with a sheet. Dear Lord, no! came Kane's silent scream. Glenna with another man!

"What in the hell do you want, mister?" growled the man menacingly. "What right do you have bursting into my room?"

"I have every right in the world," Kane flung back. "I paid for this room." His icy gaze never left the sheet concealing the invisible feminine form.

"Are you afraid to face me, Glenna?" Kane challenged belligerently.

Kane's words brought an exasperated grimace to the man's face. "You got the wrong room, mister. This is my room and this woman's name ain't Glenna. Now git the hell outa here!"

Kane's hands were clenched at his sides as the urge to beat the man to a pulp surged through him. But first he would deal with Glenna. "I engaged this room over a week ago for a . . . friend of mine. Glenna," his words directed at the sheet-covered woman, "are you going to explain this or are you too cowardly to face me?"

Slowly a tousled blond head peeped above the sheet followed by a pair of china-blue eyes and ruby-red mouth puckered in a moue of displeasure. "Like Barney said, mister, you got the wrong room." Her voice sounded coarse, nothing at all like the softly modulated tones he associated with Glenna. A grave error had been made somewhere. But how? Why?

"I'm . . . I'm sorry," he apologized lamely, his face going from white to bright red in a matter of seconds. I thought . . . that is . . . perhaps I do have the wrong room. I've been out of town and my friend may have changed rooms while I was gone." He backed away slowly, spreading his hands in a conciliatory manner.

"Just git the hell out of here, mister," growled Barney, already turning back toward the woman and what they had begun before being so rudely interrupted.

Kane made a hasty retreat, leaning against the closed door until his wildly pounding heart stilled to a steady beat. For a minute he thought Glenna . . . God! He should have known better. But where was Glenna? And why had she changed rooms so abruptly? When at length he gained his senses he retraced his steps to the front desk, still somewhat in shock.

"Wilton, what happened to Miss O'Neill?" he asked the clerk. "Was her room unsatisfactory? Is that why she changed?"

"She didn't just change rooms, Mr. Morgan, she moved out completely."

"Moved out! Impossible! Where would she go?"

"I don't know, sir. All I know is that she turned in the key and left bag and baggage."

Shock followed disbelief across Kane's face. "Did she leave a forwarding address? Was there no message for me?" How could Glenna do this to him? What would cause her to leave so abruptly without a word to anyone?

"She left no forwarding address, sir. But why don't you ask her yourself?" suggested the clerk. "She should be in the dining room at this hour."

"Thank God!" Kane breathed in relief. The thought that he might have lost her forever gave him a queer feeling in the pit of his stomach.

The final shock came when Kane entered the dining room crowded with the usual noon diners to find Glenna dressed in a pert black uniform covered by a voluminous white apron. The stark black, meant to convey modesty, provided a vivid contrast to Glenna's flame-hued hair pulled back from her face in a style that on anyone else would be considered severe and matronly, but on Glenna only succeeded in defining the fine bones of her delicate features and long swan-like neck. She was absolutely stunning and jealousy consumed Kane when he perceived every male eye following her small voluptuous form as she glided from table to table. She was his, no other man had the right to look at her as if to devour her! Kane fumed. More to the point, what in the hell was she doing working as a waitress? Then she saw him.

Noontime diners packed the dining room but strangely Glenna enjoyed the hustle and bustle of activity. Though it was only her second day on the job she had gotten along just fine so far. What truly surprised her was the way her tips were beginning to add up. A few months of this and she'd be able to repay Kane all the money he had loaned her. Then, as if her thoughts of Kane suddenly conjured up his image, he stood before her. The first sight of him wrenched an unrestrained cry of gladness from her throat, which she quickly stifled when she remembered Ellen, the fiancée he had deliberately failed to mention.

"Glenna, what is the meaning of this?" he frowned darkly. "What are you doing here in that uniform?"

"It should be obvious even to you, Mr. Morgan," she sniffed haughtily. "I'm working. And as you can see I'm very busy." She turned to leave.

"Glenna, wait! I need to talk to you."

"I've no time for you, Mr. Morgan."

"What in the hell is this Mr. Morgan business?" Kane fumed in impotent rage. His angry voice carried across the crowded room and several patrons stopped eating to observe them curiously, much to Glenna's chagrin.

"Please, Kane, people are staring at us," she hissed in a low voice.

"I don't give a damn. I demand an explanation."

"I'm the one who deserves an explanation, Kane," spat Glenna, green eyes blazing furiously.

"What is that supposed to mean?"

"For heaven's sake, Kane, sit down. The headwaiter is frowning at us. I need this job and I won't have you jeopardizing my position."

Kane looked up in time to see the headwaiter glaring angrily at them. Sensing Kane's distraction, Glenna took that moment to make a hasty retreat into the kitchen, affording Kane no choice but to leave or sit down and order a meal. Finding himself in need of sustenance, he chose the latter. A few minutes later Glenna gingerly approached the table, pad in hand, to take his order. He made a great show of leisurely studying the menu.

"Are you ready to tell me why you moved out of the hotel? I can understand your finding a job but am lacking a reason for your giving up your room." His stony gaze never left the menu though his tongue hurled the words in her direction.

"Why did you lie to me, Kane? Why did you use your wiles on me then pretend you cared for me?" Her tense voice betrayed her ragged emotions.

"I do care for you." Gray eyes collided with emerald fire.

"You lie!" hissed Glenna beneath her breath. "You used me for your pleasure when all along you had a—"

"Kane! You're back! It's about time," a pouty voice complained.

Kane paled, shaken to the core of his being. "Ellen! My God! What are you doing here? You're supposed to be in Philadelphia."

Though no invitation was forthcoming Ellen sat down, spreading her elegant yellow silk skirt about her in a queenly manner. "I sent you a telegram but evidently you never received it. Your own telegram postponing our wedding arrived, though, and I can truthfully say I was more than a little displeased. I found it difficult to believe a man you had never seen meant more to you than your own fiancée. Of course," she hinted slyly, "that was before I met Glenna. You forgot to mention Paddy O'Neill's daughter was young and beautiful."

Kane muttered expletives under his breath. No wonder Glenna was acting so strangely. It was his own damn fault for keeping his betrothal to Ellen a secret. Especially in view of his recent decision to break off his engagement. He had rushed to her room to tell her of his decision only to find her gone.

"You still haven't explained what you are doing in Denver, Ellen," Kane persisted. "Couldn't you wait for me at home?" Never had he regretted his proposal to Ellen more than he did at that moment.

"Someone had to do something, Kane," Ellen explained peevishly. "Another week or two and you'd have forgotten you ever had a fiancée. Especially with such . . . interesting company to keep you occupied."

Glenna bristled angrily, resenting being talked over and around and resisting the urge to lash out in her own defense. "Would you like to order?" she asked icily. "If not I have other customers to attend to."

Turning her attention to the menu Ellen gave her order followed by Kane whose appetite mysteriously fled the moment Ellen's elegantly clad figure arrived on the scene to complicate his life. Nodding curtly, Glenna whirled on her heel and departed.

"Well, Kane," Ellen smiled coyly, "I can see I arrived just in time."

"Just in time for what, Ellen?"

"If I hadn't arrived when I did no telling what that little O'Neill slut might have persuaded you into," she explained snidely. "Or have you already bedded her?" Her eyes narrowed suspiciously. "She seems the type with all that red hair and sultry looks."

"For God's sake, Ellen, keep your voice down,"

Kane glowered darkly. "Glenna O'Neill is a decent young woman interested only in finding her father's killer. I have nothing but respect for her. I explained in my wire all about Paddy. I owe it to my father to help find Paddy's murderer. I told you I'd be home as soon as the matter was resolved, why couldn't you leave it at that?"

"Your telegram arrived, Kane. That's exactly why I'm here. I'm not ignorant to the fact that you're not keen on this marriage. Nor am I unaware that you're not in love with me. But our marriage will take place," Ellen informed him with careful emphasis. "All my life I've counted on becoming Mrs. Kane Morgan and, by God, nothing will prevent it. For years both our families have promoted this union and I have waited long enough for you to settle down. No shanty Irish bitch is going to ruin my plans. I intend to remain in Denver until you regain your senses and return to Philadelphia with me."

Neither Kane's thunderous looks nor clenched fists disturbed Ellen as she smiled serenely and patted his hand as one would a naughty child. "Relax, my dear. We'll deal famously together. For the sake of your male ego I'll give you a child, but only one. The whole process is disgusting and I will tolerate the condition but once."

Throughout Ellen's entire tirade Kane sat with his mouth hanging open. It was the first time Ellen had spoken so frankly with him. If she thought childbearing and birthing so distasteful, what did she consider the act leading to that state? Was the thought of mating equally repugnant to her? He almost laughed in her face. It was inconceivable that this cold bitch should become his wife with a warm, loving woman like Glenna in his life. He considered telling her just that but this was neither the time nor the place.

Just then Glenna appeared with their meal and

silence reigned as they ate, Ellen happily oblivious to the dark thoughts occupying Kane's mind.

Glenna saw nothing more of Kane until suppertime when he escorted a beaming Ellen into the dining room to take their evening meal. Evidently they were too busy catching up, thought Glenna perversely. He could bed her morning, noon and night for all she cared. Fortunately Carol waited on them, saving her from facing Ellen's sarcasm and overbearing conceit. After their meal they promptly left and Glenna breathed a sigh of relief.

But her relief was short-lived when she nearly collided with Kane standing alone and obviously waiting for her in the doorway as she was preparing to leave the dining room after her shift ended that night. "We need to talk, Glenna."

"There is nothing left for us to say, Mr. Morgan."

"For God's sake, Glenna, stop this idiocy. Give me a chance to explain. Ellen is—"

"—Your fiancée," she finished. "When were you going to tell me? After the wedding?"

"Forget Ellen for a minute, will you? I need to talk to you about Eric Carter. Don't you want to know what I found out in Silver City?"

So immersed was Glenna in her own misery that she had forgotten the reason behind Kane's trip to Silver City. "Of course I want to know about Eric Carter. Especially if it has anything to do with Da's murder."

Kane nodded. "Not here. Come up to my room where we can talk in private."

Glenna froze, all her senses shrieking in protest. "No, Kane, I don't think that's wise."

"Don't you trust me?"

No! she wanted to scream. Nor myself! "What about Ellen?"

"She's retired for the night. This is between you and me, Glenna. A matter Ellen has no interest in."

A tense silence surrounded them until Kane settled it once and for all by taking Glenna firmly in hand and leading her up the stairs to his room. Once inside he closed the door and leaned lazily against it, a beguiling smile hanging on one corner of his mouth.

"All right, Kane, start talking," Glenna snapped, moving as far away from him as possible. "I'm tired and I want to go home."

"Just where is home, Glenna?"

"I'm renting a room from Kate Jones. She's a widow and it's perfect for me. I even have a private entrance. But more importantly, I can afford it out of my wages."

"I would have taken care of you, you know."

"Why you conceited oaf! You owe me nothing! I enjoyed you as much as you enjoyed me! What woman wouldn't? You're an expert lover," she taunted crudely. Had he uttered the words she yearned to hear she would have gladly fallen into his arms.

"Was that all I meant to you, Glenna? Someone to give you pleasure?"

"You were an expert teacher and I've come to enjoy how you made me feel. But you have Ellen and I . . . well, Denver is teeming with eligible men. Why should I settle for one man when there may be others able to do the same?" My God! she thought, shocked by her own words. Da must be turning in his grave to hear such talk coming from the mouth of his daughter.

Glenna wasn't the only one stunned. Kane stared at her in consternation. Was he the cause of her shocking disclosure? Had one little omission wrought such havoc in his fiery Glenna? Or had she hidden her true nature from him all these weeks.

"Glenna, I don't want to fight with you," he said,

stifling the angry retort on the tip of his tongue. "Sit down while I tell you about Eric Carter."

Gingerly Glenna perched on the edge of the bed, Kane taking a seat nearby. "I think I questioned everyone in Silver City who ever heard of Eric Carter, including his ex-mistress who refused to accompany him to Denver."

"He's exactly what he says he is, honey." Glenna stiffened at the endearment. "He gambled mostly at the Silver Lady Saloon and from what I gather his luck has been extraordinary. He amassed a great deal of money and decided to move on to other ventures. He came to Denver, met Paddy and you know the rest. He returned to Silver City the day after he handed over $5000 to your father. He hoped to convince his mistress to return to Denver with him but two weeks later he came back alone."

"There was nothing else in his past?" questioned Glenna. "No dark secrets?"

"Nothing to suggest he might be a murderer. Definitely a womanizer, not above participating in a scam or shady deal once in a while, but it appears Eric Carter isn't our man."

Glenna sighed dejectedly. "I was almost certain he wasn't," she admitted. "Where do we go from here?"

"We keep looking."

"But what about Ellen? Will you be married here in Denver?"

"Ellen has far grander plans. If we do marry," he said meaningfully, "half of Philadelphia will attend our wedding. She'll either have to wait until I'm good and ready to return or go back without me." A thoughtful look settled over his features. "Glenna, I told you before, nothing has to change. I'll arrange for you to travel to Philadelphia and you can—"

"—Become your mistress?"

"I didn't say that."

"No, but you implied it. No, thank you," she declined bitterly. "I aspire to far greater heights than that. You're disgusting, Kane Morgan, to even suggest such a thing. You're a liar, and a womanizer . . . and . . . and . . . a seducer of virgins!" The words curled around her tongue and she spit them out like pebbles from a slingshot. "You'll not use me again for your pleasure."

"What about your pleasure, love? Have you forgotten so soon the bliss we shared?"

Glenna smiled slyly, suddenly thinking of a way to hurt him as he had just hurt her. "You pleasured me greatly, sir, and for that much I thank you. If I find myself in need of your services again I'll let you know, if you think you're up to it."

"You want me for stud service?" Kane retorted angrily. "Is that all I mean to you, someone to satisfy your lust?"

"Is that all I mean to you?" she flung back in retaliation.

"Do you want me now, Glenna?" Kane asked, jumping to his feet, his lip curled in derision. "Let me show you another way to assuage that terrible yearning deep inside you." He was standing before her now, storm clouds gathering in his face, hands on hips, feet planted wide apart, and Glenna was instantly sorry she had attacked his virility.

"Don't touch me, Kane," she warned, shrinking before his rage. "You have no right."

"I have every right in the world. I was the first. You belong to me. If another man touches you I'll kill him."

Suddenly Glenna knew fear. This was a side of Kane she had never seen before. Stern, ruthless, a splendid violence hardening the contours of his face.

She peered sidelong at his bold profile, strong, lean, powerful. He seemed to stretch forever, with one long leg connected to another by virtue of firmly sinewed muscle and bone. Moving forward he forced her further onto the surface of the bed, his body threatening, unrelenting.

With the agile grace of a mountain lion he dropped down beside her, forcing her backward until she lay prone beneath him, a wild and frenzied look in his eyes, a savage possessive anger in his face. And then his mouth found hers, intense, crushing, punishing. She trembled, buffeted by an onslaught of emotions she had thought buried in the avalanche of pain she'd suffered at his hands.

His fingers caught at the hem of her gown until his hand caressed her bare thigh, finally resting on the soft forest at their juncture. "You drive me crazy, you red-haired witch," he groaned hoarsely. "Take off your clothes."

"Kane, please—"

"Take them off or I swear you'll leave here naked."

A seed of rage took root amidst her despair and she lashed out with both hands, nearly sending him sprawling. But she was no match for his superior strength. Firmly pinned beneath him, Kane began working furiously at the buttons of her gown, too fired with desire to listen to her pleas. Her dress fell away, then her petticoats. Lastly her chemise and stockings were stripped from her wildly resisting body to join those already on the floor. Lifting himself slightly his own clothing soon joined the pile and flesh slid against flesh in a sensual caress that caused Glenna to catch her breath painfully.

His cruel mouth plundered its way toward her breasts as he ran his tongue and lips across raised, hard nipples. She felt her heart jump to her throat and then tumble down to beat against her rib cage as his mouth sucked, teased and nibbled at the taut peaks. Secretly pleased by her unwilling response, a low, mirthless chuckle rumbled from his throat.

"Are you ready for your lesson, love?" he crooned in her ear.

Rising up he shifted downward and her sensitive skin registered the slight roughness of his dark chesthair as it rasped across her breasts and stomach. Glenna had no inkling what he intended until she felt his fingers part her tender flesh and the warm tip of his tongue take its place. She cried out, wanting him to stop, yet certain she would die if he did. Never would she have thought such a thing possible.

"Kane, stop! You can't! You shouldn't!" Glenna cried out mindlessly as his lips nestled momentarily on the reddish fleece guarding her treasure.

"I can and I will, love. Relax and enjoy it. If it's stud service you want you've come to the best."

No reply was forthcoming as he renewed his efforts, his mouth and tongue driving her to the very brink of ecstasy. Realizing she was close to her breaking point, Kane's tense voice urged her on. "Don't hold back, Glenna. Give in, love, give in."

She felt the waves of rapture begin deep down in the pit of her stomach and when they rose to the surface she cried out, writhing, pulsating with sweet, tormenting pleasure. Only when the last shudder left her body did Kane lift himself and slide full and deep inside her, his emotions flaming to even higher peaks.

His movements were strong, forceful, pushing, withdrawing, deeper, faster . . . until Glenna felt herself matching his rhythm, flesh meeting flesh, racing again to the summit, burning, melting, exploding. At the same time Kane reached his own zenith, his lips claiming hers in a devastating demonstration of his mastery.

When at last they had nothing more to give, locked together in exhaustion, limbs entwined, their breath slowing, Kane heaved a regretful sigh, rolled to his side and lay quietly. When he dared look over at Glenna he was dismayed to see her liquid green eyes awash with unshed tears, red lips quivering.

"Oh, God, Glenna, I'm sorry!" he agonized, her contorted features plunging him to the depths of remorse. "I don't know what got into me."

"Bastard!" she bit out between bruised lips. "I hate you, Kane Morgan!"

Stunned by the vehemence of Glenna's words, Kane could only curse himself for a stupid fool and watch helplessly as she flung herself from the bed and threw on her clothes with little thought of what she was doing or how. Escape from this man who had the ability to turn her into quivering jelly with a single touch was absolutely essential. Glenna forced her own self-loathing aside as she struggled with buttons and ties. Once again Kane had used her for his own gratification and she had allowed it. No . . . enjoyed it. What he had done to her was shocking, but never had she felt such total abandon, such exquisite rapture!

"Glenna, don't go!" Kane cried out before she reached the door. "I apologize for everything. You're right, I am a bastard."

"It's too late for apologies, Kane," she flung back caustically. "Your actions demonstrated perfectly what you think of me. Take Ellen and go back to Philadelphia. You deserve each other."

"I don't want Ellen! It's you I love!"

But his admission came too late, for Glenna had already flung herself through the door, unaware of a pair of icy blue eyes observing her from a short distance away. Nor did she realize that the top buttons of her bodice were buttoned crookedly or that her hair had lost its pins and hung down her back in glorious disarray.

9

Self-loathing consumed Kane. How could he act in such a vile manner toward a woman he suddenly realized he loved? Loved far more than his own life. He let his mind search for an answer and when it came, he discarded it as unacceptable. He had let his jealousy rule his head, and for that there was no excuse. He had treated Glenna abominably when all he really wanted to do was tell her he loved only her and promise to clear things up between him and Ellen at the first opportunity. Now he feared he had done irreparable damage to their relationship.

How could he be stupid enough to listen to those taunts Glenna flung at him when he knew she did so out of hurt and anger? She wasn't like that, could never be like that. He had hurt her, hurt her deeply by not telling her about Ellen and she was retaliating in the only way she knew how. As the Lord was his witness, he had never meant to hurt her, only preserve what they had together as long as humanly possible. Of course that was before he realized that he loved her.

* * *

After her disillusionment and anger abated somewhat, Glenna began thinking about the things Kane told her about Eric Carter. It was obvious she had to look elsewhere for her father's killer. After talking with Marshal Bartow she learned no other suspects had presented themselves once Carter was eliminated and he was seriously thinking of dropping the investigation. Glenna raised such a ruckus when told that he reluctantly agreed to continue his search for a few more weeks.

Glenna had seen little of Kane since that night she fled his room in humiliation. Whenever he came into the dining room he was usually accompanied by Ellen who clung to him like a leech. More often than not Carol was the one who waited on them, much to Glenna's relief. But whenever Kane caught her eye he looked at her with such yearning it was all she could do to hold on to her control. He acted as if he wanted desperately to say something to her but Glenna made certain the opportunity never arose. She had no idea why he remained in Denver since Ellen's arrival and wasn't about to ask him.

Then one day Eric Carter came into the Palace and took a room, intending to stay several days. He had come for the express purpose of hiring men to take back with him to work his claim. He wandered into the dining room and his eyes lit up the moment they fell upon Glenna.

"Miss O'Neill, Glenna, I didn't expect to find you working here."

"I have a living to make, Mr. Carter."

"Eric, please."

"How are things at Golden Promise, Eric?" she asked wistfully.

"I've panned a few nuggets, some dust," shrugged Eric carelessly. "Nothing earth-shattering, but I'm certain there's more there than meets the eye. I've decided to divert the creek and dig beneath the streambed. There's got to be a paystreak down there someplace. That's why I'm in town. To hire men and buy supplies."

"That's quite an operation," Glenna mused thoughtfully. He must be well-heeled if he planned something of that magnitude.

"Has your friend, Mr. Morgan, returned to Philadelphia yet?" Eric asked innocently.

"No," Glenna replied curtly. "But his fiancée came here to join him."

"His fiancée! I thought the two of you . . . well, never mind what I thought. Obviously I was wrong."

Glenna showed him to a table, took his order and then the noon crowd arrived leaving her no time to dwell on Eric Carter or Golden Promise. But Eric had not forgotten her. He managed a word with her before he left.

"What time do you get off tonight, Glenna?" he asked, his grin infectious.

"Seven o'clock," she replied curiously. "Why?"

"I'd like to walk you home, if I may." Now that Kane Morgan was out of the picture permanently he wanted to know the beautiful Glenna O'Neill better. Much better, he thought, smiling roguishly.

"That's not necessary, Eric, I can find my own way home," Glenna answered dismissively.

"It would be my pleasure," Eric assured her smoothly. "I'll be here promptly at seven." Then he took his leave before Glenna could utter a protest.

He'd charm the ears off a monkey, Glenna smiled to herself as she turned to meet the lowering gaze of Kane Morgan. Standing nearby he had heard every word, and liked it not one iota. Though he still hadn't decided how to break the news to Ellen about their engagement, he considered Glenna his private property. She was the woman he intended to marry. He opened his mouth to speak but Glenna had already whirled on her heel and if he spoke now it would be to her departing back. Lord, he thought despairingly, would he never work free of the dilemma plaguing him so he could get on with his life? A life that included Glenna.

Kane burned with jealousy, though he had never known that emotion before and did not like it. Possessiveness he could understand, but jealousy? Did love do that to a man?

For three nights in a row Kane watched and fumed while Eric met Glenna after work and walked her home. When he thought to intervene he was instantly rebuffed by an icy glare from Glenna. Ellen was fully aware of Kane's interest in Glenna and raged inwardly, determined to take Kane away from Denver before it was too late. Little did she know it was already too late and the only thing keeping the knowledge from her was Kane's inability to express himself with Glenna and her anger at him occupying his mind.

Since the night she saw Glenna tear out of Kane's room in a state of dishevelment, Ellen knew it was going to take all the guile and ingenuity she possessed to hold Kane to his promise. She sensed the attraction between Kane and Glenna and intuitively knew Kane was beginning to realize his own feelings where Glenna was concerned, but felt confident of her own ability to make Kane honor his commitment. She had far more to offer than a penniless Irish miss with nothing to commend her but her beauty. She also had the backing of Kane's family.

It mattered little to Ellen that Kane might be bedding Glenna, for she cared little for the physical side of marriage, even with a man as attractive as Kane. Perhaps she hadn't met the right man, mused Ellen thoughtfully. Whatever the reason, Kane could bed all the trollops he chose as long as his name and his wealth belonged to her.

* * *

Glenna enjoyed Eric's company. He was charming, amusing, generous and free with his compliments. Just what Glenna needed to take her mind off Kane Morgan. One Sunday he took her on a picnic and regaled her with tales from his gambling days. When he tried to kiss her she allowed it out of curiosity, aware from the moment his lips touched hers that it was not the same as kissing Kane whose mere touch sent her to heights of dazzling passion. Eric thought of every excuse imaginable to postpone his return to Golden Promise, a fact of which Kane was well aware.

One night Kane made a point of cornering Eric at the Red Garter where the gambler had gone in search of a friendly game. Kane had arrived at the saloon looking for a respite from Ellen's constant nagging that he return to Philadelphia and fulfill his obligation to her. What Ellen did not know was that Kane intended to send her back east alone. He had no intention now of marrying her and waited only for the right moment to tell her. In fact, his engagement to Ellen was in jeopardy from the moment he set eyes on Glenna O'Neill.

The minute Eric left the poker table, Kane was at his side. "I want to talk to you, Carter," Kane said, his voice showing the effect of consuming one too many drinks. He didn't usually imbibe so freely but concern over Glenna and the dilemma facing him had made him incautious.

"Sure, Morgan, but my story hasn't changed, I had nothing to do with Paddy O'Neill's killing." They gravitated toward an empty table and sat down.

"It's not about that, Carter, it's about Glenna." Immediately a wary look darkened Eric's features.

"What about Glenna?"

"Stay away from her, Carter. She's not for you." Kane realized that he was branding Glenna his private property but his jealousy overcame his good sense.

"Are you implying Glenna belongs to you?" Carter asked, his blond brows raised in question. "You can only marry one woman, Morgan, and from what I've seen and heard your blue-blooded fiancée has you hogtied."

"What can a gambler like you offer a woman like Glenna?" sneered Kane derisively.

"What can you offer her, Morgan?" shot back Carter. "A home? Children? Your name? She can never be more than your mistress, is that what you want for her? I care for her. I've decided to ask her to be my wife."

Stunned, Kane could only sit back and stare at Carter. If Glenna married Carter she would have Golden Promise. Could he compete with that?

"What makes you think Glenna loves you enough to marry you?" Kane asked, frowning. "As a friend of the family I feel justified in asking these questions concerning Glenna's welfare."

Carter laughed raucously. "I've seen the way you look at Glenna, like a sick puppy. You want her for yourself, Morgan, bad. Only there's Ellen Fairchild and you're too much of a gentleman to break your engagement." From the looks on Kane's face Carter knew his assumption had been correct. "Now if you'll excuse me I think I'll join the poker game in the next room. I feel lucky tonight."

Eric Carter had more than a little need for luck. He had spent nearly his entire fortune on Golden Promise. To add to his woes, he had lost heavily at the gambling tables these past few days. So much equipment and labor was needed to work his claim and he had no idea where it was coming from. All signs pointed to gold somewhere beneath the creekbed but his limited funds prevented him from putting his theory into operation. He needed equipment, men, explosives, lumber, God knows what else. Eric had hoped to obtain a grubstake while in town so he could begin diverting the creek. Gold could lay only inches below the surface but there it would remain until funds were made available to him.

To his chagrin, his hopes were dashed to the ground when he failed to find one banker or investor willing to finance his project. Paddy O'Neill was well known to them and it was common knowledge his claim was next to worthless. If there was gold beneath the creekbed, they assumed Paddy would have found it long before now. Taking up his old trade was Carter's last-ditch effort to obtain the funds he needed. Gambling was his profession; he was good at it. Once he struck it rich at Golden Promise he could think about asking Glenna to marry him. Carter had no idea why Paddy sold his claim but he believed the wily old prospector when he said there was still gold to be had beneath the creekbed. But it was obvious from their first meeting that Paddy had bigger fish to fry. It was a shame his secret died with him.

When a seat became vacant at the poker table, Carter quickly slid into place, putting all his skill and expertise into play. Kane drifted over to watch, poker not being his favorite game. As the evening wore on, Carter won steadily, the pile of chips before him increasing considerably when Judd Martin ambled over to the table. At his approach one man quickly vacated his seat as if on a prearranged signal. Judd smoothly took his place.

"Mind if I join in, boys?" Though he addressed no one in particular his eyes were on Carter, one gambler challenging another. The game continued and Kane watched, fascinated. Carter was a pro, but so was Martin, and Eric began losing heavily the moment Judd entered the game. Yet if anyone was cheating, Kane could not detect it, novice that he was.

Finally Carter sat with only a few chips before him, and the best hand he'd had all night. He'd gone in with three queens and drew a forth. He knew he had Martin this time, only he lacked the cash to either call or raise his bet. Damn! he cursed inwardly, what a time to run out of money. Taking a diamond stickpin from his cravat he placed it on the pile in the middle of the table. Judd Martin picked it up, scrutinized it closely then promptly handed it back to Carter with a sneer.

"Sorry, Carter, it's not good enough. This trinket can't be worth more than a couple of hundred."

"Then take my IOU, Martin," Eric persisted. I'll make it good."

"No dice, Carter. You're broke and we both know it. What else do you have to offer?"

Carter sweated profusely as his mind worked furiously. Reaching in his pocket he drew out his wallet, extracting a folded sheet of paper. "Will this do, Martin? I paid Paddy O'Neill $5000 for Golden Promise. This is the deed."

Martin laughed mirthlessly. "You must be joking, Carter. That claim isn't worth $5000 and everyone knows it."

"It's all I have." Desperation rode Carter as he held the claim before him.

"Tell you what," Martin suggested with a grand gesture. "Both the stickpin and the claim ought to cover the bet. What do you say?" His eyes gleamed greedily and suddenly Kane was reminded of a spider luring his prey into a web of his own making. Kane didn't like it. Didn't like it one damn bit. In fact, it stank.

To Kane's astute eyes it appeared that Carter had been skillfully led to this moment; that for some unexplained reason Judd wanted Golden Promise, wanted it bad. Bad enough to cheat and connive to get it. His mind working furiously despite the effects of too much liquor, Kane surprised himself by speaking up before Carter had the opportunity to accept Martin's offer.

"Wait!" Kane interjected, snatching the deed from the table where it now lay and turning to Carter. "I'll give you $5000 cash for the deed to Golden Promise. If you win I'll sell it back to you for the same amount. If you lose, it's mine."

Judd Martin cursed Kane and his untimely intervention roundly. "Keep out of this, Morgan. This is strictly between Carter and myself."

Eric Carter eyed both men narrowly. Of the two he was inclined to trust Morgan over Martin, despite the fact that Glenna stood between them. Somehow Carter sensed that Kane was a man of his word, especially in dealings concerning business or finance. Intuitively he knew Kane would keep his word. Ignoring Martin's violent protests he nodded to Kane, asked for a pen, and when it arrived signed over the deed to Kane. Kane in turn wrote a bank draft for the amount of $5000, grateful that he had had the foresight to wire his bank for a large amount of money when he realized he would be staying in Denver longer than he had originally anticipated.

"You all know me and my family," Kane said, handing the draft to Carter with a flourish. "The money is in the bank to be drawn on at will."

Martin nodded grudgingly. "All right, Carter, let's see that hand you're so damn proud of. It had better be good or you've just lost everything."

"Oh, it's good, Martin, or I wouldn't be risking Golden Promise." By now they were the only two men of the six seated around the table still in the game. One by one Carter placed his four queens face up on the table, smiling confidently at Martin. "Top those pretty little ladies."

Just as smugly Martin laid down his own hand. First one king, then another, and another. When he placed the fourth beside the others Carter stared incredulously at what he had just witnessed. He knew

Martin couldn't have come by the fourth king honestly because he had discarded it along with a deuce, his gambler's instinct telling him to go for the fourth queen instead of a full house by drawing for another king. And it had paid off. All this and more registered on his face as he jumped to his feet, sending his chair crashing backwards.

"You cheated, Martin, and I've caught you red-handed!" But before he could state the reason behind his accusation, Martin made a sudden downward motion, as if reaching for a gun strapped to his hip. Falling for the ruse like a naive boy, Carter went for his own weapon, only to learn too late just how gullible he had been.

"Look out, boss!" cried one of Judd Martin's bodyguards who rarely moved more than five feet from his side.

Gun in hand, Eric Carter's face went blank with shock when Martin drew back his coat to reveal he was unarmed. But by that time it was already too late, no one drew on Judd Martin and lived to tell of it. Responding to an imperceptible nod from his boss, the same bodyguard who had called out the warning fired, his bullet finding a home in the left side of Carter's chest. Carter dropped heavily to the floor as absolute silence reigned.

Suddenly a roar filled Kane's ears, releasing him from his frozen stance as he dove for Carter, checking his pulse for some sign of life. Carter was breathing, but barely. Abruptly he opened his eyes, focusing them with difficulty on Kane, signaling that he had something to say. Kane obliged by placing his ear to Carter's lips.

"He . . . couldn't have the . . . king. I . . . dis . . . carded it," Carter gasped out with his dying breath. "Take care of Glenna." He died before Kane could assure him Glenna would be well-cared for.

Rising slowly, Kane's piercing gray eyes impaled

Judd Martin, fully aware that a senseless murder had just been committed. Once Carter realized Martin was unarmed he would never have fired. But to all appearances it looked as if Martin's bodyguard was forced to shoot in order to save his employer's life. That's the story the marshal would be told, and no one would dare dispute it.

"Looks like you own a worthless claim, Morgan," Judd said, smirking. "I still have your bank draft. What say we make an even exchange? Your $5000 for the deed to the claim. I'm a gambler at heart and willing to take the risk."

"Go to hell, Martin!" Kane replied, pocketing the deed. "I don't like what I saw here tonight and I don't like you. If I have something you want I figure my $5000 well spent."

"Are you a gambler, Morgan? I'll draw you for it. Winner take all."

"Sorry, Martin, I've seen enough gambling for one night. Call the undertaker, I'll pay for Carter's funeral." Turning on his heel he stomped from the room, intending to drown what he had just witnessed in a bottle.

"Kane," a feminine voice accosted him. Glancing to his left he saw Sal standing just out of sight in the shadow of the stairway. He quickly crossed to her side.

"Don't provoke him, Kane," warned Sal, looking about furtively. "When Judd wants something he usually gets it."

"Why does he want Golden Promise, Sal?" Kane asked curiously. "It's rumored to be worthless."

"I wish I knew, Kane, but he doesn't confide in me. I'll tell you what I do know, though," she whispered in a low voice. "One day not too long ago a down and out prospector came in here asking to see Judd. They were holed up in Judd's office for a long time and when they came out I heard Judd mention

Golden Promise and the fact that it was now owned by a man named Eric Carter. Evidently whatever information the prospector gave Judd was valuable because there was an exchange of money. I saw the man stuffing it in his pocket when he came out the door."

"Why are you telling me this, Sal? I thought you were Judd's mistress."

"I've had enough of Judd Martin, Kane. I . . . he's not what I thought. I'm frightened of him but I can't let him know."

"Leave him, Sal," Kane urged.

"Not yet," Sal shook her tousled head. "But soon. It won't be long before we have enough saved to open our own house. Pearl and Candy are with me in this. I've got my eye on a place at the edge of town that would be perfect for our purposes. Several of Judd's girls have expressed a desire to join us."

"Be careful, Sal. I have an idea Judd Martin is a dangerous man when crossed. What happened to Carter just now is a good example of his ruthlessness."

Heading directly for the bar, Kane belted down several stiff shots before allowing his thoughts to dwell on Glenna and how she would react to Carter's death. One more senseless death associated with Golden Promise. First Paddy, then the girl named Conchita and finally Eric Carter. Now that Kane owned the claim would he be the next victim? If not for his fear that something unforeseen might happen to Glenna he would gladly give her the damn claim. It was nothing but an albatross around his neck anyway. There had to be some way to convince Glenna to leave Denver. His every instinct warned of danger to anyone connected with Golden Promise.

Without realizing it, once he left the saloon Kane's steps took him to Kate Jones's neat clapboard cottage . . . and Glenna. It was very late and all was dark inside, both upstairs and down. Somewhat fuzzy-headed and reeling from the effects of the last drinks he had consumed, he carefully picked his way around to the back where he once observed Glenna using the private entrance she spoke of. He knew Glenna was fond of Eric Carter and wanted no one to tell her of his death but himself. He created such a disturbance stumbling up the stairs he was surprised no one awakened, but when he knocked he received no immediate answer. Softly, he called her name through the panel. Silence. He rapped again, louder this time, waited a few minutes then rapped once more.

Coming out of a deep sleep Glenna heard the commotion at her door, instantly recognizing Kane's deep voice. Glancing out the window she surmised it couldn't be much past midnight. Jumping to her feet she gingerly approached the door, whispering hoarsely, "Go away, Kane!"

"Glenna, let me in! It's urgent that I speak with you."

Kane's slurred words alerted her to the fact that he was none too sober. "It will have to wait till morning, Kane. Go home and sober up. I'm not letting you in at this time of night and certainly not in your condition."

"I'm not drunk," Kane denied as an errant hiccup gave him away. "Besides, it's about Eric Carter I've come and it can't wait until morning."

"Eric?" A frisson of fear prickled her scalp. Had Kane discovered something terrible about Eric that had to be said tonight? "Just a minute, Kane." Hastily donning a robe lying across the foot of the bed, Glenna lit a lamp then opened the door and stood aside as Kane pushed inside, staggered slightly, righted himself then closed the door behind him.

"This had better be good, Kane," Glenna warned angrily. "I've not forgotten what happened the last time we were alone and you'll not have the opportunity to work your wiles on me again. Now, what about Eric?"

Once again his slurred words betrayed his condition. "I know you hold a certain fondness for the man so I wanted to be the one to tell you."

"You're drunk, Kane!" Glenna accused, eyeing him warily. Never had she seen him in this condition before and she had no idea how to handle him. "Did you think to use Eric as a pretense to gain entrance to my room?"

"Eric is dead," Kane blurted out.

"You killed him! My God! You killed him out of jealousy!" she cried hysterically.

A look of total astonishment crossed Kane's features. How could she think him capable of murder? he wondered dejectedly. He attempted to draw her in his arms but she pushed him away frantically.

"No, love, you've got it wrong," he tried to explain. "Carter engaged in a high stakes poker game tonight at the Red Garter and lost heavily. After Judd Martin cleaned him out Carter accused him of cheating and was goaded into drawing. As it turned out Martin was unarmed but Carter was killed by one of Martin's bodyguards. Everyone will swear Carter was killed in self-defense."

"Judd Martin owns the Red Garter, doesn't he?"

"Yes, and from what I hear he's one of the richest men in the territory. He's amassed a fortune feeding upon the misfortune of others."

"How so?" asked Glenna, stunned over Eric's senseless death.

"He buys the claims of down and out prospectors, from what I gather. Most of these men failed to find a grubstake needed to work their claim and Martin picked them up for a song, often finding gold within a short time with the aid of his ill-gotten gains used to provide workers and equipment."

Kane had learned all this in the evenings spent at

the Red Garter. It was amazing what one gleaned through idle talk with fellow drinkers and gamblers, often the same disgruntled miners who had lost their claims to Martin. Nothing Martin did was exactly illegal, just unscrupulous and unethical.

"Poor Eric," Glenna lamented, truly saddened. "He wasn't a bad sort."

"Were you . . . did you love him, Glenna?" Kane asked, his question startling her.

"Love? No . . . but I was fond of him," she admitted.

Until Glenna's answer was forthcoming Kane had no idea he was holding his breath. If her answer had been yes he had no idea what he would have done.

"Kane!" Glenna blurted out abruptly. "I just thought of something. If Eric is dead what will happen to Golden Promise? Does he have any close relatives?"

"Eric didn't own Golden Promise at the time of his death, honey. He sold it just minutes before he was killed. He had a good hand, unbeatable, or so he thought. He was forced to put up the deed as collateral but got a better deal by selling it outright."

"Who bought it?"

"I did, Glenna." Glenna's gasp of disbelief resounded loudly in the silence of the room. "I bought it with the understanding he could buy it back for exactly the same amount I paid for it immediately after he won the hand. Only it didn't work out that way. As God is my witness I have no idea why I spoke when I did, or why Carter accepted my offer."

"You're the new owner of Golden Promise? Oh, Kane, that's wonderful!" Glenna gushed excitedly. "Now we can—"

"No, Glenna, forget it," Kane shook his head wearily. "Three people have died because of that damn claim and I won't risk your life by going back there. I'd gladly give it to you but . . . but . . . no, Glenna, Judd

Martin made it clear he wants Golden Promise and you mean too much to me to endanger your life."

"Do you think Judd Martin killed Da?"

"I don't know, honey. I think he's fully capable of murder but more than likely he'd hire someone to do it for him."

"We have to find out, Kane. I have to know."

"Glenna, listen to me. This is getting too complicated. Your life is more important than a damn mine. I have no idea why Paddy sold his claim or why Martin wants it and right now I don't give a damn. You're coming back to Philadelphia with me where you'll be safe. Let the marshal worry about this."

"And what about the claim?" asked Glenna belligerently. "If you desert it now claim jumpers will move in."

"I won't abandon it entirely. I intend on hiring good, dependable men to work the claim before we leave," Kane revealed. "If there is anything of value out there we'll find it."

"Somehow I don't think Ellen will appreciate my coming to Philadelphia."

"She'll have no say in this. For the time being you can live with my mother as a companion."

In Kane's mind it was all settled. What he neglected to tell Glenna was that he intended to ask her to be his wife once he returned to Philadelphia and explained to his family why he couldn't marry Ellen. Had his brain not been so fuzzy he would have realized his glaring omission and righted it.

Glenna bristled indignantly. "I'm not going, Kane. I'm supporting myself quite nicely, thank you. Go ahead and leave if you want but I'm going to see this mystery solved. You'd better leave now, I'm tired. The news of Eric's death has left me drained."

Wanting only to offer comfort, Kane reached for

her, pulling her into his arms. With a sharp cry of wrathful indigination she tried to push him away but his strength far surpassed hers. Stepping closer, he tangled his hand in her hair, loving the soft feel of the gossamer strands. It never failed to give him a sense of pleasure as the fiery tresses fell through his long fingers.

"Not this time, Kane!" Glenna insisted hotly, feeling the bold proof of his virility hot and hard prodding her thigh. "I won't be seduced again!"

Ignoring her protests his mouth caught hers in a kiss so deep that tiny buds of sensation burst softly into bloom. Valiantly she fought his passionate onslaught as well as her own treacherous nature as she finally broke his grip. Stumbling backwards she nearly fell over the nightstand, suddenly remembering her father's old pepperbox she kept in the drawer, grasped the weapon and waved it menacingly in Kane's astounded face.

"You want to shoot me?" Kane asked softly, his gray eyes glued to the barrel of the gun.

"I will if you don't leave me alone, Kane," she threatened. "I can't take your constant assault on my senses. I'm not a plaything you can toy with whenever it suits your fancy. Leave me my pride, for God's sake!"

Kane quirked a dark brow as a derisive grin broke out and displayed pearly white teeth against his tanned face. "I saw you kissing Carter. Why won't you afford me the same treatment?"

"Eric wasn't engaged," shot back Glenna. Suddenly she realized what Kane had just admitted. "You spied on us!"

Kane shrugged. "Perhaps. I told you once you belonged to me. I . . . want you. I want to make love to you."

"And I want you out of here! Go make love to Ellen!"

"By God I will!" shouted Kane, by now so

consumed by anger and befuddled by drink he could scarcely think. Turning abruptly he stormed from the room with savage strides, slamming the door behind him. Glenna made a mad dash to throw the bolt before he changed his mind.

Once outside, Kane's face went blank with confusion. What had he said to inspire Glenna's outrage? Didn't she want to marry him? He did ask her, didn't he? Suddenly he went still, searching his brain furiously for an answer to that question. Had he neglected to tell her he was done with Ellen and their engagement? That he loved only Glenna and wished to marry her?

Dear Lord! What an addle-brained fool he had been! From this day forward he vowed never to touch hard liquor again for it had stolen his reasoning from him. He had almost decided to turn around and pound on the door once more when his better judgment finally asserted itself. Glenna was far too upset to listen to his feeble explanations, especially coming from a man far gone in his cups.

But of one thing Kane was certain. He must tell Ellen immediately that he was definitely not going to marry her, that it was Glenna he loved. He had been sitting on the fence long enough waiting for the right time to present itself. And that time had finally arrived.

Kane's quickening steps took him to the Palace and ultimately he found himself standing before Ellen's door. Allowing himself no opportunity to change his mind, he rapped softly. It took several minutes before Ellen's muffled reply came through the panel.

"It's Kane, open up, Ellen."

"Kane! What do you want? It must be terribly late," Ellen whined petulantly.

Sighing sleepily Ellen knew Kane well enough to

realize he wouldn't go away until she learned what he wanted. "Just a minute," she called grumpily, flinging a sheer robe over a revealing nightgown. She stood with the light at her back, the soft glow outlining every lush curve of her tall, lithe form. Kane drew in his breath sharply, never realizing that Ellen's body was so lovely. But he did not allow the seductive sight to sway him from his chosen course.

Ellen shivered, suddenly aware of how she must look to a virile man like Kane. Primly she crossed her arms over her breasts, succeeding only in drawing his attention to the beckoning triangle between her thighs.

"Stop gawking, Kane, and tell me why you've come here at this time of night," she said coolly.

Kane walked further into the room. "I've come to tell you once and for all that our marriage will never take place. We don't love each other, Ellen. It would be a terrible mistake. Glenna is the only woman I'll ever love."

"What! You're crazy, Kane. Or drunk," she said, eyeing him narrowly.

"I may be drunk," conceded Kane, "but I've never been more serious in my life."

"You're not getting out of this so easily, Kane. You know both our families will exert pressure to bring this marriage about."

"Let them try, Ellen. My mind is made up." Suddenly a crafty look settled over his features as he thought of a perfect way to solve his problem and rid himself of Ellen once and for all. "Perhaps I could be persuaded to change my mind after all," he acknowledged thoughtfully. "Let me make love to you. Show me that we will deal well with one another as man and wife."

"What! It's bad enough to permit that disgusting act after we're married, but before? Heaven forbid! Oh,

I know men get pleasure out of debasing their wives in such a vile manner but I for one will not allow it too often. I will give you one child, and once I conceive I expect you to consider my delicate condition and take your filthy habits elsewhere."

Ellen's words splashed over Kane like a dash of cold water. The sight of Ellen standing before him wearing her righteous indignation like a cloak chilled his bones. Was this vain creature the woman he had thought to spend his life with? Kane asked himself disgustedly. She couldn't hold a candle to his vibrant Glenna who made love like an angel. This haughty bitch was a cruel imitation of a woman—a woman he could do without.

"Ellen, if you don't allow me to make love to you here and now our engagement is definitely off," Kane insisted, smiling deviously. He had hit upon the perfect way to end this farce once and for all, for he knew beyond a doubt that Ellen had little use for him as a man.

Ellen froze. Did he mean it? Would he actually walk out on her if she refused to accommodate him despite the wishes of his family that he marry her? Staring fixidly into eyes the color of cold cement, Ellen realized Kane meant exactly what he said. Was it worth the pain and degradation to become Mrs. Kane Morgan? Yes, she calculated slyly. Anything was worth marrying into the prestigious Morgan family. Besides, Ellen hadn't forgotten the night she saw Glenna O'Neill stealing from Kane's room. She knew exactly what was going on between them and wasn't about to stand idly by while the little slut moved in to take her place. Gritting her teeth, Ellen decided she would do anything to keep Kane Morgan.

"You win, Kane," she agreed slowly, praying her flesh wouldn't crawl when he touched her. She glided to the bed, drew off her gown and arranged herself seductively on the smooth surface beneath her.

Kane stood as if transfixed. Not in a million years did he think she would be willing to go to such lengths to hang on to him. He had thought it the perfect opportunity to demonstrate just how wrong marriage between them would be. He still doubted she would go through with it, and grinning mischievously, decided to see just how far she actually would go. Removing his jacket, shirt and tie as he went, Kane approached the bed, watching Ellen's reactions closely. A slight tensing of her muscles revealed her revulsion, but he had to give her credit, she remained cool and detached.

Kane knew Ellen to be a virgin who probably had never been touched intimately. Lying down beside her he kissed her deeply, her rigid lips firm and unyielding. She started violently when his tongue pushed past the barrier of her teeth to explore while his hands sought her breasts, working them expertly into stiff peaks. Ellen gasped in revulsion but lay still beneath his onslaught. Then suddenly she could bear no more of his groping and fondling as she wrenched violently away. Kane sighed in relief for he had no intention of carrying the charade farther than he already had.

"Kane! I've changed my mind," Ellen screamed urgently.

"Too late," Kane replied grimly. His hand searched downward, and against her renewed struggles the firm, strong fingers found the silken crevice between her cringing thighs.

Kane desisted immediately the moment Ellen's frightened sobs commenced. His flesh felt no surge of power, no thrill of desire. Ellen's cold-blooded approach to making love left him with a feeling of emptiness in the pit of his stomach. With a snort of disgust he heaved himself away.

"Does this mean we're no longer engaged?" Ellen asked with a tinge of bitterness.

"You don't know the first thing about being a woman, Ellen," Kane accused derisively. "Glenna has more passion in her little finger than you do in your whole body."

"Ha!" gloated Ellen, covering herself with the counterpane. "I know you've been bedding the Irish slut! Well, you can have her, but only to bed. I've waited a long time to become your wife and I won't be denied." It was as if Ellen had not heard a word Kane said.

"Ellen, it won't work," Kane said with more patience than he thought possible given the circumstances. "I want a wife who'll come to my bed willingly, who'll give me children. If you can't or won't give me those things we don't belong together."

"You're wrong, Kane. We have other things in common. We come from the same background, we have the same friends. That should count for something."

"It's not enough, Ellen." Afraid that his temper would explode and he wouldn't be responsible for his actions, Kane snatched up his discarded clothing and stood glaring down at her. "Go back to Philadelphia, Ellen, I'm not going to marry you. It's Glenna I love and Glenna I'll marry."

"We'll see about that, Kane," threatened Ellen. "Both my parents and your family will have something to say about this. I'm staying right here to remind you of your responsibility. You'd probably marry Glenna the moment I left town."

"You're right about that, Ellen," nodded Kane emphatically. "But I doubt she'd have me now. I've been a damn fool."

A week passed and Glenna felt herself suffering under the strain of seeing Kane daily yet ignoring his attempts at reconciliation. He had no right to torment her so, no right whatsoever. What puzzled her most was the fact that Kane and Ellen no longer appeared in the dining room together, taking their meals at separate times.

Kane was suffering in a hell of his own making. Never did he think a woman could come to mean so much to him. But somehow Glenna had crawled under his defenses. He had seduced her under a misapprehension, but it had been her choice to make love again. She wanted him as much as he wanted her and at long last he had come to the conclusion that they belonged together. Since that scene in Ellen's room the other night he had insisted repeatedly that their engagement was a thing of the past, and he meant it. The problem was that Glenna refused to allow him near her long enough to explain.

Then one day Kane received a telegram from his mother that changed everything. His brother was in the hospital after an emergency appendectomy and Kane was needed immediately to run the business during his brother's recuperation. Kane made hasty plans to return to Philadelphia, taking Ellen with him. Before he left he visited a lawyer who agreed to handle a few pressing legal matters in his absence. He hoped what he decided wouldn't place Glenna in any kind of danger but he felt strongly about doing the right thing by her. That taken care of, he went quietly about locating two honest, dependable men, relying heavily on the word of Marshal Bartow. That left only Glenna to confront and talk some sense into.

Kane accosted Glenna as she left work that night. Her faltering steps alerted him to the fact that her day had been long and hard and she was wilting from exhaustion. Deliberately he waited until she was well away from her place of work before hailing her. She started abruptly when he softly called her name. She whirled, wavering between running or pulling the pepperbox that she had begun carrying for protection from her purse, when fright gave way to recognition. A look of vexation crossed her weary features.

"What do you want, Kane? Can't you see I've been trying all week to avoid you?"

"I couldn't leave without telling you goodbye, Glenna."

"You're leaving?" Thought it was exactly what she wanted, a look of dismay settled over her face.

"My brother is ill. I received a telegram from my mother asking me to return."

"I'm sorry, Kane," Glenna replied, her features softening.

"I don't want to leave, honey, I want to stay here with you."

"Damn it, Kane, we've gone over this before. You're not free to say those things to me."

"I am now. I'm not going to marry Ellen, love. I've already told her it's you I love." Glenna stared at him in consternation. "Did you hear me, Glenna? I've called off our engagement. I'm taking Ellen back to Philadelphia and I'll explain to both our families that it was all a mistake. Ellen and I don't belong together."

"Does Ellen feel the same?" Glenna asked once she found her voice. "I thought she loved you."

"Ellen wants me only for my name and wealth. There is no love involved for either of us. There never has been," he emphasized. "Now that I have found someone I can really love I can't go through with this farce my family forced on me. I only agreed because until now I hadn't found a woman I could love so I thought to please my family for once. I've always been sort of a black sheep who's gone his own way and done his own thing most his life."

"And . . . and you have found someone you can

love?" Glenna asked quietly, still unable to believe she was the woman Kane loved.

"Yes, you little fool. It's you I love, almost from the first moment I set eyes on you. Do . . . do you think you could learn to love me?" he asked guardedly.

"Oh, Kane!" Glenna cried, throwing herself into his arms. "I've always loved you!"

The words were like music to his ears as Kane slipped his arms around her, kissing her deeply. It mattered little to him that they were standing in the street, for there was little traffic at this time of evening. "Darling, we can't talk here and there's so much to say before I leave."

Taking him by the hand she led him to her lodgings, up the back stairs and into her room. After lighting a lamp, she turned to him, suddenly afraid that she had misunderstood, or dreamed up his declaration of love and would awaken at any minute to find herself alone. Kane smiled, the spark of hope lighting her eyes instilling in him the courage to speak.

"It's true, love. Every word. I swear. I want you for my wife."

Abruptly she sat down, overcome with happiness, until a sobering thought came unbidden to her mind. When he left she would be alone. She couldn't go east with him at this time. Not until she found her father's killer. "Do you have to go, Kane?"

"Yes, darling, I have to. But my brother is a hardy soul, he should recuperate swiftly. And I owe it to my mother and the Fairchilds to explain about . . . about my decision not to marry Ellen. But I promise I'll return the moment my brother is on his feet again. Will you wait for me?"

"You know I will, Kane. I'll be here waiting for you when you return. Only hurry back, my love, hurry back." Glenna expected him to take her in his arms, to make love to her before he left the next day. Instead he rummaged around in his pocket for something, found it and handed it to her.

"What is this?"

"I've made you part owner of Golden Promise. It always was yours, honey. I've kept part ownership only to assure myself that you'll allow me to provide the funds to work the claim. Also as a precaution to insure no one will try to cheat you out of what's rightfully yours."

Glenna stared in disbelief at the deed to the claim. She thought Golden Promise lost to her forever only to have it restored by the man she loved.

For Kane it had been a difficult decision. Not because he wanted the claim for himself, but because he feared placing Glenna in danger. In the end he did it as an act of love, to prove to her that he would return. "There is a condition, Glenna."

"What kind of condition?" she asked, instantly wary.

"I've hired two trustworthy men to work the claim," he explained, sensing her skepticism. "They are both old friends of your father's—Zach Kimball and Will Davis. I've left them instructions to report their findings to you during my absence. I hope you don't mind but I took the liberty of telling them about the float you found. They're both good men and experienced miners. But you've got to promise not to move out to the claim. At least not until I return."

"But, Kane—" she protested feebly.

"No, honey, hear me out. I'd die if anything happened to you while I'm away. For some unexplained reason Judd Martin wants the claim and he's a ruthless man. Until I find out your father's secret I'll rest easier with you living in town. Will you promise to obey me in this?"

Glenna swallowed the lump forming in her throat.

Giving her promise not to go out to Golden Promise now that it belonged to her again would be difficult, but wasn't trust a part of love? If she could trust Kane to return to her, he certainly should be able to trust her to keep her word.

"Yes, Kane," she nodded solemnly. "I'll do as you say. Just return quickly," she pleaded, her voice husky with emotion. "I love you. I love you so much."

Nothing could have kept Kane from Glenna's side that night. Nor would she have allowed him to leave. Soft light touched the room with shadows, creating a haven for the lovers and locking them away from the outside world. With a low animal sound wrenched from the back of his throat Kane reached out and pulled her against him, lowering his head to kiss her fiercely, to wipe out all memories of the past, and leave room only for the present. Glenna felt herself caught in the web of his intoxicating gaze as his eyes turned smoky and, in unison they sought the comforting folds of the bed.

She responded to his touch, his voice, his ardor, until the fires of smoldering passion ignited. Then they came together in explosive need, sating the bright flame of love until completion burst upon them in a blaze of glory.

10

Had it only been a week since Kane left? It seemed like forever. Glenna still remembered the look on Ellen's beautiful face when Kane sought her out in the dining room of the Palace to bid her goodbye. Though they had just parted at dawn after a long, wild night of lovemaking and exchanging promises, somehow Kane couldn't bring himself to leave without one last farewell. It was too public a place to kiss her but his eyes revealed all he longed to do and say.

Ellen's hate-filled, pale eyes blazed at Glenna when she wandered into the dining room looking for Kane to take charge of her bags. If looks could kill Glenna would already be dead. She read more than mere hate in Ellen's sullen expression. She realized instinctively that Ellen would do her utmost to hold on to Kane despite the fact that Kane obviously was done with her. Did the Morgan name and wealth mean so much to Ellen? Glenna wondered. Funny, she would want Kane if he didn't possess a dime and came from the poorest family.

By the end of another week Glenna could picture in

her mind's eye Kane's joyous welcome home and how perfectly he fit in at fancy dinners, parties, the opera . . . And she began to doubt his willingness to leave all that behind and return to a rough mining town like Denver. Where were all those words she spouted about trust? she wondered despondently as the days flew by with no word from Kane.

And then one day a man came into the dining room. Tall, extremely thin, a narrow moustache gracing his full upper lip, a chill of foreboding pierced Glenna when his colorless eyes lingered on her. Because Carol was busy with another customer she was forced to wait on the man.

"So you're Miss Glenna O'Neill," the man said thoughtfully when Glenna took his order. He was told that Glenna was a stunning redhead, but what he discovered for himself was that Glenna went beyond stunning. She was absolutely gorgeous.

"Do I know you, sir?" Glenna asked courteously.

"I'm Judd Martin, Miss O'Neill. Perhaps you've heard of me."

Glenna's mind worked furiously. Judd Martin! Indeed she had heard of him. And not only from Sal. He was the man responsible for Eric Carter's death. The man who wanted Golden Promise. "I . . . I believe I have heard of you, Mr. Martin. Don't you own the Red Garter?"

"That's correct, Miss O'Neill. Perhaps you've been there."

"Me?" squeaked Glenna indignantly. "I think not."

"You should visit it sometime. The Red Garter is far more than just a gambling hall or saloon. The meals served in the dining room are among the finest you'll find anywhere in Denver. Upstairs are private rooms used for . . . er . . . to conduct business."

"I'll keep that in mind, Mr. Martin," Glenna said

dryly. She took his order then left, feeling his eyes devouring her as she flitted about the room. When she presented him with his bill she learned exactly what had brought him to the Palace dining room. And she didn't like it.

"Miss O'Neill," Judd began smoothly, "I learned through the grapevine that Morgan made you part owner of Golden Promise. That's quite a responsibility for a young woman like yourself. Especially since he left town with his fiancée."

Glenna grimaced but chose not to apprise him of the truth about Kane and Ellen. It was none of his business that Kane no longer planned on wedding Ellen.

"Golden Promise should rightfully be mine," Glenna informed him coolly. "Kane is the son of my father's old friend and he was gracious enough to deed half interest back to me. What is your interest in the claim, Mr. Martin?" she asked candidly. "I understand that nothing has been taken from the creekbed in several months but sand and gravel."

"If that's so, Miss O'Neill, then I'd be doing you a favor by buying your half interest in the claim. If you recall, I'm a gambler by trade. I've bought dozens of worthless claims in the past few years."

"Why?" asked Glenna curiously.

"I thrive on speculation. Or you could say I felt sorry for the owners of those claims, men down and out of luck who needed a helping hand."

Glenna nearly laughed in his face. She felt certain Judd Martin had never felt sorry for anyone in his life.

"I'm sorry, Mr. Martin, but Golden Promise is not for sale. Not my half, anyway. And I feel qualified to speak for Kane when I say he'd also be reluctant to sell. Now if you'll excuse me I have other customers to attend to."

"Miss O'Neill, Glenna, wait!" exclaimed Judd when he realized she was about to leave. "What do you earn in a place like this? Eight, ten dollars a week? You're worth more than that, much more."

Turning, Glenna regarded him curiously, deciding to bide her time in order to learn exactly what he had on his devious mind. She was willing to bet it was nothing good.

"I am in need of a hostess for my dining room. My last girl ran away with a salesman. It suddenly occurred to me you'd be a perfect addition to my establishment. Will you accept the job, Glenna?"

"As hostess, Mr. Martin?" Glenna asked doubtfully, one delicate eyebrow quirked upward.

"Just as a hostess, Glenna," assured Judd, highly amused, using her first name with a familiarity that irked Glenna. "You're far too fine to waste on the miner and prospectors who come into the Red Garter looking for loose women. I promise to protect your reputation with my life. Your duties would consist of nothing more than presiding over the dining room. The pay is twenty dollars a week and meals," he added, hoping to entice her with an offer she couldn't resist.

Glenna's mind whirled with speculation. Exactly why did Judd Martin want her in his saloon? Though he turned on the charm Glenna was astute enough to realize he was far from beguiled by her beauty. There was more behind his offer than met the eye. According to Sal women had no important function but one in Judd Martin's life. What kind of game was he playing? Only one answer was forthcoming. He wanted Golden Promise. But why? Since Glenna was a woman who knew her own mind and used it, she fully intended to find out exactly what Judd intended. Though the weight of Kane's disapproval sat heavily upon her small shoulders, Glenna hesitated the barest instant, her thoughts only on finding her father's killer and discovering the reason behind his murder. Thankfully, Kane was not here to voice his objection. He was hundreds of miles away in Philadelphia.

Pretending to mull over Judd's offer, Glenna replied slowly, "I must admit your offer is tempting Mr. Martin. The wages I earn now barely cover necessities let alone provide for the usual comforts a woman craves. But before I give my answer I have to be absolutely certain I won't be expected to perform . . er . . . other duties."

"Glenna, the only men you take to your bed will be of your own choosing." His frankness brought a redness to her cheeks that caused Judd to chuckle. "All I'm asking is that you act as hostess. You need never leave the dining room if that is your wish."

"Then I'll take the job, Mr. Martin. I'll start Monday if that's agreeable."

"Perfectly agreeable as long as you call me Judd. And by the way, your hours begin at four o'clock in the afternoon and end at midnight. My establishment doesn't cater to breakfast and noon patrons, only to those interested in gambling and . . . er . . . other entertainment which begin later in the evening."

Kate's expressive face registered shock when Glenna told her about her new job. "But, Glenna, my dear, surely you don't mean to work in a saloon!"

"Only in the dining room, Kate," Glenna assured her. "The pay is twice what I'm earning now and I'm only required to act as hostess."

"But . . . but—" she sputtered. "Whatever will that nice Mr. Morgan think? Didn't you say he'd be returning soon? I thought he was sort of your guardian." Before Kane left Denver Glenna had introduced him to Kate and the two took an immediate liking to one another.

Glenna swallowed the laughter bubbling from her throat. Kane was anything but her guardian. "I'll cross that bridge when I come to it," she said cryptically.

At precisely fifteen minutes before four on the following Monday, Glenna stood before the Red Garter, drew a deep breath to quell her nervousness, then entered the opulent atmosphere of the saloon, and was properly bedazzled by the magnificent decor. For several spellbound minutes she could do little else but stand gawking just inside the doorway. Never had she seen anything so grand!

Walking down the stairs wearing a vibrant blue gown that enhanced her blond loveliness, Sal was the first to spot Glenna, gasping in disbelief. "Glenna! What in the hell are you doing here?" Not one to divulge his plans or business dealings unless it suited his purposes, Judd had told no one about Glenna accepting a job in his establishment.

"I'm going to be working here, Sal," Glenna replied. Astonishment closely followed by strong disapproval marched across Sal's face. "Oh, no, it's not what you think!" she added hastily. "Mr. Martin hired me for the dining room. I wouldn't have agreed to anything else."

A look of consternation came over Sal's features. "Honey, do you know what you're getting into? True, your work might never get you out of the dining room but Judd Martin never did anything without a motive. Have you thought this over carefully?"

"He offered me twice what I was earning at the Palace," Glenna contended defensively.

"Is money what lured you here? Honey, I don't like it. What does Kane have to say about all this? I haven't seen him around lately."

"Kane doesn't know," Glenna admitted somewhat guiltily. "He was called back to Philadelphia unexpectedly."

"To marry his fiancée!" Sal snorted derisively. She thought it despicable of Kane to lead Glenna on without telling her about his wedding plans.

"Kane broke off his engagement," Glenna confided. "He asked me to marry him when he returns to Denver."

"Oh, Glenna, that's wonderful!"

"What's wonderful?" Judd finally spied Glenna as she stood talking to Sal and hurried over to welcome her to the Red Garter.

"That Glenna is . . . going to work here," amended Sal hastily when she noted the look of warning on Glenna's face.

"My sentiments exactly," smiled Judd smoothly. "I'll take over from here, Sal. You can go about your business."

Giving Glenna an inscrutable look, Sal nodded and made a reluctant departure. From her close association with Judd Martin she instinctively knew he had something devious in mind when he offered Glenna a job. At first she was thrilled to become his mistress, but now she anxiously awaited the day he tired of her and found someone else to take her place. Not Glenna, though. Glenna was too good for a man like Judd Martin. Sal was positive Judd was up to no good where Glenna was concerned, but had no idea what. She vowed to watch over the girl like a mother hen in order to keep her out of harm's way.

Another thing bothering Sal was Glenna's reason for accepting the job Judd offered. Knowing Glenna as she did, Sal was certain there was more than money involved in her decision. If Kane were here he certainly would put a stop to all this foolishness, Sal reflected. But of one thing she was positive—she would keep a protective eye on Glenna while at the same time making damn certain Judd kept his lecherous hands off her. Not that she was jealous, heaven forbid! In the weeks she'd been Judd's mistress she found herself wishing daily she had never accepted the position. There were too many facets to the gambler she neither liked nor understood.

Glenna proved an instant success in the Red Garter dining room. She had purposely chosen from the extensive wardrobe Judd made available to her a dress as demure as possible given her surroundings. As hostess she was free to dress much as she pleased, whereas the waitresses and bar girl were expected to flaunt their charms in vivid-hued, short ruffled skirts that stopped at mid-calf, and low-cut blouses.

Glenna's dress, fashioned of dark green satin worn off the shoulder, was in no way vulgar or suggestive. What she wasn't aware of was the subtle way the color enhanced the warm vibrancy of her hair, the flawless creaminess of her skin and displayed her perfect figure to the best advantage.

Occasionally women were present in the dining room, either accompanying their husbands out of curiosity or were mistresses of rich, influential men. But mostly they arrived very early in the evening and left shortly after dining. The majority of the patrons visiting the Red Garter were men with either gambling or women on their minds, or both.

From the beginning they recognized Glenna as being different from the other saloon girls and treated her accordingly. Though not a night went by that Glenna wasn't invited upstairs, it was soon understood that Miss Glenna O'Neill was off limits to all, that she was a young woman who performed her job and nothing more.

After a few days on the job Judd Martin made a public display of paying special court to her, much to Glenna's consternation. Though it fell in with her plans of learning exactly what Judd knew, if anything, about her father's death, she cared little for his attention. But she tolerated it, for soon Kane would return and force her to quit. She shuddered to think of his rage when he found her working at the Red Garter. Had the marshal found her father's killer she would have given up her job in a minute, but it looked as if it was left to her to do whatever was necessary to bring Da's killer to justice.

Then one day a man Glenna hoped never to see again came into the saloon and approached Judd. Judd appeared visibly annoyed by the man's presence and the two quickly disappeared behind the closed door of Judd's office. Glenna had reported to work a half-hour early that day to visit with Sal and was on the stairway heading toward Sal's room when a man she recognized immediately slunk in the door, unaware of Glenna's slight figure hovering in the shadows.

"What the hell are you doing here, Wiley?" Judd asked the moment the door closed behind them. "I told you to stay out of sight until you find out what's going on out at Golden Promise."

"That's exactly why I came back, boss," whined Wiley Wilson in a nasal drawl. "There's somethin' funny going on up there. Both Zach and Will seemed real excited when they came in last evenin'. I hightailed it back here so's I could tell you about it and find out what you wanted me to do next."

Judd was silent a long time, carefully weighing Wiley's sketchy information. "If you're right one of them will report their find to Glenna, and if they do I'll know about it. Keep out of sight until I send for you. There's an empty room above a warehouse I've recently acquired. You can stay there."

He gave Wiley directions then motioned him toward the door, anxious to be alone to plan his next move. But Wiley hung back, something else obviously on his mind. "Well, Wiley, is there something you haven't told me?" Judd asked curtly.

"I'm a little short of cash, boss," Wiley complained, licking his lips nervously.

"What did you do with the $5000 you took from old man O'Neill?"

"It don't go far once it's divided three ways," explained Wiley. "Besides, you owe me. If not for me you'd never know about O'Neill's strike. I was the one in the assayer's office that day he brought in his samples."

"Pah!" Judd scoffed derisively. "A hell of a lot of good it did me! He sold the claim shortly afterwards and all you got for your troubles was the money instead of the deed you were supposed to bring me."

'How was I to know he sold Golden Promise to that Carter fella?"

Cursing loudly, Judd exclaimed, "It was your business to know. Besides, if those samples were as rich as the assayer claimed, why did Paddy sell his claim? Unless . . . unless he made a deal with Carter to buy it back later," he mused thoughtfully. "Paddy O'Neill was a wily old coot and I'm betting he did it to fool everyone into thinking his claim was worthless. It makes sense. That's why I offered O'Neill's daughter a job. If anything is going on out there at the claim she'd be the first to know. And now you say the two men Morgan hired have found something?" Wiley nodded enthusiastically.

"I knew I was on to something big when you told me about Paddy's samples. The assayer was happy to show me the report once he learned I intended to inform his wife about his visits to Pearl if he didn't. The samples were rich in gold but that wasn't all. Until Paddy had it assayed he wasn't even aware himself of the value. What that old bastard found was the richest vein of silver yet to be found in Colorado. The gold was incidental, assaying out to $250 a ton while the silver exceeded $7000 a ton."

"Don't forget, boss, I get a share of all that,"

Wiley reminded him slyly.

"So far I haven't been able to lay my hands on the claim, Wiley," Judd spat disgustedly. "Perhaps things will change now that the O'Neill girl has fallen into my hands, so to speak. I've got plans for her, big plans."

"I'd like to go at the red-headed witch myself," Wiley said nastily. "Because of her my two partners Jimbo and Lem are dead. Her and that damn Morgan did them in."

"If your brains weren't in your pants your friends would be alive today," snorted Judd in disgust. "After you told me what happened out there in the hills I could have killed you myself. I was waiting for the O'Neill girl to return to Denver in hopes Carter might offer to sell her back the claim. Then you and your friends decide to rape her. Sometimes a woman needs to be handled with a heavy hand in order to be controlled, but rape is another thing altogether. There are too many willing ones around to resort to force. It isn't my style."

"Aw, boss, you told us to lay low until the stink about O'Neill died down. We was drinkin' and feelin' randy when we come upon the woman. Hell, we didn't even know who she was. If that damn Morgan didn't have a soft streak in him I'd be dead myself."

"At least we won't have him meddling in our affairs," Judd remarked. "By now he has probably married that fiancée of his and is in no hurry to leave his new bride. For awhile I thought . . . but thankfully it didn't work out like that. For some reason Morgan seemed to prefer the lifeless blond to Glenna, paving the way for me and my plans."

Suddenly tired of Wiley's company, Judd opened his safe, drew out a slim sheath of bills and tossed them to the scruffy prospector who caught them deftly. "Thanks, boss, you won't be sorry."

"Get out of here, Wiley. I don't want Glenna to see you. It would spoil everything if she found out you're working for me. If you need to contact me come early like you did today, before Glenna reports for work."

"I'm goin', boss," Wiley said, opening the door. "If you want me to go back out to the claim just send word. I won't need that room you offered, I'll be holed up at Molly's Place on the other side of town. It ain't as high class as this but her whores are clean and willin'." Then he was gone, closing the door behind him and slinking through the saloon just beginning to come alive with boisterous customers streaming through the door.

The moment the office door closed on Judd and Wiley Glenna crept stealthily forward. Mindless of her own safety should she be discovered eavesdropping, she tiptoed to the door and pressed her ear against the panel. But to her chagrin she could hear nothing save for low mumblings and an occasional unintelligible outburst. Cursing her luck she tried the keyhole, only to find the key still in place inside. The minutes flew by while Glenna's frustration escalated, terrified lest she be discovered by one of Judd's hired guns.

Then Glenna froze as the doorknob slowly rotated. Fear freeing her numb legs she darted around the corner, flattening herself against the wall. She heard rather than saw Wiley leave Judd's office, catching only fragments of his last words. He mentioned Golden Promise which proved to Glenna that Judd Martin had an unnatural interest in her father's claim. But seeing Wiley here had come as a shock. Where did he fit in and what was his connection with Judd Martin? Glenna wondered curiously. The answer to that question lay in her ability to worm her way into Judd Martin's confidence.

Though Glenna kept her eyes peeled the next few days she was disappointed by Wiley's continued absence. It seemed almost as if she had conjured him up from some bad dream. Even Sal noticed her preoccupation the times they talked before duty called them to their separate ways.

Though Pearl made it a point to ignore Glenna, Glenna and Sal remained friends though they were poles apart in all aspects of their lives. Candy chose a middle ground, becoming neither too friendly nor openly hostile. Though Candy and Pearl remained close, Candy refused to anger Sal since they were to work together in their own business one day soon.

By dint of their earlier friendship struck up on the train, Sal remained Glenna's staunchest friend. And except for Kate Jones, virtually her only friend. Thus when Sal questioned her strange behavior these past few days Glenna was at odds whether or not to confide in Sal. The only thing stopping her was the intimate relationship between Sal and Judd. Glenna had no idea how far Sal would carry her loyalty to Judd.

"I know something is bothering you, honey. Would you care to tell me about it?" urged Sal as they sat over a cup of tea early one afternoon.

"Sal, what makes you think—"

"I don't think, I know," Sal interrupted. Has it got something to do with Judd? If that bastard has touched you I'll—"

"No, Sal, it's nothing like that," Glenna insisted. "I know how you feel about Judd and I wouldn't—"

"You don't know how I feel, honey," she confided in a low whisper. "I can't stand the man. At first he was everything I've ever wanted or dreamed about. That's why I consented to become his mistress. But it didn't take long before I found out he's not at all the charming man he portrays. There's another side to him. A side you're better off not knowing."

"If that's how you feel why don't you leave, Sal?" Glenna advised cautiously.

"I will, honey, soon . . . soon. Truth to tell I'm afraid of him. I think he's tiring of me and when he does I'll be free of him for good. It won't be too long before we have enough money saved up to start our own place. It won't be as fancy as the Red Garter but a hell of a lot better than Molly's Place across town."

Molly's Place! Wasn't that the name Glenna heard Wiley mention? Abruptly she came to a decision. "Sal," she began in a confidential manner, "I'm going to ask you about something that I'd like kept private." Sal nodded, drawing her chair closer.

Then Glenna proceeded to describe Wiley, finally asking if Sal had seen the man in the Red Garter at any time talking to Judd.

Sal concentrated a few seconds then brightened. "Sure, I remember him. Came in to see Judd a few weeks ago. Didn't stay long, though."

"You . . . you didn't by any chance hear what they talked about, did you?" Glenna asked hopefully.

"Sorry, honey, but the thought never occurred to me. Is it important?"

"I think so."

"If it means that much to you, I'll keep my eyes and ears open. Do you want to tell me what this is all about?"

"Not yet, Sal," Glenna shook her head, sending flame-colored curls swirling about her shoulders. "It's just a feeling I have. I know the man I just described. His name is Wiley Wilson. He and two of his friends tried to rape me but Kane arrived in time to stop them. Kane killed two of the men but let Wiley get away. At this point the relationship between Wiley and Judd is only conjecture, but I know it's got something to do with Da's death and the claim."

"Whew, honey, you sure are looking for trouble," Sal replied worriedly. "If you want my advice you'll wait till Kane returns to pursue this. Have you heard from him?"

"No, but I expect word soon telling me when he'll be arriving. By now his brother should be well on his way to recovery."

"Be careful, Glenna," cautioned Sal. "Something tells me you're getting in over your head. Perhaps you should talk to the marshal."

"I will, Sal, as soon as I have something concrete to base my charges on. And I promise to be careful."

While Glenna and Sal talked quietly, their heads bent together over the table, Judd watched from the doorway, his eyes narrowed speculatively. The growing friendship between the two women had not escaped his notice, and he filed it away for future use. Nothing was too devious or unscrupulous should he be forced to resort to such means. Something told him Glenna O'Neill was not one to be easily persuaded and that he would need extraordinary means to force her to his will.

That same night Zach Kimball called on Glenna. His first words were in the form of a rebuke. "Miss Glenna, Pete over at the livery told me you quit your job at the Palace and was working for Judd Martin here at the Red Garter. Does Mr. Morgan know about this? I ain't your pa, Miss Glenna, but I know he wouldn't like it. Neither would Mr. Morgan."

"Zach, I know what I'm doing," Glenna assured him. "And as for Kane, well, I've heard nothing from him. If he was so concerned about my welfare he'd be back by now." She seated Zach at a nearby table and joined him, it still being rather early and customers scarce. "What do you have to report?"

"Something exciting, Miss Glenna," replied the wiry prospector. Well past middle age, his graying hair and lean frame belied his strength and capability. "Me and Will were working upstream a few days ago when we found more float. It's the same blue color as those pieces Mr. Morgan showed us. I don't want to get your hopes up, but I'd be willing to swear that Paddy found the mother lode; a lode far richer in silver than gold. But it will have to be assayed before we can be sure. I took the liberty of dropping off the samples at the assayer's office. You're to pick up the report in a day or two."

"If Da found the lode why did he sell Golden Promise?" puzzled Glenna.

"Judging from where the float was found I've formed an opinion you might be interested in, Miss Glenna," Zach confided.

"Anything you or Will have to say interests me, Zach," Glenna assured him. "Kane trusts you and so do I."

"I think I know why Paddy sold his claim." So engrossed were they in their conversation that neither noticed Judd standing only a few feet behind Glenna, clearly within hearing distance. Since Zach had no reason to suspect Judd as Glenna did, he paid little heed to the gambler.

"I would be forever grateful if you could clear up that mystery for me," Glenna replied softly. Could this grizzled prospector really have stumbled upon Da's secret where Kane and the marshal failed? Glenna asked herself wonderingly.

"I think Paddy found the mother lode, all right, but it wasn't within the boundaries of his claim," Zach revealed. "I'd stake my life on it. And if I'm right and if I were Paddy I'd beg, borrow or steal the money needed to file a new claim, buy equipment and hire miners."

Total shock suffused Glenna's face. "It makes sense, Zach," she exclaimed excitedly. "All except for one thing. Where is the deed to the new claim? I can understand, though, why he sold Golden Promise if he needed funds to get to the gold, or silver, as it turned out. It even explains why he wrote to Patrick Morgan for help."

"You knew your pa best, Miss Glenna, isn't there someplace he might have hidden the deed and the assayer's report?"

"I haven't been home in four years, Zach, and things change. But I will think on it. And I'll go to the claims office first thing in the morning to see if Da filed a new claim. I'll also question the assayer about a report he might have prepared for Da."

"You do that, Miss Glenna," Zach nodded. "I'd best leave now. I'm staying at the Denver Arms but plan on leaving early tomorrow after I buy supplies."

"Don't leave until I learn whether your theory about the new claim is correct, Zach," Glenna advised. "God, I wish Kane were here! I don't know what's keeping him so long, but until he returns I'll handle this by myself. Keep your views to yourself, Zach, and I'll see you tomorrow."

Having heard all he needed to, Judd hurried away while Zach wandered off toward the bar, feeling in need of a drink and female companionship.

The next morning Judd appeared at the claims office a full hour before Glenna, received the information he sought, then left to find Wiley, an idea already forming in his mind. An idea that, should it succeed, would enmesh Glenna in a plot that would alter the entire fabric of her life. A plot in which Kane Morgan had no place.

11

The reason behind Glenna's failure to reach the claims office ahead of Judd caused her a great deal of disappointment. As she was walking past the telegraph office the clerk, recognizing her flaming hair, came running out waving a piece of paper in his hand.

"Miss O'Neill!" he hailed, capturing her attention. "A telegram arrived for you last night. I was about to have it delivered when I saw you passing by."

"Thank you," Glenna replied eagerly, reaching for the message. It could only be from Kane, she surmised, with information about his arrival. She had been expecting word daily. But dismay replaced pleasure as Kane's words leaped out at her from the printed page, settling about her like a blanket of gloom.

Kane's brother had developed an infection and he couldn't leave Philadelphia just yet. He would wire when he was able to leave. He ended by saying he loved her.

Visibly shaken by Kane's continued absence, Glenna could not stop herself from brooding, wondering if Ellen had anything to do with his delay. Then she chided herself roundly for succumbing to her loneliness and thinking the worst. Hadn't Kane said he loved her? But try as she might Glenna couldn't help thinking about his family and their desire that he marry Ellen no matter what Kane had decided. She knew Kane felt a certain responsibility to do what his family wanted, especially since he had gone his own way most of his life. His father's death had placed a heavy mantle of guilt upon his shoulders and made him aware of his duty where his family was concerned. Marrying a woman of his own station was expected of Kane. Could he in all conscience refute the wishes of his family to marry a woman miles below his social standing? Glenna wondered glumly. Only time and a few prayers thrown in for good measure would tell.

Thus it was that Glenna entered the claims office much later than expected, unaware that Judd had already come and gone.

"May I help you, miss?" asked the young clerk, immediately impressed by Glenna's beauty. Being relatively new in town he did not recognize Paddy O'Neill's daughter.

"I hope so." Glenna smiled brightly, sending the young man into a tizzy. "I'd like to know if my father filed a claim recently. Could you please look it up for me?"

"Shouldn't be any trouble, miss, if you give me your father's name."

"O'Neill, Paddy O'Neill. I'm his daughter, Glenna."

If the clerk thought it odd that two people came to his office within an hour of each other requesting the same information, he did not mention it. Although the information was not private and anyone could inquire, his senses warned him that Judd Martin was not a man he'd want for an enemy. He had heard about the gambler, had seen him several times during his visits to the Red Garter and wisely decided to hold his tongue. He truly hoped the gambler meant Glenna O'Neill no harm and reminded himself that it was none of his business.

It took him only a few minutes to locate the correct files, having already done so once that morning. "Here it is, Miss O'Neill," he said, pointing to a recent entry. "Several months ago Paddy O'Neill filed a claim on land located very close to his first claim. Within a mile or two, I'd judge."

"Zach was right," thrilled Glenna, green eyes shining with delight. "I'll need a copy of the location and its boundaries," Glenna directed in a rush of words.

"Certainly, Miss O'Neill," nodded the clerk. "But that information should be on the deed."

"Da died before he told me where to find the deed. Is that a problem?"

"Shouldn't be. There's a record of the transaction right here in the office. As long as he didn't sell it to anyone before he died it's all yours."

Glenna found Zach waiting anxiously for her at his hotel. He let loose a jubiliant hoot when told his hunch had been right on target. After what she had just learned it seemed increasingly evident that somewhere within the boundaries of the new claim they'd find the mother lode. Not an inconsiderable task, but at least now they had some idea where to search.

"It might take a while, Miss Glenna, but me and Will will find it," Zach assured her confidently. "I'll let you know just as soon as we find anything. Until then I suggest we keep mum about all this."

"Don't worry, Zach," Glenna replied in a low voice. "I don't want this getting around any more than you do. The last thing we need is to have the area overrun by prospectors and claim jumpers. If only Kane were here," she sighed wistfully.

That same day Judd Martin launched a concentrated effort to woo and win Glenna. Once he learned about Paddy's new claim and the rich lode, he found Golden Promise no longer held any interest for him. From what he learned earlier it appeared the new claim belonged exclusively to Glenna, and he aimed to have it even if it meant marrying her to get it. Thus began a campaign by Judd to win both Glenna and her rich claim without revealing to her that he had discovered Paddy's secret.

Truth to tell, Glenna did not enjoy Judd's attention, but accepted it with resignation, knowing that it was the only way to induce him to tip his hand. He couldn't know about Da's new claim, she decided, and thought it was still Golden Promise he desired, using his considerable charm to fleece her out of what was rightfully hers. With grim determination she forced herself to play at his dangerous game in hopes he might inadvertently reveal a connection to her father's death.

Judd began his ruthless pursuit of Glenna by inviting her out for a drive on her day off. This naturally progressed to picnics on those long afternoons. The first time Judd tried to kiss her they were sitting on a blanket beneath a stand of tall aspens. The day was lovely and the view spectacular. When he pulled her into his arms she stiffened, shuddering with revulsion.

"Glenna, don't pull away, my dear," Judd murmured, sensing her withdrawal. "I've waited a long time to kiss you."

"Judd, please, I hardly know you," Glenna protested.

"That's not true, my dear," Judd denied suavely. "This is the third time I've taken you out riding and you've worked for me many weeks now. Time enough for us to become acquainted."

"I . . . I don't feel for you in that way," Glenna resisted.

"Glenna, I'm beginning to care for you." His voice sounded so sincere that had Glenna not known better she could have truly believed him. "Do you have any feelings at all for me?"

"I like you," hedged Glenna cautiously. "Besides, what about Sal? I thought you cared for her."

"Sal is . . . well, you know what she is. She certainly isn't a woman I'd want to marry. All you need do is say the word and I'll no longer . . . have anything to do with her."

Glenna knew for a fact Sal was anxious to see the end of her relationship with Judd. Sal feared Judd, and with good reason. Perhaps it was within her power to perform a small service for Sal, Glenna thought slyly. "Somehow you don't seem the marrying kind," she baited.

"I could easily be with the right woman," Judd hinted. "Most men want a respectable wife, children. You'd do any man proud, my dear."

Most men but not you, Glenna thought wryly. Aloud, she said, "Are you asking me to be your wife, Judd? Perhaps I might consider it one day but certainly not now. Of course, keeping a mistress does little to commend you."

Judd cursed beneath his breath while struggling to maintain a charming facade. The little bitch! he thought in sarcastic fury. Just wait until she was legally his. He'd show her she couldn't dictate to him. Swallowing his anger, he said smoothly, "Sal means nothing to me. I was tiring of her anyway."

Then he pulled her into his embrace, pretending passion where none existed while Glenna deftly turned her face so that his kiss fell harmlessly on her cheek. It was a baiting game, one a novice like Glenna had no chance of winning.

"What are you up to, Glenna?" hissed Sal, pulling her into the kitchen a few days later. "First Judd makes a big play for you and then he dumps me. You're getting in a little deep, aren't you?"

"Are you angry with me, Sal?" Glenna asked, worried. "I thought . . . that is . . . do you love Judd?"

"The only thing I'm angry about is the certain knowledge that you are playing a dangerous game and are likely to get hurt. I don't give a damn about Judd, I'm well rid of him, but I am concerned about you. I know you can't stand Judd so why are you letting him court you?"

"I have my reasons," Glenna said cryptically. "And I can take care of myself."

Sal threw up her hands in disgust. "I give up, Glenna. Please be careful. I'm sure Judd has some ulterior motive where you're concerned. He never does anything without a reason. I don't mean to hurt you, honey, but you just ain't his type."

Glenna laughed dryly. "I know that better than you, Sal, and believe me I'm aware that Judd wants more from me than my hand in marriage."

Though Glenna was of the opinion she could take care of herself, Sal wasn't so easily convinced. Glenna was but an innocent babe compared to Judd's ruthlessness and worldly experience. Thus Sal experienced no remorse over sending Kane a telegram requesting he return to Denver as soon as possible, hinting that Glenna needed him desperately. If that didn't bring him quickly to Denver nothing would.

That evening Judd insisted on walking Glenna home and she reluctantly agreed, busying herself in the nearly deserted dining room while she waited for him to finish up in his office. From the corner of her eye she noticed a shadowy figure sidle into the partially opened door and some second sense urged her to follow. She breathed a grateful sigh when she found that Judd's late visitor had been careless enough to leave the door ajar. Making herself as small as possible she listened intently to the low murmur of voices, recognizing immediately the whining tones of Wiley Wilson.

"It's about time you returned," Judd barked impatiently. "What's going on out at the claim?"

"They did just what you said they'd do, Mr. Martin," Wiley cackled gleefully. "They abandoned Golden Promise and built a crude camp about two miles upstream."

"Have they found the lode yet?"

"Not so far as I can tell. They panned some nuggets, found significant pieces of float but that's about all. Won't be long, though, before they find the source. Both Zach and Will are experienced miners. I predict old Paddy's daughter will soon be the richest silver baron in the territory."

"She'll be sharing her fortune with her husband," Judd smirked complacently.

"Husband? She ain't married," scoffed Wiley.

"She will be soon if I have my way."

"To you?" Judd nodded. "You sure are smart, boss," guffawed Wiley, obviously delighted. "I knew you'd find some way to get what you wanted. What does the girl think about all this?"

"The stupid bitch thinks I'm in love with her," bragged Judd. "But I couldn't care less about her."

The bastard! fumed Glenna, red dots of rage bursting inside her brain. He'd be shocked to learn exactly what she thought of him! But what truly amazed her was that he knew all about Da's new claim and the silver. She'd received the assayer's report only a day or two ago herself. Did he have eyes everywhere? What really angered her was that he had sent that snake Wiley to spy on Zach and Will. Was he also capable of murder?

"What the hell are you doing out here spying on the boss?" a harsh voice challenged.

Glenna whirled, her heart thumping in her chest. Towering before her stood one of Judd's bodyguards, his eyes glinting dangerously. "I . . . I—" stammered Glenna, fear forming a lump in her throat that refused to be dislodged.

"What's going on out there?" Judd demanded when the ruckus outside his door alerted him to the fact that he and Wiley were not alone. His eyes narrowed coldly when he saw Glenna in the clutches of one of his men. "What are you doing with Glenna, Duke?"

"I found her listening outside the door, boss," Duke explained, his heavy hand bruising the tender flesh on Glenna's upper arm.

"Is that true, Glenna?" asked Judd quietly, his tone sending chills racing up her spine.

"No, Judd, of course not," she scoffed, slanting Duke a haughty glare. "Your man is sadly mistaken. The truth is I got tired of waiting and came to see if you were ready to leave."

Just then Wiley sidled from behind the door and stared at Glenna, his lascivious gaze raking over her insolently. Glenna's eyes bulged in dismay, looking at a man who had come so close to raping her was more unnerving than she would have imagined. Judd noticed the direction of Glenna's gaze and cursed loudly at Wiley who stood at his elbow.

"Damn you, Wiley, I told you to keep out of sight!"

"What does it matter now, boss? Duke just told us he caught her listening at the door. She probably heard everything."

Judd's voice was cold and accusing. "Did you hear what we said, Glenna?"

"I . . . no . . . I—" Glenna's slight hesitation damned her, and she knew a moment of panic until she quickly gathered her wits about her and attempted to undo the damage already done. "Of course not, Judd. How can you think I'd do such a thing?"

Judd's smile failed to reach his eyes. "Come inside, Glenna," he invited in a voice as smooth as oiled silk.

"If it's all right with you, Judd, I'll wait out here until you finish your business," Glenna declined sweetly. Judd nodded to Duke who immediately pushed her inside the room, abruptly releasing her arm, causing her to stumble against Wiley who took advantage of the situation by dragging her against his chest.

"Let's see you get away this time." Wiley sneered, his arms like steel bands about her body.

"Judd, what's the meaning of this?" Glenna demanded, the stench of Wiley's unwashed body sickening her. He smelled as if he hadn't bathed in years.

"Let her go, Wiley," Judd ordered curtly.

"Aw, boss," Wiley complained, "I was only having a little fun."

Judd glared at him then turned to Glenna, impaling her with a piercing gaze. "How much did you hear, Glenna?"

"N-nothing, Judd, I heard nothing," insisted Glenna, assuming a facade of innocence.

"Glenna, I don't hold with rape, but if I have to I'll give you to Wiley."

"I'm not yours to give!" Glenna spat furiously.

"There are three strong men in this room," threatened Judd. "I can do anything I please. Now, tell me what you heard."

"Enough to put you and Wiley in jail!" declared Glenna hotly, disregarding her own imminent danger.

"That's where that foul creature Wiley belongs anyway. He tried to rape me! And you're no better!"

Significant glances were exchanged between Wiley and Judd. "And what would you charge me with, Glenna?"

There was no turning back now. "Murder!" The word rolled around her tongue and she spat it at him. "You either killed Da for his claim or ordered it done! And you can forget about marrying me. You're nothing but a slimy toad. I wouldn't marry you if you were the last man on earth!" There, it was all out in the open. "I'm sure the marshal will be interested in what I know."

"You heard nothing and know even less," Judd's cold voice warned her. "Not once was murder mentioned tonight in this room. Your imagination is working overtime. You're obsessed with your father's death. Perhaps you are even becoming unbalanced."

Was that a threat? Glenna wondered in a surge of renewed anger. "Do you think Marshal Bartow will believe that?"

Judd's pale eyes assessed her slowly. "Obviously you don't know the law. A wife can't testify against her husband."

"We're not married, Judd, nor likely to be!" scoffed Glenna.

"That's where you're wrong, my dear, we're getting married tonight," Judd smiled deviously.

Glenna gave an involuntary shudder, fear feeding her anger. "I'm getting out of here, Judd, you're mad!" she retorted, whirling on her heel. At Judd's nod Duke reached out to put an end to Glenna's short-lived flight, tossing her toward Judd like a rag doll.

"Duke, where is Carl?" Judd asked, referring to another of his bodyguards.

"He's somewhere in the saloon keeping an eye on things," Duke said.

"Go find him, Duke, and bring him here," Judd ordered brusquely. Duke left to do his bidding while Glenna stood fuming in the circle of Judd's arms. A full five minutes passed before Duke returned with Carl, an overgrown brute hired strictly for his brawn.

Carl stared stupidly at Glenna before acknowledging Judd. "You wanted me, boss?"

Judd nodded. "Where is Sal?"

"Sitting with one of the customers, do you want her?"

Glenna had no idea what Judd intended but intuitively knew she would not like it. His answer not only stunned her but fortified her belief that he was the man responsible for her father's death.

"I don't want, Sal, Carl, I just want you to go out and keep an eye on her. Don't let her out of your sight."

"Is that all, Mr. Martin? Just keep an eye on her?"

Judd grinned craftily. "No, that's not all, Carl. When I give you the sign you're to take Sal out in the alley and kill her. Make it look like she was attacked by a drunk—you know—rough her up some. The marshal isn't going to worry too much about the death of another whore." Acknowledging the order with a nod, Carl left, obviously willing to earn his pay by murdering in cold blood.

"No-o-o-o," screamed Glenna, struggling to escape Judd's cruel embrace. "What kind of a monster are you? Why would you kill Sal?"

"I'm not stupid, my dear. I know you and Sal have become friends. If you refuse to marry me she'll be the one to pay for your stubbornness. Are you willing to sacrifice her life to remain free?"

"I don't believe you," Glenna scoffed, disbelief turning her eyes a dark emerald green. "An act such as that goes far beyond mere cruelty."

Judd turned to Duke. "Give Carl the word, Duke," he instructed calmly and concisely, leaving

Glenna no doubt as to the veracity of his words. In that instant she realized that Judd would stop at nothing to gain his own ends, and would feel no remorse at murdering an innocent victim.

Duke had his hand on the doorknob before Glenna found her voice, nearly choking on the words. "Wait! Don't do it, Judd! I'll marry you!" Then she collapsed in a storm of tears, thoughts of whatever happiness she and Kane might have shared washing away with the downpour. Where was Kane when she needed him?

A caustic smile curved Judd's lips. He had known all along that Glenna would capitulate once he showed her he meant business. "Forget it, Duke," he countermanded. "Tell Carl to keep close tabs on Sal in case I change my mind." Duke nodded and left.

"I told you I'd marry you, leave Sal out of this," Glenna pleaded desperately, teetering on the brink of hysteria.

"Oh, no, my dear, Sal is my ace-in-the-hole. We'll be married tonight but I want no hysterics, no last minute denials. You'll stand calmly by my side and speak your vows loud and clear. If you falter or voice any objection whatsoever Carl will be waiting in the wings to carry out my order. Is that clear?"

"Perfectly," spat Glenna in impotent rage.

Just then Wiley let out a nervous guffaw and both Glenna and Judd turned in his direction, surprised to find him still in the room.

"Go get the preacher, Wiley," Judd ordered curtly. "Drag him out of bed if you have to, but have him here in fifteen minutes. Tell him it can't wait till morning."

"Sure, boss," Wiley sighed regretfully. "Sure wish you'd let me have her first."

"Get going, Wiley!" After a baleful glance in Glenna's direction, Wiley scooted out the door.

"Well, Glenna, soon we'll be man and wife," Judd smiled complacently.

"I've consented to become your wife," replied Glenna, her mind working furiously, "but we both know we can't stand one another. That's the only way I'll agree to this farce. Otherwise you'll have to kill me as well as Sal, and it will all gain you naught. I don't want you anywhere near me."

"As long as we'll be husband and wife we may as well benefit from this marriage," Judd winked lewdly. "I'm a good lover, ask Sal if you don't want to take my word for it."

"You could be the best lover in the world for all I care," bit out Glenna hatefully. "I loathe you. You killed Da and would have killed Sal without a second thought. You might wed me but you'll never bed me. I'd kill myself before I'd allow you to rape me!"

The word rape immediately turned Judd off and he slanted Glenna a look of pure disgust. "What makes you think I'm interested in you in that way? Well, think again, you haughty bitch. All I want from you is that claim and the mother lode hidden within its borders. I have no need to resort to rape. There are plenty of women around willing to accommodate me. With you in my bed I'm liable to take a chill and die," he insulted crudely.

"You can have your own room and sleep in your own cold bed for all I care, but once that preacher says the words over us you will live here with me. I insist on that for appearance's sake. Nor will I be made a laughingstock of by an unfaithful wife. I'll kill any man you take to your bed. It's me or no one, is that clear?"

My God, what am I getting myself into? panicked Glenna. Yet was she given any choice? It was either yield to Judd's demands and watch her father's dreams go up in smoke or refuse and stand helplessly by while an innocent woman was killed. Could she in all conscience sacrifice Sal to save herself? In her hands lay the choice of life and death and Glenna saw no way out but to marry Judd. Hopefully a way to extricate herself from an intolerable situation would present itself later. At least she had gained one small concession. If Judd could be believed, he would not force himself on her. For that much she was thankful.

Glenna's dark thoughts were rudely interrupted by Wiley's return, dragging in a disgruntled preacher who had been roused from bed only minutes before. "This had better be important, Mr. Martin," blustered the preacher, hastily buttoning his jacket over his paunchy middle.

"It is, Reverend, very important. I want you to marry Miss O'Neill and myself."

"Now?" asked the astounded man. "It's after midnight. Can't it wait until morning?"

Judd's arm inched around Glenna's waist, giving it a fond squeeze. "Reverend, Miss O'Neill is a decent woman and we . . . er . . . suddenly find we cannot wait. What would you have us do?" He smiled apologetically as Glenna cringed inwardly, his bold words sounding as if they had already consummated the wedding. Nothing could be further from the truth.

The preacher sent Glenna a mildly disapproving frown. "Miss O'Neill is of a different religious persuasion, I believe."

Judd cursed beneath his breath then walked around to his safe, reached inside and withdrew a small pouch heavy with dust and nuggets. He tossed it to the surprised man of God. "As I said before, it is imperative that we marry immediately. Perform the ceremony now and this is yours. Might be enough here to build that bigger church you've been talking about."

The reverend hefted the bag in his hand, mentally weighing the contents and calculating its worth. It must have made up his mind for he turned to Glenna and asked, "Are you willing to abide by the marriage vows spoken over you by a man of God other than that of your own faith?"

Judd's intense blue eyes bore into Glenna, warning her of the dire consequences should she give the wrong answer. Silence. The constriction in Glenna's throat prevented her from forming a reply.

"Glenna, my dear," Judd encouraged, "the Reverend is waiting for your answer. Tell him, darling, tell him what you want." A gasp escaped her lips as he cruelly prodded her in the ribs.

"Yes," squeaked Glenna, her voice fragile and shaking.

"Yes, what?" prompted Judd relentlessly.

"Yes, I want the Reverend to marry us."

"Very good," nodded Judd contentedly. "Wiley, go tell Duke and Carl there is to be a wedding and everyone is invited. I want the whole town to rejoice with me and celebrate my good fortune. Have the gaming room set up and we'll be married there."

"In a saloon gambling hall?" protested the reverend vigorously. "I had thought the office would suffice. A private ceremony, you know."

"Sorry to disappoint you, Reverend, but as I said before I want all my friends around me on this festive occasion. It's not every day a man gets married. Join me while I attend to the arrangements." Then he turned to Glenna. "I'll send Sal in. She can act as your bridesmaid."

Abruptly he burst out laughing, causing the preacher to shake his head, thinking the whole business crazy but the recompense too generous to refuse. Besides, he was astute enough to realize that being a man of the cloth would offer him little protection should he anger a ruthless man like Judd Martin.

* * *

"My God, you can't be serious!" exclaimed Sal the minute she rushed through the door. "Judd is out there telling everyone you're getting married tonight and inviting them all to stick around for the ceremony. Have you lost your mind?"

Her words went on and on, causing Glenna to press her hands over her ears and turn her back to Sal. "Enough!" she shouted, quickly reaching the end of her tether. "I know what I'm doing, Sal. There's nothing you can do or say to change my mind."

"But you hate Judd. You think he killed your father. Why are you doing this?"

"I have my reasons," Glenna said cryptically.

"Glenna, honey," Sal cajoled, "we've been friends a long time. If Judd is forcing you to do this we can go to the marshal. He'll protect you."

Glenna eyed Sal sadly, thinking of her reasons for agreeing to Judd's scurrilous plan. If she refused her friend would die, but under no circumstances could she confide in Sal, or even the marshal. Too many lives could be lost by doing so. Glenna knew Judd would suffer no qualms in killing the marshal should she run to him for help. He was too near retirement to enmesh him in Judd's nefarious plot. Not only that, but once she was rushed through this ceremony her testimony would not hold up in court.

Sal wrongly surmised that Glenna's uneasy silence meant she was wavering and renewed her efforts to stop what she considered madness. "What about Kane? I know you love him. And he loves you. Think what this will do to him."

Truth to tell, Glenna tried desperately not to think about Kane and what he would feel or do when he learned of her hasty marriage to Judd. Nor was she likely to have the opportunity to explain, not if Judd had anything to say about it. "Sal, you're just going to have to accept my word that I have to do this and trust me."

Sal searched Glenna's face for an answer to her strange behavior, and when none was forthcoming was left no choice but to nod her reluctant agreement. "Judd asked me to act as witness, me and Duke. Are you sure I can't talk you out of this folly?"

Heartsick, Glenna shook her head dumbly. Her mouth opened as if she intended to speak but nothing came out. Then it was too late as the door opened and Judd swaggered inside, holding his hand out to her. With a sense of impending doom, Glenna stepped forward, accepting the challenge that fate had dealt her.

12

Two incredibly long weeks had passed since Glenna stood before a room crowded with drunken, cheering men and exchanged vows with Judd Martin. Afterwards he ordered drinks on the house and forced her to remain at his side to accept congratulations from scores of well-wishers until she was certain the false smile on her face would crack and sheer exhaustion claimed her.

The reverend had left immediately after filling out the necessary papers legalizing her marriage to Judd but Glenna was not so lucky. Only when pink tinged the western sky did Judd allow her to escape to one of the empty rooms above stairs that was to be hers. Locking the door behind her she fell atop the bed and was asleep almost instantly, her mind and body existing in a void from which there was no escape. She later found out that Judd spent his wedding night with Pearl, and blessed the woman for taking her place in his bed.

The most difficult task facing Glenna was informing Kate Jones of her marriage and moving her things to the Red Garter. Judd sent Duke with the carriage to help Glenna with her trunk so she was unable to say much to Kate by way of an explanation. She was certain Judd sent Duke along to spy on her so she deliberately ignored Kate's probing questions about her hasty marriage as well as her accusing glare.

"I don't think I'll ever understand this, Glenna," the older woman said disapprovingly, wagging her head from side to side. "I thought I knew you but now I'm not so sure. I'm glad Paddy's not here to see this."

"So am I, Kate, so am I," Glenna agreed sourly, further confusing the poor woman. Then Duke returned to the room and Glenna took her leave, loath to return to the place she had come to think of as her prison.

A scant few days after the wedding Judd left for Glenna's claim, which she had begun referring to as simply Promise Two, taking Carl and two hired men with him. Upon reaching the claim Judd's first act was to inform Zach and Will of his marriage to Glenna, after which he fired them. At first both prospectors were skeptical, scoffing openly at the idea of Glenna marrying the gambler no matter how attractive he might be. But when Judd showed them the marriage papers he had brought along for just such a purpose, they had no choice but to believe the man claiming to be Glenna's husband. Besides, no resistance was possible with four armed men facing them. Regretfully they packed their meager belongings and left.

Though the two men had been hired by Kane and technically were working for him, Kane had left Glenna in charge, giving her the right to fire and hire as she wished. With Kane still gone and Glenna married to Judd Martin, the gambler now had the right to act in Glenna's stead, leaving Zach and Will no recourse but give in to Judd's demand that they be replaced by men loyal to him.

Judd spent two weeks at the new claim site,

searching for the mother lode he now knew for a fact existed somewhere other than in the mind of a dreamer. But to no avail. Situated on the west bank of Clear Creek, Promise Two existed in a thicket of dense brush amid outcroppings of rock rising from a steep hillside. It was already the end of August, and Judd hoped to find the lode before snowfall and commence digging come spring, even if he had to hire a hundred men to join the search.

Those few days following the wedding and before Judd left for the claim proved a nightmare for Glenna. Except for two rare occasions she kept to her room. Once to retrieve her belongings from Kate's house and again to accompany Judd to the dressmaker. At first she balked at being completely outfitted for her new role as Judd's wife, but acquiesced when Judd threatened to have her tied and carried to the dressmaker's. Nor was she allowed to continue her job in the dining room because Judd decided that his wife had no need for gainful employment. Existing on the fringes of respectability most of his life, Judd had high hopes for gaining wealth, respectability and respect through his marriage to Glenna.

The day Judd left for the claim with his men Glenna breathed a welcome sigh of relief. He came to see her shortly before he left, barging into her room as if he had every right. Glenna had just eaten breakfast with Sal and hadn't bothered to lock the door after her return.

"What do you want?" she barked as Judd sauntered boldly into the room.

"Do I need special permission to talk to my wife?" he asked sarcastically. "I thought you'd be interested to know I'm leaving and won't be back for a week or two."

"Good riddance!" replied Glenna caustically, deliberately turning her back.

Glowering with rage Judd reached her side in two strides. "Listen well, my dear bride, you're lucky I don't beat you for that remark. I'm a firm believer that women have but one function in life and you sure as hell don't know yours. When I return things around here are going to change. Hiding in your room will no longer suffice for I've decided you'll share mine."

"Over my dead body!" bit out Glenna sharply.

"That too can be arranged," Judd smirked knowingly. "No matter what happens to you the claim is mine. I no longer need you."

Stunned, Glenna recoiled, knowing that nothing would prevent Judd from committing murder again. Every minute she remained with him she placed her life in danger. "You'd probably enjoy seeing me dead, wouldn't you?" she challenged defiantly.

"No, my dear," Judd denied, raking her from head to toe with deliberate thoroughness. "I've decided you make me a perfect wife, except for one little detail which I expect to remedy upon my return."

"I won't share your bed. You promised!"

"Promises are made to be broken. Until my return enjoy your solitude. I'm leaving Duke orders to watch over you. If you do or say anything out of the ordinary he will carry through my instructions concerning Sal."

"You cold-blooded bastard! Am I to consider myself a prisoner here?"

"Of course not," scoffed Judd. "The carriage is at your disposal and you may move about town freely. With Duke to accompany you, naturally. I want all of Denver aware of what a beautiful woman I married and how happy we are together. Be sure to smile on your outings, my dear, and tell all your friends what a wonderful husband I am." His raucous laughter still rang in her ears long after he was gone.

For days afterwards Glenna fumed and raged in her room, cursing the fates that brought her into contact with Judd Martin and the Red Garter. She also cursed Kane Morgan for leaving her alone to deal with these things beyond her ken.

Then one day she was searching through her possessions for a cameo that belonged to her mother and realized she had left it in a small case shoved beneath her bed at Kate's house and promptly forgotten. Deciding a visit to Kate was called for, Glenna left her room above the Red Garter intending to walk the short distance to Kate's house. Almost immediately Duke fell into step behind her. "Where are you going, Mrs. Martin?" he asked, his voice courteous but patronizing.

The last thing Glenna wanted was Duke trailing behind her like a watchdog. "Down to the dining room for lunch," Glenna lied, her mind working furiously. "Have you been instructed to choose my meals for me?"

Her mild rebuke worked like magic as Duke, scowling darkly, ambled into the saloon instead of following her into the dining room. Somehow Glenna was determined to escape from Duke's constant surveillance. She was halfway through her meal when Sal sauntered through the door, spotted her and seated herself at the table.

"It's good to see you downstairs, honey," she smiled amiably. "I'll bet it's lonesome without Judd."

Glenna's reaction was vehement and immediate, serving to fortify Sal's belief that Glenna had not married Judd willingly. "I'd be grateful if he never returned!" grimaced Glenna distastefully. "I wish I'd never laid eyes on that despicable man!"

"Glenna," Sal said in a confidential whisper, "why

don't you tell me about it? You can trust me. Perhaps I can help you."

"No one can help me," Glenna countered bleakly. "Certainly not you." Sal's hurt expression caused her to add, "I mean it would take a miracle to get me out of this one."

"Maybe a miracle will turn up one of these days," hinted Sal slyly. "In the meantime, what can I do to help you?"

Discouraged, Glenna sighed. She could only think of one miracle and that was for Kane to appear. But after so long a time that was not likely to happen. In all probability Kane had succumbed to his family's wishes and married Ellen after all. There was no other explanation for his continued absence with no word save for that one telegram weeks ago. All this and more went through Glenna's mind while Sal waited patiently for Glenna to speak.

"Did you hear me, Glenna? How may I help you?"

Glenna sighed again. "I'm afraid there's nothing you can do, Sal, unless—" Her eyes shifted to the doorway where Duke now stood with his back against a pillar. "Maybe there is something—" She hesitated doubtfully.

"Well, spit it out."

"Can you keep Duke occupied for a time? Judd appointed him my keeper and I need to go off on my own for awhile. I want to visit Pete, Kate, and maybe the marshal. If you could do that for me I'd be grateful."

Sal's delighted giggle floated around the nearly deserted room. "Say no more, honey. That bastard has had the hots for me for a long time but until now was afraid of Judd. If you'd like I'll keep him so busy all afternoon he won't have the time to think of anyone but me."

"Sal," Glenna said guiltily. "I wouldn't want you to do anything you find . . . distasteful."

"Distasteful?" Sal scoffed merrily. "It's my business to keep men occupied and happy. Truth to tell, the big son-of-a-bitch kind of turns me on so don't you worry your head about me. I can handle him just fine."

Glenna flashed Sal a grateful smile, still somewhat perturbed over what Sal intended. "You're sure?"

"Positive. Now, here's what you do." Then she proceeded to give Glenna instructions on how they were to continue.

A short time later Glenna rose and left the dining room, purposely snubbing Duke as she walked by. When she reached the doorway she turned back to Sal and announced in a loud voice, "I'm going to take a nap, Sal. Please wake me at six o'clock if I'm not up by then." Sal waved a hand in reply then watched smugly as Glenna disappeared up the stairs.

When Duke made to follow Sal called his name, drawing his attention from Glenna. After a long, thoughtful look at Glenna's departing back he shrugged then turned his steps to join Sal. He'd had his eye on her since she first showed up at the Red Garter but Judd had claimed her as his own. Now that Judd had taken a wife Duke meant to turn his sights on Sal.

Truth to tell, he preferred Judd's red-headed wife to any woman he knew but Duke was no fool. Though Judd had married Glenna O'Neill for the claim left to her by her late father and cared little for her as a woman, Judd expected his wife to remain sacrosanct. He jealously guarded his possessions and Glenna was now one of his possessions. Though it was common knowledge Pearl still shared Judd's bed on occasion, Glenna was the woman who bore his name. It was hands off where Glenna O'Neill Martin was concerned and Duke was satisfied to turn his amorous attentions to blond, bubbly Sal.

It took Sal but a few minutes to coax Duke into her bed. In no time at all he was in her room and in her arms.

Listening at the door for fading footsteps, Glenna hesitated only a moment after she heard the door to Sal's room close with more force than necessary. It was the signal agreed upon. Drawing in a deep breath she slipped from her room, raced down the stairs and out the door without being seen by any of the girls starting to drift downstairs—except for Pearl who barely caught a glimpse of her making a hasty departure.

Pete appeared glad to see Glenna though he was reserved and somewhat cool. "I reckon congratulations are in order, Miss Glenna," he said after they'd exchanged a few words of greeting.

"Don't think too badly of me, Pete," Glenna said, her eyes begging for understanding.

"I ain't judging you, Miss Glenna. That's only for the good Lord to do. I am a mite disappointed, though. Never thought you'd wed a man like Judd Martin."

"Maybe one day you'll understand, Pete," Glenna said cryptically. Aware of Judd's ruthless nature she had no wish to jeopardize Pete's life by revealing too much.

"You'll always be Paddy's daughter to me, Miss Glenna," Pete assured her kindly. "And should you ever need help you can depend on me."

Tears of gratitude gathered in Glenna's green eyes, turning them to shimmering pools. "Thanks Pete, I appreciate that."

Finding herself suddenly bereft of words Glenna made her goodbyes and turned her steps toward Kate's house, deciding to visit with her former landlady and retrieve the small case forgotten in her hasty packing.

Kate greeted Glenna with tears in her eyes. "I've been so worried about you, Glenna. I wanted to come and see you but . . . but . . . I didn't feel right coming to that . . . saloon. You understand, don't you, dear?"

"I understand, Kate," Glenna assured her, patting her chubby hand.

Soon they were seated in Kate's spotless parlor sipping tea and munching on delicious cookies, talking about everything but Glenna's marriage to Judd Martin. After much beating about the bush Kate finally broke the ice.

"You are happy, aren't you, dear? Being married to Mr. Martin, I mean."

"I'm fine, Kate, really," Glenna lied, swallowing the lump forming in her throat.

Kate did not believe her one bit. "But Glenna, why—"

"Please, Kate, don't ask. Just be my friend."

A puzzled frown worried Kate's wrinkled brow but she reluctantly honored Glenna's wishes by changing the subject. After a few uncomfortable minutes their conversation once again found its footing and they resumed their pleasant chitchat.

At length Glenna asked, "Have you rented my room yet, Kate?"

"Not yet, dear. As you well know I won't rent it to just anyone."

"One of the reasons for my visit today is to retrieve a small case I'd forgotten when I moved out," Glenna revealed. "I shoved it under the bed and only remembered it when I looked for a piece of jewelry that belonged to my mother. Do you suppose the bag is still there?"

"Heavens yes, dear," Kate exclaimed in a rush. "I've only been up there once since you moved out and discovered you left it so clean I had nothing further to do."

"Do you mind if I go up now and look?"

"Of course not, child," Kate smiled fondly, "but

do you mind going up by yourself? I'm due at the dress-maker in a few minutes. I'll give you the key and when you're finished just slip it under my front door."

"You go about your business, Kate, I won't take long," Glenna promised.

"Take your time, dear. Look around for anything else you might have left behind. You did leave in a hurry," Kate reminded her with gentle reproof.

A few minutes later Glenna found herself climbing the stairs to her old room wishing she still lived there and all that had transpired since then was nothing but a bad dream. But the moment she opened the door to a room bereft of all her personal belongings Glenna realized it was not a bad dream she had been thrust into; it was cold, hard reality.

She found the case exactly where she had placed it under the bed. Inside was her brooch as well as several other personal items. Placing it beside the door she roamed aimlessly about the room, randomly opening drawers but finding nothing else she might have forgotten. Deliberately she prolonged the moment of departure, dreading her return to the Red Garter and Duke's relentless scrutiny.

Fearing to linger longer lest Duke somehow track her down, Glenna reluctantly prepared to leave, turning her steps toward the door. Suddenly the unlocked door burst open and Glenna's heart did flip-flops when Kane, appearing more powerful and dynamic than she remembered stood framed in the doorway. The moment she had dreamed of for weeks was abruptly upon her and she could do little more than stand and gawk like a smitten schoolgirl. Until he opened his arms and Glenna nearly tripped over her feet in an effort to reach that safe haven.

Forgotten was Judd Martin and her forced marriage. Forgotten was Golden Promise as well as Promise Two. At that precise moment nothing mattered but the man she loved; she was suddenly lost in a whirlwind of emotions that scattered her thoughts and reasoning.

"Kane, oh Kane!" she breathed ecstatically as his lips swooped down to claim hers in a possessive kiss that branded her his forever. "I thought you'd forgotten me."

"Forgotten you!" exclaimed Kane in a voice bordering on astonishment. "My darling, not a minute went by that I didn't yearn to hold you like this. I alienated family and friends to return to you but it mattered little for I knew what treasure awaited me here in Denver."

Then his lips captured hers again and Glenna found herself drowning in the familiar manly fragrance that infiltrated her senses. Her heart was thundering in triple time, her body aching to mold itself to the hardness of his.

The feel of her supple curves beneath his hands was maddening. He wanted to undress her slowly, to touch every delicious inch of her, find each sensitive point, stir the passion that simmered just beneath the surface. His caress wandered over her breasts then ascended to draw the gown away from her shoulders.

Everything about her pleased him, Kane mused as his hand slid over her hips, outlining her trim waist. By now Glenna's wits lay in shambles and she voiced no objection when the dress fell in a pool at her ankles. His fingers worked on the stays of her petticoat then slid it from her hips. The rest of her underclothes quickly followed.

"I am desperate to make love to you, Glenna," Kane groaned as if in pain. "I need to prove to myself that you are real and that we are finally together again. It's been so long, love, so long—"

Glenna trembled beneath his exploring caresses, pleasurable tingles of desire rippling across her bare flesh and then searing her with white-hot fire.

Instinctively she curled her arms around his neck, tunneling her fingers through his raven hair, drawing him closer, aching to be consumed by the only man who could drive her to the brink of insanity with his tantalizing caresses.

With one hand curved beneath her knees, Kane lifted her with ease, placing her gently on the soft down mattress. His clothes fell away like magic and then he was stretched out beside her. She felt the outline of his mouth on her lips, his breath mingling with hers as his kiss deepened to plunder her mouth with hungry impatience. His hand glided back to her breast and then his mouth left hers to wander over the slope of her shoulder. His tongue flicked across her flesh to the pink bud of her breasts, teasing it to tautness, and Glenna closed her mind to all except the tide of rapture that flooded over her, leaving her drifting on a sea of pure enchantment.

As his caresses descended across her abdomen to her thighs, waves of desire towed her into a sensual whirlpool. His knowing fingers delved into her womanly softness, arousing her until she cried out for him to sate the maddening craving he had nurtured deep within her. But Kane continued relentlessly and she caught her breath as another round of wild sensations swept over her.

With a will of their own her fingertips delved into his dark hair then traced the pulsating column of his neck, moving down to his muscled shoulder then explored the expanse of his broad chest. She loved touching him. He was all bronzed muscle—a powerful creature whose magnificent body always intrigued her.

Her hand gently curved the firm line of his jaw, guiding his head to hers. Her lips parted invitingly as her emerald eyes took him prisoner and held him suspended in the depths of her longing gaze. His kiss took her far beyond passion, beyond mere physical desire and into the realm of everlasting love.

Kane's muscles turned to a mass of quivering jelly under the soft hands that explored the length of his body and he closed his eyes in sheer ecstasy. Then her moist lips hovered on his skin, tasting every inch of him. Glenna felt as if she were starving and only this man had the power to offer her sustenance as her teasing kisses totally devoured him.

Kane moaned, feeling himself burn with the fires of hell as the tips of her breasts skipped across his flesh branding him with a flame that blazed out of control. Beyond reason now, he wanted her, needed to appease the torment she had wrought with her hands and mouth. He lifted her above him, guiding her hips until he was a flame within her, pulling her satiny skin against his chest. Passion was eating him alive as he set the sweet, wild rhythm that began their rapturous journey.

Glenna clung to him in pleasure as ecstatic feelings coursed through her. Then suddenly Kane changed their positions, rolling her beneath him. "Glenna—" Her name trembled from his lips in a maddening groan.

Her eyes fluttered open to regard the lithe, powerful man who hovered above her. His silver gaze was potent, burning with a living fire. She was his alone. Glenna had taken him farther than he had ever been before. Making love to this tempting vixen sapped his strength and demanded his heart, a forfeit he was more than willing to pay.

They moved in perfect rhythm as he thrust against her, unable to control the wild urgency that drove him. Kane strained above her, overwhelmed by the fierce emotions controlling his mind and body. She was his sun, his moon, his beacon to guide him in the darkness. His arms tightened around her as if he never meant to let her go. Then they were soaring, hot, cold, trembling, one in body and soul. Like a bomb bursting, passion exploded through Glenna while Kane shuddered above her, burying his head against the thundering pulsations in her neck. Then slowly they tumbled from the heights and drifted back to reality like a feather gently settling down to earth.

Rolling to his side, Kane smiled lazily. "Nothing has changed between us, love. We were created for one another. Nothing would please me more than to make love to you every night of my life."

Glenna sighed happily, in perfect agreement with Kane. What they had together was so special it was awesome. She loved this man beyond reason, beyond life. "I love you, Kane," the words tumbled forth.

"And I love you, my darling. I promise we'll never part again. We'll be married the moment I can make the arrangements."

Kane's words blasted her like a dash of cold water in the face, bringing with them the harsh reality of what had transpired during his long absence. Though her marriage to Judd Martin was a sham she had no right to enjoy or accept Kane's love. Some people might brand her an adultress for what she had just done and she loved Kane far too much to complicate his life. The very best she could hope for was that once Kane learned how Judd had forced her into marriage he would understand, perhaps even offer his help after she explained about Da's new claim and the silver.

Suddenly Kane caught her hand and brought it to his lips, smiling affectionately as he kissed each fingertip. "What are you thinking, love?"

Glenna attempted to pull away but Kane grasped her arm and tugged her firmly back into his embrace. "Kane, I have to talk to you." She began to tremble, searching desperately for the least painful way to break the news about her marriage.

"Later," Kane murmured, his appetite for her insatiable. "I can't seem to get my fill of you. You're a witch; a beautiful, desirable witch, and I love you."

She could not resist the playful expression that settled on his handsome features. There was a boyish quality in his grin that lured her away from her heavy thoughts and back into his waiting arms.

Again passion flowed like a river flooding its banks after a spring thaw. He whispered words of need as his hands began once more to weave their glorious magic, leaving her pliant and responsive beneath his bold touch. She was like clay beneath the hands of a master craftsman, molded and formed to respond to him. Unable to bear another moment of such exquisite torture, Glenna reached out to him, her hand closing about his bold manhood as she led him to the moist softness of her womanly body. Perfectly attuned, they achieved bliss together before returning to the real world. Glenna released the breath she had been holding as Kane slumped beside her, totally content, completely exhausted, but exquisitely happy.

"From the moment I saw you again you had my brains so scrambled I didn't stop to ask why you no longer work at the Palace," Kane said when his breathing finally returned to normal. "When I inquired about you they told me you had found other employment. I did little more than order my bags taken to my room before I rushed over here in hopes of finding you home. What is this all about, honey?"

Heaving a regretful sigh Glenna knew the moment of revelation had arrived and she could no longer delay telling Kane about Judd and the underhanded methods he used to coerce her into marriage. What a relief it would be to finally unburden herself. She prayed Kane's violent temper would not cause him to act imprudently where Judd was concerned and that together they could find a way to extract her from this intolerable situation.

"I quit the Palace several weeks ago, Kane," Glenna began hesitantly. "A . . . a better job came along and I took it."

"I would have thought the Palace offered the best there was in town," Kane contended. "Where do you work now?" Before she could form an answer he added, "Actually, you had no need to work, honey. I told you I left money on deposit for you at the bank."

"I know, Kane," Glenna hedged, "but I would feel useless if I didn't work." She fell silent.

"Well, where are you working? And how is it I found you home at this time of day?"

"I took a job at the Red Garter. In the dining room," she added hastily when she saw the storm clouds gathering in Kane's face.

"You did what!" Shock followed by disbelief marched across his face. "You're actually working for Judd Martin? A man who may be involved in your father's murder? My God, Glenna! I gave you credit for having more sense than that! You're going to quit today. Get dressed and I'll go with you. I won't have that bastard intimidating you."

"I . . . I no longer work, Kane," Glenna admitted, her nerves taut as a bowstring.

"Thank God," Kane breathed, relaxing against the pillow. "Would the day after tomorrow be too soon for our wedding?" he teased, his good humor restored.

"Dear Lord, Kane, I can't let you go on like this! I have to tell you."

"Tell me what?"

"I'm already married. I married Judd Martin a few days ago."

Absolute silence filled the room and Glenna thought her heart would stop beating if Kane didn't say something. With deliberate slowness he rose from the bed to stare down at her, unaware of his nakedness or what it did to her. Disgust and loathing distorted his features as he spoke. His voice was tight, brittle with barely controlled rage, and for the first time in her life Glenna was afraid of this stranger who had just made such tender love to her.

"You slut!" he spat, his fists clenching tightly at his sides. "Couldn't you wait until I returned? Did you hunger for a man so badly that you fell into bed with the first one to catch your fancy? I could have forgiven you for that, but marriage? What in the hell were you thinking of? I thought you loved me!"

"I did! I do!" declared Glenna in a rush for words. "You don't understand!"

"Oh, I understand, all right. Only too well. It's wealth you hunger for and you thought Judd richer than me. How soon after I left before you fell into his bed?"

"No, it's not like that!" Glenna denied vehemently. "Please, Kane, let me explain. If you love me you'll hear me out."

"Love? Bah! You don't know the meaning of the word. You lured me with your womanly wiles then used me, all the while accusing me of using you. And I, like a fool, fell into your trap. All you've ever wanted from me is your father's claim. Well, you've got it now, at least half of it. I hope you're happy. You and Judd deserve one another. Both of you are ruthless and greedy. It galls me to think you let me make love to you without a word about your marriage. Have you no scruples?"

"About as much scruples as you have!" Glenna shot back hurtfully.

Kane began tearing about the room, frantically pulling on his discarded clothing, ignoring the tears shimmering in Glenna's green eyes and the soft pleas falling from her lips. Never had he been so disgusted with himself. His love for Glenna had left him open and vulnerable. She had stolen his heart and ripped it to shreds. Never again, he vowed silently, would a woman chew him to pieces and spit him out.

"Kane, please let me explain," Glenna gulped in a final attempt to vindicate himself. "I didn't want to marry Judd but he—"

"—Forced you?" laughed Kane nastily. "Your lies are pathetic, Glenna. I know you. Nobody could force you into anything. And if there was any truth in what you say you could have gone to the marshal for help. I'm sorry, Glenna, but I guess I never really knew you. I may have been the first with you but I sure as hell won't be the last. I hope Judd appreciates my efforts."

Angrily he stomped toward the door, refusing to acknowledge Glenna's pleas, for never in a million years would he understand her reasons for marrying Judd Martin.

"Kane, wait, don't . . . go!" But her words never reached his ears as he strode out the door and down the stairs. Stopping at the first saloon he came to he gulped down two whiskies in quick succession, bought a bottle then hastened to his room to drown those glorious memories of the woman he loved; a woman he could have sworn loved him in return. So much for love.

It mattered little to Glenna that Duke spotted her the moment she returned. Nothing mattered now that Kane thought her capable of all those terrible things he accused her of. If only he'd listened to her! If only he'd allowed her to explain. She had wounded his pride and nothing she'd said made the slightest impression on him. But some day, Glenna resolved, he had to listen. Perhaps when he cooled off. . . . No matter what difficulties she had to surmount she was determined to tell him about her father's new claim and the rich vein of silver concealed somewhere within its boundaries.

Kane stayed drunk for days. Finally exerting great effort, he pulled himself together, determined to vanquish the demons tormenting him. He accomplished it in the way his nature demanded, by facing the source of his agony and rising above it. Kane hoped that seeing Judd and Glenna together would cure him of his addiction to the little witch once and for all. Thus it was that he found himself walking into the Red Garter, a forced smile on his face and a chip on his shoulder.

Wandering aimlessly about, he saw neither hide nor hair of either Glenna or Judd. Perhaps it's too early, he concluded, finally taking a table and ordering a drink. From across the room Sal spotted him immediately, wrinkling her brow worriedly. Had he learned about Glenna's marriage to Judd? she wondered distractedly. If he did he seemed to accept it calmly enough, which was quite out of character for Kane Morgan. Yet if he didn't know she certainly didn't want to be the one to tell him.

Abruptly Kane spied Sal and motioned her over. Reluctantly Sal sauntered up to the table, taking the seat he offered. "Good to have you back, Kane," she greeted breezily.

"I got your wire, Sal, but obviously not in time," Kane returned glumly. "You could have told me what Glenna planned."

"Honestly, Kane, I hadn't the slightest inkling what Glenna intended," responded Sal, interpreting Kane's words to mean he already knew about Glenna's marriage to Judd. "Nearly two weeks ago he summoned the preacher to the saloon at midnight and married Glenna in front of a hundred people."

"Didn't you try to stop her?" reprimanded Kane brutally. "What kind of a friend are you?"

"Lord, yes, I tried, but you know how stubborn Glenna can be. It was as if some secret force was compelling her to act as she did. There was no stopping her. I'm sorry, Kane, I know how you must feel."

Kane scowled darkly, his narrowed silvery gaze searching the room restlessly. "Where are the newlyweds? Too enamored of one another to leave the privacy of their bedroom, I suppose," he growled sarcastically.

"Kane, there's something funny about that marriage," Sal murmured in a confidential tone.

But Kane barely heard her words, so engrossed was he in his thoughts of those rapturous hours spent in Glenna's arms before she had the decency to tell him about her recent marriage.

"Kane," Sal repeated urgently, "did you hear me? I said Glenna's marriage is—"

"Kane!" Sal's words were obliterated by Pearl's high-pitched squeal. "What are you doing back in Denver?"

"Er . . . business, Pearl," Kane hedged.

"Have you heard about Glenna's marriage?" gushed Pearl with feigned innocence. Now that Glenna was no longer competition she hoped to have Kane all to herself. If he turned to her for consolation she'd be only too happy to oblige.

"He's heard," Sal clucked, warning her to hold her tongue. A warning Pearl chose to ignore.

"Wasn't it romantic the way Judd got the preacher out of bed to marry them because they couldn't wait?" she sighed dreamily.

"Pearl!" Sal chided sternly. "You know as well as I, better, perhaps, that Glenna did not—"

"Stop!" Kane demanded angrily. "I don't want to hear about Glenna and her husband. What they do is none of my concern. And if either of you want to retain my friendship you will never mention Glenna to me again."

"That's fine with me," Pearl shrugged carelessly. "I never liked her anyway. Those innocent ones are always the worst."

Sal refused to comment, preferring instead to drop the subject. After a while she drifted off to join a group of men clamoring for her attention, leaving Kane to Pearl's tender ministrations. Never one to mince words, Pearl immediately invited Kane upstairs, hinting at the pleasure he would find in her room. Kane smiled wryly, knowing full well that he could never hope to duplicate what he experienced with Glenna. He was on the verge of declining in favor of drinking himself senseless in spite of his earlier resolve when suddenly Judd Martin breezed through the door, greeting his friends effusively. It was obvious from the rough clothing he wore and the saddlebag draped over one arm that Judd was just returning from a journey. Duke immediately confronted his employer and began whispering frantically in his ear.

"Where in the hell has he been?" Kane asked Pearl, nodding toward Judd.

"Who knows?" shrugged Pearl. "He doesn't confide in me. All I know is that he left a few days after his wedding."

"Odd," muttered Kane, thinking that he wouldn't have tired of Glenna so soon had she married him. Now the very sound of her name drove him into a rage. Hate took up residence where love once thrived.

Then abruptly Judd spotted Kane, and for a brief moment the sight completely unsettled him. But in the space of a heartbeat he regained his wits, a wide smile painted across his handsome face.

"What brings you back to Denver, Morgan?" In truth Judd had hoped Kane would stay in Philadelphia and their paths might never cross.

"I own half interest in a claim, remember?"

Judd laughed harshly. "Oh, yes. I believe my wife," he emphasized, "owns the other half. You've heard, of course, that Glenna and I are married?" He didn't wait for Kane's reply before adding, "You'll be dealing with me now in regard to Golden Promise. Not that there's much of value left to deal with." Judd's colorless eyes defied Kane to object, but Kane chose to ignore the challenge at this time.

"Congratulations, Martin," he said tightly. Then he stared pointedly at Judd's traveling gear. "Have you been away? It must be rough tearing yourself from the arms of your bride so soon after the ceremony."

"Ah, yes, my bride," smiled Judd lewdly. "A tempting morsel, Morgan. Or perhaps," his eyes narrowed suspiciously, "that's something you already know."

What in the hell was he getting at? Kane wondered. Had Judd already learned that he and Glenna had spent an afternoon in bed in Glenna's old room? Somehow Kane doubted that. He probably was referring to the fact that he had not taken a virgin bride and wondered if Kane had been there first.

"Glenna and I are . . . old friends," Kane acknowledged. "I am well aware of her . . . endearing traits."

"Stay away from my wife, Morgan," Judd warned ominously. "She belongs to me and I won't have you or any other man sniffing after her."

"Your wife holds no interest for me," Kane contended. "Just remember that half of anything to come out of Golden Promise belongs to me. I'll check with my men to see what's going on up there."

"If you're talking about Zach Kimball and Will Davis, they no longer work for you. Glenna saw fit to fire them. I put three of my own men in charge."

Kane groaned in frustration. One more mark against Glenna, he calculated morosely. Was there no end to that woman's deviousness? "What gave her the right to fire two good men?" Kane demanded to know.

"You weren't here, she could do as she pleased."

"Do as you please, you mean."

Judd shrugged carelessly. "You'll have to excuse me, Morgan, my wife is anxiously awaiting me in our bedroom. I've been gone a long time and we've got a lot of catching up to do." Nodding to Kane and bestowing a benign smile on Pearl who had sat silently through the entire exchange, Judd strode through the saloon, taking the stairs two at a time.

Kane glared menacingly as Judd bounced up the stairs, across the overhanging balcony and entered a room situated at one end of the long aisle. With Judd's bold entry into the room he obviously shared with Glenna, Kane lost whatever good sense he possessed as he looked at Pearl through new eyes, seeing in her an answer to all his yearnings and frustrations.

"Where's your room?" he asked harshly.

Pearl grinned slyly. "Just follow me, handsome. I'll make you forget Glenna ever existed. The little two-timing bitch doesn't deserve you."

"You talk too much, Pearl," Kane growled, sweeping her into his arms and racing up the stairs amidst cheers and lewd encouragement from patrons viewing his hasty exit.

13

Kane had no way of knowing that the room Judd entered was his own; one not shared with Glenna. Judd knew better than to enter his wife's room for he realized full well it would be locked against him. And after an exhausting two weeks searching for the elusive mother lode and the long ride back to Denver, he was in no mood for a battle. Especially with Kane Morgan gloating in the background. A confrontation with Glenna was long overdue but not until Judd was rested and better equipped to deal with his recalcitrant wife. If there was any truth in what Duke had hurriedly whispered in his ear just moments ago she had much to account for.

His face set in harsh lines, Kane followed Pearl's directions, soon setting her on her own feet in a large, gaudily decorated room embellished with fripperies in varying shades of red. Pearl's arms slipped around his neck, drawing him into a kiss that was devouring in its intensity.

"I've waited a long time for this, Kane," Pearl whispered hoarsely, working frantically on the buttons of his shirt.

"See to yourself," Kane growled, shoving her hands aside in order to complete the chore himself.

Pearl gave him a withering look but fell to unfastening her own clothing, shedding her short skirt, boned, low-cut bodice and petticoats before Kane did little more than remove his shirt. She gave an exasperated snort then moved to help him.

"Slowpoke," she chided in a sexy chortle.

But before Pearl could so much as loosen the fastenings on Kane's trousers he scooped her up and tossed her on the bed, dropping to one knee beside her. "Slowpoke, am I?" he crowed, raking her voluptuous form from head to toe with his silver gaze. Pearl reached for him, her hands passing over the huge bulge pressing against the front of his trousers, her fingers nimbly releasing his throbbing strength.

Straddling her prone form his hands roamed freely over her soft flesh as his tongue flicked hungrily at the large, dusky pink nipples cresting the generous mounds of her breasts. Pearl moaned and Kane renewed his efforts, his tortured mind picturing Judd similarly engaged with Glenna.

Glenna! Oh God! How could you? Kane raged inwardly as Pearl writhed beneath him. He gained scant comfort in the knowledge that the soft, pliant body moaning in pleasure beneath him was not the firm, silken flesh he yearned for. How in the hell did he expect to gain pleasure with a practiced whore while the woman he desired above all others lay in her husband's arms but a few feet away? The hell with Glenna! he thought furiously. She made her choice and I've made mine. But when he closed his eyes, only one face rose before him, and his desire wilted as swiftly as it was born.

Cursing violently he flung himself from Pearl, snatching up his shirt and lurching toward the door. "Kane, what's wrong? What have I done?" Pearl cried out in dismay.

"Nothing, Pearl," Kane threw over his shoulder. "I've changed my mind, that's all."

"You bastard! How dare you bring me this far then leave me dangling!" Kane mumbled something unintelligible then slammed the door on Pearl's frantic ravings.

Kane stumbled down the stairs, his thoughts dark and forbidding. Damn you, Glenna! he raged beneath his breath. The little bitch finally succeeded in emasculating him. Never had he been so humiliated! In all his years not once had he failed to perform to the satisfaction of both himself and his partner. But Glenna had changed all that in a matter of minutes, making it impossible for a practiced whore like Pearl to arouse him. What kind of man was he to allow a scheming witch like Glenna to turn his life upside down? No answer was forthcoming as he shoved his way angrily through the crowded saloon and out the door.

Glenna had no idea Judd had returned until he presented himself at her door the next morning. "What do you want?" she asked as he pushed his way inside, slamming the door behind him.

"It's good to see you too," he replied sarcastically.

"Did you expect a loving welcome? If you did you came to the wrong place."

"I expected you to greet me as a proper wife should. We happen to be married."

"In name only," returned Glenna acidly.

"Until I decide otherwise," Judd informed her. "I thought you might be interested to know about my trip to the claimsite."

"You went to Promise Two?" queried Glenna.

"Did . . . did you find what you were looking for?"

"If you're talking about the lode, no, we failed to find it. The men and I must have tramped over every square inch of that ground with no luck. But if the lode is there we'll find it."

He droned on for several minutes but Glenna had already shut out the sound. Since Kane's return she could think of little else but his anger at her and his refusal to allow her an explanation. And now he hated her and she couldn't blame him. How could he believe she had betrayed him when their loving had been on a plane above anything they had ever known? When ecstasy splintered through her she knew Kane had experienced the same rapturous sensations.

"Did you hear me, Glenna?" Judd demanded to know when he felt Glenna's mind wandering.

"What! What did you say?"

"I asked if you knew Kane Morgan was back in town."

"Why, no, was I supposed to?"

"Duke told me that you disappeared for several hours a couple days ago. Were you with Morgan? Is there something going on between the two of you?"

"It's none of your business, Judd," Glenna raised her chin defiantly. "You've got what you wanted, now leave me alone."

"I've decided I want more from you than what you've already given me, which isn't much. If you're handing out your favors I'm entitled to more than I'm getting."

"We made a bargain," Glenna insisted. "There are plenty of women available to take my place in your bed."

"Listen, you red-headed witch," ground out Judd remorselessly. "You're my wife and I've decided I want you."

"Even if you have to rape me?"

Judd frowned darkly, grasping Glenna by the upper arm. "I don't like rape, Glenna," he emphasized. "Using force holds little appeal for me. But if I have to I'll use blackmail, or better yet, let my men do the convincing. One way or another I'll have you when I'm good and ready. In the meantime keep away from Morgan. Don't even think about telling him about our little arrangement. It would be easy for Duke to pick him off in the street one day. He's just waiting for me to give the order."

"You wouldn't!"

"Try me," smiled Judd viciously. "If you don't come to my bed willingly when I want you you'll find yourself minus two friends."

Abruptly he released her and Glenna recoiled in aversion. The man was a devil. Evil, corrupt and totally unscrupulous. It wasn't enough that he had the claim, now he wanted her. Would she be able to give in to him in order to save the lives of two people she cared about? She hoped she'd never be put to the test.

Judd watched the play of emotion rushing across Glenna's face. At first he cared little for the woman herself, wanting only the claim she owned and what it represented. But in the two weeks spent tramping through the wilderness he began to think of her in other terms. She was breathtakingly beautiful; fresh and tempting to a man accustomed to nothing but whores for bed partners. The longer he dwelt on the womanly curves hidden from his eyes and the seductive way she carried her lissome body, the more he wanted her. Being away from her had done what her close proximity had failed to do. Besides, she was probably a virgin and the thought was a tantalizing one, feeding his desire. Unless that damn Morgan had already gotten to her. If Judd had his way he would find out soon enough.

He'd allow her to stew a few days before he made his demands, Judd thought slyly. Once she realized he meant what he said about her friends she'd come to him willingly enough. He wanted her soft and pliant beneath him, not screaming and fighting. Though Judd Martin felt little remorse over ordering violence committed in his name, he abhorred doing it himself. But one way or another, he vowed, Glenna would soon be his wife in every way.

"I expect you to show yourself downstairs tonight," Judd ordered brusquely. "I want everyone to see for themselves what a happy couple we are."

"I think not," demurred Glenna coolly.

"I left instructions for Duke to bring you down, either on your own or with his help," he continued, ignoring her protests. "Wear one of your new gowns." Then he was gone, leaving Glenna with nothing but a bruised arm and a head swimming with murderous thoughts.

Kane was so disgusted with himself he could barely stand the sight of his own reflection in the mirror. Time and again he chided himself for being a fool where Glenna was concerned. After that fiasco the night before he had no business returning to the Red Garter. It gained him nothing but heartache to view Glenna prancing about on her husband's arm, but some perverse instinct drove him there tonight. He'd be damned if he'd permit Glenna to see how deeply she had wounded him.

He leaned against the bar, just another man quenching his thirst, when Sal strolled up to him. She motioned with her head toward a table and he picked up his drink and followed. Once they were seated, Sal asked, "What did you do to Pearl last night? She seemed pretty upset after you left."

"Ask Pearl," Kane muttered sourly.

Sal shrugged. "Since you two didn't hit it off maybe you'd like Candy." Kane shook his head negatively. Silence. "Kane, I'd be glad to—"

"No, Sal, thanks," Kane smiled dryly. "I'm . . . I'm not fit for female companionship right now. Some other night, perhaps."

"Sure, Kane, anytime. But I don't expect to be here much longer. You'll have to come to Sal's Place to take advantage of my offer."

"Sal's Place?"

"Remember what I said when we first met? About opening my own place, I mean."

"Of course," Kane recalled. "You, Pearl and Candy were saving to open a house of your own. I didn't think it would be this soon, though."

"This is a generous town. But we still have a ways to go," confided Sal. "There's a large house on the other side of town I've had my eye on for some time. I checked yesterday and it's still vacant. We need only a couple more thousand to buy it. Then of course there's furnishings and such."

"Are you that anxious to leave, Sal?"

"I can't wait to get out of here, Kane. Lately I've had the queerest feeling that I'm being watched. I don't know what Judd is up to but I don't trust him. It's beyond my ken how Glenna could—" Kane's warning frown stopped her in mid-sentence.

"What would you say if I loaned you . . . say . . . five thousand dollars? I'd like to become a private investor in your . . . er . . . enterprise."

Sal squealed in delight. "You'd do that, Kane? You'd invest in a bawdy house?"

"Why not?" laughed Kane. "It's a wise investment and I'm sure to earn a good return on my money. Meet me at the bank in the morning and I'll see you get the funds."

Suddenly Sal's face sobered. "It's what I've wanted for a long time . . . yet—"

"What is it, Sal? What's bothering you?"

"I don't like to leave Glenna. I'm afraid for her, Kane, truly."

"I fear your concern is misplaced," laughed Kane harshly. "Glenna is a big girl and she made her choice. Her kind will always land on their feet."

"But, Kane," protested Sal vigorously. "What if she needs—"

"Take care of your own affairs, Sal," Kane advised sternly, "and let Glenna see to hers."

Soon afterwards Sal was imparting her good fortune to a breathless Pearl and Candy. Though Pearl was somewhat reluctant to leave a lively spot like the Red Garter where life had been good to her, she nevertheless agreed to throw in with Sal's plans. They had been friends a long time. And besides, it would be good to be her own boss for a change. Beautiful but featherheaded Candy happily went along with anything Sal suggested.

Kane sucked moodily at the amber liquid in the glass he held carelessly in his hand, his eyes staring fixedly into space. Yet he knew instinctively the moment Glenna entered the saloon on the arm of her doting husband. As if on cue all eyes turned in their direction, most of them riveted on the lovely redhead elegantly gowned in emerald silk that bared a large expanse of pale skin above a daring decolletage. Her waist seemed miniscule in comparison to the billowing skirts swirling about slender ankles also clad in green silk.

Playing the proud bridegroom to the hilt Judd led her around the crowded room, stopping here and there to exchange words or introduce Glenna to a friend. From her painted smile Kane had not the slightest inkling that anything was amiss; she portrayed the radiant bride extremely well. In reality Glenna was but a shell of her former self. Being on display, so to speak, and forced to play a role she abhorred was painful as well as difficult. She was living a lie and hating every minute of it.

From across the room Glenna felt the pull of Kane's magnetic gaze, two silver orbs narrowed in hateful contemplation. Inwardly she cringed, her own eyes pleading for understanding, but he denied her that satisfaction as he deliberately turned aside, welcoming one of the bar girls who had sidled up to him, pulling her into his lap in a display of ardor he was far from feeling. Though he gained a modicum of satisfaction from the look that flickered across Glenna's face, it was short-lived as he helplessly watched Judd's cruel fingers bite into the tender flesh of Glenna's waist the moment he noticed the direction of her gaze. Then he was guiding her out of sight and abruptly Kane released his hold on the girl occupying his lap and sent her on her way with a friendly pat on her generous bottom.

"I saw the way you looked at him, my dear," Judd snarled jealously from the corner of his mouth.

"Who are you talking about?" Glenna asked innocently.

"I think you've developed an itch for Kane Morgan," Judd accused nastily. "Just remember I'm the only one with the right to scratch that itch."

"How dare you talk to me like that!" Glenna hissed, pulling away from his grasp. "I refuse to stand here and be insulted." Whirling on her heel she fled from the crowded saloon and up the stairs to the safety of her own room, locking the door securely behind her.

Eyes narrowed thoughtfully, Judd watched avidly the seductive sway of her skirts as she disappeared through the door. So certain was he that she had locked the door behind her that he deliberately refrained from charging after her although he yearned to do so. But that didn't keep him from his lustful thoughts—thoughts of the treasure that lay hidden beneath those swinging skirts. Soon, he smiled wolfishly. Soon. . . .

The following morning Sal met Kane at the bank, and after the funds he promised her were transferred to her own account she spent the remainder of the day making arrangements for the move to the spacious house soon to become one of the most successful bawdy houses in Denver.

Two days later while Judd was out conducting business of his own, Sal left, taking Pearl, Candy and two other girls from the Red Garter with her. Her first act as madam of her own house was to hire four strong men willing and able to handle Judd Martin and his hired guns should they come calling. By the end of the week Sal's Place was receiving its first customers, word of mouth being its best advertising. From the first it was a resounding success and soon Kane had good reason to applaud his wise investment.

Glenna was the only person outside those involved in the move to learn of Sal's plans, and in her own way was instrumental in making certain the girls' departure went smoothly. When Glenna was told by Sal of her plans, omitting only Kane's involvement, she puzzled Sal by her exuberant approval.

"Thank God you're leaving," breathed Glenna, obviously relieved.

"Will you be that glad to be rid of me, honey?" frowned Sal. "I thought we were friends."

Glenna looked stricken. "Oh, Sal, I didn't mean it like that," she quickly amended. "I know how much you wanted this." Glenna was ecstatic to know that Sal would no longer be available to be used as a hostage by Judd to force her compliance to his will. Perhaps with luck she would soon find a way to escape this intolerable situation.

Not a day went by that Judd did not follow

Glenna's every move with lust-filled intent. Stricken, she realized it would be only a matter of time before he demanded his rights as her husband, and that was something she could not endure. Locking herself in her room proved futile, for of late Judd demanded her presence in the saloon at least during part of the evening. He paraded her around like a pet monkey and she doubted she could stand much more of it. But wisely she kept her own counsel. Sal was better off not knowing how Judd had used her as a tool to force Glenna into marriage. Once Sal was out of Judd's reach that left only Kane to worry about. Would Judd actually harm Kane should she openly defy him by attempting to leave? Glenna wondered distractedly. Of course, she answered her own question. He's killed once and would not hesitate to do so again.

What she did was hatch up a scheme to keep Duke occupied while Sal and the girls packed their belongings and made their move without complications. The day Judd left Glenna decided on the spur of the moment to go on a shopping spree. And since Judd left strict orders that she be accompanied at all times, Duke felt obligated to follow her about town as she made purchase after purchase, piling them all into his reluctant arms.

Judd was in a rage when he returned and found five of his best girls gone. He fumed and ranted, blaming Glenna for dragging Duke away when he should have remained in the saloon keeping an eye on things. He went so far as to send two of his men to Sal's Place, but they were promptly repulsed by the four burly men hired by Sal that very day.

Enraged, Judd was astute enough to realize that he no longer held the upper hand where Glenna was concerned, that nothing was preventing her from going to the marshal, or even Morgan, with her story. He felt strongly that it was long past the time to consummate his marriage. Unless he took her to his bed immediately it would be far too simple for Glenna to obtain an annulment. At first Judd didn't desire her in that way, his tastes leaning more toward the flamboyant, but as the days passed he became more and more obsessed with her as a woman. The subtle perfume she wore clung to her body, teasing him unmercifully. The firm curve of her breasts enticed him, as did the seductive sway of her hips, and her haughty indifference served only to whet his appetite for more than she was willing to give.

For an entire week Judd watched and waited, and then one day he took the key from Glenna's door while she was out. That day he drank heavily, fueling his anticipation until the time was ripe to go to her. He sat in on a poker game and his luck proved incredible. The cards fell in his favor like magic and to Judd's befuddled mind it was but a portent of what the night would bring. In his mind's eye he pictured Glenna's white body spread beneath him. Though he wanted her eager and willing, Judd had no false notions about her complying without a fight. Though he cared little for the exertions of a struggle before lovemaking, he had been fortifying himself all day for the ensuing battle and by evening was well-prepared to broach those virgin portals. For despite his accusations to the contrary, Judd still believed Glenna too prudish to give up her virginity to Kane Morgan without the benefit of marriage.

The saloon fairly bulged with patrons, a floor show was in progress and the gambling tables were operating at capacity. Grinning like a cat who had just consumed a canary, Judd hauled himself out of his seat and, staggering slightly, unerringly stumbled up the stairs amidst the noise and din created by scores of men engaged in pleasurable pursuits. The time was right and Judd knew it.

Glenna had taken supper downstairs earlier than usual and retired to her room immediately, relieved that for once Judd hadn't insisted she stroll about the crowded room on his arm. Even from afar Glenna was aware that Judd had been drinking heavily and her fear escalated. Normally Judd drank sparingly or not at all. His success as a gambler demanded a clear head and steady hand and Glenna's suspicions were aroused by his extraordinary behavior. Was tonight the night Judd meant to make good his threat to take her to his bed? Glenna worried, wringing her hands in desperation?

That terrifying thought consumed her and she became convinced that Judd was fortifying himself for the ordeal ahead. If so, Glenna prepared to put up the battle of her life. But what good was her meager strength pitted against a man like Judd? Without a weapon she was virtually helpless. Suddenly she remembered Da's old pepperbox hidden in the bottom of her trunk and immediately felt better.

Hurrying through her meal she rushed to her room and began digging around in her trunk for the weapon. Heaving a sigh of relief her fingers closed on the gun and drew it out. But when she rummaged further for the ammunition she experienced a sharp pang of disappointment. There was none. Somehow she had forgotten to pack the ammunition when she left the cabin at Golden Promise. Dejected, she sat down to think. Abruptly she remembered she hadn't locked the door behind her and rushed to complete the task, only to discover the key missing from the lock.

"Damn you, Judd Martin!" she cursed aloud, dropping to her knees and scrabbling on the floor for the key, knowing all along she wouldn't find it.

Suddenly the door flew open and Judd entered, grinning from ear to ear. "Are you by chance looking for this?" he asked, holding up the missing key.

Still crouched on the floor, Glenna leaped at Judd. "Give me that!" she demanded. "And then get out of here!"

Easily holding her at bay with one arm, Judd swiveled, fitted the key in the lock and turned it dropping it in his vest pocket after removing it from the door. Immediately Glenna began backing away.

Advancing slowly Judd removed his coat, dropping it carelessly on the floor, followed by his cravat. "It won't do you any good to fight, my dear," he slurred drunkenly. "I've made up my mind about this. It's past time I've done my duty by you. A pregnant wife is less likely to stray from her husband's bed. And make no mistakes, my dear, if I have my way you will be pregnant soon . . . very soon."

If the situation hadn't been so desperate Glenna would have laughed in his face. Never would she carry a child of Judd Martin's! "You can't bully me, Judd!" she spat contemptuously. "Sal is no longer available to use as a weapon against me. She's out of your reach now and you can no longer threaten me into compliance."

"Kane Morgan is still walking the streets," he hinted craftily.

She slanted him an uncertain look. "Kane can take care of himself."

Judd swore, making a grab for her. One step ahead of him, Glenna ducked sideways, leaving Judd with nothing but a handful of lace as the neck of her bodice split, revealing two heaving mounds of pearly white flesh. Judd's eyes bulged appreciatively and the tempting sight of exposed flesh caused him to renew his efforts, strong drink and lust turning him wild with desire for his red-haired wife. How could he ever have thought her undesirable? Judd wondered, lunging at her again. Once more Glenna neatly sidestepped, but her billowing skirts proved her undoing.

Clutching at the swaying material Judd drew Glenna inexorably toward him, grinning with salacious intent as she struggled to escape. "Oh, no, you don't my red-haired vixen,'' he crowed delightedly. ''I've got you now. Your virginity belongs to me and I intend to relieve you of it without delay.''

''My virginity!'' snorted Glenna without a thought to the consequences. ''I gave it up months ago to the man I love!''

Red dots of pure rage exploded behind Judd's eyes. ''You slut!'' he bellowed, backhanding Glenna across one side of the face. Glenna reeled from the blow, only Judd's cruel grip keeping her from falling. ''How dare you give away what should be rightfully mine! After I beat you to within an inch of your life I'm going to kill Kane Morgan!''

''I don't remember mentioning any names,'' Glenna insisted, more frightened than she had ever been in her life. As angry as Judd was she'd be lucky if he didn't kill her. She had never seen him so drunk or so enraged.

''You didn't need to name your lover. It's obvious Morgan bedded you while the two of you stayed alone at Golden Promise all those weeks. And the day you disappeared for hours was the same day Morgan returned to town,'' Judd accused remorselessly. ''It's one thing to let him screw you before you were my wife but another to allow it after we were married. I told you I wouldn't stand for any hanky-panky from you and I meant it.''

Glenna cringed as his heavy hand struck out blindly, his blow sending her reeling against a small table where she often took her meals. Grasping the edge and levering herself upwards, Glenna prepared herself for another vicious attack, biting her bottom lip to keep from crying out. Stubbornly she vowed Judd would gain no satisfaction from hearing her beg for mercy or scream from the pain he was inflicting on her.

His next blow glanced off her shoulder as she turned her back toward him, clutching at the table she was leaning against. Without its support she would have fallen. When he began to remove his belt from his trousers, Glenna reacted instinctively, thinking of nothing but survival.

When she swiveled to escape Judd's blow her eyes fell on something she had missed earlier in her frantic search for a weapon. After breakfast she had carried a bowl of fruit upstairs to enjoy at her leisure, forgetting entirely the sharp knife stuck in a juicy apple. A slender blade, capable of inflicting grave damage despite its innocuous appearance.

Her back to Judd, Glenna grunted in pain as he wielded the belt with dexterity, her shoulders hunching in agony. Like a caged animal reacting instinctively against a tormentor, Glenna grasped the handle of the knife and whirled just as Judd prepared to strike again. When he saw her feeble attempt at defense his face screwed up and he began jeering at her cruelly.

"You can't hurt me with that toy, Glenna," he chortled mirthlessly. "Drop it or it will go harder with you." He took a step forward, his face dark with menace.

"Stand back!" Glenna ordered, threatening him with the ridiculously small knife. Though she hardly expected to maim him permanently she hoped at least to halt his abuse of her. Then she would flee. As far away from Judd Martin as possible.

Still chortling over her futile attempt at bravery Judd snatched at the knife, but only caught more of Glenna's bodice, leaving it shredded about her slender waist. Glenna saw red as her temper exploded, stunning Judd as the lethal blade whizzed harmlessly past his face, missing him by mere inches.

"You bitch!" he screamed. "You nearly blinded me!"

"That was my intention," panted Glenna, making another swipe with the knife and missing as he leaped backwards. Still having the advantage, she lunged again, but by this time Judd had regained his wits and was ready for her, catching her wrist in mid-stroke.

Exerting his mastery over her, Judd wrestled her to the floor, falling heavily atop her. He tore at her clothes, so enraged he completely forgot his earlier resolve vowing he no longer wanted her. He wanted her all right. If only to prove to her that she belonged to him, that she was not Kane Morgan's plaything. First he'd rape her, then beat her. After that he'd kill her lover.

But Glenna had other ideas. Well aware of what Judd planned for her, she lay helplessly pinned beneath his sweating body, vowing to resist or die trying. Layer by layer Glenna's clothes left her body until she lay clad in nothing but a thin shift. Conserving her strength Glenna waited, the knife still curled in one fist; the fist Judd held immobile in his large hand. Anticipating Glenna's surrender, Judd released his grip on Glenna's wrists in order to remove his own clothing. In so doing he made a fatal error considering Glenna's desperation. The moment Glenna felt her hands freed, she reacted instinctively. As if in slow motion the arm wielding the knife made a descending arc, gathering force and speed until it found its mark in Judd's chest. His eyes widened in disbelief and he grunted once before collapsing in a heap atop her.

The urgency of the moment past, Glenna allowed herself the luxury of tears, shoving furiously at the dead weight of Judd's body. Only with the warm, wet trickle of blood oozing from his body onto hers did Glenna come to full realization that Judd might be dead. Finally succeeding in squirming from beneath his prone form, she turned him over, trembling as she drew a deep, shuddering breath.

He's dead! her mind screamed. I killed him! Certainly she would hang for this night's work! Judd's friends would enjoy seeing her hang for murder, she rationalized. No matter how she tried to explain, no one would believe she was protecting her honor. Judd was her legal husband, a man who had every right in the world to her body.

Judd lay still—so still, Glenna thought, horrified by what she had done. And the blood. There was blood everywhere, on her hands, her clothes, staining the floor. She had to escape, now, before she was found and taken to jail. But where? Where could she go?

The sound of footsteps passing in the hallway released her feet as she dashed for the door, suddenly realizing the key lay within Judd's vest pocket. Fighting her revulsion Glenna approached the body, closing her eyes as she gingerly reached into Judd's pocket with two fingers and withdrew the key, unaware that she had been holding her breath until she began to grow dizzy from lack of air. Inhaling deeply she backed toward the door, pausing once again when she recalled her state of undress. Rushing to her wardrobe she grabbed a cloak, threw it over her bloodstained shift and unlocked the door, thankful that she was still in possession of her shoes.

Struggling to retain her scattered wits, Glenna had the presence of mind to check the hallway before charging out and to lock the door behind her. If luck was with her no one would discover Judd's body before morning. Hugging the wall Glenna inched her way toward the back stairs; the same stairs used by customers who feared being recognized leaving the room of one of Judd's whores. Luckily the chorus girls were peforming on stage and Glenna traversed the hallway and stairs virtually unseen, soon finding herself in the back alley outside the Red Garter, her relief so great she nearly collapsed on the spot. Suddenly a terrifying thought came unbidden to her mind. To whom could she turn to for help?

Kane! Kane would help her. But as quickly as the thought came she discarded it. Kane hated her. Knowing how he felt would he come to her aid? Of course, she decided. He loved her once and love does not die so easily. But still she hesitated, unwilling to place his life in danger. After she hurt him so badly she owed it to him not to involve him in her troubles. Besides, she hadn't seen him in days and for all she knew he could have returned to Philadelphia.

But Sal! Sal would help her, Glenna rationalized with a grateful sigh. If she could find Sal's Place perhaps she could be persuaded to offer Glenna refuge until she found way to leave town. Trains came and went regularly now and Glenna fully intended to be on one very soon. The farther away the better.

Her mind made up, Glenna emerged from the alley, heading in the general direction of Sal's Place. She knew the house to be on the edge of town situated on the west side of Cherry Creek and began the long trek across town, keeping to the shadows wherever possible. She shivered beneath the cloak, the long days of summer already turning into autumn's chill nights. But her steps did not falter as they carried her away from the Red Garter.

Suddenly, from out of nowhere, two burly men blocked her path and a scream of terror froze in her throat. "Were you lookin' fer us, little lady?" asked one of the men whose rough voice tugged at her memory.

"Hell, Wiley, who'd look fer an ugly brute like you?" guffawed the second man whose unkempt hair and scraggly beard reminded Glenna of a shaggy dog. A vicious shaggy dog.

"You ain't such a prize yerself, Lars," grumbled Wiley. Then he turned to Glenna whose face was partially hidden by the hood of her cloak. "Let the little lady decide which of us she wants."

"I want neither of you! Leave me alone!" Glenna retorted hotly, attempting to sidle around them. But escape was made impossible as Lars grasped her arm, hauling her around to face him.

"If ye can't choose then me and Wiley will share you." He began dragging her into a darkened alleyway, Wiley following close behind, now and then patting her rounded buttocks through the lightweight cloak.

Abruptly Glenna twisted violently, startling Lars who suddenly found himself in possession of nothing but an empty cloak. Wiley, filled with more than his share of liquor was unable to act swiftly enough as Glenna darted past him, her long hair flowing like a red river behind her, the moonlight clearly outlining her shimmering nude body beneath the thin shift she wore. Recognition came instantly to Wiley.

"Well I'll be damned!" he mouthed, astounded. "What in the hell is Judd Martin's red-haired wife doing out in the streets this time of night?"

"Judd Martin's wife? Are ye certain?" Lars asked, thinking that the gambler's retribution would be swift and lethal should his wife come to harm at their hands.

"Ain't no one else in Denver with hair that color," declared Wiley, his suspicion aroused. "Think I'll mosey on over to the Red Garter and call on old Judd jest to see what's goin' on. Something smells fishy to me. It ain't like Judd to let his woman roam the streets in her chemise this time of night. Yer comin', Lars?"

"I don't want no part in this," Lars waved his hand. "See ya around, Wiley." Wiley watched wordlessly as Lars hurried off in the opposite direction. Shrugging indifferently he turned his steps toward the Red Garter.

14

Shivering from the cold, Glenna crouched in the shrubbery growing behind Sal's well-lit house, eternally grateful that all she had lost in the scuffle with Wiley and his friend Lars was her cloak. In a daze she walked for what seemed like miles, wondering if Wiley had recognized her, thankful at least that they hadn't followed. Then abruptly she had come upon Sal's Place, easily distinguishable by the steady stream of men coming and going; laughter, music and bright lights flowed from nearly every window. From all indications Sal's Place had been an overwhelming success.

Glenna's first inclination was to rush headlong into the house and into Sal's comforting arms. But then good sense prevailed and she stumbled around to the back, intending to remain concealed until the wee hours of morning, if need be, when Sal's customers had found their way home and the girls were safely tucked into bed. Only then would she consider venturing forth. The fewer people who saw her the better for everyone involved.

Her teeth chattering from the cold, Glenna huddled amidst the damp brush for what seemed like hours, her body stiffening and chilled. Would they never leave? she wondered dismally as the revelry continued far into the night. Just when she thought she could stand it no longer, one by one the lights in the house began to blink out. At length all but one lamp had been extinguished, and that came from a back room Glenna assumed was Sal's office. Uncoiling her shivering form Glenna moved woodenly from her concealment, intending to alert Sal to her presence by tapping on the window. Then abruptly something happened to send her scurrying back to the shelter of the surrounding darkness.

The sound of loud, angry voices sent a chill of foreboding racing along Glenna's spine; the boisterous exchange taking place at the front of the house and the persistent banging on the door speaking eloquently of danger. When Sal finally answered the summons disjointed bits of conversation drifted to where Glenna lay huddled in the bushes.

"Where is she, Sal?" demanded a gruff voice Glenna recognized instantly as belonging to Duke.

"Who in the hell are you talking about?" Sal asked belligerently. "It's late and all my girls are sleeping. Or they were before you came banging on my door."

"Don't play dumb with me, Sal," Duke warned ominously. "There's only two places that red-haired bitch could go and she ain't at that Jones woman's house, we checked there first. So save us both time and trouble, Sal, and tell us where you're hiding her."

'Are you talking about Glenna? My God! What has she done?"

"We're going to search the house whether you like it or not, Sal," Duke insisted in a threatening manner. "The little bitch stuck a knife in Judd Martin and we aim to see her punished for this night's work."

"Is . . . is he dead?" Sal was stunned. If Glenna stabbed Judd no doubt she had been goaded beyond reason.

Thought Glenna strained her ears she could not make out Duke's response. But in her heart she knew Judd had to be dead. There was too much blood for him to be alive.

From her concealment Glenna watched with trepidation as one after another the lamps flared on throughout the huge, rambling house. Even the attic was thoroughly searched for Glenna saw lights winking from the window facing the backyard. Thank God, she thought fervently, that she had the foresight to wait outside until everyone had left. Had she not she was sure to have been discovered and punished on the spot by Duke, or turned over to the marshal for hanging.

Nearly an hour elapsed before the lights were extinguished, once again plunging the house into darkness. Duke's voice carried through the stillness as he and his men trooped out the front door.

"I could have sworn we'd find her here," he grumbled. "You'd better not be holding out on us, Sal. I'm not done with you yet. If we don't find her tonight we'll be back tomorrow to continue the search."

"I told you she wasn't here," Sal shot back angrily. "And now you've got my girls all upset with all that traipsing in and out of rooms. If you do come back, Duke, you'd better come well-armed 'cause I'm hiring extra men tomorrow. Now get the hell out of here!" Glenna heard the door slam and then the rumble of voices disappearing into the encompassing darkness.

Her mind working furiously, Glenna reluctantly decided that by following her course of action and seeking help from Sal she would be deliberately placing her friend in danger. The less Sal knew about the situation the better off she would be. Judd's friends were sure to demand retribution should Sal be found guilty of harboring a criminal. And that's exactly what she was, Glenna thought glumly. A murderess. Though she had killed in self-defense, nevertheless she had killed.

Rising stiffly, Glenna's primary concern was finding proper clothing for herself. She could hardly leave town clad in a torn, blood-stained shift. Perhaps she could steal some clothes from someone's clothes-line, thereby compounding her crime by adding theft to the growing list. But just as she was about to withdraw from the thick shrubs and flee, the back door flung open, revealing Sal's voluptuous form outlined in the spill of light coming from the lamp raised aloft in one hand. Glenna froze as Sal's hoarse whisper reached her ears.

"Glenna! Are you there?" Perched on the horns of dilemma, Glenna hovered between showing herself and fleeing in the opposite direction. "Please, Glenna, if you're out there, show yourself. They're gone now, no one will harm you."

With a will of their own Glenna's feet followed a path to Sal's door. "I . . I don't think I should come in, Sal," she said from between chattering teeth.

"My God, you're half-naked!" exclaimed Sal, shock and compassion making her voice tremble. "I thought—that is, I hoped—you'd be out there. Come in, honey, and warm up while you tell me what happened."

Though by this time Sal was made shockingly aware of the deplorable condition of Glenna's face, she set her mouth in a grim line and said nothing. Both Glenna's eyes were beginning to blacken and large purple bruises marred the tender skin of her pale cheeks. Long, jagged scratches oozed blood on her shoulders and across the tops of her breasts. If Judd wasn't already dead she'd kill him herself for this night's work, Sal vowed grimly.

Glenna hung back. "I don't want to make trouble for you, Sal. I heard what Duke said."

"Don't worry about me, I can take care of myself," scoffed Sal, urging her inside. When Glenna made no further protest Sal guided her into the kitchen and sat her in a chair, then busied herself with the coffeepot, pretending not to notice the blood-soaked shift inadequately covering Glenna's shivering form.

While the coffee perked Sal disappeared, returning almost immediately with a soft wool blanket she wrapped around Glenna's shoulders. Wearily, Glenna flashed her a grateful smile. Consumed by misery, Glenna offered nothing by way of an explanation until Sal had poured them both a cup of coffee and settled down in a seat across from her. Glenna wondered where to start but Sal saved her the trouble by speaking first.

"Do you want to tell me what happened, honey? Were you outside when Judd's men came looking for you?"

The aftermath of shock rendering her nearly speechless, Glenna nodded. "I . . . I saw them. That's why I wanted to leave before you discovered me. I didn't want to involve you in this mess."

"In what mess? You know you can trust me."

"I know, Sal. But are you sure you want a murderess for a friend?"

"Then it's true," breathed Sal in an outpouring of compassion. "But you're not a murderess, not yet, anyway. Duke told me Judd was still alive. Just barely, but still alive, nonetheless. He said the next hours would be crucial ones for him."

Glenna looked up sharply. "He's still alive? Thank God! I . . . I never meant to kill him, you know." So great was her relief that she began sobbing hysterically, choking and gasping to catch her breath. Sal did nothing to stop her, allowing her time to vent her grief until the tears finally slowed to a trickle and the sobs fell off to an occasional hiccup.

"How did it happen, honey?" Sal restated her question. "I know it couldn't have been pleasant for you to be driven to attempt murder."

"At first Judd tried to . . . to exert his husbandly rights," Glenna shuddered in revulsion. "But later—"

"You mean," interrupted Sal incredulously, "that in all these weeks you've been married to Judd you never . . . he never—"

"Not once," admitted Glenna solemnly. "It was part of our bargain."

"Bargain?"

Glenna nodded. "It's too complicated to go into now, Sal, but suffice it to say I didn't marry Judd willingly."

"I suspected as much," Sal acknowledged grimly. "Go on, honey."

"When I resisted, he flew into a rage. He'd been drinking heavily all night and . . . and something I said sparked his anger. He began beating me." She winced and gingerly touched a finger to her bruised cheek, vividly recalling those desperate moments.

"The bastard!" growled Sal beneath her breath. "Go on."

"I couldn't stand it any longer, Sal. He would have killed me! I . . . somehow my hand found the fruit knife left in a bowl of fruit sitting on the table, and self-preservation drove me to react as I did. But I didn't mean to kill him, just stop him from abusing me."

"You stopped him, all right, honey," laughed Sal mirthlessly. "Now all we have to do is think of some way to get you the hell out of Denver. If Judd recovers—the bastard's too ornery to die—he'll spare no expense nor leave no stone unturned until you're found. You can be damned certain he'll make you pay, and pay dearly. Maybe we ought to send for Kane. He'll know exactly what to do."

"No!" Glenna panicked. "Not Kane! Promise me, Sal." On the verge of hysteria, she grasped Sal's hand, bruising it in an effort to give emphasis to her words.

"Whyever not, Glenna? If I know Kane he'll want to help you."

"I can't involve him in this, Sal, no more than I want to involve you. Judd already has reason to hate him and he's threatened to kill him on more than one occasion."

"I know they don't like each other, but why would Judd want to kill Kane?"

"It . . . it's something I said, Sal. Oh, I can't explain now. Just promise you won't tell Kane I'm here."

Unwilling to distress Glenna further, Sal nodded. "All right, honey, I promise. I'll do all in my power to keep you out of Judd's clutches without Kane's help."

A fit of shivers shook Glenna. Just the thought of Judd laying hands on either Sal or Kane filled her with dread. "I can't stay here, Sal. Each minute I remain increases your danger."

"It's you I'm worried about, honey. But you should be safe here at least for a day or two. That ought to give us enough time to decide what's to be done. Right now you need rest. You've been through hell and are in no condition for anything but sleep."

Meekly Glenna followed Sal from the room, heeding her warning for silence as they tiptoed past several closed doors to a narrow staircase leading to the upper floor. Sal wisely decided, and Glenna wholeheartedly agreed, that no one should know Glenna occupied the attic.

Glenna collapsed in a boneless heap on the lumpy cot set against one wall while Sal fetched warm water and towels which she used to bathe Glenna's bruised face and body. She also pressed a heavy sack of coins on Glenna to be used to aid her escape once a viable plan was agreed upon. But within a few minutes Sal found she was talking to herself for Glenna had fallen sound asleep before she could be eased out of the blood-soaked garment she wore.

Glenna struggled up through the heavy blanket of sleep pressing her into the darkness. The sun was but a pale globe in the eastern sky when something roused her from slumber. Disoriented, she sat up, the dust-coated relics in the attic bringing reality flooding back in a rush of panic. Dear God! Glenna screamed in silent supplication. If only the events of last night were nothing but a bad dream and she'd wake up safe in her own bed at Golden Promise and Da would still be alive. But when loud voices drifted up to her Glenna realized with a jolt that this was no dream and that far from being safe, she was the object of a manhunt.

"She's got to be here, Sal!" the voice that had awakened her insisted.

Kane! Glenna's heart thumped dangerously in her breast when she recognized the voice of the man she loved. It took every ounce of willpower she possessed not to rush down the stairs and throw herself into Kane's capable arms.

From the gist of the conversation it was evident that Sal's words did nothing to discourage Kane. "Starting with the cellar I'm going to search every inch of this house until I find Glenna, Sal, and when I do I want to know what in the hell is going on!"

I have to leave! Glenna thought furiously. But how? She had no clothes, no money. Then her eyes fell on the sack of coins Sal had pressed on her last night. Though half asleep she vaguely remembered Sal talking about buying a train ticket to Silver City—which happened to be the first train out of Denver today—and bringing her something to wear. But Kane's precipitous visit early this morning had necessarily delayed those plans. After the initial shock of what she had done passed, and fortified by a good night's sleep, Glenna felt renewed strength and determination. Possessed of courage, fully capable of controlling her own life, Glenna now drew on that strength to plot her own course, even if it meant existing without the man she loved. Whatever the future held she was determined to face it and live with it. She alone was responsible for her actions last night. She alone must pay.

With a decisiveness that surprised her, Glenna began a frantic search of the attic and crowed jubilantly when she discovered an old trunk filled with boys' clothing. Probably left by the former owner, Glenna assumed. Selecting baggy trousers, shirt, vest and heavy woolen jacket, Glenna flung off her blood-stained shift and quickly donned the more serviceable attire. She even found a pair of sturdy boots that fit reasonably well and a hat she jammed on her head, stuffing her bright hair inside. Pocketing the sack of money she hurried to the door, but the commotion on the floor below halted her steps. How in the world would she get out of the house without being seen?

The window! From where she stood Glenna noticed the nearly bare branches of a huge tree brushing against the side of the house. With no other means of escape available she decided to take the chance, thanking her lucky stars that the window faced the back of the house.

Easing herself from the windowsill, Glenna grasped a sturdy branch and swung free, catching her breath painfully as she dangled helplessly in the chill morning air. Suddenly her feet touched a lower limb, hugging the trunk as she inched herself downward until she hung a scant six-feet from the ground. Clinging by her fingertips, abruptly she released her hold, dropping heavily to the earth below, shaken but unhurt. When no warning cry was issued her feet grew wings and she took off in a burst of speed.

"Damnit, Sal! Glenna has to be here!" Kane's angry voice insisted. "There is no place else for her to go!"

"I tell you she's not here!" rejoined Sal, equally adamant. "You've searched the whole house and haven't found her." Dear God how she hated to lie to Kane. If only she hadn't made that stupid promise to Glenna.

"There's still the attic," Kane said, screwing his head around to peer up the narrow staircase.

Sal nearly sighed aloud, grateful when Kane started up the stairs, certain that he would find Glenna and relieve her of the responsibility of saying nothing. She was positive Kane wouldn't let anything bad happen to Glenna once he took charge. But when Kane burst through the attic door the room appeared empty. A more thorough search turned up nothing save a bloody shift, rendering Sal absolutely speechless, so certain was she they would find Glenna cowering in a far corner.

Holding up the irrefutable proof, Kane asked calmly, too calmly to suit Sal, "How do you explain this, Sal? I assume it's Glenna's?"

Sal nodded, looking goggle-eyed and confused. Surely Glenna couldn't have disappeared into thin air, could she?

"Why in the hell didn't you tell me she was here before she pulled a disappearing act?" raged Kane.

"I . . . pr—promised," stuttered Sal.

"The hell with promises! Don't you realize she's in danger? Judd is still alive and all his men are out looking for her. How did it happen? At first I refused to believe it when I heard Glenna tried to kill Judd. The whole damn town is talking of nothing else. But if the bastard was abusing her she had every right in the world to defend herself."

The bloody chemise still dangling between two fingers, Kane grimaced with distaste. "I hope this is Judd's blood, Sal, and that Glenna isn't hurt. If he's harmed her in any way I'll finish where Glenna left off."

The deep timbre of his voice sent a chill racing down Sal's spine. "As you suspected, Glenna was defending herself, Kane. Judd beat her when—"

"The bastard!" he spat contemptuously.

"She's bruised and battered but unhurt," Sal continued, leaving her previous sentence unfinished. "What puzzles me is how she got out of here, and what she was wearing when she left."

Kane had already figured that out as he pointed toward the open window. Peering over the sill Sal's heart stood still when she visually measured the distance Glenna would have fallen had she lost her grip on the tree growing outside the window. "She sure as hell couldn't have climbed down that thing naked," commented Sal wryly.

Glancing about Kane spotted a trunk whose lid stood ajar and he flipped it open, revealing a treasure trove of boys' clothing.

"An enterprising young woman," he mused, rummaging through the trunk. "No one would be looking for a smooth-faced lad. Did she say where she might go?"

"I did mention the train," Sal said brightly. "But Glenna was nearly dropping from exhaustion and I didn't think she heard me. Do you suppose—"

"I hope to God I find her before Judd's men get to her," Kane fervently prayed.

"Are you going to the depot?" Sal called to his departing back. "That's probably the first place she'll go. I gave her enough money to see her safely to any destination she chooses."

"It's a starting place," Kane flung over his shoulder. "I'll check back with you later."

Pulling her hat more firmly over her eyes Glenna walked swiftly toward the center of town and the train depot. Both her ankles smarted from her drop from the tree but not enough to keep her from proceeding at a fast pace down the street just beginning to come alive with activity. Little heed was given to the youth hurrying on his way, his furtive side-to-side glances, as if he half-expected to be pounced upon at any time, hardly deserving a second glance.

Maintaining a brisk pace Glenna soon came within sight of the depot, panting breathlessly when she saw the train sitting in front of the station discharging and taking on passengers. Hastening her steps she entered the depot office intending to purchase her ticket, and nearly collided with Duke who was patrolling back and forth before the ticket window, scrutinizing each and every person who approached.

Would she pass such close inspection? Glenna asked herself, thinking furiously. When Duke glanced her way she ducked her head and left, deciding retreat was the better part of valor. Instead, she prepared to board the train and purchase her ticket from the conductor once they were underway. But once again Glenna experienced the pang of bitter disappointment. Guarding the boarding platform stood two of Judd's hired men. They were bound to recognize her, she rationalized, even dressed as she was. But perhaps they wouldn't, she countered hopefully. To her knowledge there was only one way to find out.

Mustering her courage, Glenna sauntered toward the boarding platform, her head bowed, eyes cast downward, fearful lest her distinctive green eyes give her away. But as luck would have it Duke chose that precise moment to leave the station and approach the two men guarding the boarding platform. From where she stood a short distance away Glenna eavesdropped on their conversation.

"I don't know how the little witch managed to escape us," complained Duke bitterly. "Judd was positive she'd try to board the first train out of town."

So, he still lives, Glenna thought, uncertain whether or not she was pleased to learn that Judd was still alive.

"Is the boss going to be all right, Duke?" questioned one of the men.

"He lives a charmed life, Mac," laughed Duke. "The knife deflected off his rib and missed his heart by mere inches. Had he been allowed to bleed all night he would be dead, but as luck would have it he was discovered soon after it happened. He owes his life to Wiley Wilson."

"How so?" asked Mac curiously. He hadn't heard the whole story and wondered how a frail little lady like Judd's wife could hurt him so badly. And why.

"Wiley came busting into the saloon late last night demanding to see Judd. When I tried to stop him he kept shouting something about seeing Judd's red-haired wife running down the street half-naked. Now that just didn't make sense so we went upstairs together. I knew Judd was in Glenna's room but when I knocked there was no answer. The door was locked so we were forced to break in. We found the boss sprawled on the floor bleeding like a stuck pig."

Duly impressed, both men shook their heads in amazement. "Did Judd tell you it was his wife who stabbed him?" asked the second man.

"He sure did, Lacy," nodded Duke eagerly. "While we waited for the doc to arrive he regained consciousness, told me what happened and made me promise to find her no matter what it took. I aim to keep that promise. Are you certain neither of you noticed her boarding the train? I picked you because you've both seen her often enough to recognize her."

"I'd recognize that red hair anywhere," Mac contended smugly.

"And those green eyes," added Lacy for good measure.

Suddenly Duke's gaze fell on Glenna where she stood by the baggage cart pretending to be searching through the luggage. He studied her intently, lids slitted thoughtfully before calling out, "You there! Boy!"

Panic-stricken, Glenna could not think beyond fleeing for her life as her feet took wing, all thoughts of boarding the train long forgotten.

"What in the hell is the matter with him?" asked Mac, watching Glenna's hasty departure.

"Beats me," shrugged Duke carelessly. "I had it in mind to ask the kid if he saw anyone matching Glenna's description. I figured he worked for the stationmaster and might have noticed her. No matter, we'll find her."

"Yer ugly mug probably scared the kid off," guffawed Mac, earning himself a look of pure disgust.

"Forget the jokes and keep your eyes peeled," Duke ordered brusquely. "There's more trains through here today and Glenna's bound to try boarding one of them." Then he returned to the station to continue his own vigil.

What do I do now? Glenna's brain screamed as her feet carried her away from the depot. The train whistle let loose a tremendous blast and she choked back a sob of dismay. Within minutes the train would leave without her.

Maybe she ought to turn herself in to the marshal, Glenna considered desperately. At least he'd be able to keep her safely out of Judd's clutches. And as long as Judd still lived they couldn't hang her, could they? But in the end Glenna did not turn herself in to Marshal

Bartow, for it suddenly occurred to her that should Judd choose not to press charges she would end up exactly where he wanted her—under his control. Her best bet was to find a way out of town . . . and soon.

Everywhere Glenna looked she saw one or more of Judd's men patrolling the streets, their eyes searching restlessly for a red-haired woman. Thank God for her disguise! So far she had been able to pass undetected under their noses. But how long before one man more observant than the others recognized her? she ruminated bleakly. If the option of leaving by rail was closed to her then she'd do the next best thing—buy a horse. A horse, a gun, and supplies were essential for a trek through the wilderness. Though she dismissed a visit to the general store as entirely too dangerous, Glenna knew exactly where she would find each and every item on her list.

Pete at the livery stable failed to recognize her, for his eyesight over the years had steadily deserted him. But he did catch a glimpse of two black eyes and a bruised face. "You been in a fight, sonny?" he asked as he saddled a feisty bay Glenna had just purchased with part of the money Sal gave her.

"Sort of," Glenna hedged in a voice pitched deliberately low.

"This here's a nice piece of horseflesh you just bought, lad. I hope you take good care of him. You goin' on a trip?"

Though Pete usually minded his own business, the badly used youngster intrigued him. Where had he come by the money to buy an expensive animal like the bay?

"My pa's waiting for me outside town," Glenna lied smoothly. "We plan on doing a little prospecting and he wanted me to have a good horse."

"You from Denver? I don't recollect seein' you before?"

"Naw, we're from Dodge City. Just arrived yesterday by train. They say there's still plenty of gold to be had up in the foothills."

"Well, good luck to ye, young fella," Pete cackled, displaying a nearly toothless grin. "I predict you'll be back soon, though. Won't be long before snow flies and you'll be lookin' fer a place to hole up fer the winter."

"I reckon you're right," mumbled Glenna, counting out the gold pieces to pay for the horse and saddle. Then she wasted no time vaulting on the bay's back and urging him forward, calling over her shoulder, " 'Bye, Pete, take care."

Pete waved jauntily before the realization struck him that the lad had called him by name though he didn't remember giving it out.

Kane reached the depot only minutes after Glenna left, his eyes the color of cold cement when he recognized Judd's men patrolling the surrounding area. They're hunting her down like an animal, he thought disgustedly. Then he recalled that she was disguised as a boy and might have gotten by Judd's men and boarded the train safely. He decided to find out as he leaped aboard and slowly walked through every car, carefully scrutinizing each passenger. After making the long trek forward and then back again he was dead certain Glenna was not on the train. No doubt she had been scared off by Judd's men.

Then the whistle blasted and a cloud of steam escaped the engine, signalling its imminent departure, and Kane hopped off the platform just as the train jerked forward. He waited around a short time in hopes that Glenna might appear to purchase a ticket for the next departure due later in the day, but when he saw Judd's men settle down for a long stay he instinctively knew Glenna would not show up.

Now what? he asked himself grimly. Where would she go? What would she do? And why did he care so much? The last question was the easiest to answer. No matter how much she had hurt him, no matter that she was another man's wife, he loved her still and would do everything in his power to keep her out of harm's way. Even as he thought the words he vowed to keep his feelings to himself, for never again would he become vulnerable to a woman's wiles. Glenna had played him false once and though he loved her still she would never have that weapon to use against him again. Nor could he bring himself to stand idly by while trouble courted her and she needed him.

Slowly Kane made his way back to his hotel wondering what to do next when suddenly it hit him like a bolt of lightning. Of course! He knew exactly where Glenna would go. She might not stay long but the small cabin at Golden Promise would afford her a certain measure of security after the terrible upheaval of the last hours. It took him only two short hours to gather up his gear, including warm clothing, supplies and weapons, and take to the trail, making but two brief stops along the way. One to inform Sal of his destination and another to the livery stable where he questioned Pete carefully and learned that his assumption had been correct. A young lad had bought a big bay horse and headed west out of town barely two hours ago. Though Kane wisely kept his own counsel he knew Glenna was the boy and it was to Golden Promise that she was headed.

Kane's bulging saddlebags were a precaution in the unlikely event Glenna was not at Golden Promise and he was forced to broaden his search. There was a good chance one or more of Judd's men were still working the claim and occupying the cabin. Of course Kane had no knowledge as yet of the new claim or that Golden Promise had been abandoned long ago in favor of Promise Two where Judd's men had settled in for the winter.

A thick, encompassing darkness settled over the land as Glenna reached Golden Promise, and she kept to the cover of the trees and brush surrounding the camp for a good fifteen minutes, watching intently for any sign of occupancy. From talk overheard between Judd and Duke she doubted that anyone would be about. Carl and the two men working the new claim supposedly occupied the cabin on the property. From all appearances Golden Promise lay abandoned and forgotten.

Urging her mount forward, Glenna moved from her concealment, reining the bay before a makeshift stable where she dismounted, removed the saddle and left the weary animal with a forkful of hay to feed upon. He isn't the only one tired, thought Glenna drearily. How she longed to throw herself on her bed and lose herself in the welcoming arms of sleep.

Moonlight lit her path as Glenna trod lightly toward the cabin. Cautiously she listened at the door before trying the knob, hearing nothing but night sounds from the surrounding wilderness. The door opened beneath her touch and she entered the dark interior. The fall of pale moonbeams illuminated the emptiness of the room and Glenna allowed herself to relax as she fumbled in the dimness for a lamp, finding and lighting it. A hasty inspection proved that though incredibly dirty, the cabin remained much as she had left it.

Too tired to scounge around for a meal, though she hadn't eaten all day, Glenna entered her bedroom, grimacing distastefully at the filthy sheets covering the unmade bed. Luckily she found a set of clean sheets, made the bed and fell into it clothes and all. Sleep came instantly; even before she could reach over and extinguish the lamp.

Behind Glenna by mere hours, Kane followed her

trail to Golden Promise. Darkness had slowed them both, making the twenty mile trip seem endless. He found no indication that Glenna meant to camp on the trail so he plodded onward, reaching the claim shortly after midnight. He stabled his horse beside Glenna's bay who neighed a welcome and moved aside to share his supper with the tired newcomer. A light shining through a side window drew Kane's immediate attention and within minutes he was peering through the pane at a sleeping form sprawled atop the bed dimly illuminated by light falling from a bedside lamp. Fully clad except for the battered hat which had fallen to the floor, Glenna's red hair tumbled about her like a living flame.

Kane drew in his breath sharply, mesmerized by the intriguing sight. She lay on her stomach, the tender curve of her buttocks clearly outlined and defined by the tight boy's breeches she wore. Stupefied, Kane stared fixedly as she turned on her back, her plaid shirt pulled taut against full breasts. She was breathtaking, Kane thought, marveling at the beauty of her body. Memories merged with dreams as he recalled the last time they were together; the fire, the passion that had consumed them. And then she had told him about her marriage to Judd and the entire structure of his life crumbled around his feet.

Moving away from the window Kane approached the front door, cursing when he found it unlocked. What if one of Judd's men had reached her first? How easy it would be for one of them to just walk in and overpower her. Thank God he had found her before anyone else thought to come out here. But Kane knew it would be just a matter of time before Judd would think to send someone to Golden Promise. By then he hoped to have Glenna safely away.

The room was dark and cold. Frost covered the ground nearly every night now at this time of year and the first snowfall could be expected at any time. Pausing until his eyes became accustomed to the darkness, Kane found a lamp, lit it and began laying a fire in the fireplace, grateful that the woodpile was well-stocked. Not a whimper was heard from the bedroom where Glenna slept soundly through it all.

Soon the fire was emitting a welcome warmth and Kane shed his jacket, dropping into a nearby chair. He glanced longingly through the open door into Glenna's bedroom, then promptly denounced himself for harboring thoughts that sent liquid fire spiraling upward through his hardening body.

Glenna was no longer his, he reminded himself resentfully. For reasons unknown she had chosen Judd Martin over him and nothing could change that. Though he had no idea what had driven her to attempt murder, it was something he intended to find out, but it was scant comfort to know it would change nothing. Glenna was still married, and he owed her nothing but his contempt, but to his everlasting regret he learned love didn't work that way. His love for her was blinding and constant, though intermingled with hate and resentment, and he could no more abandon her than he could cut off his right arm.

15

Kane wasn't the only one caught up in a dream. Just a few steps away in another room Glenna moved restlessly in her own dream world. A world that included Kane. She dreamed of how he had made her feel the last time they were together; how his searing lovemaking had driven her beyond the realm of endurance. He was an intense, consummate lover; tender, compassionate, more concerned with her pleasure than with his own. Then, from somewhere within her, his name came trembling from her lips, brought forth by a force more powerful than any she had ever known.

Caught in the strange half-world between sleep and total awareness, Kane heard the desperate summons wrenched from Glenna's throat. Urged forward by the age-old siren's song, he shook himself awake and approached the bed, surprised to find Glenna thrashing about restlessly, his name tumbling from her lips. Instantly he was beside her, his strong arms a soothing balm as she immediately calmed down and snuggled into the curve of his hard body.

Her eyes screwed tightly shut, Glenna knew she was dreaming, knew that it was only her intense yearning for the man she loved that had conjured him up from the depths of her heart. Not that it mattered. If she could be with Kane like this only in her dreams she never wanted to awaken.

But to Kane the warm, vibrant body he held so tenderly in his arms was very real. And despite the fact that he had no right to her, despite his earlier resolve to remain immune to her feminine wiles, he wanted her. And judging from the way she had called out his name, as if driven by desperate need, he knew she wanted him too. Reverently his lips touched and tasted the tears that lay upon her cheeks, amazed that she still slept while he never felt more awake in his life.

Of their own violition his fingers released the buttons on her blouse, revealing in the flickering light twin mounds of pure alabaster crested by deep pink buds already tautening beneath his avid gaze.

"Glenna, look at me," Kane said softly, urging her to awaken. His fingertips traced up her throat lightly and rested beneath her chin, holding her face tilted upwards. Drawn from her dreams by the sound of his voice, she opened her eyes and found herself being devoured by velvety pools that possessed the power to turn her into molten lava.

"No!" Glenna cried out, screwing her eyes tightly shut. "I don't want to wake up. Let me dream a little longer."

"Glenna, love, open your eyes, I'm no dream. See, I'm real," he insisted, pressing his lips to hers. "I'm flesh and blood and right here beside you. I won't let anyone hurt you, I promise."

Reluctantly Glenna raised her lids until the firm, bold lines of Kane's face came into view. "Kane? It is really you? Oh, God! Why? Why did you follow me?"

"I want to help you, Glenna."

"No! You don't now what you're getting yourself into!"

"I know exactly what I'm getting myself into."

"I don't deserve you, Kane. Not after what I did to you. Please leave. You don't understand. I . . . I nearly killed a man. Perhaps he's already dead."

"Your husband!" he spat the words as if ridding himself of something distasteful, "isn't dead nor is he likely to be. Before I left I heard the wound you dealt him isn't nearly so grave as first supposed. All that blood made it seem worse than it really was. What in the hell drove you to do it?"

Suddenly he shifted and the light hit her face just right, causing Kane to gasp aloud in shock as she regarded him through bruised and swollen features. The sight spoke more eloquently than words. "The bastard!" he ground out from between clenched teeth. "Killing isn't good enough for him. Why, Glenna? Why did he do this to you?"

Intuitively Glenna realized that if she told Kane that Judd beat her because she all but admitted she and Kane had been lovers, Kane would fly into a rage and demand retribution. And the outcome of that confrontation would be disastrous. Judd's men would make short work of Kane and that Glenna couldn't bear. She was determined to do or say nothing that might endanger Kane's life. She loved him far too much to cause his death.

"I . . . something I said angered him, Kane," she admitted cautiously. "He had been drinking heavily and . . . and it just happened. I'm not sorry I stabbed him," she defended staunchly. "I used whatever means necessary to defend myself. Only . . . I never realized so little a weapon could inflict that much damage. It wasn't my intention to kill him, only stop him from . . . from hurting me."

"Oh, God, Glenna, I could kill him myself for doing this to you."

"Do you still care that much, Kane?" asked Glenna hopefully.

"I wouldn't like to see a dog hurt the way Judd hurt you," Kane deftly eluded, unwilling to admit his true feelings. "If only I could understand your reason for marrying Judd it would make things a lot easier." No matter whose woman she was his body reacted violently to her nearness, making him oblivious to all but the need to make love to her. Here. Now.

Glenna's thoughts closely paralleled Kane's as she felt herself responding to his need, wanting only to experience this man's love one last time. Tomorrow was time enough to bare her soul, to explain about the new claim and Judd's reasons for forcing her into a loveless marriage. An unconsummated marriage, albeit a legal one.

"If you'll listen to me, Kane, and try to understand," Glenna promised breathlessly, "I'll tell you everything. Only not right now. The shock of what I've done and all I've endured is still too raw an emotion to reveal tonight. Later, Kane, please."

"I'll hold you to that promise, Glenna," Kane said pointedly. "I do want to understand how all this came about. Truly, I do."

"Just hold me, Kane," Glenna pleaded, moving restlessly against him. "I need your strength right now more than I've needed anything in my entire life."

Kane groaned as if in pain, his big hands guiding his hips to hers, letting her feel his need for her, leaving her hot and cold and trembling beneath his familiar touch.

"Can you feel how much I want you, love? I know you're another man's wife but I can't help myself."

"Forget Judd. I need you too much to let him come

between us now."

"Brave words," murmured Kane, nibbling at her ear. "But I'm not afraid of him or his men."

What did bother him, he thought but did not say, was the fact that Judd Martin had probably held Glenna in his arms and loved her much as he was doing now. What's more, he had every right in the world to do so. How many times had Judd made love to her? How many times had Glenna responded? Those thoughts nearly drove him wild with jealousy. Desperation consumed him as he strove to drive all memory of another man from her mind. He wanted her body to remember only his lovemaking, his touch, as he launched an attack against her senses that left her breathless and sighing.

His clothes melted away like magic, tossed aside in his eagerness to claim the woman he loved. Then he turned to Glenna, no word of consent necessary as he slowly peeled the shirt from her shoulders and down her arms, flinging it to the floor. His greedy kisses blazed a searing path across her flesh, leaving a white-hot fire smoldering in their wake. He lowered his head to nuzzle the pink crests of her breasts, and a sweet warmth plowed through him as the small buds bloomed full and erect, flowering under his ardent attentions. He cradled the delicate weight of her breasts in his hands, his thumbs circling the engorged nipples, and Glenna sighed in response.

Easing his hands beneath the waistband of her boy's trousers he skillfully pulled them down her thighs and legs, her hips lifting eagerly to aid him in his endeavor. Then she lay nude and magnificent beneath him. Light, fleeting kisses moved against the skin of her rib cage, the curve of her hip, the flat expanse of her stomach, and paused to lovingly circle the triangle of tight, gleaming ringlets nestled between her slender thighs. She gasped, an aching need soaring to life inside her. But the kisses continued against the velvet softness of that sensitive flesh, causing her to cry out in supplication.

"Not yet, love," he chided gently, stilling the movement of her hips with his big hands. "After tonight you'll have no memory of another man ever having made love to you."

"But, Kane, no one—"

"Shhh, love, lie back and let me love you."

He tightened his hands around her waist to hold her close as he continued to probe her with his tongue until she caught fire, his every movement bringing her to exquisite pleasure—more pleasure than she had ever known. He buried his face against her, cupping her buttocks now, his tongue moving faster as she writhed in his grasp. Relentlessly he pushed against her, his mouth warm and moist as she helplessly succumbed to the erotic torture he brought her. He felt pleasurable ecstasy shudder through her body and he wanted only to give her more.

Desisting only when the last tremor left her body, he burrowed himself eagerly between her thighs and thrust himself joyfully within her, moving with lazy precision to draw her once again to the edge of rapture. With gentle, subtle movements he began the rhythm of love, the impetus of his thrusts increasing with the sound of his deep, ragged breathing.

The moment before his thunderous climax overtook him he captured her lips, imparting her own essence into her mouth as his tongue took up the same rhythm of his pounding hips, carrying her to the brink of ecstasy when only moments before she had thought herself completely sated. Kane was proving his total mastery over her body as he thrust, probed and drove her inexorably toward a plane above mere ecstasy, beyond desire into the realm of the sublime. With a shout of joy he joined her in her tumultuous journey into a world of their own making.

At last they clung together in exhaustion. Kane rolled off her with a deep sigh and lay quietly beside her, for the moment sated but far from satisfied. Would he ever get enough of her? Somehow he doubted it. A lifetime with this red-haired enchantress wouldn't be enough. Absently he caressed the pale globe of her stomach, his mind working furiously. It gave him little pleasure to realize that his dreams of the future included this special woman, for she was a woman he had no right to claim.

"What are you thinking, Kane?" Glenna asked curiously. The expression on his face was dreamy and soft.

"I'm trying to decide where to take you," Kane replied with alacrity. "Someplace where Judd Martin has no power to demand your return."

"You'd risk that for me?" said Glenna whimsically.

"That and more," nodded Kane tersely.

"I'd give anything if I could change things, Kane; if I could turn back the clock."

"Would you agree to a divorce, Glenna, if I could get you safely away from here?" he surprised himself by asking.

Stunned, Glenna could only stare at Kane dumbly. "You still want me? But you said—"

"Forget what I said," he replied gruffly. "I never stopped wanting you."

"Oh, Kane," she breathed ecstatically, throwing herself into his arms.

His hands slid from her stomach and at the curve of her waist his fingers spread around it and massaged lightly before slipping down over her hips to cup her buttocks. His palms rasped deliciously over the raised flesh, smoothing it as her breath hissed between her teeth. Was it possible to feel desire so soon after being so thoroughly sated? Evidently it was, for the fires of response kindled in her anew.

His lips found hers as his kiss expressed his hunger, possessing her utterly. She sighed with languid delight as his hand played between her legs, drawing pleasure from her. Her body was aflame, consumed and fed by his desire, and his need became her own. Her hands found his shoulders, and beneath her stroking fingertips she felt his tempered strength, the firm skin and rippling muscles that shifted beneath her touch like steel sheathed in velvet, and reeled in his masculinity.

Delicious passion consumed them and Glenna's legs opened joyfully as he slid inside, his bold staff tall and thick, a pale tower of ivory fashioned expressly to bring her pleasure. Love was in his eyes and lay unspoken on his lips as he strained over her pliant flesh. Though no words were spoken they reveled in delights that transcended mere physical desire and made them one, body and soul.

Thoroughly exhausted, Glenna relaxed and let slumber draw a veil over her as she lay contentedly in the curve of Kane's body. She felt loved, protected, and safe for the first time in months.

Weary, yet too keyed up to sleep, Kane shifted restlessly, his agile mind planning furiously. At first he thought to take Glenna to Philadelphia, but upon further consideration decided too many problems faced them at his home. There was still Ellen eager for him to "come to his senses" and honor his promise of marriage. His mother was disgusted with him and his brother thoroughly denounced his "irresponsible" behavior. Not to mention Ellen's parents who condemned him out of hand. Thrusting Glenna into a lion's den, so to speak, leaving her open to ridicule for deserting her marriage, was definitely out of the question. No, Kane decided emphatically, the answer lay in another direction.

California, Kane decided. He would take her south to Pueblo and board a train there for California. God knows he had plenty of money to see him anyplace he wanted to go. Once her divorce was granted they would marry and he'd never let her out of his sight again. Maybe they'd even raise a whole brood of red-headed kids. Everything finally settled in his mind, Kane slipped into the world of darkness as sleep carried him away.

Glenna awoke with a start to find Kane fully dressed and throwing together a breakfast of sorts. From his gear he had taken bacon, frying it in a pan placed over the glowing coals in the fireplace rather than cleaning up the dirty kitchen and starting up the stove. The tantalizing aroma of freshly brewed coffee tickled her senses and started her mouth to watering.

"Kane, what are you doing?" Glenna called, stretching luxuriously. They had slept long past sunrise and the night chill had given way to weak rays of sunshine beating down to earth.

"Fixing breakfast, sleepyhead," he sent back over his shoulder. The delicious odors emanating from the fireplace sent her taste buds into a spin. She had eaten nothing in twenty-four hours and was starving. But at the moment another need took precedence over hunger.

"Do I have time for a bath?"

Kane laughed. "If you hurry. I already had mine in the creek and it wasn't too bad if you're an eskimo."

Glenna slanted him an oblique look then slid from the bed, wrapped a blanket around her slim form and padded from the bedroom. "Do you have any soap?" she asked.

"The soap is on the table."

Clutching the blanket tightly she retrieved the soap and started for the door, her bare feet already aware of the chill.

"Glenna, wait!" Kane laughed teasingly as a col blast from the door she had just opened nearly change her mind about a bath. "That won't be necessarily. I se a pot of water to boiling for you. It won't be the same a immersing yourself in the icy creek but at least yo won't freeze your . . . er . . . toes." He quirked a dar brow as a wolfish grin broke out, displaying pearl white teeth against a deeply tanned face.

For the first time Glenna noticed the huge kettl swinging over the coals and she expressed he appreciation while Kane lifted it down from it supporting arm and carried it to where a shallow tub h had found in the shed was waiting to receive it Wordlessly he carried the empty pot to the creek fo cold water and soon had the bath prepared to th correct temperature.

"Your bath, my lady," he bowed gallantly.

Glenna giggled, feeling suddenly lighthearted an free. "Thank you, kind sir," she returned saucily. The she boldly dropped the blanket and stepped into th shallow water, squealing when Kane aimed a playfu swat at her bare behind.

She washed quickly while Kane busied himself wit their breakfast, every now and then sending her a loo of such longing she had to struggle against laughing a his obvious discomfort. Suddenly Kane decided he ha had enough. Glenna had just given her hair a final rins when he slammed down the frying pan and vaulte across the room, reaching down and hauling her out o the tub in one impatient motion.

"Kane!" she shrieked, "I'm getting you all wet!"

For an answer he dragged her close, water drippin down her body and hair to gather in a puddle aroun their feet. His hands searched downward, and his firm strong, fingers found their way to her silken crevice Before she could voice a protest he captured her mouth her lips alive with sensation, wondrously tasting of hi being, her tender flesh burning with the touch of his hands as they moved lightly, searching out each tingling part.

"I'll never get enough of you," he whispered against her ear.

"Kane, I'm cold." Her soft plea bore a note of light reproach, but her protest died a sudden death when he swept her off her feet and carried her to the rumpled bed. Needless to say the coffee was too strong and the bacon burnt by the time they got around to eating. But to Glenna it was a feast fit for a queen. As long as Kane was nearby to share her throne all was right in the world.

While they ate Kane revealed his plans, thrilling Glenna with his obvious desire to share his life with her, although she realized that leaving Judd meant she must abandon all claim to Promise Two and whatever riches it produced. Abruptly she recalled Kane still did not know about the new claim Da filed on before his death, deciding it was long past the time to explain to him her reason for marrying Judd Martin.

She began by telling him about the new claim located just a few miles upcreek from Golden Promise, and Paddy's reason for selling Golden Promise in the first place. She left out only her suspicions that Judd was responsible for her father's death, hiring Wiley to do the dirty work for him and stealing the deed to the claim. Her reason for omitting that piece of information was simple. Once Kane learned of Judd's guilt he was certain to rush off to avenge Paddy's death and perhaps lose his own life in the bargain.

A low whistle escaped Kane's lips. "So Paddy really did find the mother lode." Then his face screwed up in puzzlement and anger. "So help me I don't know whatever possessed you to marry Judd. Thanks to your marriage he now owns the new claim as well as half of Golden Promise. Has he found the lode yet?"

Glenna sensed Kane's keen disappointment with her and she knew the time had arrived to reveal everything to him. But perhaps, she reconsidered thoughtfully, she should wait until they were far away, too far for Kane to return for a confrontation with Judd.

"As far as I know Judd's men haven't found the lode yet. They're staying in a cabin on the claim and intend to remain there all winter. To protect it against claim jumpers, I suppose."

"Last night you promised you'd tell me why you married Martin."

"And I will, I want to," she said evasively. "But right now I think we should leave here. Knowing Judd it won't take him long to figure out where I am. I'll tell you everything once we are safely out of Judd's reach."

Kane leveled her an assessing look, wondering why she was being so evasive. Gray eyes that but a short time ago sparkled with inner fires now impaled her with icy shards. "Why are you deliberately putting me off, Glenna? If you have any feelings at all for the man you married, tell me now and I'll get out of your life. What are you hiding? Perhaps you have no desire to be 'saved' from him. Perhaps he has no intention of punishing you or harming you in any way. But judging from those bruises on your face I seriously doubt that."

"Kane, the minute we're out of danger of being discovered by Judd's men I'll tell you everything," Glenna promised, flashing him an affronted look. "And when I do I know you'll understand why this marriage was necessary."

Openly skeptical, Kane nodded, for the time being appeased but far from satisfied.

A short time later Kane packed whatever staples were still available in the cupboards and saddled their horses while Glenna went through her father's trunk for a change of clothes. Around midmorning they rode away from Golden Promise, tears hovering in the corners of Glenna's eyes. It was sad leaving for she seriously doubted she'd ever see the claim again.

They followed the trail through the woods for a distance, glancing over their shoulders from time to time to make certain they weren't being followed. Brilliant sunlight flashed through the bare branches overhead dispelling the morning chill. The serene silence which pervaded the forest was broken only by the echoing sound of their horses' hooves and the twittering of birds. Suddenly the trail widened and Glenna kneed her mount into position beside Kane.

"Do you think we're being followed, Kane?" she asked, hearing nothing but forest noises all around her.

"It's difficult to say," judged Kane. "The leaves underfoot muffle all sounds of pursuit."

"Oh, look, Kane," pointed Glenna delightedly. "There's a small stream ahead flowing from between those rocks. Can we stop?"

"Only for a few minutes, love. Long enough to fill our canteens and water our horses."

When they approached the small waterfall Glenna slid gratefully from her horse, stretched her legs and knelt to fill her canteen and moisten her hands and face in the icy brook. The peacefulness of the place, she decided as she thoughtfully surveyed her surroundings, would provide a perfect setting in which to tell Kane all about Judd and how he had blackmailed her into marrying him.

"Kane, I'd like to tell you now about Judd and our marriage, if you think we're no longer in danger."

Kane nodded, preparing to dismount, when suddenly he froze in the saddle, all his finely honed senses screaming a warning.

"Get back on your horse, Glenna," he ordered curtly. "Hurry!"

"Kane, what is it?"

"Don't argue, just mount up and ride like hell!" He eased his shotgun from his saddle holster while Glenna sprinted to her horse, vaulting onto its back in a single leap as the hackles rose at the back of her neck.

Without warning four riders emerged from the thicket surrounding them and Kane reached over and slapped Glenna's horse on the rump, causing it to jerk into motion with Glenna clinging to the saddlehorn and the reins trailing on the ground.

"After her!" a familiar voice ordered, and Glenna turned her head around as one man broke from the group and thundered close on her heels.

Suddenly a shot rang out and from the corner of her eye Glenna saw her pursuer fall from his horse as Kane's shot found its target. "Go, Glenna, get out of—"

Glenna screamed as two more shots rent the air and Kane's words halted in mid-sentence. "No-o-!" The word was torn from her throat in the form of an agonized denial of what her heart told her had just happened. The very thing she had tried to prevent had finally come to pass.

For weeks she had endeavored to protect Kane from Judd and his men but in the end had caused his downfall. Had she the reins in her hand she would have turned her mount and ridden back to him, regardless of her own danger.

Her eyes blinded with tears, Glenna was unaware of the horse and rider pounding after her, or of the long arm reaching out to grasp the trailing reins, urging the bay to a halt. Only when she looked into Duke's grinning face did she realize that all her efforts had been for nothing. Because of her Kane lay on the frosty ground either dead or dying. Glenna offered no resistance as Duke led her back to the spot where the other three men—one bleeding profusely from the shoulder—stood in a knot staring at a motionless figure sprawled at their feet. Sliding from her horse Glenna dropped to her knees at Kane's side, cradling his head in her lap, tears of pain and anguish blurring her vision.

"You've killed him! Damn you, Duke, you've killed Kane!" Two bright splotches darkened Kane's shirt, one just above his belt on the left side and the other on the upper right side of his chest. In a daze she noted that his breathing was labored, each breath shallow and pained. Congealed blood formed a puddle on the ground beneath him and Glenna began tearing frantically at her shirttail thinking to make a cloth to staunch the endless flow of blood.

"Is he dead?" Duke asked laconically.

"Naw, not yet," answered one of the men who prodded him ungently with the toe of his boot. "Won't be long though if he keeps on bleeding like he is."

"Good riddance," Duke shrugged carelessly. "We've done the boss a favor by ridding him of the bastard. Morgan's been a thorn in Judd's side ever since he came to town."

Grasping Glenna by the arms he attempted to pull her away from Kane. "No!" she screamed, nearly demented by grief. "He'll die if he isn't taken care of right away. Help me, Duke! We've got to stop the bleeding before he dies."

But Duke was relentless as he finally managed to tear her away from Kane, dragging her kicking and screaming from the white-faced, still form of her lover. "You're coming with us, Mrs. Martin," Duke snorted, tossing her onto her horse, requiring the help of two men to subdue her. Swiftly he tied her hands to the pummel and her feet together, running the rope beneath the bay's belly. Then he took up the reins and urged the animal forward.

"He'll die if we leave him!" Glenna wailed, twisting her head around for one last look at the man she loved. "If his wounds don't kill him wild animals will. Please, Duke! Please don't leave him like this. I'll go back with you peacefully if only you save Kane." Her entreaties earned her nothing but a nasty laugh from Duke and a slap to her horse's rump by the man directly behind her, causing the bay to move smartly ahead.

The trip back to Denver was a nightmare in which Glenna could think of nothing but Kane lying on the ground, his lifeblood slowly spilling from his gravely injured body into the frozen earth. He was dead! Because of her Kane had died before she had the opportunity to tell him her reasons for marrying Judd. Had she even thought to tell him she loved him? How could life be so unfair?

Because of the lateness of the hour they were forced to camp beside the trail that night. Glenna was untied long enough to see to her needs and eat the makeshift meal provided by Duke. But food held no appeal as Glenna shoved it aside, glaring hatefully at Duke. "Murderer!" she spat, her body rigid with contempt.

Duke smirked. "You'd better eat, Mrs. Martin. You'll need your strength to face what the boss has planned for you. He won't be too pleased when he learns we found you with Kane Morgan."

Glenna chose not to respond, staring sullenly into space. Duke glanced surreptitiously about him, noted that his men were grouped around the campfire, then sidled closer to whisper in Glenna's ear. "There is an alternative to facing Judd, you know," he hinted slyly. Glenna regarded him coldly. "I've got some money put aside, quite a lot should the truth be known. If you agree to come with me, be my woman, I'll forget all about Judd Martin. I always did fancy you, Mrs. Martin—Glenna. We could go east, west, anywhere you say."

"You're . . . you're despicable, Duke! What

makes you think I'd trade one depraved animal for another?''

Undaunted, Duke nuzzled the fragrant red curls tumbling in delightful disarray about her shoulders. ''You'd have my promise that I'd treat you right, while you have no guarantee that Judd will do the same.''

''Don't touch me, Duke!'' Glenna hissed angrily, impaling him with spikes of green flame. ''Do you think I could ever forget that you killed Kane? I'll take my chances with Judd.''

Put off by the open hostility and contempt she displayed, Duke spun away, jumping to his feet. ''You've made your choice, Mrs. Martin,'' he flung at her. ''Before Judd finishes with you you'll wish you'd listened to me.''

Sour-faced and grim he joined the men sitting around the fire, thinking how much he'd like to be in on the punishment doled out by Judd, knowing it wouldn't be very pleasant. Shortly afterwards one of the men approached Glenna, retied her hands and feet and carried away her plate of untouched food. Soon they were settling down for the night and Glenna squirmed uncomfortably on the cold ground, prepared to spend a miserable few hours tyring to keep warm. She was surprised when Duke sauntered over and flung a blanket over her shivering form.

''The boss said you were to be returned in good health.''

Dressed as she was in boy's clothing with a hat jammed down over her ears, completely concealing her red hair, Glenna's return to Denver passed unnoticed. With little regard for ceremony she was hustled into the Red Garter, escorted upstairs and into the room she had previously occupied, and locked in. Shortly afterwards a bath was carried up to her and while her hands moved mechanically with the mundane chores of bathing and dressing, her stomach churned with apprehension and her nerves grew taut as a bowstring.

Was Judd well enough to see her? Glenna wondered distractedly. Would he have her beaten? Or turn her over to the marshal? Why had he provided her with a bath and given her ample time to rest before apprising her of her fate? Perhaps Judd lay near death, she reasoned, and no one knew what to do with her. Not that she cared what the future brought. With Kane dead—surely he had been too gravely wounded to survive—Glenna's life held no meaning. She had caused his death as surely as if she had pulled the trigger.

For days Glenna languished in her room, her meals brought to her by either Duke or another of Judd's hired men. From Judd she heard nothing. Once she gathered her courage and asked Duke if Judd were dead.

"Don't you wish," grinned Duke nastily.

After that she did not bother to ask, patiently resigned to whatever fate willed. One day she could have sworn she heard Sal's voice wafting up the stairs and through the hallway. But when nothing came of it she decided that in her desperation she had conjured up the voice of her friend.

Never had Glenna felt so bereft, so completely alone. Kane's death had robbed her of the will to live. In her heart she knew she could love no other man and deplored the anguish she had caused him by marrying Judd. She had deliberately ruined the happiness they might have shared together as man and wife and inadvertently caused his death. Had she been wiser and stronger she would have thrown caution to the wind and refused Judd, letting the cards fall where they may. Yet in her heart she knew she would never have allowed Sal to be harmed as long as the choice lay with her. To a ruthless man like Judd, murdering innocent people to get what he wanted was a way of life. Hadn't her own father been a victim of Judd's foul play?

Finally the day came when Glenna was ushered to Judd's room. He appeared pale and wan and she experienced a pang of remorse, until she remembered that he probably would have killed her if she hadn't stopped him as she did. Though the wound she dealt him had not proved fatal his great loss of blood rendered him weak as a newborn kitten. To add insult to injury an infection had immediately set in causing him to burn with fever then shake with chills.

Finally brought face to face with her husband, Glenna could not force herself to feel sorrow at what she had done. Because of Judd Kane was dead, coldly shot and his body left for wild animals to devour. The thought was nearly more than she could bear.

Judd Martin was a mere shadow of the man he once was. For twenty-four hours after his stabbing he hovered near death. Who would think such an innocuous weapon could inflict go grievous a wound? Had he been allowed to bleed but a few minutes more, the doctor had told him, it would have been too late. At least that old coot Wiley Wilson had redeemed himself by showing up at a crucial time demanding to see Judd, alerting Duke to his great need. And now the woman responsible for his near demise stood before him, unrepentant and dry-eyed, contempt visible in every line of her tense body.

Glenna stood ramrod straight, chin tilted defiantly, hands clenched at her sides. "What are you going to do to me, Judd?" Though she tried desperately, she could not control the slight quiver in her voice. Not that it really mattered, she thought dismally. What happened to her was trifling indeed compared to what Kane had suffered.

Judd must have glimpsed the despair and finality in her face, and for a brief moment his eyes softened.

Though Judd knew she had been the cause of his suffering and pain, he still wanted the lovely witch. For she had truly bewitched him. He had searched his mind long and hard for a fit punishment, one deserving of all he had endured at her hands. One by one they were all discarded. Perhaps the best punishment would be no punishment at all, he mused thoughtfully.

"Does it make you happy to think you nearly brought about my death?" he rasped weakly.

"Does it make you happy to kill a man?" she countered defiantly.

"Ah, yes, Kane Morgan, your lover. I didn't order his death, you know," revealed Judd. "In fact, I had no idea you were with the man. I thought he was still back east."

"But you're not sorry he's dead," accused Glenna, her voice dripping venom.

"That's neither here nor there," shrugged Judd, the effort bringing a wince of pain to his face. It was obvious the interview was rapidly draining his meager resources. "What puzzles me most is what I'm to do with you. What do you suggest, my dear? Do you think you should go unpunished?"

"Do what you will, Judd. It matters little to me," shrugged Glenna carelessly.

"Did you love him so much, Glenna?"

Slowly Glenna nodded, the lump in her throat preventing her from uttering a word. An angry flush suffused Judd's face.

"Duke!" Judd called abruptly, startling Glenna when he fell back against the pillow, his face suddenly paling from red to ashen.

Duke came bounding in, glaring at Glenna reproachfully. "What is it, boss? Should I call the doctor?"

"No," Judd gasped, his voice a hoarse whisper. "Get her out of here." He nodded toward Glenna.

"Lock her in her room. I don't want to see her again until I'm ready to deal with her."

"That's it?" Duke grumbled. "Just lock her in her room? She deserves—"

"I'm aware of what she deserves," Judd grimaced. "Until I decide what to do with her she's to come to no harm. Do you understand?"

Duke nodded, and shortly Glenna found herself being hustled back to the same room and four walls she had stared at for days, her fate still undecided. Which in truth was the worst fate of all.

While Judd lay recuperating a slow transformation altered his attitude. Not that he was changed overnight from a ruthless gambler with little respect for life into a soul of kindness, but rather the change was in how he came to regard Glenna and their future together, if he decided there was one. Having nearly met his death at her hands he felt something akin to remorse at the vile way he had treated her that night she had stabbed him, which truly puzzled him. He had literally backed her into a corner and forced her to lash out at him in order to save her life, for as drunk as he was he might have killed her when he learned Morgan had already partaken of what rightly belonged to him. Learning that he wouldn't be the first with her had driven him beyond sanity.

It galled him beyond measure that he still wanted her. Yet want her he did. Wanted her warm and willing in his bed. Witchery, sorcery, call it what you like. Judd Martin, womanizer, gambler, schemer, had met his match in a red-headed virago who had somehow gotten under his skin. With Kane Morgan no longer a contender for her favors Judd intended to have her, in his bed and in his life.

Still the question remained. Should he punish Glenna? Hell no! he argued with himself. Did he want to keep her with him even if it meant using unscrupulous methods? This time the answer was a resounding yes. Call it lust, call it possessiveness, maybe even love, he thought perversely, but one day he'd have Glenna O'Neill where he wanted her. Exactly how he would accomplish this miracle was unclear, and no doubt would take time. But Judd Martin had time to spare.

16

During the two long months it took Judd to recuperate, boredom and restlessness became Glenna's constant companions. While Judd regained his former robust health, Glenna grew increasingly wan and listless. Completely recovered, Judd now faced the problem of deciding upon Glenna's fate. Frantically, he searched for a way to convince her to willingly remain at his side and share his bed though he knew she professed nothing but contempt for him. So far the answer to his dilemma had escaped him. Until Glenna herself gave it to him.

What Glenna only began to suspect after an entire month of seeing no one but Duke and an occasional maid, became an absolute certainty before another month had elapsed. She was pregnant with Kane's child! Conceived that rapturous night spent in his arms at Golden Promise. Unexpectedly she was presented with a reason for living at a time when she thought her life at an end. For the first time since Kane's death she truly cared what happened to her for she was determined to fight like a tigress to keep Kane's child safely within her.

Her thoughts consumed with Kane's babe as well as her own plight, Glenna was totally unprepared to find Judd standing just inside her room, his back to the door. So immersed was she in her thoughts that she had not heard him enter. Being ignorant of Judd's plans for her was the worst torture imaginable, but then she supposed Judd already knew that. It was the way he operated.

He looked a thousand times better than he had weeks ago lying in bed all white-faced and weak. With a sense of fatalism she squared her small shoulders and faced him defiantly. "You're looking better, Judd," she intoned dryly.

Judd smiled, sauntering into the room with much of his old cockiness restored. "That's quite a concession coming from you, Glenna." Though she wanted desperately to turn and run she bravely held her ground, giving Judd ample cause to admire her courage. What a mate she'd make for him, he thought with a sense of wonder. No other woman had inspired him to make such a statement. And to think he had once considered her unworthy of his regard and felt no desire for her. What a fool he had been!

"Have you come to a decision?" was her only comment.

"About what?"

She looked at him austerely, waiting, unyielding, stubbornly defensive. She was a woman with a child to protect.

While Judd had not actually come to a firm decision concerning Glenna he had spent long hours during his recuperation considering every aspect of their relationship to date. It came as no surprise when he realized he had given her nothing of himself to admire. Would she think differently if he showed her a another side of himself, a side rarely seen by any of his friends? "Regardless of what you think I'm not out for vengeance, Glenna," he said, shocking her to the core. "I won't harm you."

Glenna's startled face betrayed her skepticism. "What are you up to, Judd? Have you forgotten so soon that you nearly died at my hand?"

"I've forgotten nothing," he admitted grimly. "As I recall, your attack was not without provocation."

Stunned by Judd's statement, Glenna cried out, "Am I free to go? Is that what you are telling me?"

"No! Never! You're my wife and my wife you'll remain. I want you to be a real wife to me. In every sense of the word."

Now it was Glenna's turn to protest, using his very words. "No! Never! I love Kane! I'll always love him."

"Kane Morgan is dead," Judd goaded cruelly, struggling to contain his anger in a fruitless attempt to present a new image. "You have nothing, no one. You could learn to love me, my dear, if only you'd allow yourself to."

"Love you? Bah! You flatter yourself, Judd. Even if you didn't order Kane's death you still were responsible for having my father killed. I don't forget or forgive so easily."

"Contrary to your beliefs I had nothing to do with your father's death," Judd contended smoothly.

"I don't believe you!" spat Glenna scornfully. "You and Wiley planned it all. You found out all about Da's new claim, and the fact that he found the mother lode. You married me in order to gain control of that claim. Why did you see fit to murder Da? Obviously it gained you nothing."

"I knew nothing about your father's death until after it happened, having only a nodding acquaintance with Wiley Wilson at the time," Judd explained cautiously. "He happened to be in the assayer's office when Paddy brought in those rich samples, naturally thinking they were from Golden Promise and that your father had finally found the mother lode.

"Wiley had no idea Paddy sold his claim to Eric Carter, or that he filed a new claim. That came later. Intending only to frighten Paddy into surrendering his claim, Wiley and his two partners waited until he left town then jumped him, demanding he sign the deed to Golden Promise over to them. When Paddy insisted he longer longer owned the claim Wiley lost his temper and killed him. That's when Wiley came to me. He was scared and thought I'd help him in return for his information about Paddy's rich find."

"You knew Wiley killed Da yet you did nothing about it," accused Glenna hotly.

"Of that I'm guilty."

"And you killed Eric Carter to get the deed to Golden Promise."

"That was an unfortunate accident. Duke is paid to protect me. He knew I was unarmed."

"You planned it all!"

"You can't prove that, my dear. It was self-defense. Duke thought Carter was drawing on me," Judd allowed. "I'll admit I'm greedy and calculating but that's one murder I won't confess to."

"You'd have killed Sal for no reason other than that she was my friend."

"You don't know that. I threatened to have her killed. There's a big difference between that and the actual deed."

"I don't trust you, Judd. And I don't believe you. Even if you did have nothing to do with Da's murder—which is highly unlikely—your words fail to convince me that you are innocent of any wrongdoing. I want nothing further to do with you."

The strain of attempting to portray someone completely out of character was beginning to take its toll on

Judd. Never before had he been obliged to answer to anyone save himself for his actions. His intense desire for Glenna had wrought a change he cared little for. And truthfully, he was at the end of his tether, fully aware that nothing he said seemed to make a modicum of difference in her opinion of him.

"Damn it, Glenna!" he exploded in a fit of pique. "I've made every effort to treat you with kindness. To show you in deed as well as word that I . . . I've come to care for you. I want you. I want you to be a real wife to me and forget all what went before. But now I'm beginning to lose patience with you."

Rendered speechless by Judd's astonishing declaration, Glenna burst out laughing. "You care for me?" she gasped, panting with hilarity. "You are incapable of caring for anyone but yourself!"

Red dots of rage exploded behind Judd's eyes and he grasped Glenna's arms and pulled her close, molding her soft body to his. "I'll show you just how capable I am!" he shouted, lifting her off her feet and tossing her onto the bed, crushing her beneath him. "I'll make you forget Kane Morgan if it takes the rest of my life. I'm going to make love to you until you either beg for mercy or cry for more."

Glenna felt her bodice rip, cool air fanning her skin as Judd clawed at her clothing, determined that this time nothing would keep him from possessing his wife. The sight of tempting mounds of tender flesh caused him to groan aloud. It was all he had dreamed about for weeks. His mouth lowered to possess the cherry buds cresting those glorious peaks while Glenna struggled frantically against his ardent assault.

"No, Judd, please!" Glenna begged, pinned helplessly beneath his straining body.

"I'd rather make tender love to you, Glenna," he panted raggedly, "but if you want it rough I'll gladly oblige. Sometimes it's better that way."

Glenna gasped and choked as her skirts were flung over her head. Then she felt Judd's hands groping between her legs, hurting her. Suddenly she thought of her baby, that tiny, unformed being resting beneath her heart whose life she was responsible for. Nothing must happen to Kane's baby! It was all she had left of him. Judd mustn't harm that precious life she nurtured.

"Judd, stop!" she cried out, her voice muffled by her skirt and petticoats. "Don't hurt me! I'm pregnant!"

Driven by lust, Judd nearly missed her last words, but when they finally reached his brain it was like a dash of cold water in his face. For weeks he had been searching for a way to force her to honor their marriage vows and she had unwittingly handed him the very weapon he needed. Raucous laughter bubbled from his lips as he threw himself onto the bed beside her. Smoothing her skirts down over her limbs, Glenna sat up, expecting anything but mirth in response to her startling announcement.

Greatly relieved, she wrongly assumed that Judd no longer wanted her now that she was carrying Kane's baby. Would he consent to let her go? She allowed herself a glimmer of hope. She waited for him to stop laughing, her body taut with apprehension.

"It's Morgan's brat, I presume," Judd finally said. There was a hint of something in his voice Glenna found difficult to decipher. An emotion akin to envy tinged with hate. She nodded, lumps as large as stones forming in her throat. It was still too painful to speak of the man she loved.

"Do you want this baby, my dear?" he asked slyly. Again Glenna nodded, trusting him not at all. And with good reason. "Then I suggest we have a long talk."

"I've nothing to say to you, Judd, except to demand that you leave my room."

"You're wrong, wife of mine," he mocked sarcastically. "You're married to me yet find yourself carrying another man's child. That alone is worthy of discussion."

"What is there to discuss? I'm having Kane's baby in seven months whether you like it or not. I assume you'll want me out of your life now and I'm perfectly willing to make my own way."

"You've got gumption, I'll give you that," Judd allowed grudgingly. "How do you propose to make a living? I'm sure Sal could make room for another whore but what happens when your belly gets too big to accommodate your customers?"

"You bastard! How dare you talk to me like that! Just let me go, I can take care of myself."

"I should beat you to within an inch of your life for what you've done," Judd taunted cruelly, "and no one would blame me. First you attempt to take my life and then you cuckold me. What do you think would happen to you if it was Morgan you wronged? I doubt he would be as lenient as I."

Glenna doubted it too. But Judd did nothing without a motive. What did he want from her? She found out all too soon.

"Women have been known to lose babies, you know," he hinted slyly. "I have complete control over you. If I found I no longer wanted you myself I could give you to Duke. He's long expressed a yen for you. You'll find him not so gentle as I. In his lust he might accidentally do you harm . . . or—" he paused dramatically, "harm your child. Is that what you want, my dear?"

Glenna gasped, clutching her stomach protectively. "You'd see an innocent babe harmed?"

"Not I, my dear, but Duke. He cares only for that soft white body of yours and his own satisfaction."

"What do you want from me, Judd? Why are you telling me all this?"

"Isn't it obvious, Glenna? I want your promise that you will be a wife to me in every way, and in return I'll swear to protect you and Morgan's child with my life. I'll see that no harm comes to either of you."

"And if I don't?"

"As I said before, Duke fancies you, so do a lot of other men I know. How long would you keep your baby with men lined up outside your door?"

"You heartless creep! Even you couldn't be so cruel."

"Try me and find out." Should the truth be known he doubted he could do it, but Glenna had no way of knowing that. "I care nothing for that brat you're carrying, it's you I want. But be a real wife to me and I'll treat it the same as the children we'll have together."

Glenna shuddered. Have Judd's children? Never! "You'll see that no harm comes to us?" she repeated, her mind working furiously. Judd nodded. Even if she promised her word would mean nothing because it was given under duress. But Judd need not know that. Yet if she agreed she didn't want him touching her intimately. No man but Kane had that right and he was dead.

"Before I agree to anything," Glenna said evasively, "I want your word on something."

"Go ahead and ask, I'm in an expansive mood right now and can afford to be generous." And in truth he was. If her request wasn't too outlandish he'd grant it. If need be he'd promise to harm neither Glenna nor her child, but once it was born he intended to farm it out to people who would raise it as their own. He would put his own baby in her belly to take its place; one every year if that's what she wanted. He'd make damn sure she'd be too busy to think about Morgan or his child.

"I don't want you touching me until my baby is born," Glenna blurted out defiantly. "I'll be your wife, but in name only until after I've recovered from childbirth.'' That should give her plenty of time to find a way to leave Judd, she thought deviously. ''And I won't be shut up here any longer,'' she added for good measure. ''I want to be able to come and go as I please.''

Judd eyed her narrowly, his gaze cool and assessing. When he finally made love to her, he decided irritably, he wanted it to be with nothing on her mind but him. He knew she still mourned for Kane Morgan and worried about the baby she carried. He prided himself on his prowess in bed and taking Glenna now would do nothing for his male ego. If need be he could make do with whores until she was rid of her burden. Besides, he thought distastefully, soon her belly would be too big an obstacle to surmount. If it gained him a willing wife he could afford to be generous, at the same time giving her reason to be grateful.

''All right, my dear, have it your way. Go ahead and revel in your pregnancy, but afterwards, you're all mine. Agreed?''

''Agreed,'' lied Glenna, crossing her fingers behind her back.

''Just keep one thing in mind, Mrs. Martin,'' he grated threateningly. ''Double-cross me and I'll never trust you again. Not only will you be made to suffer but so will your brat. Understand?''

''Yes!'' Glenna hissed contemptuously. Why did you have to die, Kane? her heart cried out.

''Then let's seal the bargain,'' he grinned, pulling her into his arms, ''with a kiss.'' And kiss her he did, deeply, crushing her mouth beneath his, parting her lips with his stabbing tongue. It was a cruel kiss, one without tenderness, clearly meant to prove his mastery over her.

She felt his manhood against her thigh and turned cold as stone, a lump of clay beneath his hands and mouth. Just when she thought she had bargained in vain Judd broke off the kiss and shoved her away.

"Remember that, Mrs. Martin," he jeered crudely. "One day you'll beg me to bed you. You're a woman newly awakened to sexual pleasure and one day you will plead for me to satisfy you."

Cringing inwardly at the thought, Glenna said nothing, glaring balefully as he left the room. Though Glenna's imprisonment had ended, her struggle to survive had just begun.

Glenna put Judd's words to the test almost immediately as she left the Red Garter that next day, visiting the dressmaker and ordering an entire wardrobe to fit her growing figure and charging it to Judd Martin. It serves him right, she thought spitefully as she chose only the best materials. Next she purchased soft white goods with which to make baby clothing. By the time she returned word had circulated that she was expecting.

After the success of her first outing, Glenna was certain she wasn't being followed and immediately launched a plan to visit Marshal Bartow, certain she could depend on his help once she told him about Judd and Wiley and how they schemed to get her father's holdings.

The next day it snowed heavily so it was several days before Glenna could put her plan into action. As luck would have it Judd intercepted her as she left the saloon. "Where are you going, Glenna?"

"To buy some thread I had forgotten to purchase the other day. I'd like to start making a layette."

"Judging from the size of the bills that have been arriving since your last shopping spree I had assumed you'd forgotten nothing."

"Would you prefer I not spend any of your money, Judd?" she asked sweetly.

"Spend away, my dear," he smiled blandly.

"Come spring we're certain to find the mother lode and then we'll have all the money we need or want. Don't tire yourself," he added with mock concern.

Taking a circuitous route and keeping an eye peeled lest Judd decide to have her followed at the last minute, Glenna soon stood before the marshal's office, pausing a few moments to gather her wits before stepping inside. The man sitting behind the desk looked up, smiling when he recognized her.

"Good afternoon, Mrs. Martin. To what do I owe this pleasure?"

"You're not Marshal Bartow!" blurted out Glenna, recognizing instantly a man she'd seen many times at the Red Garter. Usually he was seen talking to Judd with whom he appeared to enjoy a close friendship.

"I'm glad you noticed," laughed the man, who was much younger than the previous marshal. "I'm Marshal Dawson. I've seen you many times at the Red Garter. I was lucky enough to be present when you married Judd Martin."

"What happened to Marshal Bartow?"

"Retired. A month ago. I was appointed by the town council to fill in. Did you wish to see Bartow about anything special?"

"N-no," Glenna stammered, confused. This unexpected turn of events put a whole new light on things. Dawson was obviously Judd's man and would report back to him should she tell him what was on her mind. "This is just a social call," she improvised. "I had no idea Marshal Bartow retired. He's an old friend of the family. I'll just call on him at home."

"Won't do you any good," Dawson grinned. "He took his wife back east to visit their daughter. Are you certain I can't help you?"

"Positive," Glenna insisted curtly. "Good day to you, sir."

"Good day, Mrs. Martin," Dawson smirked. "Come back any time."

Damn! Damn! Damn! Glenna silently raged all the way back to the Red Garter. What rotten luck! Was her life to be one bitter disappointment after another? She desperately wanted to visit Sal but snow began to fall again and she reluctantly returned to the saloon.

Two days later Judd did something that stunned her. He bought a house.

"A saloon is no place to bring up a child," he explained tersely. "Nor a proper atmosphere for an expectant mother. I think you'll like the house. I've even hired a full complement of servants to staff it. We should be quite comfortable there."

"We?" squeaked Glenna.

"Of course. Did you expect to live alone? I've turned much of the running of the Red Garter over to Duke so I will no longer be tied to this place full-time. I'm independently wealthy, expecting my first child and mean to spend more time with my bride."

His words offered her little comfort for she knew exactly how he felt about her pregnancy and Kane's child. Did he mean to keep her under his thumb by not letting her out of his sight? Had Marshal Dawson told him of her visit and was this Judd's way of showing her he didn't trust her? If he remained constantly underfoot how would she manage to escape? All these questions and more raced through her brain.

Glenna had to admit the house Judd bought was a vast improvement over the boisterous atmosphere of the Red Garter. They moved in during the first break in the weather, which had been terrible of late. The city appeared surrounded by an endless vista of white, beautiful but confining. The servants Judd chose were well-trained, the house itself tastefully furnished, and if Glenna found anything to complain about it was Judd and the way he goaded her constantly with his cloying attention.

Glenna discovered Judd's house, sitting on a hill overlooking the city, was but a few short blocks away from where Sal conducted business, and she yearned to see her friend again, but she did not relish trudging through the snow. When she voiced her desire to Judd he coldly informed her that his wife had no business consorting with whores. So she bided her time, waiting for a day to plan her visit when duty claimed Judd's presence and weather permitted a trek through the snow.

Dressed in a flowing dressing gown, despite it being nearly noon, Sal answered Glenna's knock. The sight of Glenna standing on her doorstep rendered her nearly speechless.

"Glenna! Thank God you're all right. I've been so worried about you. I tried to see you several times but that bastard Duke turned me away. Finally I gave up."

"As you can see, Sal, I'm fine."

"Come in, come in," Sal urged, pulling her inside. "God, it's good to see you! But whatever happened to Kane? The last time I saw him he was chasing after you. Obviously he didn't find you 'cause you're with Judd again."

She ushered Glenna into her office and shut the door, scrutinizing her thoroughly. "Really, Sal, I'm fine," Glenna insisted, flushing.

"What did Judd do to you when he caught up with you?" Sal asked, concern coloring her words. "Why wouldn't he let me see you?"

"Actually," Glenna explained slowly, "Judd did nothing to me except keep me locked in my room for weeks and weeks until I thought I would die of boredom."

Amazement furrowed Sal's smooth brow. "Honey,

I know Judd and he's not one to forget and forgive so easily. And what about Kane? Where has he been all this time?"

"Oh, Sal, he's dead! Kane is dead. Duke killed him."

"Dead? Kane dead? Oh no, honey, you must be mistaken."

"There's no mistake, Sal. I saw the whole thing. Kane lay on the ground bleeding to death from a gunshot wound when Duke dragged me off, leaving him for wild animals to finish off." Tears flowed down her cheeks in torrents, moving Sal to offer comfort.

"Glenna, think positive. A miracle could happen."

"A miracle? Bah! If something like that did happen where is Kane now?"

Sal had no answer. "Is that why Judd decided not to punish you? Because Kane is no longer a threat to him? Did he know you and Kane loved each other?"

"If he didn't, he does now," Glenna admitted wryly. Sal cocked her head, waiting for Glenna to explain. "I'm carrying Kane's child."

Sal paled visibly. "And you admitted it to Judd?" Glenna nodded. "I'm surprised he didn't kill you." She regarded Glenna narrowly. "He wants something from you, that's why he hasn't harmed you! What is it, honey? What did you promise Judd in return for your child's safety?" she asked astutely.

"I . . . I swore I'd be a . . . wife to him."

"But you're already his wife."

Glenna shook her head. "Not in the way he means."

"He wants you to share his bed," Sal snorted in disgust.

"Exactly," Glenna admitted dryly.

"Why did Judd marry you?" Sal asked curiously.

"For Da's claim."

"Golden Promise?"

"No. Judd forced me into marriage to gain control of a new claim Da filed shortly before his death."

"And you agreed? Somehow that surprises me."

"I didn't want to, Sal. But Kane wasn't here and I had no one to turn to for help."

"What about the marshal?"

"There . . . there's another reason. Judd threatened to . . . to kill you if I didn't comply with his wishes."

Comprehension dawned. "You went through all this to protect me?" Glenna nodded as misty tears blurred Sal's vision. "I don't deserve a friend like you, Glenna. I only hope that one day I can show you how much your friendship means to me."

They embraced affectionately as Sal wiped blindly at the tears forming in the corners of her eyes. "You've always been my friend, Sal," Glenna smiled through a watery mist.

"What are you going to do now, honey? Do you trust Judd to keep his word? Has he already demanded payment?"

"Somehow I convinced him to wait until after my baby is born to . . . to come to my bed. And, no, I don't trust him to keep his word. He'd do well not to take mine seriously either. I'll never consent to share his bed. One day when he least expects it I'll just quietly disappear. I'm no longer guarded. He thinks that pregnancy has clipped my wings. He knows I have no money, nowhere to go, nothing. That's why I'm confiding in you, Sal. One day soon I might need your help."

"You have my help and anything else you might need. But I think you should talk to the marshal first."

"Marshal Bartow has retired."

"I heard that."

"One of Judd's men has been appointed to fill Bartow's term. I've already thought of asking him for help but the moment I saw Dawson sitting behind the marshal badge I knew I'd find no help there."

"If only Kane were still alive," Sal sighed regretfully. "What a waste."

"What!" cried a voice behind them. "Kane Morgan is dead?"

Both Sal and Glenna swiveled to face the woman who stood in the doorway. They were so intent upon their conversation that they hadn't heard Pearl enter the room.

"I didn't hear you knock, Pearl," Sal reprimanded coolly.

"There's no need," flung back Pearl defiantly. "I still own an interest in this establishment. And for your information, I did knock but apparently you didn't hear me. Now, what were you saying about Kane being dead?"

"It's true," Glenna answered, meeting Pearl's hateful glare. "I saw him die myself. He was shot by Duke and left in the woods to die."

"It's all your fault!" Pearl spat venomously. "Wasn't one man enough for you? Did you have to claim the two most eligible men in town?"

"That's enough, Pearl!" Sal ordered curtly. "It wasn't Glenna's fault and she's suffered enough already without your recriminations. Besides, Kane made it clear he wanted nothing to do with you, though Lord knows you tried hard enough to lure him to your bed. Men like Kane don't marry whores."

"Is that why he didn't marry Glenna?" Pearl asked sweetly, malice coloring her word. Then she turned abruptly on her heel and stormed from the room, leaving Glenna and Sal staring after her in astonishment.

Shortly afterwards Glenna left, promising to return soon, only the weather failed to cooperate and it was nearly a month before Glenna called on Sal again. By this time she had grown thoroughly sick of having Judd dogging her steps, his gaze lingering obsessively on her growing girth. By now well into her fourth month, Glenna's breasts severely strained the seams of her bodice but her softly rounded stomach remained cleverly concealed beneath her full skirts. Although it wouldn't be long, Glenna conceded, before the bulge became obvious to all.

Glenna had yet to experience the first stirrings of life but anxiously awaited that event, cherishing the tiny being growing within her as a remembrance of the man she loved.

So far Glenna had found little opportunity to flee, time and weather combining to work against her. It appeared Judd was taking no chances where she was concerned, keeping her under constant scrutiny at all times. Occasionally he left her for short periods while he conducted business, and Glenna kept a bag packed against just such an occurrence. But the time had yet to arrive for her to take advantage of his leaving. Judd's absences were usually of short duration and failed to coincide with the departure of the train, the mode of travel she intended to use to make good her escape.

In mid-February a brief respite in the weather occurred, resulting in a welcome thaw and milder temperatures. When Judd informed Glenna he had business in Pueblo and would be gone a few days, Glenna rejoiced, until she learned one of Judd's men would be keeping an eye on her. But it really didn't matter for somehow she'd find a way to leave Denver.

No sooner had Judd's train chugged out of the depot than Glenna was walking briskly down the street toward Sal's house. Behind her trailed the man hired to guard her. Suddenly she made a sharp turn down an alley, coming out on the street housing the general store. Glancing surreptitiously about as she entered, Glenna breathed a sigh of relief when she noted that her guard had yet to emerge from the alley. She spoke briefly to the clerk then began wandering aimlessly around the tables laden with merchandise, pretending to study each item intently. The moment the clerk's attention was turned to another customer Glenna scurried toward the back of the room, slipping unnoticed through the curtained doorway and out the back door into the alley. Fifteen breathless minutes later she was ushered into Sal's house and safely ensconced in her office.

"That is it, Sal," Glenna revealed excitedly. "Judd is gone and won't be back for several days and I've managed to elude the man guarding me. While he's out scouring the town for me I hope to make good my escape. Even the time is working to my advantage. The next train leaves within the hour and I intend to be on it."

"Where will you go?"

"Wherever the train is headed."

Sal stooped before the safe sitting in the corner, fiddled with the dial and swung open the heavy door. "How much—"

A high, piercing scream originating from the front of the house halted Sal's words in mid-sentence. "What in the hell—" she muttered, rising to investigate the cause of the commotion. She rushed out the door followed closely by Glenna. When they reached the front hall both women froze in their tracks, their mouths wide open in shock.

Standing in the hall looking pale and pounds lighter stood Kane. Not a ghost but a flesh and blood Kane who was being literally devoured by Pearl who clung to him as if she never intended to let him go.

"Kane!" squealed Sal, every bit as excited as Pearl. "You're alive! Thank God!"

Glenna could do little more than stand as if rooted to the spot and stare. Kane alive? How could it be? With her own eyes she watched helplessly as his life's blood drained from his body. Then Kane saw her, poised on the balls of her feet. Rudely he shoved Pearl aside, opening his arms to her. Glenna took one shaky step forward, then another, but that was as far as she got before great waves of vertigo assailed her and her head began to spin dizzily as she desperately struggled against the darkness threatening to engulf her. She began her slow descent to the ground long before she reached those welcoming arms. and Kane reached her long before she touched the ground, scooping her limp body tenderly in his arms and carrying her to one of the empty bedrooms indicated by a concerned Sal.

Slowly coming out of her swoon, Glenna's blurry eyes focused on Kane. He sat on the bed in the garishly furnished room murmuring soothing words she failed to understand. Tentatively, afraid lest he disappear in a puff of smoke, Glenna reached out and touched his cheek, her eyes misty pools of emerald green.

"I'm real, love," Kane said, gently kissing the fingers that lingered on his lips. "Do you think you could get rid of me so easily?"

"Kane, Kane!" Glenna rejoiced. "How? Why? I saw your wounds and the blood pouring from them. Where have you been? How is it possible?"

"One question at a time, love," laughed Kane, helping Glenna to sit up. "First, I owe my life to Zach and Will, the two miners your . . . husband saw fit to dismiss." Glenna winced at the word. "After they were let go they staked a claim not far from Golden Promise and built a cabin, intending to pass the winter in the mountains. They were out hunting the day I was shot by Duke. They heard the shots and found me bleeding to death."

"Oh, Kane, I wanted to die myself when I thought you were dead. Duke dragged me away and left you to the mercy of wild animals."

"You were the one I was concerned about, sweetheart. Thank God Judd did you no harm. All those weeks I lay on my back weak as a kitten I imagined all sorts of terrible things."

"I'm . . . fine, really, Kane," Glenna hesitated.

"I lay in a stupor for days," Kane continued thoughtfully. "Many times Zach nearly gave up on me but my concern for you kept me going and gave me the will to recover. Slowly I began to mend but it was weeks before my strength returned. I lost a tremendous amount of blood but Zach proved a skilled healer. He dug out the bullets and cauterized the wounds to stop the bleeding. I owe him my life."

"I feel as if I'm just awakening from a bad dream," Glenna sighed happily. "But you look so pale."

"Enough of me," Kane said, his gray eyes intent upon her face. "At the first break in the weather I left the mountains and came directly here, hoping Sal might know what became of you. Imagine my surprise to find you standing before me. Have you been staying with Sal?"

There was much Glenna had to tell Kane, but not yet. "Later, Kane," she murmured, nuzzling his neck affectionately. "Kiss me, my love, please kiss me. I still can't believe you're alive."

Happy to comply, Kane captured her lips in a demanding kiss and she responded instantly, her head tilted backwards and her lips parted hungrily to take him. He obliged by slipping his tongue between her teeth, exploring the velvet moistness within. The kiss held, deepened, their breaths mingling as passion exploded.

His hands roved restlessly over her body as his lips left hers and traced the curve of her cheek, then trailed down her white throat and across her smooth bosom.

His nimble fingers unfastened the hooks that held her bodice, slipping it away, and the chemise with it. He lifted her skirt and his hand went beneath it, stroking the smoothness of her thighs, the soft mound between them. He felt her moistness between his fingers and his own passion mounted.

Then as if by magic her dress lay in a heap on the floor, soon followed by Kane's restricting clothing. His lips lowered to taste a swollen nipple and caressed it with his tongue. Her hands tangled in his thick black hair and drew him closer, closer . . .

She could feel his response to her, feel the tension in the lean, hard body she clutched ecstatically to her own. She rejoiced at his swift response to her kisses, the slow exploration of his tongue between her parted lips, the bold thrust of his manhood against her thigh. His hands slipped downward over the soft bulge of her stomach and he paused, frowning thoughtfully.

"You're putting on weight, sweetheart," he teased. "Even your breasts seem larger, but I like them that way. Your nipples are like dark red cherries, but taste even sweeter. Dear God, how I love you!"

He slipped downward, nuzzling the soft fur shielding her womanhood, and then his lips found her, parting the tender folds with his tongue. Glenna shuddered, all thoughts focused on her body and what Kane was making her feel. "Kane!" she gasped, ecstasy spiraling through her. The first penetration of his tongue sent a searing jolt through her veins which stole the breath from her body.

Then a moan of disappointment escaped her throat as Kane's lips left her and he surged forward, filling her, joining them, making them one. With words, sighs, gasps, she encouraged him, confessing that he brought her boundless pleasure. He moved in an easy rhythm, drawing her inexorably into the vortex of the tornado he was creating with his driving hips. His head rolled from side to side and she breathed erratically as his mouth feasted upon breasts swollen with passion.

"Come with me, Glenna," he panted, his eyes glazing over with ecstasy. "Let go, love."

He strained over her, his loins nearly bursting, his tempo increasing. Trembling on the edge of ecstasy, pleasure blazed through her like a bright flame. Her dramatic response drove him over the brink, unable to hold back a moment longer as his hoarse cries of joy filled her ears.

"I love you," she whispered as the earth settled down around them. "I love you, Kane."

17

Momentarily sated, Kane lay on his side, idly stroking Glenna's stomach. "How did you get away from Judd?" he asked, his curiosity far from satisfied. Knowing the gambler as he did Kane doubted he would allow Glenna to walk out of his life so easily. Especially after her attack upon him. Something just didn't sound right and he wanted to know what had happened.

Glenna smiled a secret smile. Now she would tell him about the baby and watch his face glow with happiness, and shock, no doubt. They hadn't ever discussed children but she assumed Kane wanted them. Didn't all men want an heir? No time like the present to find out, she decided.

"Gaining a little weight, aren't you?" Kane asked again before Glenna could form the words she longed to say. His hand paused on the slight mound of her belly, a puzzled frown wrinkling his brow. Could it be? Was Glenna . . . ?

Glenna gulped nervously. "That's what I wanted to tell you, Kane, only I didn't know how to begin."

His gray eyes went murky as a frisson of apprehension stiffened his spine. "Suppose you start at the beginning." A note of despair crept unbidden into his voice, but in Glenna's excitement over the news she was about to impart, it went unnoticed.

"I'm pregnant, Kane, and I hope you—"

"You're carrying Martin's baby!" Kane's shocked voice accused unjustly. "You certainly wasted no time falling into his bed once you thought I was dead." Given Kane's frame of mind it followed naturally that he should assume the baby belonged to Judd, completely ignoring the fact that he might have fathered the child himself. Consumed by visions of Glenna lying in Judd Martin's arms, responding to him, conceiving his child, jealousy reared its head like an ugly monster, making coherent thought impossible.

"Kane! Oh no!"

"I can see I'm neither needed nor wanted in your life now. Go back to your husband where you belong, Glenna, and raise your child together."

Struggling into his pants and gathering up the rest of his clothes, Kane stomped from the room while Glenna was still stuttering out an explanation. Once again his hot temper and pride had sent him fleeing without allowing Glenna's words ample time to register. His name was still on her lips as he sprinted down the stairs past a surprised Sal and out the door, pulling on his clothes as he went.

"What in hell is the matter with him?" Sal asked Glenna as she barged into the room without bothering to knock. If she found it odd that Glenna lay naked in bed, she said nothing. In truth she had suspected such an outcome when she left Glenna and Kane alone. It was the strange ending to their reunion that she hadn't anticipated.

"Sal, what am I to do?" wailed Glenna, clenching her fists in frustration. "I started to tell Kane about the baby but he wouldn't listen. He thinks that Judd and I . . . that Judd is the father. How could he think such a thing when he knows how much I love him?"

"Because he thinks with his heart instead of his brain," Sal said, exasperated. "Don't cry, honey, he'll soon come to his senses and realize the baby is his."

"By then it will be too late," Glenna groaned in frustration. "I have to leave Denver before Judd returns. I intend to be on the next train out of town. If Kane doesn't want me I'll make my own way." Her chin rose belligerently as she hurriedly began to dress. She had another life to think of now and when Kane finally came to his senses he could damn well come looking for her.

"You already missed the train, honey," Sal imparted belatedly. "The next one's not due till morning."

"Oh God," Glenna moaned, thoroughly disheartened. "Can I stay here, Sal? If I go home now there is no way I can slip away tomorrow. After today Judd's man isn't likely to be so careless again and I doubt I'll have the opportunity to leave."

"Sure, honey. Just stay put. No one needs to know you're here. I'll talk to the girls and caution them to keep quiet."

"Thanks, Sal. I don't know what—" An insistent clatter at the door prevented Glenna from finishing her sentence.

"What is it?" called Sal through the closed door.

"It's Pearl, Sal. Someone's here to see Glenna."

"Kane!" squealed Glenna, rushing to open the door. "He's come back, Sal!"

"Glenna, wait!"

But Sal's words of caution failed to register as Glenna flung open the door, gasping in shock at the hulking form of Judd's henchman, looking decidedly disgruntled at having been outsmarted by a mere woman. Her stricken gaze flew immediately to Pearl whose gloating smirk spoke volumes.

"Why, Pearl? Why did you do it?" Glenna choked out, her voice quivering as defeat stared her in the face.

"Damn you, Pearl!" Sal berated angrily. "Do you realize what you've just done?"

"Why no," replied Pearl with mock innocence. "When Bert came asking for Glenna I didn't think to lie. Why should I?"

"Why indeed?" muttered Sal darkly. "All right, Pearl, you can go now. I'll deal with you later."

A satisfied smile curving the corners of her mouth, Pearl nodded, quirked a slim brow at Glenna and left.

"I'll escort you home now, Mrs. Martin," Gordy announced gruffly, his eyebrows meeting at the bridge of his nose in a ferocious frown. "You shouda told me you wanted to visit Sal. I would have seen you got here safely."

"I did get here safely," Glenna retorted huffily. "And I wish to remain with Sal."

"I don't mean to argue with you, Mrs. Martin, but I've got my orders. The boss hired me to look after you in his absence and I don't think he'd like you associating with a bunch of whores. This is no place for a woman in . . . er . . . your condition."

Glenna flushed indignantly. Did everyone in Denver think she carried Judd's baby? But naturally Judd would want it that way. Sighing in resignation, Glenna nodded to Sal and prepared to leave with Gordy. Not only had she been betrayed by Kane but by Pearl as well—although Glenna had no idea what Pearl hoped to gain by her action—and she felt she no longer had a choice.

Sal watched in consternation as Glenna left with Bert, turning back once to wave. Cursing Kane for a fool, the madam decided to take matters into her own hands. Deliberately waiting until evening when Pearl was engaged by one of her many customers, Sal pulled on a hooded cape and slipped out the door into a waiting carriage she had ordered earlier. She was driven directly to the Red Garter where she sent her driver inside. A short time later he returned, shaking his head. From there they went to the Palace where her luck proved no better. Cursing the turn of events and all men in general, Sal reluctantly returned home.

Glenna's words boldly announcing her pregnancy still ringing in his ears, Kane rushed from Sal's house as if the devil himself were after him. Vaulting on his horse and spurring him ruthlessly, Kane relied on the cold wind and pelting sleet which had just begun to fall to blow the cobwebs from his muddled brain. He knew he shouldn't have run out on Glenna like he did but how could she expect him to remain while she carried Martin's baby? Did she have no feelings for him? Granted, she thought him dead, but did that make it right to fall into the gambler's arms so soon? Yet it wasn't as if she were betraying him, Kane realized with a smart of guilt. She was married to Martin, after all, and had every right in the world to conceive her husband's child. But damn it! Kane fumed unreasonably. By all rights the child should belong to him.

Bypassing the Red Garter, Kane reined his mount in front of the Silver Slipper, secured him to the hitching post and entered the warm, noisy atmosphere of the saloon, pulling his slouch hat over his face in order to avoid recognition. As it turned out no one spared a glance to the stranger who wandered in from the cold and ordered a bottle, drinking it in solitude at a corner table well out of the mainstream.

But despite his heroic efforts, Kane could not get drunk, failing miserably in his attempt to drown his sorrows in a bottle. Finally he gave up, returning to the Palace Hotel where to his surprise he learned his room was still being held in reserve for him with all his belongings and valuables intact. According to the desk clerk, it was assumed he would return. No one thought him dead but Glenna and the men involved in his shooting, for Judd had no wish to advertise the fact that Kane had been killed by one of his men. After paying his considerable tab he sought the sanctuary of his room only minutes after Sal had left.

Disdaining sleep, Kane set about packing his bags, intending to draw his money from the bank the next morning and leave Denver for good, for there was no longer a valid reason to remain. Once his packing was completed, he paced endlessly, lost in painful contemplation, picturing Glenna as she had looked when he made glorious love to her mere hours ago, her eyes dreamy, words of love tumbling from her lips. It couldn't have been pretense! Kane insisted stubbornly.

His mind worked furiously, bringing him abruptly to the realization that he had done Glenna a grave injustice by taking flight in anger without allowing her the courtesy of listening to her explanation. God! How could he be so obstinate? He loved her and owed her his trust. The least he could do was stand by her and take care of her if she needed him. But before his mind had time to adjust to that thought a knock sounded on his door. His hand on the gun strapped to his waist, Kane turned the knob. As far as he knew no one suspected he was in town but he was fully prepared to defend himself should it be necessary.

A man Kane recognized immediately stood in the opening. He had seen him many times evicting rowdy customers from Sal's Place. The man's name was Phil. "What can I do for you, Phil?" Kane asked curiously, intuitively aware that he had been sent by Sal.

"Sal sent me, Mr. Morgan. She wants to see you right away."

By now Kane's emotions were totally drained,

leaving him exhausted and out of sorts. "Can't it wait till morning?" he asked grumpily.

"I'm afraid not," Phil shrugged apologetically. "Sal said it was urgent."

"All right, Phil," Kane sighed wearily. "You go on ahead and I'll be there directly."

"If you don't mind, Mr. Morgan, I'll wait. Sal will have my hide if I come back without you."

Fifteen minutes later Kane sat facing Sal in her cozy office, thoroughly puzzled by her odd behavior as she glared daggers at him. "You really outdid yourself this time, Kane Morgan!" She spat the words out like bullets, each one finding its target.

"What in the hell are you talking about, Sal?" Kane shot back.

"I'm talking about Glenna, you bastard!"

"I should have known," muttered Kane. "I guess you know all about her being pregnant with Martin's child."

"I know Glenna's pregnant," Sal acknowledged. "She told me some time ago."

"What do you expect me to do about it? Rejoice?"

"A man usually does when he's told he's about to become a father."

"I'll leave the rejoicing to Martin, thank you."

"Then you're a bigger fool than I thought! The baby is yours."

"Mine? But how—"

"You could answer that better than me," snorted Sal disgustedly. "Do you consider yourself sterile, or unable to father a child? Did you completely ignore the fact that you might have impregnated Glenna when you found her at Golden Promise?" Kane opened his mouth to speak. "No, don't say anything, just listen," Sal ordered, jabbing a finger at his chest.

"Don't deny you bedded Glenna at Golden Promise 'cause I know better, randy goat that you are."

"If the baby is mine why didn't Glenna say so?" Kane asked belligerently, although in his heart he suspected Sal spoke the truth.

"Did you give her a chance?" retorted Sal scathingly. "You lit out of here like a scared rabbit."

Kane frowned, still not thoroughly convinced. "What makes Glenna so certain I fathered her child? It's entirely possible that Martin—"

"He's never touched her!"

"What! They've been married for months. Am I supposed to believe Glenna and Martin never shared a bed?"

"Believe what you want but it's the truth."

"You're treating me like an idiot, Sal. The man had every right in the world to bed her."

Sal frowned in consternation. "Didn't Glenna tell you why she married Judd?"

"Somehow she never got around to it."

"No wonder you're confused," Sal mused thoughtfully. "Let me explain. Judd forced her into marriage. He wanted her father's new claim and threatened to have me killed if she didn't comply with his wishes and marry him. When she still balked he used her love for you, telling her you'd be killed too. She had no choice. Judd backed her against a wall and demanded her surrender."

"So she married him," Kane said bitterly, sorry he had never killed Judd when he had the chance. "How is it that he never bedded her? He's hardly the type to deny himself the pleasure of her body."

"Why do you think she stabbed him?"

"He was beating her and she attempted to defend herself."

"You're damn right she was defending herself! Against his unwanted attentions. And after she was returned to Denver by Duke, Judd was too badly hurt to continue what he started. During his recovery Glenna discovered she was pregnant and received Judd's promise not to harm the baby or try to bed her until after she recovered from childbirth if she complied with his wishes and afterwards became a wife to him in every way. A promise she never intended to keep. She'd promise anything to protect your child."

Rendered speechless, Kane could only stand and stare stupidly at Sal. Everything she had told him made sense. Why did his pride and temper forever interfere with his common sense, causing him to reject Glenna for the second time without allowing her the benefit of the doubt? he asked himself glumly.

"I wouldn't blame her if she never wanted to see me again," lamented Kane, feeling nothing but disgust for himself.

"She loves you," Sal reminded him tersely. "What are you going to do about it? Judd is due back any day now."

"It wouldn't take much persuasion to kill Martin and make Glenna a widow," Kane mused thoughtfully.

"And rot in jail?" scoffed Sal. "Not on your life. Glenna needs you to protect her. Get her out of here as fast as you can."

"I love Glenna, Sal, and would do nothing to jeopardize her life or that of my unborn child. You're right, killing Martin would prove nothing. I've got to get Glenna away from Denver and Judd Martin."

"Kane, wait! There's a watchdog guarding Glenna."

Kane stopped, his mind racing furiously. "He shouldn't be too difficult to dispose of. How loyal is he to Martin?"

"That depends. Money buys a man's loyalty out here," Sal grinned mischievously. "Are you richer than Judd Martin?"

Kane stood beneath Glenna's window in the driving sleet, watching impatiently as the last light in the servants' quarters of the large house Sal directed him to blinked out. It was very late, long past midnight, and the streets in the quiet neighborhood Judd had chosen were deserted, all traffic driven inside by the lateness of the hour as well as the inclement weather. In one hand he clutched the key to the back door, meekly surrendered to him by Bert whose loyalty wavered dramatically once Kane mentioned the huge amount of money that would be his once he agreed to Kane's demands. Thank God he made a habit of carrying a large amount of emergency cash stashed in the false bottom of his suitcase and that it had remained untouched all this time in his room.

Slipping to the back of the house Kane inserted a key in the lock and held his breath, letting it out again when the door opened easily on well-oiled hinges. Having taken the precaution of learning the layout of the house from a cooperative Bert, Kane lit a match and proceeded cautiously through the kitchen and into the hall. The match flickered out but not before he noted the staircase leading off to the right.

Glenna slept fitfully, too distraught to allow the respite of healing sleep. Kane—why wouldn't he listen to her? Kane—why didn't he love her enough? Kane—Kane—Kane. Her mind was so filled with him that she dreamed she heard him calling to her, his voice tense with longing. Rolling over in bed her eyes popped open, certain she hadn't been dreaming. Somewhere on the wings of night came Kane's voice.

"Glenna, wake up, please!"

Rearing up, Glenna hugged the blanket to her breasts, suddenly alert, her ears trained on the soft murmuring coming from the other side of the door. Gingerly she climbed out of bed, trailing the blanket behind her. She knew the door was securely locked so felt no fear approaching it, only a strange prickle of apprehension. The disembodied voice called out again and Glenna's heart lurched with joy as recognition came swiftly.

"Kane?" Could it possibly be . . . ?

The answer was brief but authoritative. "It's Kane, Glenna. Let me in."

Releasing the lock Glenna stood back, allowing Kane to slip inside the darkened room. "Kane, how did you get in here?" Glenna asked incredulously.

"With a key," came the terse reply. "No more questions, just get dressed and pack a small bag. We're getting out of here."

"I don't understand. A little while ago you said—"

"Forget what I said. I know the baby is mine and know your reason for marrying Judd Martin. From now on I'm going to take care of the both of you. Now hurry. And wear something warm."

Glenna's heart swelled with love as she quickly lit a lamp and drew the proper clothing from her wardrobe, struggling into them. Kane moved to help her with the buttons at the back of her dress then searched through her garments for a heavy cloak and threw it over her shoulders.

"Put a change of clothes in a bag, darling, and let's get out of here."

Glenna surprised him by rummaging around under the bed and retrieving a small suitcase already packed and ready to go. "I . . . I planned on leaving at the first opportunity," she hastily explained.

Kane grabbed the bag, blew out the lamp and steered Glenna toward the door. "Wait!" Glenna balked, refusing to budge another inch. "There's a guard somewhere in the house. Judd left him to keep watch over me. How did you get by him?"

"Don't worry about Bert, I took care of him."

"You . . . killed him?" Glenna shuddered.

"There was no need," Kane said cryptically.

"What about the servants? Are they usually about this time of night?"

"N-no, they won't be stirring until dawn. Oh, Kane, thank you, thank—"

"Later, love. Here, take my hand. I don't want you falling down the stairs." Cautiously he led her down the stairs, through the darkened house and out the back door, carefully locking it behind him.

Only when they were both settled on Kane's horse and moving slowly through the empty streets did Glenna allow herself to relax, praying that they would soon be far from Denver and Judd Martin. "Where are we going, Kane?" she asked abruptly.

"We're going to my room at the Palace. So far the desk clerk is the only person who's recognized me. And I intend to make it worth his while to forget he's seen me."

"What if he recognizes me?"

"No chance. Pull your hood over your face and keep your head down. He'll think I'm bringing a whore to my room for the night."

Glenna flushed, grateful that her head was averted so Kane couldn't see her expression, for in truth was she any better than a whore? She was married to one man while carrying another's child. But she and Kane loved each other. And she had been forced against her will into marriage to Judd. If Judd hadn't interferred in her life she and Kane would now be married, and their child legitimate.

"What then, Kane? I can't remain hidden in your room forever."

"There's an eastbound train out of here in the morning. We'll take it and make connections in St. Louis for Philadelphia. I'm taking you home, darling. To my home."

Suddenly the thought of meeting Kane's family terrified her. "Kane, you can't! We're not married!

What will you tell your mother? Your brother? Oh, what a terrible thing I've done to you!"

Just then they reached the hotel and Kane had time for nothing more than a reassuring murmur, delaying longer explanations until they were safely in his room. "Lower your hood, Glenna," he urged in a hoarse whisper as they entered the welcome warmth of the all-but-deserted hotel lobby. But as it turned out Kane's precautions proved unnecessary as the night clerk sat dozing behind the desk, his head cradled in his arms. In less time than it took to breathe they were up the stairs and in the safety of Kane's room where Glenna collapsed breathlessly in his arms.

"I've been a fool, love, please forgive me," Kane murmured soothingly into her ear. "I know everything now and if I weren't worried about your safety and that of my child I'd wait around for Judd and kill him for what he's put you through."

"You know everything? How—"

"Sal told me, and thank God I had sense enough to listen."

"And . . . the baby? You're happy about the baby?"

"The only thing that would make me happier is if we were married. But it will happen, love, you'll see. You'll be introduced to my family as my wife. They all know I returned to Denver to marry you. Who's to know any differently? In the meantime I'll instruct my lawyer to quietly arrange a divorce. It shouldn't be too difficult since the marriage was fraudulent as well as never consummated."

"Is . . . is that possible?" Glenna asked hopefully. "What if someone finds out we're not married?"

"No one will, love. My lawyer is the soul of discretion. And, yes, divorce is possible under certain conditions. I'd say your chances are better than average."

Clinging to him in relief, Glenna allowed Kane to lead her to the bed and help her remove her clothes, gently tucking her beneath the covers. "Get some rest, darling," he smiled tenderly. "There are still a few hours left till daylight."

When she tried to draw him down with her he resisted only a moment then reclined fully dressed at her side, drawing her into the curve of his body. Even before he had placed a gentle kiss on her forehead she was asleep.

Glenna awoke to find herself alone, and panic swept through her. A quick glance around the room told her that Kane's luggage was missing as well. Had he changed his mind and deserted her again? Surely not, she reasoned, her mind in a turmoil.

A great sigh of relief escaped her lips when the door opened admitting Kane carrying a tray with her breakfast. He smiled, a dimple forming in each cheek. "I've taken care of everything, love. Our bags are at the depot waiting to be loaded on the train and after you've eaten we'll leave ourselves."

"What about the clerk? Do you think he'll recognize me?"

"Keep your head down when we walk past. There's no need for you to even look his way. Besides, I've good reason to believe he'll be on his way to California very soon. He's always wanted to go there but never had the funds."

"And suddenly he finds himself with money to spare," Glenna laughed impishly.

"Exactly," Kane twinkled. "Will you be sad to leave Denver, Glenna?"

"No, I'll be happy wherever you are, Kane," she admitted sincerely.

"What about your father's claim? Do you have any regrets about the way things turned out?"

"Someday we'll come back," Glenna said wistfully. "With our children."

The train pulled out of the depot in a blinding snowstorm. Few people were on hand, allowing Kane and Glenna an inconspicuous departure. Not one hardy soul was about to mark their exit from the hotel or their short trudge through the snow to the depot mere minutes before the train whistle signaled a warning blast.

Kane's money bought them first-class accommodations and the trip to St. Louis, though hardly pleasant, was not unbearable. The cold proved their worst enemy and the small stoves kept burning in each car did little to ward off the chill that settled unbidden in Glenna's bones. The wind rattled the windows and found its way into every crack and corner. The day they reached St. Louis was one of the happiest of Glenna's life. She was with the man she loved, carrying his child, and safe at last. But the long ordeal she had endured had taken its toll.

No one needed to tell Kane that Glenna had reached the end of her endurance, or that she was exhausted to the point of becoming physically ill if she weren't allowed a respite in their journey east. Thinking only of Glenna and his child, Kane secured a room at the best hotel St. Louis had to offer and settled them in for as long as it took Glenna to rest and recover her strength.

Their time in St. Louis was well spent. During their sojourn in the city Kane ordered an entire wardrobe for Glenna, to make up for having to come away from Denver with little more than a change of underwear and a few mementos that belonged to her parents. A long, unbearable week passed before he attempted to make love to her, and when he did it was accomplished with such tenderness and caring that Glenna could have cried with happiness.

"Are you certain it won't harm either you or the baby?" he asked solicitously as he settled down in the bed beside her. "I want to make love to you more than I want food or drink but I'll wait if you say so. I'll wait for as long as it takes."

Her hand fluttered then settled on the crisp fur covering his chest, causing him to gasp aloud. Smiling seductively her hand roamed downward, feeling the strength of the muscles rippling across his rib cage beneath her questing fingertips.

"Making love won't harm me, darling," she put his mind at ease. "What would hurt me is if you didn't."

Kane's stomach tightened as he felt her hand slide down into the pelt crowning his manhood. Kane's groan fired her own need as he suddenly came alive beneath her hands and lips. Grasping her waist in both hands he balanced her above him and slowly, carefully lowered her onto him. Throwing her head back in sublime pleasure, Glenna rode him as she would a wild stallion until Kane easily flipped her on her back, never missing a stroke as his skillful thrusts carried them both into a world ablaze with fire and lights; a world where love and ecstasy went hand in hand.

Later, with the first heat of passion sated, they made love again more leisurely. Kane called her his love, his life, his wife, and for the first time in months Glenna felt secure.

18

Patting a stray curl in place and securing the fashionable little hat Kane had bought her atop her flaming tresses, Glenna glanced at Kane hesitantly and sighed. "Do I look all right, Kane? Do you think they'll like me? Oh, Lord, I'm scared."

"Honey, relax. They'll love you as much as I do."

Grasping her hand securely in his he confidently led her onto the platform and down the steps, allowing Glenna her first real glimpse of Philadelphia since their train had chugged to a halt. She knew little about the city except that it was located on the Delaware River which gave it ready access to the Atlantic Ocean eighty-eight nautical miles away. The shipyards were the most extensive in the east and the city now rivaled European cities of comparable population. It boasted public street lighting, paved streets and pumps supplying citizens with water.

According to Kane Philadelphia was a center of learning and culture as well as trade and industry, by both American and European standards. The city was also a leader in still another area—finance, a business in which the Morgan family excelled. The Pennsylvania Railroad was considered one of the great railroads of the world.

With little effort Kane efficiently dispatched their luggage to his house, hired a hack and soon had them on their way to Vine Street, the northern boundary of the city. Though Kane had scoffed at Glenna's fears concerning her reception by his family, in truth he suffered those same fears. When he had returned to Philadelphia from Denver with Ellen, announcing the dissolution of their engagement and his intention to marry Glenna, his reception had been anything but warm. His brother's keen disapproval had been expected but he hadn't anticipated his mother's reaction. In no uncertain terms he was coolly informed that one does not break promises to a member of the Fairchild family.

At that time he expeced to marry Glenna and never return to Philadelphia, but circumstances had decreed otherwise. His brother James had been absolutely livid over Kane's breach of promise. The Fairchilds, though no longer as prosperous as they once were due to bad investments, still wielded considerable influence in the world of finance. James once confided that he would have married the chit himself were he not so old and in need of a wife long before Ellen was ready for the marriage market.

Kane shuddered to think what his family and the good citizens of Philadelphia would say should they learn he and Glenna were not husband and wife but living scandalously in a state of sin. The fact that Glenna already had a living husband only complicated matters and the illegitimate child she carried added further to the dilemma. But Kane would rather cut off his right arm than see any harm come to Glenna and their child. Then all thought ceased as the hack ground to a stop before the largest, most imposing house Glenna had ever seen.

Constructed of brick, the bowed-out front was supported by four huge wooden pillars three stories high. More windows faced the quiet residential street than Glenna cared to count. Its imposing dimensions intimidated her and if Kane hadn't been clutching her arm she would have turned and run.

"Don't be frightened, love," he whispered as he led her to the door. "Remember, you're my wife and we're expecting our first child."

If only it were true! Glenna thought passionately. The part about their being married, that is. But no words were forthcoming as Kane rang the front doorbell and waited for the butler to answer the door.

"Chin up," were the last words she recalled before the door swung wide revealing a tall, thin elderly man dressed in severe black livery.

The man's eyes lit up at the sight of Kane. "Welcome home, Master Kane," the butler intoned dryly, the hint of a smile softening his stern features.

"Thank you, Perkins," Kane grinned easily. Then almost as an afterthought he pulled Glenna forward. "This is my wife, Perkins."

If Perkins was surprised he did not show it, his bland features displaying no emotion whatever. He was the perfect example of the well-mannered servant as he inclined his head in Glenna's direction. "Welcome to Morgan Manor, Mrs. Kane." His voice held the proper note of respect and his manner suggested only polite interest in the goings-on of the family he had served faithfully for many years.

"Where is everyone, Perkins?" Kane asked, noting that the house seemed deserted.

"Both your mother and Mrs. James are out and Master James is at the bank. No one is home at the moment but the servants."

Kane nodded dismissively. "See to our luggage when it arrives, Perkins. For the time being my wife and I will share my room."

"Certainly, sir," intoned Perkins dryly. "Is there anything else you'd like?"

"A bath!" Glenna blurted out, blushing profusely at her temerity.

"See to it, Perkins," ordered Kane, smiling fondly at the woman he loved more than his own life. "And send up something light to eat in an hour or so."

"Very good, sir," Perkins replied as he watched the couple climb the wide staircase arm in arm.

Though he seldom voiced an opinion, nor was he asked to, he thought Master Kane's wife a vast improvement over the insipid, thoroughly spoiled Fairchild woman who had long aspired to the title of Mrs. Kane Morgan. But Perkins knew the poor red-headed child was in for a bad time once Master James and his mother returned and found the new bride firmly ensconced in the family home. No doubt there would be the devil to pay, not that Master Kane gave a hoot what the rest of the family thought, Perkins smiled in a rare display of emotion. He always was a wild one who lived his life according to his own dictates. Life wasn't going to be too pleasant around the Morgan home for awhile, Perkins decided, but it definitely would be interesting. If he were a betting man he would place all his money on Kane and his little bride eventually winning the family over.

Though the room Glenna was to share with Kane was masculine in decor, she had never seen anything more magnificent. The entire cabin at Golden Promise would fit comfortably inside these four walls. Done in shades of green and brown with hunting scenes decorating the walls, its dark, highly polished furniture suited Kane perfectly. The huge bed was covered with a hunter-green velvet spread and the thick rug beneath her feet boasted green and brown scenes much like the ones decorating the walls.

"I know it's far from feminine," Kane apologized, "but you can change anything you like. Better that than separate rooms!" He leered wolfishly.

Before Glenna had time to comment on the room, she was informed that her bath was prepared and waiting by a timid young maid named Annie who had been assigned by Perkins to see to her needs. Imagine Glenna's surprise to find a separate room devoted to nothing but bathing, containing every accessory imaginable, all more luxurious than any Glenna had ever seen. In fact, she was so pleased she spent more than an hour lolling in the large porcelain tub, giving Kane more than ample time to speak to his mother who had just returned home with his sister-in-law Winnie. He went directly to her room where no prying ears could overhear.

"Kane, Perkins told me you came home," she greeted, presenting a still smooth cheek for its customary kiss. Kane quickly obliged, for no matter how often his mother chided him for his irresponsible ways or tried to change him, he loved her.

A slim woman of medium height, Beth Morgan did not look her sixty years. Her beautifully coiffed black hair was shot with strands of silver and her blue eyes lit up the pale oval of her unlined face as she regarded her willful son. Her quick, bird-like movements clearly proclaimed her displeasure with her second son and she sighed distractedly, wishing he were more like the docile James who was content to remain firmly ensconced in the family fold and see to business. The only fault she could find in James was that after ten years of marriage to Winnie he had produced no children and Beth had all but given up on him. She had hoped that Kane's marriage to Ellen Fairchild would prove more fruitful.

But then Kane had broken his engagement and announced his plans to wed a prospector's daughter. A woman with nothing to commend her save that her father was a friend of Patrick's from the old country.

"You're looking well, Mother," Kane said after the dutiful kiss.

"Too bad I can't say the same for you, son," Beth remarked after carefully scrutinizing Kane's pale face and too-thin frame. "From the looks of you I'd venture a guess that all is not well with your marriage."

"Perkins must have told you I brought Glenna back to Philadelphia." Tight-lipped, Beth nodded, her disapproval apparent. "I wanted to talk to you about Glenna before you met her."

Beth motioned Kane into a chair, then began pacing. "Is your recent marriage an unhappy one, Kane? Is that the reason you brought your bride home? From what you said previously I assumed you'd make your home in Denver near her father's claim."

"Sit down, Mother," Kane invited, exasperated. Wordlessly, Beth obeyed. "Glenna and I are still very much in love. And . . . and we couldn't be happier. But things have changed, Mother. Not the way Glenna and I feel about each other, that will never change. But certain . . . elements working against us made our leaving Denver at this time imperative."

"What elements?" Beth asked, alarmed. "Kane, are you in trouble?"

"No, Mother, it's nothing like that," he lied convincingly. "I just thought it best to get Glenna out of Denver for awhile. And speaking of Glenna, I expect you and James to make her feel welcome here."

"I know my manners," Beth reproved, giving her son a hurt look. "But you must admit I'm justified in being upset with you. The Fairchilds hardly speak to me these days and Ellen becomes absolutely livid at the mere mention of your name. You must remember that she is not so young anymore and has waited a good many years for you to set the date."

Kane sighed distractedly, obviously getting nowhere with his mother. "Mother, Glenna needs all the encouragement she can get right now. She is pregnant. She's expecting my child and your first grandchild," Kane blurted out. If nothing else worked in Glenna's favor perhaps the certain knowledge that Glenna would soon produce a Morgan heir would.

"Your . . . your wife is expecting? So soon?"

"Not so soon, Mother, we've been married for months. Ever since I returned to Denver." Hopefully no one would bother to check the veracity of his claim, Kane thought to himself. "Glenna is in her fourth month."

"A child!" gloated Beth, appeased as well as vastly pleased. The long overdue grandchild was finally on its way! "Is Glenna well?" she asked sharply. "Have the servants taken good care of her? Honestly, Kane, sometimes you are downright perverse. Why didn't you tell me Glenna was pregnant before you let me ramble on?"

"I wanted you to like Glenna for herself, not for the heir she's about to give me."

"I can't say I'm entirely happy with your choice, son, but as long as Glenna is your wife and already expecting your child she'll be made welcome by me."

"I knew I could count on you, Mother." Kane smiled winningly. "I only hope James is of the same mind."

"I think you'll find your brother somewhat bitter. As you well know, James and your father promoted the match between you and Ellen. James was all set to undertake a new business venture and Joseph Fairchild used his considerable influence to obtain the backing necessary. But after your engagement to Ellen was broken he convinced the investors to abandon James and his project. Your brother is absolutely livid."

"I don't wish to quarrel with James, Mother," Kane contented, "but I've always lived my life the way I saw fit. He may have ten years on me but I make my own decisions and take charge of my own affairs."

When Glenna entered the parlor that evening all conversation stuttered to an abrupt halt. After her bath earlier in the afternoon Kane persuaded her to nap until dinner, and she gladly complied, having no desire to be presented to his family until she looked her best.

On that score Glenna need not have worried. Still flushed from her nap and a thoroughly satisfying bout of lovemaking, Glenna was a veritable vision as she entered the room on Kane's arm. Wearing one of her new gowns fashioned in velvet, the green color added sparkle to her emerald eyes and enhanced her creamy complexion. Annie had done wonders with her unruly mass of flaming red hair and only wispy tendrils strayed from the top of her dainty head to frame the perfect oval of her face.

The fitted green bodice of her gown emphasized her generous breasts, the tops of which gleamed whitely against the darker hue of the gown. Thankfully the full skirt was designed to disguise her pregnancy, though Glenna realized that in a few weeks nothing would conceal her growing girth.

Beth Morgan was the first to react to Glenna's entrance into the room, grasping both her hands warmly in her own. "Welcome to Morgan Manor, Glenna," she said brightly to cover her confusion. She had expected Glenna to be lovely but not nearly so dazzling as the fairy creature facing her. No wonder her son had fallen under the spell. Unconsciously her eyes dropped to the barely perceptible bulge hidden beneath Glenna's skirt, bringing a flush to Glenna's face. She was aware that Kane must have told his mother that she was expecting.

"Th-thank you, Mrs. Morgan," Glenna stammered, sick over the lie she was forced to perpetrate.

"Please, my dear, won't you call me Beth? Mrs. Morgan sounds so cold. Have you been taken care of? If there is anything you need or what please fell free to ask. After all, this is your home now."

Glenna murmured an appropriate reply while from the corner of her eye she watched Kane's brother approach, and she steeled herself, sensing his disapproval.

"Glenna, this is my brother James and his wife Winnie," she heard Kane saying as she turned her attention to the couple standing before her.

James Morgan looked every bit the ten years that separated him from Kane. Tall, impeccably attired, with tinges of gray touching his temples, Kane's brother presented the perfect picture of a successful businessman. Though not so tall as Kane nor so ruggedly handsome, James's keen gray eyes studied her with intense interest. Perhaps the pair inherited their gray eyes from their father, Glenna noted idly, for Beth's were a bright blue.

James's diminutive wife Winnie looked to be about the same age as her distinguished husband. Though pretty enough, she appeared but an extension of the husband she clung to so possessively. Her eyes evidenced neither friendship nor animosity, satisfied to follow her husband's lead in the matter of her brother-in-law's wife, though she did feel sorry for poor Ellen Fairchild who had been literally abandoned at the altar.

"So you are the woman who stole my little brother's heart," James said, the same warmth extended by his mother moments before sadly lacking.

"James!" Kane objected violently. "I may be younger but by no means little."

"Sorry, brother," James slapped Kane's back good-naturedly. "I couldn't resist."

All his life Kane had looked up to and respected his

father and older brother, only escaping their authority when they tried to dictate his future. He still loved James and knew the feeling was reciprocated.

James studied Glenna avidly, and against his will found himself admiring what he saw. He was fully prepared to dislike the woman, for her marriage to Kane had cost him a fortune. His enterprise would have greatly enriched the Morgan coffers had it not been for her untimely intervention. His own marriage, though he had grown to love his little Winnie, was originally one of convenience, one that added much to the Morgan holdings. His one regret was that they had produced no children and at this point in his life James was unwilling to set his wife aside for her barrenness. He counted heavily on Kane to provide the future heirs to the Morgan dynasty.

He had thought Ellen perfect for that role, and so had their father, for a deal was soon struck to wed Kane to Ellen, thus combining wealth with an old and distinguished name. Though the Morgans possessed great wealth, James was under no illusions when it came to their standing in the snobbish social community. His father Patrick was an Irish immigrant, a newcomer in a city boasting of old family names. James's marriage to Winnie had helped break down those barriers and Kane's marriage to Ellen was the final coup needed to establish the family firmly in the bosom of society.

But Glenna O'Neill, a prospector's daughter from a rough mining camp outside the raw town of Denver had changed all those grand plans. Yet, coming face to face with Kane's beautiful wife, James couldn't really fault him for falling in love and marrying her before someone else grabbed her up. Besides, their marriage was already an accomplished fact, he assumed, forcing him to make the best of it. In James's opinion, keeping harmony in the family was far more important than the prestige of joining the Morgan and Fairchild clans, although the astute businessman in him still chafed at the loss.

So it was entirely understandable that James's greeting should be somewhat stilted and less than enthusiastic. Even so, it was more than Glenna could hope for. His smile was genuine, but not one to openly display his emotions, James formally welcomed her into the family. Winnie, following her husband's lead, shyly clasped Glenna's hands and murmured appropriate words.

The ordeal of meeting his family finally over, Glenna clung to Kane's arm for support. Her legs felt wobbly beneath her and she knew her face had visibly paled during the introductions. Now an uncomfortable pall settled over those assembled and Beth, ever the consummate hostess, jumped into the void.

"I hope you were able to rest this afternoon, my dear," she said, addressing Glenna. "We want to keep you and that baby healthy."

"Glenna!" James exclaimed with a start. "You're pregnant already?"

Glenna flushed, her face nearly as bright a red as her hair. But she was saved from answering by Kane who proudly announced, "It's true, James. Glenna is expecting our child in five months."

Strange as it may seem, James experienced a surge of joy at Kane's words. After ten years of marriage to his Winnie he realized their union was unlikely to produce offspring and the family's hopes for an heir lay solely with Kane. His congratulations were warm and sincere, exhibiting more exuberance than he had previously.

"I can't fault you for wanting to start a family right away," grinned James. "Especially with a wife like Glenna." Beth made a chiding sound with her lips at James's crude remark but did not reprimand him. "In fact, this is terrific news."

"I'm so happy for you, Glenna," Winnie said with a wistful smile. Her own childless years weighed heavily upon her but did not diminish her happiness for Glenna. "And I assure you I'll be a doting aunt so be prepared to have me hovering over the crib."

Touched by Winnie's words, Glenna was astute enough to realize her welcome wouldn't have been half so warm had she not been expecting Kane's child. But her guilt over living a lie was such that she was willing to accept whatever crumbs came her way. Then Winnie said something that stunned her.

"Oh, James, we simply must give a party in Glenna's honor. I'm certain all our friends are anxious to meet Kane's wife. And the sooner the better, given Glenna's condition. It's been ages since we've had a party and the coming holiday season is the perfect time to make it a gala affair."

James feigned indecision, but in truth the idea appealed to him. What better way to introduce Glenna into society and demonstrate the Morgan's approval of their newest family member than to hold a reception in honor of the bride and groom?

"An excellent idea, Winnie!" Beth agreed wholeheartedly.

"Oh, no!" Glenna objected strongly. "I don't need a party, truly."

"We insist," James lent his support. "Besides, you're a Morgan now and since you were married without benefit of family it's no more than right that a reception should be held in honor of your marriage." Being the male head of the family James felt qualified to make the final decision. "It seems to me that New Year's Eve is a fine time for a party."

"Kane!" Glenna implored, her green eyes conveying her panic as they begged him to intervene. How could they honor a marriage that never took place?

"James, I hardly think this is the right time to give a reception. Perhaps after the baby—"

"Nonsense!" scoffed James. "Why, if you hadn't told me Glenna was pregnant I would never suspect it. We'll launch your wife in grand style. Mother, you and Winnie can work out the details. There now," he smiled benignly, immensely pleased with himself, "it's all settled."

Kane shrugged helplessly as Glenna gave him a pained look. But there was nothing he could do. The Morgan family had made up their minds and to them the matter merited no further discussion. Heaving a sigh of acquiescence, Glenna realized the situation was out of her hands and inevitably she would be introduced to Philadelphia society as the legal wife of Kane Morgan.

It seemed impossible to Glenna that she had been living with Kane's family for all of two weeks. In that time she had grown truly fond of both Beth and Winnie, although she realized that in all likelihood they were just making the best of an uncomfortable situation. It was really Ellen whom Beth wanted for a daughter-in-law even though the woman freely offered her friendship and kindness. Truth to tell, it was Glenna's own conscience that prevented her from being truly happy with the situation. Yet somehow she struggled through Christmas, acknowledging that it was the best since leaving her father's small cabin over four years ago. The warmth displayed by the family group brought tears to her eyes.

Even James appeared willing to accept Glenna into the family. But in his daunting presence Glenna felt somewhat more reserved. His piercing gray eyes seemed to probe her very soul. And she had far too much to hide to feel truly comfortable in his company.

Now suddenly New Year's Eve was upon her, Glenna thought moodily as she watched from the bedroom window as their guests began to arrive, expecting to greet Kane's new bride. A little sob escaped her throat, sounding much like a hiccup being choked back.

"Glenna, what's wrong, love?" Glenna whirled to find Kane standing behind her looking handsome and debonair in his black evening clothes.

"How can we go through with this . . . this sham, Kane? It isn't right!" His arms curved comfortingly around her and she felt safe and protected, but only for as long as they remained in this room.

"It is right, love. If it weren't for Judd Martin we'd truly be man and wife."

"But we're not!" she insisted stubbornly.

"I've got the best lawyers in Philadelphia working on your divorce. It's a slow process, I admit, but take heart, darling. It will all work out. We just have to be patient."

"And in the meantime your family thinks we are wed. Think what it would do to them if they found out the truth."

"They won't. No one knows where you are except Sal, and she'd never tell. No doubt Judd Martin is still under the misapprehension that I am dead. Now, put on your best face and come downstairs. Mother sent me to fetch you. She wants us in the reception line."

"Do I look all right?" she asked, moving out of his embrace and stepping back in order to give him the full benefit of her magnificently clad figure.

"You're absolutely radiant," Kane whispered, awestruck. He had seen Glenna unclothed as well as garbed in various outfits since he had known her but never had he seen her looking as beautiful or as desirable.

Her lowcut gown was fashioned of layer after layer of black and silver tulle. Puffed sleeves sat low on her upper arms baring creamy white shoulders. Her neck, 'as adorned with a diamond necklace Kane had preented to her at Christmas.

"You look pretty good yourself," Glenna compliiented, inspecting his tall, muscular frame from eneath a fringe of sooty lashes. "Quite the handsomest ian I've ever seen."

"Just keep that thought in mind tonight when all he men are clamoring for your attention," Kane varned with mock severity, happy to see her dark mood ad lifted.

"You're the only man for me, Kane," Glenna ssured him with a saucy look.

"Don't forget it, love. Come," he smiled, gallantly resenting his arm, "shall we go down and greet our uests?"

Glenna met more people that night than she had in er entire life. She was in turn congratulated, hugged, issed and inspected by every person present—which anged upward of one-hundred and fifty—until faces nd names whirled around in her head, making it ache. ut far worse as well as completely unnerving was aving to extend a welcome to Ellen Fairchild and her arents. The cool blond beauty flashed her such a look f loathing that Glenna was struck nearly speechless, vobbling dangerously on knees suddenly gone numb.

"Are you all right, love?" Kane asked, slipping a upporting arm around her waist.

"I'm fine, Kane," she assured him, recovering uickly. "But I'll be glad to sit down again."

"Then you're in luck. The last guests have arrived nd dinner is about to be announced. You'll have a hance to rest before the dancing begins."

Truth to tell, Glenna enjoyed herself more than she vould have thought possible. She had danced little in er life and after being partnered by Kane and James for the first two dances, she was whirled around the floor by a succession of men both young and old who were obviously captivated by Kane's young bride. Only Ellen's baleful glare kept her from being completely at ease.

When Kane claimed Glenna for another dance later that evening he wisely suggested a short respite and she readily agreed. Arm in arm they left the crowded ballroom and entered the library, a cozy room Glenna had grown to love. From a short distance away Ellen tracked their slow progress, eyes narrowed jealously. After a short interval something perverse inside her persuaded her to dog their steps. To anyone who cared to look it appeared that Ellen was going off to visit the powder room.

Glenna collapsed in a stuffed leather chair and slipped off her dancing slippers, propping her aching feet on the footstool placed conveniently nearby. Kane smiled affectionately. "You looked as if you needed a rest."

"You're very perceptive," Glenna nodded wearily. "I didn't realize how tired I was until I sat down."

"Do you know I'm the envy of every male in the room regardless of age?"

"Truly?" Glenna asked with feigned surprise.

"You little witch!" Kane laughed. "You know you've been the center of attention all evening."

"Especially the center of Ellen's attention," muttered Glenna beneath her breath.

"What did you say?"

"Why was Ellen invited?"

"Her family and ours have been friends for years. It was inevitable. Has she bothered you?"

"Not unless you call those dark looks bothersome."

"I'm sorry, darling, but I did jilt her. In a way I can't blame her for being bitter. I just thank God you entered my life in time to prevent me from marrying her and making the biggest mistake of my life."

At that moment Glenna loved him more than she had ever thought possible. "I cringe to think what might happen should Ellen learn the truth about us."

Outside the partially opened door Ellen pressed closer in order to catch every word being spoken by the man she still wanted despite having been rejected by him. What was Glenna saying? What "truth" was she speaking of? Ellen wondered curiously. A feeling that she was on the verge of learning something that might be of great value to her in the future caused her breath to still in anticipation.

"You are worrying needlessly, darling," Kane contended. "There is no way Ellen could know you are married to Judd Martin. Denver is hundreds of miles away. And besides, why would she even suspect such a thing?"

"But what will happen if your lawyer fails to obtain a divorce? What if—"

"Glenna, don't do this to yourself."

"But, Kane, what if Judd somehow learns where to find me? He has every right in the world to demand my return and claim our child."

"Over my dead body!" Kane protested violently. "You belong to me, Glenna. You're carrying my child. No one will take you from me. No one!" he repeated forcefully. "I'll kill Martin before I let him have you."

Having heard all she needed to know, Ellen slunk away in the direction of the powder room, nodding absently to an acquaintance whom she passed in the hall. Her mind working furiously, Ellen carefully digested all she had just overheard. If Kane could be believed, and she had no reason to doubt him, he and Glenna were not legally married; that in fact Glenna was the wife of Judd Martin, although Kane had freely admitted having fathered Glenna's child. That piece of information was a total surprise to Ellen for she had no idea Glenna was expecting.

Why had Glenna left her husband? Ellen mused. Even more puzzling was Glenna's reason for marrying Judd Martin in the first place. Judging from their conversation it was obvious Judd hadn't let Glenna go willingly and had no idea where to find her. It was equally obvious that Kane's family knew nothing of this astonishing development. They would be horrified to learn they were harboring an impostor under their roof. The whole situation would bear some serious thought, Ellen decided spitefully. But of one thing she was certain—as long as she was in possession of this incriminating bit of information Kane and Glenna would definitely not live happily ever after.

Kane helped Glenna slip back into her shoes, massaging her ankles and calves with loving care. "It's almost midnight, love," he said after a quick glance at his watch. "Shall we join our guests and welcome in the New Year? We have much to look forward to in the coming year." He patted the mound of her stomach and helped her to her feet, but temptation got the best of him as she rested briefly in his arms.

As it always happened whenever he was near her, the urge to kiss her became too urgent to resist as she nestled in his embrace. He gazed at her and their souls met. Words too meaningful for speech were silently conveyed and answered in their hearts. Then he captured her mouth, gently, with his full emotion in check, but with enough force to transmit his desire. Glenna melted in his arms, her lips willingly opening beneath his probing tongue. With the deepest reluctance he broke off the kiss and offered his arm.

"It wouldn't look right to desert our guests now," he twinkled, his eyes a smoldering gray. "We'll continue this later, love, in the privacy of our room. If you aren't too tired," he added solicitously.

"I'm never too tired for you, Kane," she replied, rolling her eyes suggestively. "Let's sneak away as soon as we welcome in the New Year. I much prefer a private celebration."

With those words written indelibly in his brain, Kane guided her out the door and into the crowded ballroom just as the countdown began announcing the New Year and in time to steal another kiss, this time beneath a spray of mistletoe hanging from the chandelier.

19

Over two months elapsed before Ellen came to a decision concerning Glenna and her adulterous relationship with Kane. She knew what she had been contemplating was despicable, but hadn't Glenna stolen her betrothed without a shred of remorse? Besides, Ellen considered it her duty to bring the deplorable situation into the open. The Morgans deserved better from Kane and the whole mess begged for exposure.

Once her decision had been made Ellen acted swiftly, dispatching a telegram to Judd Martin in Denver. But as luck would have it an early spring storm whipped through the area snapping the telegraph lines and the message never reached him. Of course Ellen did not know this as she patiently waited for an answer.

One month passed, then two, and the full bloom of spring burst upon the countryside while Ellen fumed in impotent rage. By now Glenna was close to delivering her child and grudgingly Ellen decided to wait before trying to communicate with Judd Martin again. Though she'd go to any lengths to have Glenna out of Kane's life she drew the line at deliberately endangering the life of an innocent babe. She wasn't completely without scruples, she just wanted what was rightfully hers.

On the first day of August, Ellen decided a visit to Morgan Manor was in order, hoping to learn firsthand information about Glenna and her confinement. She had seen Glenna only infrequently since the New Year's Eve reception, and always in Kane's company. It was disgusting how he constantly hovered at her side, she snorted derisively. The waiting and doing nothing about her secret information was beginning to grate on her nerves and Ellen wasn't certain how much longer she could keep that knowledge to herself.

It was a warm, bright day full of promise when Ellen presented herself at Morgan Manor. Upon being informed that both Beth and Winnie were shopping, she asked to see Glenna, whereupon she was politely shown to the parlor while Glenna was summoned. She grimaced in disgust as Glenna awkwardly wielded her bulk into the room, panting from the exertion of negotiating the stairs. Then and there Ellen decided she would never allow herself to suffer through a pregnancy.

"You wished to see me, Ellen?" Glenna asked as she carefully lowered herself into a chair. "I can't imagine why," she added warily. Though Glenna's figure was no longer svelte her looks had not diminished. Ellen was chagrined to see how impending motherhood had enhanced her already considerable beauty.

"It was remiss of me not to call sooner," Ellen revealed. "I've been a friend of the family for years." She stared pointedly at Glenna's protruding abdomen. "Exactly when are you expecting the blessed event? From the looks of you you must have conceived on your wedding night. Or did you wait that long?"

Fuming inwardly, Glenna slanted Ellen a

venomous glare. "When I conceived is none of your business," she declared stonily. But Ellen remained undaunted.

"Does your husband know you are expecting?" Ellen remarked casually.

"Are you mad? Of course Kane knows!"

"I'm not speaking of Kane," Ellen retorted smugly. "We both know you are married to Judd Martin. How can you be certain it's Kane's child you're carrying?"

Glenna's stomach somersaulted into her throat and her face drained of all color. "Wha-what are you talking about?"

"Don't pretend ignorance, Mrs. Martin," she emphasized spitefully. "You're living a lie. Think what it would do to the Morgans should word leak out about your adulterous affair with Kane."

"How . . . how did you find out?"

"That's none of your business. Suffice it to say that I know and will employ any means necessary to rid this family of the shameless hussy they're harboring under their roof."

"If you have any compassion at all you will say nothing," Glenna pleaded urgently. "Allow Kane to solve this problem in his own way. "I . . . I've grown very fond of the Morgans and would do nothing to dishonor them or cause them embarrassment."

"If you truly meant that you would leave. Immediately!"

"Leave? But . . . You must be mad to even suggest such a thing at a time like this."

"Mad? Hardly," taunted Ellen cruelly. "But I warn you I mean to claim what is mine. One way or another I will be Kane's wife. And if your concern for the Morgan family is genuine you'll quietly disappear."

"Are you threatening me?" Glenna asked.

"There's no need," Ellen shrugged carelessly. "I

know you'll do the right thing where the Morgans are concerned."

"The right thing?"

"Of course. There's no place in Kane's life for a married woman and her bastard."

"Don't you ever call my baby a bastard! Our child was conceived in love and has a father. You know Kane will come after me if I leave. Do you think he'd allow me and his child to disappear from his life so easily?"

"If you're wise you'll go where you won't be found. I hear there are a multitude of opportunities for a young woman in California."

"And if I refuse?"

"You'll be hurting no one but the Morgans if you refuse to heed my . . . advice. Do you want all of Philadelphia to learn that you are married to another man while posing as the wife of Kane Morgan? It will make it look as if the entire Morgan family condones the affair. They will be shunned by society. And all because of you. Do you want that?"

Put in that light Glenna could not fault Ellen's reasoning. "Well?" Ellen prodded remorselessly. "Which will it be? Will you leave of your own accord or do I inform them and all their friends of your true marital status?"

When Ellen first entered Morgan Manor her purpose wasn't to demand Glenna's departure. Not until after her baby was born, that is. But the moment she encountered Glenna in all her maternal radiance envy and jealousy caused her to cast aside all her good intentions, such as they were. Consumed with the need to banish her competition, Ellen could no longer hold her tongue, demanding in no uncertain terms that Glenna leave. No doubt the child wasn't even Kane's but belonged to Judd and Glenna was foisting it off as a Morgan. Kane would be well rid of the devious chit, Ellen decided spitefully.

Glenna bowed her bright head and made a half-hearted attempt to brush away the tears gathering in the corners of her eyes. Faced with the choices Ellen offered, Glenna felt pushed into a corner with no place to turn, nowhere to go. Could she in all conscience remain and stand helplessly by while the Morgan name was dragged through the mud? The answer was clear in her mind. No matter how much she loved Kane she had to leave.

Heaving herself to her feet, she glared into Ellen's gloating face. "You win, Ellen," she ground out from between clenched teeth. "I'll leave but . . . oh—" she gasped, clutching her stomach and doubling over in pain.

"What is it?" Ellen asked sharply, expecting some ruse.

"The . . . the baby! It's coming!"

"Are you certain? Or are you trying to play on my sympathy? Because if you are—"

"Oh God, Ellen, call one of the servants to go for the doctor," Glenna pleaded, writhing in agony. "Quickly!"

Convinced that Glenna was truly in pain, Ellen turned to summon help. But at the last minute she whirled to face Glenna. "Do I have your word that you'll leave Kane?" she prodded heartlessly. "Or do I set the wheels in motion to expose you?"

"I'll leave!" moaned Glenna. "What other choice have you given me? But don't expect Kane to turn to you once I'm gone. He'll move heaven and earth to find me. Now get out of here and let me have my baby."

"Leave Kane to me." Ellen smiled deviously as she slipped through the door where she encountered Perkins and promptly relayed Glenna's message.

Then she left Morgan Manor, her thoughts consumed with all the ways she planned on consoling Kane once Glenna was out of the way.

* * *

Daniel Morgan made his appearance just before midnight, nearly three weeks early and protesting lustily despite being somewhat smaller than a full-term baby. Kane resolutely remained by Glenna's side throughout the ordeal which, all things considered, proceeded without complication.

Danny's birth affected the entire Morgan family. Kane was ecstatic, and within minutes the tiny mite had captured the hearts of the Morgan household. It was obvious to all that Beth doted on her only grandson and that Winnie and James were equally besotted by their small nephew.

"Thank you for my son, darling," Kane murmured as he tenderly ruffled the dark fuzz capping the baby's head. He looked so natural in the crook of Glenna's arm.

Exhausted after giving birth, Glenna could only smile weakly before nodding off to sleep. Kane's words came drifting to her on a cloud of euphoria. "I love you, Glenna. I love you more than my own life."

Recuperation came swiftly and within a week Glenna was once again taking meals downstairs with the family. A nurse had already been engaged for the baby and when a wet nurse was dicussed, Glenna reluctantly agreed but did not forsake entirely the pleasure of nursing her own child.

A week later Ellen paid another visit on Glenna. "I see motherhood hasn't hurt your figure," were her first words as she insolently raked Glenna from head to toe with cool amber eyes. "But now that I look closely I can see your waist is at least two inches larger than it was. Surely you're not nursing the child!" she exclaimed, aghast, her gaze settling on the generous curve of Glenna's breasts. "Women of the upper class don't nurse their own children."

"Have you forgotten that I am a prospector's daughter and those rules hardly apply to me?" Glenna retorted hotly. "Why are you here? I'm sure you didn't come to comment on my figure or admire my son."

"You're correct," Ellen admitted smugly. "You know why I'm here. It's time you left. Now. Before Kane becomes too fond of the child."

Glenna fumed inwardly, her mind working furiously. Not only would Kane be devastated should she take Danny away but James, Winnie and Beth would suffer as well. Could she do that to them? Yet she couldn't leave her baby behind. In the end there was only one answer possible. If she left her baby must go with her.

"It's not as easy you seem to think, Ellen. There is Danny's future to consider."

Ellen shrugged. "Leave the boy. Beth and Winnie will gladly raise him. To prove I mean the child no harm I will allow Kane to claim him as his heir thus relieving me of the distasteful task of childbearing. It all sounds so simple to me."

"If I go, Danny goes with me," resisted Glenna stubbornly.

"You have a week, Glenna. If you aren't gone by then I'll tell the Morgans the heir to the family fortune is a bastard." She turned to leave. "Don't bother showing me out, I know the way. Just remember, one week."

Ellen left Morgan Manor, her steps firm and decisive. In her heart she knew Kane would not allow Glenna to disappear from his life so easily, but as desperate as she was it was worth a try. What puzzled her was Judd Martin's reason for ignoring her first telegram. This time she decided to leave nothing to chance. Within an hour after her interview with Glenna a second telegram was dispatched to the gambler. A letter followed it by mere hours. But Judd did not wait for the letter. By the time it arrived he was already on a train headed east to Philadelphia.

In the solitude of her room, Glenna mulled over Ellen's ultimatum. And came to the inevitable conclusion that she was far too fond of the Morgans to cause them the pain and distress she knew they would suffer should Ellen be allowed to disclose the true status of her relationship to Kane. Until a divorce from Judd became a reality Glenna decided it was best for all involved for her to quietly disappear. If all went well she would be gone before Kane returned home from the bank where he maintained an office. James had talked him into accepting more responsibility in their father's business and Kane had reluctantly agreed. But in her heart Glenna knew that Kane would rather be living the life of an adventurer than sitting behind a desk day in and day out. With Judd Martin breathing down his neck what choice did he have? Glenna asked herself despondently. With her out of his life perhaps he would be free to live according to his own dictates. With that thought in mind her task of packing and leaving as Ellen requested was made easier but certainly not less painful.

Glenna was packed a good two hours before Kane was due to arrive home and she paced the room nervously, waiting for Beth and Winnie to leave the house on their endless round of visits before making good her escape. But fate willed otherwise. The carriage carrying the Morgan women had just cleared the gate and Danny's nurse dispatched on an errand manufactured by Glenna when Kane burst into the room, bubbling with excitement.

"Darling! I've just heard from my lawyer. Good news! Instead of divorce he's obtaining an annulment on the grounds that your marriage was never consummated. Within a month—two at the most—you'll be free. Then we can go off to a neighboring state and be married quietly. No one need ever—" Suddenly his keen eyes fell on Glenna's packed bag sitting beside the door and his words stuttered to an abrupt halt.

"Kane, I—" Glenna began hesitantly.

"What is this, Glenna?" Kane interrupted, staring pointedly at the stylish traveling suit she wore and motioning toward the suitcase. "Are we going somewhere?"

Heaving a sigh of frustration, Glenna sank to the bed, her knees threatening to give way beneath her. "I'm only doing what I think best, Kane, you've got to understand that."

"Damn it, woman! Will you make sense? What in the hell are you talking about?"

"My leaving," she blurted out. "Can't you see I'm only hurting you and your family by living with you without the benefit of marriage?"

"Leaving?" Astonishment followed by disbelief marched across his face. "Didn't you hear what I just said?" he thundered, exasperated. "Within a month or two you'll have your annulment and then we can truly be man and wife. There is no need for you to leave. We've gone all these months without mishap so why this sudden decision to leave?"

"Certain . . . things have changed, Kane," Glenna tried to explain.

"Were you intending to just up and leave without telling me?" he asked, astounded by her lack of concern for his feelings. "What about my son? Were you taking him with you?"

"It's not that I want to leave, Kane," Glenna exclaimed, his obvious hurt and bewilderment tearing her apart. "I love you far too much to remain and see your name thoroughly besmirched."

"By whom?" Kane demanded to know. "No one

besides my lawyers knows about us and they wouldn't say anything.'' Glenna visibly paled and Kane peered at her closely, eyes narrowed suspiciously as comprehension finally dawned. ''Has someone threatened you, darling? Is that why you're so set on leaving?''

Well aware of Kane's violent temper, Glenna hadn't intended on telling him about Ellen's visits or her unreasonable demand that she leave. As hotheaded as Kane was he was likely to rush out and wring her neck. Glenna was counting on leaving Morgan Manor without a confrontation with her volatile lover. But now that Kane had set her plans awry she felt compelled to offer an explanation.

''I'll tell you everything, Kane, if you promise not to fly out of here in a rage until after you've had time to cool down and think clearly,'' Glenna said, her green eyes wide and pleading.

Impatiently, Kane nodded, then dropped to the bed beside her. ''I'll try, love,'' he agreed reluctantly. ''Just tell me who is forcing you to leave. It's not James, is it?'' Though Kane loved James dearly he would not stand for his brother's interference in his life.

''No, Kane, not James,'' Glenna replied.

''Then who?''

''Ellen. Ellen Fairchild. Somehow she learned that I'm married to Judd Martin and she threatened to expose our affair unless I agreed to leave.''

''That bitch!'' exploded Kane, jumping to his feet. ''What in the hell did she think to gain?''

''You,'' revealed Glenna. ''She knew I wouldn't risk exposing you and your family to damaging gossip and acted accordingly. Once I was out of your life she intended to take my place.''

''There's no way a shallow creature like Ellen could ever take your place!'' Kane growled with bitter emphasis. ''Don't you realize that you and Danny are my life? Without you I am nothing. Even if I had never met you I doubt I could have gone through with my marriage to Ellen. Just wait until I get my hands on that contemptible witch."

He began to pace back and forth, his hands itching to feel Ellen's neck snap beneath his fingers. In fact, if he hadn't promised Glenna he'd practice caution he'd rush out this very minute and confront his ex-fiancée. Instead, he stopped before Glenna and sank down beside her on the bed, hoping to convince her that her leaving would accomplish nothing.

"It was wrong of you to try and sneak out of here without a word, love. You can see that now, can't you?"

"I was only doing what I thought best, Kane."

"We're in this together, darling," Kane pointed out patiently. "I am perfectly capable of protecting you and Danny. Ellen was just bluffing. She'd never find the courage to expose us."

"I don't know, Kane," Glenna said doubtfully. "I think you're underestimating the woman and the lengths she is prepared to go to to get what she wants."

"Leave Ellen to me," Kane responded confidently. "And I don't want to hear another word about leaving. Is that clear?" Reluctantly, Glenna nodded, still undecided as to whether or not she was doing the right thing.

"I don't want to see you or your family hurt on my account or because of Danny," she repeated in a final attempt to sway Kane's thinking.

"What will it take to make you understand that I'd never let you go no matter what Ellen did or said? I'll always love you. I can't look at you without remembering how you look lying naked in my arms, your emerald eyes glazed with passion. Few people experience what we have together, love. Do you think I'd let you go so easily? One day our son will bear my name, I promise. Trust me, Glenna. Trust me and love me."

"Oh, Kane, I do love you. That's why I agreed to leave. I never want our love to hurt you."

"No, Glenna, you'll not leave. Not now, not ever. You mean too much to me. Look at me," he said gently, tilting her chin with one finger until their eyes met. "Promise you'll do nothing foolish. Like leaving me. I'll see to Ellen and we'll be married in a few short weeks. Trust me."

"I don't ever want to be separated from you, Kane. I need you. Danny needs you."

"Not as much as I need you and our son." His gray eyes spoke eloquently of his need as he lowered his head and captured her lips, his tongue curling into her mouth, drawing from it a measure of her sweet essence. She responded instantly as his touch ignited the fires of smoldering passion in her. His fingers tunneled through the flaming tendrils that lay against her cheeks as his kiss deepened, his tongue exploring the velvet recesses of her mouth in a way that set her pulses racing. With deliberate thoroughness he let his hands roam to and fro over her supple body, rejoicing in the soft moans escaping her lips, until kisses and caresses no longer satisfied them.

Tenderly he pressed her against the softness of the bed where the downy folds embraced their bodies. His hand slipped into the opening of her bodice and his fingers found her breasts where they teased a nipple until it hardened in response and her breath quickened. Her own fingers flew to the band of his trousers where she tugged impatiently, bringing forth a delighted chuckle from his throat. The sound was a low rumble in the silence of the room.

"I know, love," he whispered hoarsely. "I want you just as badly."

Assisting one another with an eagerness born of mounting passion, their clothes soon lay in a tangled heap beside the bed. As his firm, powerful body lowered over her, she pressed upward. Slowly, with gentle thoroughness, he tensed and tantalized with lips and hands until she warmed and tingled all over. His caresses were exquisite torture and she encouraged him to continue, confessing that he brought her untold pleasure.

"Do you like it when I do this, my love?" he asked, catching an erect nipple between his teeth then drawing it into his mouth.

"Yes," gasped Glenna, lurching against the pull of his lips.

"And what about this?" he asked, his mouth trailing fire along her rib cage, pausing to sip delicately at the slight indentation of her navel before coming to rest at the forest of bright fleece shielding her womanhood.

"Oh God, Kane, yes!"

His fingers parted bright curls until his tongue found the treasure he sought, driving her to a frenzy of desire.

"Please, Kane, now," Glenna begged, tugging at his hair.

"Let go, love," Kane urged, renewing his efforts to bring her the greatest pleasure possible. "I want to give you more pleasure than you've ever known."

Glenna was soaring; her body afire, her senses reeling. Kane's tongue probed relentlessly into her throbbing flesh and she began vibrating with a need beyond defining. Just when she thought she could experience no greater joy, Kane carefully inserted a finger into her hot woman's flesh. She made no effort then to hold back as a shriek of elation ripped through her body radiating from the place where Kane lovingly toiled.

And then he was looming above her, filling her with his maleness, murmuring his pleasure at her response in her ear. Kane groaned as tight flesh enfolded him in a deep caress that nearly proved his undoing. But he wanted to be strong for her; wanted to show her, where words failed, just how much he loved and needed her.

Deliberately pacing himself, Kane began moving in long, gentle strokes, carefully stoking her need as well as his own. When he felt the flicker of response in her burst into flame, his thrusts quickened, becoming more forceful, his urgency sparking her own until Glenna found herself matching his strokes, the fire building once again.

"I can't wait much longer, love," Kane panted. Beads of sweat peppered his forehead and his face tensed in concentration. "Come with me, Glenna."

He thrust vigorously, once, twice, and Glenna needed no further urging as she felt sensation mounting, despite having been thoroughly sated only moments before. And then she was there, joining Kane in his race toward the stars. At the moment ecstasy claimed him her name slipped naturally from his lips.

Replete, they lay in each other's arms, limbs entwined, hearts beating in unison. "Now do you see why we belong together, Glenna?" Kane asked in a breathless whisper. "We were made for one another, love."

Smiling contentedly, Glenna had to agree.

The next day Kane paid a call on Ellen. Impatiently he paced the elegantly appointed parlor of the Fairchild mansion while he waited for Ellen to make her appearance.

"Kane! How nice of you to call," greeted Ellen as she breezed gaily into the room. "If you've come to see father, you just missed him. He and mother left hours ago to spend the summer at the beach. They want me to join them but I'm reluctant to leave the city for the boredom of the seashore,'' she rambled on endlessly.

''I didn't come to see your father, Ellen,'' Kane informed her bluntly. ''I think you know why I'm here.''

''I haven't the slightest idea,'' Ellen replied with studied innocence. ''Unless . . . unless you've finally come to your senses and realized that Glenna isn't the woman for you.''

''Glenna is more woman than you could ever hope to be!'' Kane thundered, impaling her with an icy glare. ''Did you think by forcing her to leave me you could take her place?''

''Did Glenna tell you that, Kane? If she did she's lying. I'd never do such—''

''No use pretending, Ellen. Thank God I arrived before Glenna was able to comply with your devious wishes. Even if she had succeeded, know that I'd never turn to you for solace.'' His face a mask of rage, Kane took a menacing step forward, causing Ellen to retreat hastily.

''Kane, what I did was for your own good,'' Ellen reasoned in vain. ''Glenna is married to another man. You are only hurting yourself and your family by defying society and living openly as man and wife.''

''How did you find out, Ellen?''

''I . . . I overheard a conversation between you and Glenna.''

''You eavesdropped, you mean,'' accused Kane hotly. ''And then you used the information to force Glenna to leave me. Well, it won't work. Have you told anyone yet? Have you already begun to spread your poison?''

''No, Kane,'' Ellen was quick to deny. ''I've told no one.'' She wasn't about to tell Kane of the telegram she sent to Judd Martin closely followed by a letter. Nor reveal the fact that she had already received a reply from Glenna's grateful husband.

"Then you can thank your lucky stars you possessed the foresight to keep your mouth shut," Kane warned sternly. "Soon Glenna will be granted an annulment and we can be married like we were meant to be. Then no one will be able to hurt her. In the meantime, I'd strongly advise you to stay away from my family and remain silent. Do we understand each other, Ellen?"

Ellen blanched, well aware of Kane's temper when crossed. He could be a hard, cruel man and she had no wish to be on the receiving end of his punishment. "I understand, Kane," she ground out from between clenched teeth. "I'll give you no more trouble."

"See that you don't," Kane said tersely. Then he whirled on his heel and left Ellen standing in the middle of the room, her knees shaking dangerously.

If Kane knew she had wired Judd Martin, Ellen thought bleakly, her life wouldn't be worth much. Fear released her feet as she raced to her room to pack a bag, thinking it was long past time to join her parents at the seashore. She wanted to be nowhere within reach when Judd Martin turned up at Morgan Manor to claim his wife.

20

In the days that followed Glenna went about her business with bated breath, certain that Ellen would spread her tale no matter what Kane said. Though Kane assured her he had taken care of the problem, Glenna still had her doubts. Somehow Ellen did not seem the type to give up so easily.

Only after two weeks passed with no hint of gossip reaching her ears did Glenna begin to relax. During that time Ellen had kept her distance. In fact, Beth told her Ellen had joined her parents at the seashore and wasn't expected back in the city anytime soon. At long last Glenna was able to accept Kane's prediction that nothing would go wrong and they would soon be man and wife, confiding to Kane that she was sorry she hadn't seen fit to trust him to handle Ellen the first time she was approached by the spiteful blond. But her relief was short-lived.

The following day Glenna had a surprise visitor. She was summoned by Perkins who informed her a man requesting to see her awaited in the parlor. Kane had left earlier to inspect a new steamship he considered buying and none of the other Morgans had yet arived downstairs for dinner.

Though the man had his back to her studying a portrait on the wall, Glenna recognized him instantly. His rust-colored hair and thin frame gave him away. As if sensing her presence, Judd Martin turned, a wide smile spread across his attractive features.

"Did you think I wouldn't find you, Glenna?" he asked, his smile turning into a snarl. "You're my wife and it's time you returned to my bed and board. You've played whore for Kane Morgan long enough." He raked his slim figure insultingly. "So you've had his bastard. Good! Soon your belly will swell with my seed."

Astounded to see Judd standing before her, Glenna could do little more than stare, mouth agape, all her senses screaming out in protest. It appeared that Ellen had gotten her revenge after all. For how else would Judd know where to find her? Just thinking of Ellen made her blood boil, releasing her from her stupor.

"Get out of here, Judd! Leave me alone. Soon our marriage will be dissolved. I'll have my annulment and then Kane and I will be married. I want nothing more to do with you."

A nasty laugh bubbled forth from Judd's throat. "If you don't have the annulment in your possession then you are still my wife, and I have every right to claim you."

"No!" cried Glenna, truly frightened. Never would she willingly place herself in Judd's hands! Never would she allow him to raise Kane's child! "There's more to consider than just myself. There's Kane's son."

"So you've given Morgan a son," sneered Judd. "Leave the brat for all I care. Just pack your bags, we're leaving."

"I'm going nowhere with you, Judd Martin! I

belong with Kane."

"That bastard has more lives than a cat. I thought he was dead."

"He's very much alive, and we love each other. For once in your life do something decent. Leave us be," Glenna implored.

"Pack your bags, my dear."

"Are you going somewhere, Glenna? Who is this man?"

Both Glenna and Judd swiveled to face Beth who happened to be passing the parlor and halted in the doorway at the sound of voices raised in anger. Immediately Judd stepped forward and sketched an elegant bow before the attractive older woman.

"Allow me to introduce myself, madam. I am Judd Martin."

"I am Beth Morgan," Beth replied warily. "Are you a friend of my daugher-in-law?"

Judd laughed raucously. "Your daughter-in-law! That is impossible, Mrs. Morgan. Glenna has no mother-in-law. I am Glenna's husband and my own mother has long since gone to her reward."

Shock marched across Beth's face and her gentle eyes showed the tortured dullness of disbelief. "You, sir, are a liar!" she accused haughtily. "Glenna is married to my son Kane. They have a child but a few weeks old."

A smug smile hanging on the corner of his mouth, Judd reached into his pocket and extracted a sheet of paper, presenting it to Beth with a flourish. "If you require proof, madam, then this should suffice."

With a sense of dread Beth glanced at the paper long enough to recognize the document as well as Glenna's signature next to that of Judd Martin, attesting to its authenticity. She raised her head, staring at Glenna with stricken eyes.

"Is this man truly your husband?" she asked, choking on her words.

With all her heart Glenna wished she had left two weeks ago as she had planned rather than see Beth hurt like this. She nodded, searching for words of explanation.

Beth blanched, thinking of the innocent babe she had come to love beyond reason. Her grandson, or so she assumed. She hesitated, blinking with bafflement and torn by conflicting emotions. "Is Danny Kane's child? Or . . . or is this man the father?" she found the courage to ask.

"In name the child is mine," Judd forestalled Glenna by answering. "But in truth he's your son's bastard. It's difficult to admit one's wife has been unfaithful, madam, but one man has never been enough for Glenna. How long do you think she'd remain with Kane? Not long, I'd wager."

Glenna gasped, her face a mask of horror. "Don't believe him, Beth!" she pleaded. "The man is despicable. You don't know him. He forced me into marriage, then stole my inheritance. He is involved in my father's murder and would stoop to any means to gain what he wants."

"What a tale you tell, my dear," replied Judd smoothly. "Why, Glenna's best friend is a whore. Certainly that reveals something about her character."

"I'm not ashamed to claim Sal as my friend," Glenna retorted thoughtlessly, suddenly realizing how her admission must sound to Beth.

See, I told you so, Judd's expression seemed to suggest as he slanted Beth a knowing smirk.

"How could you, Glenna?" Beth sobbed, her voice catching painfully in her throat. "We took you into our home, accepted you, and loved you, and you repay us by living a lie."

"Beth, please, let me explain," Glenna begged, driven by desperation.

"Explain what?" James strode briskly into the room followed closely by Winnie. His cool, gray eyes moved assessingly over Judd before settling uncertainly on Glenna. "What is this all about, Glenna? What is this man to you?"

"I am Glenna's husband, sir. Judd Martin, at your service."

"You are mistaken, Mr. Martin," James denied stoutly. "Glenna is my brother's wife."

"James," Beth interjected, sending a wounded look in Glenna's direction. "Look at this." Glenna's marriage certificate passed easily into James' hand while Judd stood by grinning.

James quickly scanned the words than handed it to Winnie, turning a disapproving frown on Glenna. "Is this true, Glenna?" Glenna nodded unhappily. "Does Kane know about your husband?"

"James, please don't condemn me without listening to my explanation. Kane and I love each other. He knows about Judd and has quietly been working on my behalf to obtain an annulment. We were so close until Ellen discovered the truth. I'm certain she's the one who informed Judd where to find me. I'm within weeks of being free. Kane and I were to wed immediately upon receipt of my annulment. Don't judge me harshly when you nothing of my situation."

"You lied to us, Glenna. I know that much. Am I right in assuming Danny is Kane's son?"

"Yes," Glenna whispered, her voice quivering with emotion. Where was Kane when she needed him?

"And you've come for your wife, is that correct, sir?" James questioned Judd curtly.

"Though she might be another man's whore, Glenna is still my wife," Judd shrugged carelessly. "I have every intention of taking her back to Denver with me."

"Then I suggest you pack, Glenna," James shocked her by saying. "But the baby remains. He's Kane's son and will be raised accordingly. Does that meet with your approval, Mr. Martin?"

"Keep the boy, if it pleases you," Judd agreed amicably. "I'm perfectly capable of fathering my own child."

"Only Kane has the right to send me away!" Glenna exploded in a fit of rage. "Don't you think he deserves a say in all this, James?"

"As head of the family, Glenna, I make the decisions. And if I say you belong with your husband then Kane has no choice but to agree."

"You have no right to decide my future, James," Glenna fumed impotently. "What makes you think I'd leave Danny behind? Besides, I'm not budging from here until Kane returns."

"I'll grant you that much," James allowed grudgingly. "We'll all wait here until Kane arrives."

Judd bristled indignantly. "I have better things to do than wait around all day for my wife's lover. I'm leaving, but expect me back bright and early tomorrow for I'm definitely not leaving town alone. Or if you decide to let Glenna go today you can contact me at Hayden House where I'm staying. Room five, first floor." He turned to leave and James nodded curtly, happy to be rid of the despicable man so easily. He'd seen and heard enough from Judd Martin for one day.

The moment Judd left the room, James whirled on Glenna. "How dare you put us in this position!" he blustered angrily. "Once this gets out we will be the laughingstock of Philadelphia."

"James," chided Beth. "You're being too hard on Glenna. "From what I understand of the situation Kane had full knowledge of Glenna's past. You can't hold him blameless in this mess."

"Nor do I," James replied coolly. "I'll say my piece to Kane when he arrives."

"Don't make Glenna leave," Winnie shocked everyone by saying. Until now she had stood silently by, taking everything in, including her husband's decision to send Glenna packing. To everyone's knowledge it was the first time she had ever disagreed with James or openly defied him. "It's obvious Glenna and Kane love each other deeply. And what about Danny? He belongs to us. You can't separate a mother from her child."

"Winnie, I think these decisions are best left to me," James frowned reprovingly.

"You know I've always deferred to you in all things, James," Winnie sniffed, "but I think this time you're wrong to summarily hand Glenna over to that dreadful Judd Martin. From what little I saw of him I don't like him."

Glenna flashed Winnie a grateful smile, then glanced hopefully at Beth, her eyes pleading. "Perhaps Winnie has a point, James," she acquiesced thoughtfully. "Kane knows what he is doing. Why not let him explain before condemning Glenna. After all, she is the mother of Kane's child."

"What am I supposed to explain?" came a well-loved voice from the doorway.

Stifling a cry of joy, Glenna launched herself at Kane, nearly knocking him over. "What is it, darling? Has something happened to upset you?" He scowled at James ferociously. "What did you say to Glenna, James?"

"Better you should ask what Glenna has done to upset us," James shot back reproachfully. "I assume you knew all along that she is married to a man named Judd Martin. How dare you foist her off as your wife!"

"Damn that little bitch," Kane cursed beneath his

breath, referring to Ellen. To James, he said, "Glenna might be Martin's wife according to the law, but she has always belonged to me. That bastard forced her into marriage, abused her and stole her inheritance. Besides, in a few weeks she'll be a free woman and can do as she pleases. My lawyers assured me an annulment is forthcoming."

"You could have had the decency to tell us all this from the first," James retorted. "We are your family."

"Would the truth have been any easier to swallow?" Kane contended angrily. James had the decency to flush. "Would you have Glenna bear my child anywhere but at Morgan Manor?"

"No!" cried Beth, siding solidly with Kane. She had come to love Glenna like a daughter and couldn't bear to part with Danny. "James, listen to Kane. If that man is as despicable as Kane says he is then I can't fault Kane for taking her away. I might not agree with his decision to keep the truth from us but I wouldn't wish Glenna back with her husband. Perhaps we can keep this quiet and once Kane and Glenna are married no one needs to know the truth."

"Mother," James said patiently. "You heard Martin. He fully expects Glenna to return with him to Denver. Does he look the type to take defeat lightly? Besides, the law is on his side. Glenna is his wife."

"I'll not go with him," Glenna vowed stubbornly.

"You have no choice," James countered sternly. "Had you confided in me from the beginning I might have found some way to help you. But now—it's too late."

"It's not too late," Kane argued. "I'm perfectly capable of solving my own problems. Neither Glenna nor Danny will leave Morgan Manor. I'd kill Martin before I'd allow him to take either of them from me."

"Kane!" gasped Beth, shocked at Kane's fervent avowal. "Don't talk like that! Taking another man's life is a serious matter."

"I've never been more serious in my life, mother. I love Glenna and no one, certainly not Judd Martin, is going to claim what's mine."

A long silence ensued, the poignant moment sharpened by Kane's determination to protect Glenna against any threat, at whatever cost. Unable to bear the dissension between family members, especially when she was the cause, Glenna jumped into the void.

"I'm sorry," she murmured, gulping back her tears. "I tried to leave two weeks ago after Ellen's visit, but Kane interfered. I never meant to hurt anyone."

"Ellen Fairchild?" James demanded to know. "What does she have to do with this?"

"Somehow she learned of Glenna's marriage and confronted her, demanding that she leave or face full disclosure," Kane replied bitterly. Then he went on to explain what happened between Glenna, Ellen and himself, ending by saying that no one but Ellen could have informed Judd Martin of Glenna's whereabouts.

"Why would Ellen do such a thing?" Beth asked, puzzled.

"She wants Kane," Winnie answered intuitively before either Kane or Glenna could form a reply.

"But to deliberately disrupt an entire family!" Beth wailed, dismayed. "I guess I never knew her."

"Nor I," admitted Winnie. "And to think I once felt sorry for her."

"This talk is getting us nowhere," James interrupted impatiently. "The fact remains that Glenna is still the wife of Judd Martin. And if he chooses he can bring the law here to claim what is legally his."

Glenna clung to Kane, using his comforting bulk as a lifeline. Why couldn't Judd have stayed away two weeks longer, when according to Kane she would have had her precious annulment? she silently lamented.

"Don't despair, darling," Kane patted her

soothingly. "I'll go and speak to Martin. I'd gladly offer all I possess if he'd agree to leave us in peace. Who knows, it just might appeal to a greedy man like him."

"I wouldn't ask you to beggar yourself for me, Kane," Glenna shook her head despondently.

"What good is all my wealth without you to share it with?" Kane chided gently.

"Hmmm, it just might work," James mused, rubbing his chin thoughtfully. "Are you determined to go through with this, Kane?"

"Determined is hardly a strong enough word, James. Glenna is my wife in all but name. And soon we'll be properly married. Martin is welcome to everything I own if he'll quietly disappear."

"I still can't forgive you so easily for deceiving us, but—well, damn it, you're still my brother and Danny is my nephew. Any fool can see that you and Glenna were meant for each other. If all you own isn't enough for Martin, you can depend on me to provide what is needed."

A suspicious moistness gathered in the corners of Kane's eyes. "Thank you, James," he said gratefully, clasping his brother on the shoulder.

"I suspect I did it for myself as much as for you. I'd never be able to live with Winnie or mother if I didn't offer. I don't condone what you and Glenna did, mind you, but I respect your motives. I agree that Glenna is worth fighting for despite my earlier misgivings. I think the appearance of Martin took us all by surprise."

"Then it's settled," Kane smiled, hugging Glenna warmly. "I'll speak to Martin as soon as possible."

Later, in the privacy of their room, Glenna voiced her doubts. "It's not going to work, Kane," she shook her head sadly. "Judd has all the money he needs. For some reason he wants me. I've rejected him so many times he's become obsessed with the need to possess me.

I think I know Judd better than you, Kane, and the man won't be satisfied with anything less than having me in his bed."

"Over my dead body!" stormed Kane, flinging himself around the room in a rage. "He'll not have you. I'll do whatever is necessary, including murder, to keep him from claiming you," he rashly proclaimed. "Trust me, darling. One way or another Judd Martin will be gone from our lives forever."

No sooner had Kane left the house to confront Judd than his words came tumbling back to haunt her. Several times this day he had threatened Judd's life. Would Kane actually kill for her if it came right down to it? Glenna asked herself, suddenly frightened. Well aware of Kane's temper when roused to anger Glenna decided he would. That thought scared the wits out of her, instilling her with the courage to somehow prevent Kane from doing something he would later regret.

Sparing a brief moment to look in on a sleeping Danny, Glenna slipped unseen from the house and traced Kane's steps to Hayden House but a short distance away. Earlier Judd had said he occupied Room Five located on the first floor, so when she reached the hotel a bare ten minutes behind Kane, she decided to locate Judd's room from the outside and peer in through the window, revealing herself only should Kane's anger explode and he attempted to make good his threat against Judd's life. She loved Kane far too much to see him punished for a crime committed in her behalf.

Glenna rounded a corner, carefully counting the windows along the side of the building until she came to what she thught was Room Five, fear for Kane hastening her steps. Suddenly she halted, her incredulous gaze following a man hurrying away in the opposite direction. Though she had caught a mere glimpse of his profile, Glenna was certain it was that despicable Wiley Wilson, the man who had killed her father. What was he doing in Philadelphia? she wondered curiously. But when she looked back to refresh her memory, he had disappeared from sight, and Glenna was no longer certain of the man's identity.

Gingerly Glenna approached the open window, surreptitiously glancing about in all directions before sidling closer. No one was about and the encroaching darkness as well as the concealing shrubs effectively shielded her stealthy movements. When no cry of warning sounded, Glenna sighed gratefully and stretched on tiptoes until she could see into the room. Her determination to protect Kane from his own folly was like a rock inside her and she forced herself into a calm she was far from feeling as her eyes anxiously scanned the room. Sheer black fright swept through her at the grisly sight that confronted her.

Kane stood over Judd's lifeless form stretched out on the floor, a smoking gun held loosely in one hand. From her perch outside the window Glenna saw all too clearly the bright splotch spreading from a central area just above Judd's heart. No sign of life remained in his rigid body. She had arrived too late! From all appearances Kane had already carried out his threat and rid them of Judd's unwelcome interference in their lives. On the verge of alerting Kane to her presence, Glenna hesitated when a loud commotion momentarily confused her. And then it was too late to reveal herself as the door to the room burst open and two uniformed policemen rushed inside.

Kane stared down at Judd's still form, intuitively aware that he was dead. The weapon in his hand was still warm. Though a man lay dead at his feet he could dredge up no remorse. Judd Martin deserved to die. His one consuming thought was of Glenna, and that now she was free to marry him. Suddenly, loud noises at the closed door alerted him to the fact that he had unwittingly placed himself in a threatening position. But before he could react, the door burst open admitting the law.

For as long as he lived Kane would wonder what provoked him into glancing toward the open window. Perhaps it was the muted sound of someone stifling a sob. Or maybe he was so perfectly attuned to his only love that he was instantly aware whenever she was near. Whatever it was, he caught a brief picture of a white face peering into the room. Glenna!

How long had she been watching? Kane wondered distractedly. And for what purpose? Suddenly comprehension dawned as the two policemen closed in on him and demanded he drop the weapon. Dragging his eyes from the window, Kane stared at the gun in his hand as if seeing it for the first time. It fell to the floor with a dull thud. Then he moved cautiously toward the lawmen in a deliberate effort to draw their attention from the open window and Glenna. If only she had the presence of mind to remain silent so as not to attract undue attention to herself, Kane silently implored. He was determined to protect Glenna at all costs.

"Stay where you are," one of the policemen ordered while the other gingerly approached Judd's body. "Is he dead, Casey?"

Casey bent over Judd's still form, felt for a pulse, then shook his head. "No need to call a doctor, Fenton," Casey said, rising to his feet. "The bullet went through his heart. He died instantly."

"Who are you, mister?" Casey demanded to know.

"Kane Morgan," Kane replied, sparing a brief glance toward the window, encountering nothing but empty space. Had he only imagined Glenna standing outside? No, of course not. A very frightened, very real Glenna had been there. Had she in fact beat him to Judd when he was delayed a few minutes by an old friend outside Hayden House? Did she have enough time to. . . . All his senses screamed in protest. Glenna must be protected no matter what the consequences.

"Did you kill this man, Mr. Morgan?" Fenton asked, keeping a wary eye trained on Kane.

A long silence ensued, a silence fraught with a multitude of decisions and unanswered questions, none of them attractive. But in the end there was but one answer possible. "Yes," he admitted dully, with finality. "I killed Judd Martin."

While Kane was handcuffed and led away, Glenna sat on the ground beneath the window, completely hidden by shrubbery, one fist stuffed in her mouth to stifle her cries of anguish. She had heard Kane admit to murder and the shock of it had rendered her numb. She had no idea how long she sat there on the damp ground after the police led Kane away, until she finally comprehended the seriousness of the charges leveled against him and the consequences that followed. Only then did she rally. He had risked everything for her and she owed it to him to keep her wits about her in order to be of any help.

Rising unsteadily to her feet, Glenna ran all the way to Morgan Manor, fighting desperately to retain her fragile control. James! She had to find James immediately and tell him what she had just seen and heard. If anyone could help Kane it was James.

Glenna was nearly hysterical when she reached the house, rushing inside just as the family was leaving the dining room. Her unorthodox entrance halted them in their tracks.

"My word, Glenna, wherever have you been?" Beth asked, noticing her sudden pallor and the disheveled state of her clothing.

"We waited dinner for you," James scowled, "but Perkins said you left the house. Surely you didn't go with Kane, did you?"

"James, oh James! Kane is in terrible trouble," Glenna gasped. "He needs you!"

"Glenna, calm down. What happened to Kane? He went to see Judd Martin. Did that man harm Kane? If he did I'll—"

"You don't understand, James," wailed Glenna, finding it impossible to steady her racing heart. "Kane killed Judd Martin! I saw him standing over the body with a gun. The police came and took him away. Oh, James, you've got to help him."

Beth collapsed in a chair making choking sounds in her throat while Winnie stood beside her, obviously in shock. "You saw Kane kill Martin?" questioned James sharply. "You're absolutely certain, Glenna? Where were you when all this took place?"

"I . . . was afraid something like this would happen so I followed Kane to Judd's hotel. Only I arrived too late," Glenna revealed, biting her lip to control her tears. A raw, primitive grief overwhelmed her as she wrapped herself in a cocoon of misery. "He did it for me and now he's in jail."

"Glenna, listen to me. Did you actually see Kane shoot Martin?" James repeated, giving her an exasperated shake.

"N-no," Glenna stuttered. "But the gun in his hand was still smoking. What else could I think? I'm certain Judd refused to relinquish his hold over me and in his rage Kane shot him. If I had left weeks ago none of this would have happened."

"Don't say that, Glenna," Winnie chided, finally finding her voice. "We couldn't bear it if you had taken Danny away. I'm sure James will straighten all this out. Won't you, James?"

Three pairs of anxious eyes turned to James. "Will you help Kane, James?" Beth added her plea to those of Winnie and Glenna. "There has to be some kind of mix-up for Kane isn't capable of cold-blooded murder."

"I'll see what I can do, mother," James sighed wearily, certain that his hotheaded brother was capable of anything in defense of the woman he loved. But if there was any way at all to help Kane he would find it. I'll go immediately to the police station and find out from Kane exactly what happened."

"I'll go with you," chimed in three feminine voices.

"No, I'll go alone," James protested earnestly. "If I'm to be of any help to Kane it's best I question him in private. I'll be back as soon as I can."

"James," Glenna said hesitantly. "Tell Kane that . . . that I love him no matter what."

James nodded, then hurried out the door before the women decided to press their suit to accompany him. He wasn't certain he could deal with their emotions when they saw Kane behind bars. For that matter he was uncertain how he would handle it himself.

Kane paced the confines of the small, airless cell, weighing the whole structure of events in his mind. His heart refused to believe what his mind told him. Glenna had nearly killed Judd once, and this time she had finally succeeded. What had gone on before he reached Martin's room? he wondered bleakly. Had Glenna arrived with the intention of killing her legal husband? Why, Glenna, why? he silently raged. Couldn't you trust me to handle it?

Kane had arrived at Judd's room only minutes after he heard the shot from the hallway and rushed headlong through the unlocked door to find Judd sprawled on the floor, dead from a bullet wound through the heart. Driven by instinct, he picked up the still smoking gun to inspect it. After that all hell broke loose, and then he saw Glenna crouched outside the open window. It took damn little imagination to convince himself of what had taken place only moments before his arrival. And he was determined to protect Glenna no matter what the cost to himself.

"You have a visitor, Morgan," a curt voice disturbed his reverie. "Five minutes is all you're allowed."

Kane looked up to see James standing behind the guard, his concerned features creased with worry. Kane waited until the guard left then asked in a low voice, "How did you find out so soon, James?"

"That's unimportant, Kane," James dismissed impatiently. "What matters now is learning the truth so I'll know best how to help you."

"I killed Judd Martin, it's as simple as that," Kane insisted stubbornly, refusing to meet James's eyes.

"Why, Kane? For God's sake, man, don't you realize the trouble you're in? Cold-blooded murder is punishable by death. At least tell me he drew first, or threatened you, anything. If only I had taken your threat to kill Martin seriously I might have prevented this. Please, Kane, tell me the truth!"

"I told you, James. I killed Martin after he steadfastly refused to leave Glenna alone."

"I don't believe you, Kane. You're not a killer. There's more here than meets the eye. Why do you persist in this folly? I can help you if you'd only confide in me."

"It's no use, James," Kane reiterated, his square chin tilted at a stubborn angle. "I'd appreciate it if you could find me a good lawyer, I don't fancy dying." Wild horses couldn't drag the truth out of him, Kane decided, clamping his teeth tightly together.

"Your five minutes are up," the guard announced curtly. But James was reluctant to leave. How could he face the women after what Kane just admitted?

"Go on, James," Kane urged. "The women will need you. "Tell Glenna I love her, and take care of Danny for me."

"Glenna sends her love to you," James remembered as he turned to leave. "And Kane, think about what I said. You're hurting no one but yourself by concealing the truth. Not for one minute do I believe you killed Martin without reason or provocation."

Glenna cried steadily for two days. By now news of Kane's dreadful crime was widespread throughout the city and talk of the upcoming trial could be heard on every street corner and perused in all the newspapers. The local tabloids labeled it a crime of passion, for it didn't take long to ascertain that Glenna was Judd Martin's wife once the marriage license was discovered on his body. Consequently Glenna was raked over the coals by the gossips, but none of that mattered when Kane's life hung in the balance. James had hired the best trial lawyer in Philadelphia but in view of Kane's confession and overwhelming evidence against him, things looked bleak indeed.

What really bothered Glenna was that she had yet to see Kane. After James's visit she had tried to gain admittance and was turned away by a guard. Then a few minutes ago James informed her that Kane was once again allowed visitors and she hurried to the jail, anxious to see and speak with her husband.

He was waiting for her when she arrived, having already been told to expect her. They embraced through the bars and Kane tasted salt on her face when they kissed. "Don't cry, darling," he whispered, brushing away the tears with the balls of his thumbs.

Peering through a watery mist, Glenna clung to him, the bars biting into her tender flesh. "I'm so worried, Kane," she sighed.

"There's no need for worry, love," Kane assured her with more confidence than he felt. "I'll protect you. No one need know what really happened." His voice dropped so low she could barely hear him.

"What?" Glenna asked, becoming instantly alert. "What are you talking about?"

"You can drop the pretense with me, love," Kane whispered, keeping an eye peeled for the guard. "I'd never betray you. What really puzzles me is why you tried to solve this on your own. Didn't you trust me enough to handle Judd Martin?"

"Kane! For God's sake, you're not making sense. I didn't kill Judd. I thought you did. I heard you admit to the police. You told James you killed him." They both froze in a stunned tableau.

"Jesus!" groaned Kane irreverently. "I saw you outside Martin's window, Glenna. He was dead when I arrived, and when I saw you lurking nearby I thought . . . that is, I naturally assumed—"

"Oh Kane!" wailed Glenna as shock shuddered through her. "Whatever are we to do? If you didn't kill Judd, and I didn't, then who did?"

Kane groaned in frustration. "And to think I confessed to a murder I didn't commit. As to the culprit, I haven't the vaguest idea. Did you see anything suspicious while you were outside Martin's room?" Then he paused, eyeing her curiously. "Just what the hell were you doing out there, Glenna?"

"I . . . I followed you, Kane," Glenna admitted sheepishly. "I hoped to prevent you from . . . doing something you'd later regret. I felt responsible for everything that happened and hid beneath the window in the event I was needed. I arrived in time to see you standing over Judd with a gun in your hand."

"It's obvious we were both mistaken," Kane allowed with a weary shrug. "I only hope it's not too late to find the real killer. If only you had seen something—or someone. The real killer had to escape through the open window for if he had gone through the door I would have seen him."

"I'm sorry, Kane, but . . . wait!" she cried,

bursting with excitement. "I did see someone, someone I recognized. It was only a fleeting glance but I could have sworm I saw Wiley hurrying away from the hotel."

"Wiley Wilson? That old reprobate who tried to rape you back in Denver? What would he be doing in Philadelphia and why would he kill Martin? Wiley was in Martin's employ."

"I don't know, Kane, but it's a start. If Wiley didn't do it maybe he knows who did."

"You're right, love," Kane acknowledged thoughtfully. "Find James and tell him all you just told me. If Wiley is still around James will find him. Then have him notify my lawyer so I can change my plea."

"Kane, I'm so frightened. What if you're convicted?"

"Trust me, darling, I won't be. It will all work out and then we'll be together like we were meant to be."

On that note they parted, Kane to continue his pacing and Glenna in search of James.

21

"I knew Kane wasn't being truthful!" proclaimed James loud enough to carry through his office door. "I don't know how we're going to undo the damage already done by his ill-timed confession. If only he had seen fit to confide in me."

"What's done is done," Glenna sighed regretfully. "I only hope it isn't too late to find Wiley Wilson and force a confession from him."

"Do you really think this Wiley character could have killed Martin?"

"He's certainly capable of it. I told you he's the man who killed Da. Do you think you can find him? Even if he isn't guilty I'm certain he was up to no good," Glenna ventured.

"If what you told me about him is true, I daresay you're right," James mused thoughtfully. "And if this Wiley is still in Philadelphia I'll find him. Now," James said, rising abruptly, "I'm off to talk to the lawyer, then I'm going to hire a private detective to find Wilson.

Give me his description and I guarantee I'll find him if he's in the city."

Glenna obliged by providing a detailed description of the scruffy prospector, then hurried off to inform Beth and Winnie of this latest development while James rushed to the lawyer's office.

Though James's search for Wiley was thorough, encompassing Philadelphia and its environs, the man was not found. He seemed to have disappeared into thin air, if indeed it was Wiley Glenna had seen. And after several fruitless days of searching, James began to think she had been mistaken, that the dim light and her fear for Kane had sparked her imagination.

And then one of the men engaged in the search brought back the disturbing news that a man of Wiley's description had checked into a rundown inn in a seedy section of town under the name of Fred Wiley. Glenna was ecstatic, thinking their search at an end until James reluctantly revealed that Wiley checked out the day after Judd's murder. He told the desk clerk he was leaving town.

"There goes our case," James lamented, cursing beneath his breath. The family was seated in the parlor after supper when James disclosed the results of his search.

"Oh, James," Beth wailed, dismayed. "What will we do now? I can't bear to see Kane wasting away in jail."

"Jail is the least of Kane's worries," James remarked grimly. "A guilty verdict could mean his death. But I haven't told you everything. Ellen Fairchild has been subpoenaed to testify for the prosecution. According to Kane's lawyer she is reported to have heard Kane threaten to kill Judd Martin."

"Oh, no, the vindictive witch," groaned Winnie,

voicing the opinion of all present. "Kane is doomed."

Beth began sobbing softly, but Glenna's despair took an altogether different turn. She grew angry. And the angrier she got the more determined she became. "I'll not let Kane suffer!" she declared stubbornly. "I'm going to find Wiley Wilson myself!"

"If only it were that simple," James responded. "We have no idea where to find the man."

"I know," Glenna speculated shrewdly. "I'm absolutely certain Wiley returned to Denver. And I'm going to be aboard the next westbound train. Don't ask me how, but one way or another I'll clear Kane's name of that ridiculous murder charge."

"I can't let you go, Glenna," James objected vigorously. "Kane would never forgive me if I let you traipse off by yourself in search of a killer. I'll send off a telegram to the marshal inquiring if Wiley is in Denver. If he is we can hire a detective to bring him back."

"That isn't any good, James," Glenna contended in a rush of words. "Time is already running out for Kane. If we're to save him it's imperative I leave immediately. Besides, I don't trust the marshal, he was Judd's man." She whirled to confront Beth and Winnie, her green eyes imploring. "You'll care for Danny while I'm gone, won't you?"

"You know we will," Beth promised. "But Glenna, it could be dangerous and Kane—"

"How much time do I have, James?" Glenna cut her off impatiently. "How soon before Kane's trial?"

"Sixty days is the best we can hope for, Glenna. Lawyer Murdoch is prepared to ask for an extension and I'm certain it will be granted."

"It's not much but it will have to do," Glenna nodded with grim determination. "I'll pack immediately."

"If you're set on this folly, Glenna, then I'll go with you," James insisted.

"No, James," Glenna refuted firmly. "You're needed at home. Kane needs you and so do Beth and Winnie. Don't forget, I'm placing my son in your care."

James sighed in resignation. Although he applauded her motives, he deplored her methods. He liked even less the idea of Glenna tracking down a killer alone, pitted against a man like Wilson and whoever hired him. For James was certain that if Wiley was indeed guilty of murder someone had put him up to it. Could he, in all conscience, allow Glenna to go? he asked himself bleakly.

"No, Glenna!" he hammered out firmly. "You're not going."

"Sorry, James. You have no right to issue orders to me. You're neither father, brother nor husband. I'm determined to see Kane's name cleared no matter what it takes."

James could see he was getting nowhere with Glenna. She was adamant about going to Denver. Perhaps . . . just perhaps, there might be a way to aid her cause, he reasoned as an idea suddenly occurred to him. "What about that marshal? The family friend you spoke of who retired."

"You mean Marshal Bartow?"

"Yes. Do you think he'll help you?"

"I . . . I don't know. I suppose it's worth a try if he's returned to Denver."

"The only way I'll let you go is if you promise to seek his help. Otherwise I could never face Kane. Will you grant me that much, Glenna?"

"I promise, James," Glenna vowed solemnly. "If Marshal Bartow is available I'll ask for his help. And James, try to make Kane understand why I must do this."

"She what?" raged Kane in a voice loud enough to raise the dead. "Are you mad, James? How could you let Glenna do anything so foolish? She's throwing herself into a den of lions. If anything happens to her I'll never forgive you!"

"For God's sake, control yourself, Kane. I tried to stop her," James defended, "but Glenna has a mind of her own. She's bound and determined to find Wilson and clear your name."

"I'd rather die for a crime I didn't commit than see Glenna harmed."

"You know Marshal Bartow better than I, do you think he'll help her if asked?"

"Yes, thank God for that much," Kane breathed gratefully. "I would have liked to see her before she left, perhaps I could have talked her into being sensible."

"There was no time, Kane. The train left early this morning. But she promised to send a wire the moment she arrives. God willing she'll be able to shed some light on this mystery."

Eight days later the Union Pacific chugged to a stop in Denver station discharging Glenna and a plethora of other weary travelers. She hired a hack to convey her, along with her luggage, to the Palace Hotel where she engaged a room. After a hot bath and supper she fell into bed and slept eighteen straight hours. When she awoke she felt revitalized, ready and able to do whatever was necessary to clear Kane of the murder charge hanging over his head. But where should she start? She guessed the best place would be with Marshal Bartow. James's idea had been a sound one. If anyone could help her it would be the retired lawman.

After sending a telegram to James as he requested,

Glenna set out for Marshal Bartow's neat cottage located near the center of town. His wife Hilda answered the door.

"Why, Glenna, it's been ages since we've seen you in Denver," the good woman ventured. "We were sorry to hear about your husband. News came over the wire a few days ago. I can't imagine that nice Mr. Morgan committing such a terrible crime."

Would the woman never stop rambling? Glenna wondered impatiently. "Kane didn't kill Judd, Mrs. Bartow. That's why I'm here, to prove his innocence."

"You've come to Denver to prove Mr. Morgan's innocence? What makes you think Judd Martin's killer is in Denver? My oh my," clucked the inquisitive woman.

"Why, if it isn't Glenna," boomed a voice from inside the house. "I never expected to see you back in Denver. Come in, come in. What can I do for you?"

"You can help me find Judd's killer," Glenna revealed. "If I don't, Kane is likely to die for a crime he didn't commit."

"Come into the parlor, Glenna. Hilda will get you something to drink while we talk."

Hilda Bartow recognized a dismissal when she heard one and automatically turned to the kitchen to do her husband's bidding. She had been a lawman's wife far too long to interfere in his business. "I'll make us some lemonade and bring cookies," she called over her shoulder. "Yell when you're ready."

"A good woman," the marshal smiled before turning his attention to Glenna. "Now, Glenna, how can I help you? You know I retired some months ago. In fact, me and Hilda were away on an extended trip back east. I wasn't even aware of your marriage to Judd Martin. Quite a shock, I have to admit."

Immediately Glenna launched into a spirited telling of the facts behind her marriage to Judd Martin.

Bartow spoke little during the recital, only nodding from time to time. If he was shocked by her tale, Glenna wasn't aware of it, for he didn't blink once when she revealed that Wiley had killed her father under Judd's direction and that Judd had married her for the claims, both Golden Promise One and Two that naturally passed to her upon Paddy's death. Only when she revealed that she bore Kane's child did Bartow make any kind of comment.

"I thought there was more than mere friendship between you two. It was obvious to me that Kane's feelings went deep where you were concerned."

"We love each other, Marshal," Glenna admitted shyly. "That's why I'm here."

"So you've been in Philadelphia with Kane all this time," Bartow mused thoughtfully. "How did Martin find you? Judd hinted that you were back east on an extended visit with relatives. Only I knew you had no relatives in this country."

"Somehow Kane's ex-fiancée, Ellen, found out that I was still Judd's wife and informed him where to find me just weeks shy of obtaining my annulment. Judd arrived in Philadelphia to claim me and you know the rest."

"Where does Wiley Wilson fit into all this?"

"I wish I knew," sighed Glenna bleakly. "I saw him, or thought I did, outside Judd's hotel the night he was killed. There has to be a connection and I intend to find it. If you could help me locate Wiley then I—"

"Glenna," Bartow interrupted. "I'm sorry to be the bearer of bad news."

Panic seized Glenna as her mind jumped on Bartow's words and their obscure meaning. "What . . . what is it, Marshal?"

"Wilson was knifed two days ago in an alley behind the Red Garter. He died before naming his killer. It was assumed he was killed for the money he had on him at the time. He won heavily at the poker table that night."

Intense dismay touched her pale face and Glenna merely stared, tongue-tied, and very shaken. "Dead! Now we'll never know if he was Judd's killer," she wailed despondently. "Do you know if he was gone from Denver during the time Judd was in Philadelphia?"

"I don't know, Glenna, but it shouldn't be difficult to find out. If you'd like I'll put out a few feelers and learn what I can."

"I hoped you'd offer," Glenna nodded somberly. "Although I don't know what good it will do now."

"Don't give up, Glenna," Bartow patted her hand in a fatherly manner. "I let you down once when I retired before I found your father's killer, but perhaps it's not too late for Kane."

"I hope you're right, Marshal," Glenna said doubtfully.

They sat in silence for a few minutes, then Bartow asked, "What do you intend to do about your husband's property? I'm sure Martin's lawyers will be glad to see you. From what I understand he left a considerable estate."

The heavy lashes that shadowed Glenna's eyes flew up and she stared at Bartow in surprise, recalling with a start that she was Judd's widow. To her knowledge he had no living relatives, which left her in sole possession of his worldly goods. "To tell the truth I hadn't thought much about it," she stammered.

Later that day Glenna left the law office of Murphy and Conroy, her head whirling in confusion. She had no idea Judd was so wealthy. It seemed that he had been amassing gold and property for years. Besides several working mines yielding both gold and silver, there were two buildings housing a mercantile and hardware store, three tenements, shares in two railroads, the Red Garter, and the house she lived in but briefly. And of course the thousands in the bank accounts that were now hers. Yet she wanted nothing except what was rightfully hers. Her father's claims were all of Judd's property she was the least bit interested in. From the lawyer Glenna also learned that Duke was now in charge at the Red Garter and had been for some time, since before she left Denver with Kane. It amused Judd to play the gentleman while Duke ran the gambling saloon.

Exhausted from her day of surprises, not all of them welcome, Glenna decided to wait until the next day to visit the Red Garter and confront Duke. She hated the man for shooting Kane and leaving him for dead and couldn't wait to dismiss him now that she owned the saloon. Even if she was forced to close the doors to business she meant to be rid of Duke. Lawyer Murphy told her she had every right in the world to do as she pleased with Judd's property. She gave instructions to sell the house but left the firing of Duke to herself. It would do her heart good to witness his dismay after what he did to Kane.

The next morning Marshal Bartow was at her door before breakfast. Arising bright and early that day, Glenna let him in instantly. He offered to buy her meal and over coffee told her what he had learned the previous night.

"Wilson disappeared from town shortly after Judd Martin left," Bartow revealed in a hushed voice. "He returned less than a week ago and was mysteriously killed two days later."

"I can't help but think that—"

"—Wilson was killed to keep him quiet," Bartow supplied, answering Glenna's supposition.

"Exactly. It seems that one murder triggered the other. If only I knew what it all meant," Glenna moaned in desperation. "Time is running out for Kane."

"I learned something else, Glenna," Bartow divulged confidently. "On more than one occasion Wiley was seen conferring with Duke in private. Once they were heard arguing and another time money changed hands. I don't want to raise your hopes needlessly but Wiley could have been paid by Duke to kill Judd."

"By Duke?"

"It's a distinct possibility. But you can't condemn a man on such flimsy evidence. I no longer have the authority to open an investigation and the present marshal and Duke are close friends. He was Judd's man but upon notification of Martin's death he transferred his loyalty to Duke. You know Duke is running the Red Garter and has been for some time, don't you?"

"Yes, Judd's lawyer told me as much. And my first official act as Judd's heir will be to dismiss Duke. That despicable man shot Kane and left him for dead." Bartow gasped in dismay, prompting Glenna to tell him how Duke had shot Kane when he attempted to take her from Judd and how for months she thought him dead.

"Duke isn't a man to be trifled with," Bartow predicted ominously. "In many ways he's worse than Martin."

"I don't want the man in my employ," Glenna ground out remorselessly.

"Don't do anything foolish, my dear," Bartow warned sternly. "Somehow I'll contrive to remain near at hand should you need me. Though I still command a certain amount of influence with the territorial law I am no longer the dispenser of justice in Denver, so I advise you to act prudently at all times. Duke could be extremely dangerous should he think you suspect him of ordering Judd's murder."

It was still early when Glenna entered the Red Garter. Only a few customers were clustered around the bar at this early hour and not more than two or three bargirls sat at a table drinking coffee and talking. Glenna recognized none of them. Even the bartender was totally unfamiliar to her. It looked as if a complete turnover of employees had taken place during her long absence. It amazed Glenna to think she was the owner of a gambling hall. With a sense of wonder her eyes wandered over the rich furnishings and flamboyant interior.

Then abruptly she noticed Duke ambling down the stairs, and their eyes clashed. If ever Glenna recognized shock, it was written all over Duke's face as he turned ashen beneath his deep tan. After a moment or two he gathered his scattered wits and picked his way around the empty tables to her side. He fidgeted nervously, giving Glenna the distinct impression she was the last person in the world he expected or wanted to see.

"Mrs. Martin, Glenna, this is a surprise. I suppose you were notified of Judd's death. A terrible tragedy. I never would have thought Kane Morgan capable of murder. But then, jealousy does strange things to people." He stared at Glenna intently, waiting for her response. No mention was made of the fact that Duke had shot Kane and for months thought him dead.

But Glenna wasn't about to be baited by the likes of Duke. Her one consuming thought was ridding herself of his unwanted presence and doing it as soon as possible. "Death never is a pleasant thing to contemplate," she replied evasively. "Did you know Judd was in Philadelphia?"

"I . . . yes, he told me about you and Morgan. I was here when he received the telegram from some woman back east. He told everyone you were visiting relatives and he was going to fetch you home. Of course

I know the truth. Judd trusted me to keep his secret."

"I'm certain he did," Glenna said disparagingly. "You were two of a kind."

"What's that supposed to mean?" Duke growled, jumping to his own defense.

"Can we talk in private?" Glenna asked, suddenly aware of the curious stares turned in their direction.

"The office should do," Duke replied shortly, leading her into the room Judd always used to conduct his private business. He motioned her to a chair but Glenna preferred to stand. Abruptly she whirled to face the man she despised.

"You must be aware that I'm Judd's sole heir and am now in possession of all his holdings."

Duke nodded warily, certain he knew what was coming next. "I know Judd had no relatives but—to tell the truth I never expected to see you back in Denver. I assumed you and Morgan would marry to legitimize your child and ignore Judd's holdings. I know how you felt about him and Morgan is rich in his own right."

"Do you also know that Kane has been accused of Judd's murder?"

A pointed silence elapsed during which Duke's throat worked convulsively before he formed a reply. "That was a stroke of luck I hadn't counted on," he muttered, half to himself.

"What! What did you say?" demanded Glenna, more certain than ever that Duke was the man behind Judd's murder.

"N-nothing," he stumbled, suddenly aware that he had nearly tipped his hand. "What I meant was that I was surprised to hear that Kane had killed Judd. It's . . . not what I expected of him."

"Kane didn't kill Judd," Glenna refuted hotly. "He was unfortunate enough to be in the wrong place at the wrong time. Someone else beat him to it."

"Did . . . did Morgan see anyone? Do the police

seem satisfied that Morgan did it?" In Glenna's opinion his anxious words were more than enough to convict him.

"I speak the truth when I say Kane didn't do it," Glenna insisted, for the time being keeping to herself the information concerning Wiley being spotted fleeing from the scene of the crime. If Duke paid Wiley to commit murder she didn't want him to think he was suspect.

"I'm surprised you'd leave your lover languishing in jail to come to Denver," Duke contended shrewdly.

"Kane's brother and lawyer expect to have him free soon," Glenna lied convincingly. "My time in Denver is limited since I came only to claim Judd's estate. It's no secret I hated Judd but at least he left me a wealthy widow."

"Did you come to lay claim to the Red Garter?" Duke demanded to know.

"I haven't decided what I want to do with it yet, but of one thing I am certain. I want you out of here, Duke. I never liked you and I don't trust you. When you shot Kane and left him for dead you proved just what a miserable human being you really are."

"What do you mean you want me out of here?" blustered Duke, his temper exploding. "I run the Red Garter! Without me you have nothing. Judd trusted me so why can't you?"

"I'd close the doors before I'd allow you to remain."

"Why didn't you stay in Philadelphia where you belonged? You weren't supposed to come back, ever. Of all the damn rotten luck! I could have taken over here and in time bought the place from Judd's estate for a song."

In face of his implacable fury Glenna took an involuntary step backwards. Had she acted rashly by demanding that Duke relinquish his position? Perhaps her loathing for the man had caused her to act unwisely and she had done more harm than good. With Wiley dead she hadn't one chance in a thousand of proving Kane innocent of Judd's murder. In the course of their conversation Duke had admitted to nothing, nor was he likely to.

"I've always hankered after this place," Duke continued angrily. "Did you think I intended to remain Judd's lackey forever? There's more to life than being a hired gun. I deserve better treatment than to be booted out on my ear. Judd owes me for all my years of loyalty."

"Judd is dead and I owe you nothing," Glenna declared haughtily. "I want you out of here by noon tomorrow."

"Sell me the place, Glenna," Duke persisted eagerly. "The saloon means nothing to you. I have some savings and could sign a note for the rest."

"Tomorrow noon," Glenna repeated firmly, edging toward the door.

"Who will you find to run the place on such short notice?" Duke continued to resist.

"That is my problem." With her hand on the doorknob she turned to face Duke, her eyes shards of green ice. "It's too bad about your friend Wiley. Do you know who killed him?"

"Wiley was no friend of mine!" he protested sullenly. "He was Judd's man."

"I could have sworn I saw him in Philadelphia around the time Judd was killed," Glenna let drop casually. Then she was gone, leaving a stunned Duke in her wake. On her way out she was relieved to see Marshal Bartow lounging at the bar, making good his promise to keep an eye on her.

What did the little witch know? Duke asked himself as he watched her jaunty progress out the door. Nothing, he assured himself confidently. Judd was dead and so was Wiley. Nothing or no one could link him to the two murders. That Kane Morgan became involved at all was a stroke of luck he hadn't counted on. He also hadn't expected Glenna to come rushing to Denver at the first opportunity to claim Judd's estate. The cold-hearted little gold digger, he thought disgustedly. Well, she wouldn't get away with it. On way or another he would own the Red Garter and command the wealth and recognition he so richly deserved.

The next day Glenna paid a call on Sal. It was still early and she found the house quiet and the girls still abed after their late night. A Chinese houseboy showed her into Sal's private office and promptly went to summon his mistress. A full five minutes elapsed before Sal breezed in, her lush figure draped in a pale pink wrapper, her blond hair falling in disarray about her satin-clad shoulders. Judging from her tousled appearance it looked as if she had just stepped out of bed.

"This had better be important," Sal grumbled crossly as she slammed the door behind her. "I don't make a habit of rising so early. If it's about a job, you . . . my God! Glenna!" she squealed joyously.

At first glance she failed to recognize Glenna. Not only was she still fuzzy-headed from having just been awakened, but the sun streaming through the window behind her visitor momentarily blinded her. But the moment Glenna stepped out of the glare recognition came instantly.

"God, but it's good to see you, honey. I heard about Judd and I can't say I'm sorry. Is it true Kane killed him?"

The two women embraced, still friends despite being poles apart. "Kane didn't kill Judd, Sal, but he'll hang for it unless I find the real killer. They're calling it a crime of passion but Judd was already dead when Kane entered his room."

"I knew it!" exclaimed Sal, slapping her thigh. "Not that I'd blame him if he did do the skunk in, but it hardly sounds like something Kane would do." She paused, her curiosity clearly piqued. "What in hell are you doing back here at a time when Kane needs you most?"

"Kane is exactly why I'm here, Sal." Then she proceeded to explain how she saw Wiley Wilson outside Judd's hotel at the time of his murder, finally following him to Denver only to find him dead.

"Why would Wiley want Judd dead?" puzzled Sal. "The old bastard wasn't smart enough to do anything on his own."

"He did kill my father," contended Glenna.

"But killing Judd doesn't make sense."

"That's why I came to you. I figured if anyone knew anything about Wiley's death or his mysterious trip to Philadelphia it would be you."

"Gosh, honey, Wiley was a closemouthed old coot, but Candy might know. He kind of took a liking to her and visited her every few days or so. I'll call her."

Glenna fidgeted the whole time she waited for a sleepy-eyed Candy to make her appearance. And when she did she proved friendly and cooperative, providing Glenna with valuable information.

"Wiley visited me quite often," Candy acknowledged with a tiny shrug. "I couldn't stand the randy old goat but he always left a big tip. The last time I saw him—the night before he was killed, I guess—he flashed a big bankroll. He was pretty drunk and said he had been away for awhile. I wondered why I hadn't seen him for a few weeks. I figured he was doing some prospecting."

"Did he say where he went?" Glenna quizzed

anxiously.

"Not exactly," Candy replied. "He just said 'back east' somewhere."

"Did he mention Duke? Or where he got the money?"

"N-o-o-o," drawled Candy thoughtfully, "but he did admit to doing a favor for a friend who paid him extremely well."

"Are you thinking what I'm thinking, Glenna?" Sal asked, her eyebrows arched in sudden comprehension.

"What are you talking about?" Candy asked curiously.

"Glenna hesitated, unwilling to involve Candy in her affairs. "For your own good, Candy, it's best you don't know. Suffice it to say it doesn't involve you."

Candy shrugged. Her frivolous nature left no room for concern or undue curiosity in something not directly involving her. Especially if that knowledge might prove harmful. "Suits me fine. It's too early in the morning for serious discussion anyway." In a swirl of frosty lace decorating her flimsy chemise, she flounced from the room.

"Do you think Duke is behind Judd's death?" Sal asked the moment Candy was gone.

"It's a distinct possibility," Glenna confirmed candidly. "But I'll never get him to admit it."

"What about the Red Garter? Hasn't he been managing it for Judd?"

"Not anymore. I let him go. He has till noon tomorrow to clear out."

"My God!" groaned Sal. "Don't you realize what kind of man you're dealing with?"

"I think I do," Glenna reluctantly agreed. Her face went grim. "And I've probably ruined what little chance I had of finding Judd's murderer. Not that I had much of a chance once I learned Wiley was dead. I've failed Kane miserably."

"You had no business traipsing out here on your own anyway," Sal scolded sternly. "I strongly advise you return east immediately. Let the lawyer clear Kane's name."

"Not yet, Sal. Soon, maybe, but not yet. There's still a remote possibility I might discover something. Right now I have a favor to ask of you."

"Anything, honey," Sal offered.

"Manage the Red Garter for me until I decide what to do with it."

And so it was settled. Pearl and Candy eagerly agreed to run the house while Sal moved over to the Red Garter.

Later, seated across the table in the Bartow kitchen, Glenna imparted all she had learned to the ex-lawman.

"You made a powerful enemy, Glenna," Bartow shook his grizzled head. "Surely you didn't expect him to admit he paid Wilson to kill Martin, did you?"

"I don't know what I expected, Marshal. I just knew I couldn't allow that man control of my property a moment longer than necessary. Sal agreed to manage the saloon for me. In the meantime I'm going to wire James and tell him about Wiley's death. I may be forced to leave Denver without ever learning the truth," she lamented.

22

Two days later an answer to Glenna's wire sent her heart leaping with joy. Though she had despaired of leaving Denver without accomplishing the task she set for herself, James's communication revealed that clearing Kane's name was no longer necessary. At the last minute two very reliable witnesses had come forward with some vital information placing Kane still in the hallway some distance from Judd's room when the shot was heard, supporting Kane's contention that he didn't enter Martin's room until after his death. James expected Kane to be released from jail soon and the case reclassified as an unsolved murder. Clearly and succinctly James urged Glenna to return to Philadelphia immediately.

Marshal Bartow couldn't have been happier when told of this startling development. "I'm glad you're leaving, Glenna. Messing with Duke could bring you nothing but trouble. I was prepared to go to any lengths to protect you but I'll admit I was worried. When are you leaving?"

"Tomorrow," Glenna replied a bit wistfully. She was truly fond of Marshal Bartow. "But I'm certain we will return one day. Kane is hardly the type to be content sitting behind a desk in a stuffy office. Now that Judd is no longer a threat to me I'm certain he'll want to return to Denver. I've still not given up on Golden Promise. Somewhere out there Da's dream is waiting to be discovered. I owe it to him to find the lode he gave his life for."

"I wish you luck, Glenna," Bartow extended. "Call on me if and when you return. If I don't see you before you depart please give that young man of yours my best. I hope he'll have the good sense to marry you the moment you step off the train."

By the time Glenna left the Bartow house it was too late to call on Sal and tell her that Kane was all but free and she was returning to Philadelphia the next day. Sal was certain to be immersed in duties at this time of evening, leaving no time for a private talk. Glenna decided there would be plenty of time left tomorrow before departure to bid Sal goodbye.

Sal had been in charge of the Red Garter since noon of the day before and Glenna had neither seen nor heard from Duke who was gone when Sal arrived to take his place. Knowing Duke she was hardly surprised when Sal informed her that the low-down skunk had departed with all the money in the safe, including the receipts that had accumulated since Judd's death. Glenna thanked her lucky stars that he had left without causing a ruckus. But had she really seen the last of him? she cautioned herself.

After taking supper alone in the dining room, Glenna paid her hotel bill and arranged with the clerk to have her bags, which were already packed, picked up and taken to the depot the next morning and placed aboard the ten o'clock train. She instructed him to take the bags even if she was not in her room for she planned on departing early to bid a friend goodbye. Then she returned to her room, laid out the clothes she intended to wear the next day, slipped on a nightgown and climbed into bed. Then she spent some tearful minutes thinking of Danny and how much she missed him. She had been gone just over two weeks but it seemed more like months.

Then she thought of Kane and the love they shared. Soon they would be together, married as they were meant to be. She loved the way he smiled; the dimple on one side of his cheek deepening and his eyes crinkling at the corners. He made love to her as if each time was special, caressing and titillating her with hands, lips and mouth until her world tilted crazily and nothing mattered but consummating their love in every way possible. Her pleasurable musings soon lulled her to sleep.

A knock on the door roused Glenna from a deep sleep. Automatically she checked the watch pinned to her nightgown and noted in the dim lampglow that it was only two in the morning. Confused as well as somewhat disoriented, Glenna called out sleepily, "Who's there?"

A soft, feminine voice replied, "It's me. Sal. Let me in. I have to talk to you."

Sal! Had something gone wrong with the Red Garter? Had Duke returned to make trouble? "Just a minute, I'm coming." Reaching for her wrapper, she shrugged into it, holding it together loosely with one hand while unlocking the door with the other.

The hallway was shrouded in darkness and all she could make out was a feminine form outlined in the doorway, when suddenly the figure was shoved rudely aside by a masculine arm reaching out from the shadows. A rough voice growled, "Get out of here, Lil,

I owe you one." From then on everything happened quickly.

A gag was stuffed into her mouth before the scream left her throat. A scratchy blanket smelling of horse was thrown over her head and Glenna felt herself suspended in air and upended over a muscular shoulder. Though she was blinded, Glenna surmised by the length of time it took that she was being carried down the back stairs, through the deserted kitchen and out the rear door to the alley. When she felt herself being hoisted onto the back of a horse she knew her assumption had been correct. But who would want to kidnap her? Duke! she answered her own question as a warm body settled behind her in the saddle. Why? What did he hope to gain?

Finding her hands suddenly free she began to struggle, striking out blindly. A groan followed by a curse erupted from her captor's throat when her fist connected with something soft, providing her a moment's satisfaction. But it was short-lived. A clout to her head rendered her momentarily senseless. "Keep that up and you'll get more of the same," the gruff voice spat in her ear. Still reeling from the blow, Glenna retreated behind a wall of silence in order to muster her strength. Once it returned she intended to put up the fight of her life, for she'd be damned if she'd allow Duke the satisfaction of subduing her.

Keeping to the side streets and alleyways, Glenna's abductor wound a circuitous route around the sleeping city. Nestled in the woods just beyond the outer fringes of the sprawling town, a deserted, rundown shack sat in the middle of brush and tall pines. Originally it had been built by prospectors, but as the city outgrew its limits the shack had been abandoned to civilization and allowed to decay to its present dilapidated state. Duke had discovered it long ago, claimed it for his own and made it barely habitable. He had been staying there since Glenna threw him out of the Red Garter. It was close enough to the city to keep him informed of all the goings-on yet secluded enough to be private. It was here that he took Glenna.

After what seemed like hours the horse was reined to a stop and Glenna was unceremoniously hauled down and propelled forward. Perceptively she realized she was being led into a building of sorts for she heard the squeak of a door and stumbled over the threshold, her bare feet padding across a dirt surface worn smooth by years of use. A door slammed behind her and instinctively she whirled in the direction of the sound. Through the thinness of the blanket Glenna was aware of a glow of light as Duke lit a lamp. At the end of her endurance, she clawed at the musty covering impeding her sight and whipped it over her head, tossing it to the floor with a grunt of disgust. Next she attacked the gag as she yanked it out of her mouth, spitting out the foul taste it left. Then her eyes fell on Duke, leaning arrogantly against the door of the rude cabin and grinning smugly.

"What do you mean by this, you contemptible bastard?" she spat angrily. "You can't abduct me and get away with it."

"No? Who's to stop me?" smiled Duke nastily.

"What do you want?"

"Sit down and I'll tell you."

Glenna glanced about the sparsely furnished room, spied a table and two chairs and, choosing one, sat down with all the aplomb she could muster under the circumstances. "All right, Duke, I'm waiting."

Plopping down in the other chair, Duke propped his feet on the table, shoved back his hat and grinned like a cat who had just consumed a bowl of cream. "I want two things," he informed her, his hot eyes raking her thinly clad figure insolently. The satin wrapper hugged her generous curves which the thin gown beneath did little to disguise, making it difficult for him to keep his mind from wandering in other directions. But business first, Duke warned himself sternly, sighing regretfully. Once he got what he wanted from her he could take his pleasure from her body.

"Well, spite it out!" Glenna shifted uneasily beneath Duke's silent appraisal. She knew exactly where his thoughts led him and if he tried anything with her she'd make damn certain he didn't escape unscathed.

"I want the Red Garter and both claims. Sign them over to me and you can leave here unharmed."

A stunned expression settled over Glenna's beautiful features. Give up Da's dream? Never! "You can have the Red Garter," Glenna offered eagerly, hoping to placate him by giving in to half his demands. "But you'll not have either claim. They mean nothing to you. In all this time the mother lode has never been found and more than likely never will."

"It's there, all right. I suspect that no one has looked in the right place," Duke convinced himself. "Do you think the Red Garter will make me wealthy? Bah! Not the kind of wealth I want. I want more, Glenna, and you'll provide me with the means. Do you think Judd got rich from gambling alone? Not likely."

"Take what I'm willing to give and count yourself lucky, Duke. I'll gladly sign the Red Garter over to you immediately if you let me go. No one need know what happened tonight if you return me unharmed. I had planned on leaving town in the morning anyway."

"It's not good enough, Glenna. I want it all. The gambling saloon and the claims." To a man who had nothing all his life, Duke was now greedy to possess it all. What he thought was his had been abruptly snatched away beneath his nose and he wasn't about to let the little witch escape so easily.

"Take it and be satisfied, Duke. Besides Kane and our child those claims are the only things that mean anything to me."

"Then you'll stay here until you change your mind. I told you before I won't settle for half."

"You're crazy! Someone will miss me."

"Who?" laughed Duke nastily. "You said yourself you were leaving in the morning. You paid your hotel bill last night and arranged to have your luggage put on the train. It could be weeks before anyone discovers you're missing." It was obvious to Glenna that Duke had done his homework before planning all this.

"You're wrong!" Glenna denied. "Kane is expecting me. If he comes to Denver looking for me there's no place you can hide to escape him."

"From the looks of things Morgan will be in jail a good long time. If he's convicted of murder he could hang."

"Wrong again, Duke," sneered Glenna imperiously. "Kane has been completely exonerated of Judd's murder. Two reliable witnesses placed him outside the room when the shot was fired. No doubt he's already been released from jail."

"You're lying!" Duke accused, a frisson of fear prickling his spine. "I've heard nothing about that."

"I received a telegram from Kane's brother just yesterday telling me about this latest development. Why do you think I was leaving Denver?"

Duke shrugged. If what Glenna said was true he'd have to act fast in order to force her to give up the claims. But he still wasn't completely convinced she spoke the truth. Until he learned otherwise he would work on the assumption that Morgan was still in jail.

"There's paper and ink sitting on the table, Glenna. It takes but the stroke of a pen to set yourself free," Duke persisted. "You can still leave town as planned."

Glenna hesitated but a moment before grasping the pen and dipping the tip in the inkwell. Smiling gleefully,

Duke shoved a clean sheet of paper beneath her fingers. She wrote several short sentences, waved the paper back and forth to dry, then handed it to Duke. With smug satisfaction Duke took the sheet, read it, then in a rage tore it into bits.

"I can see I'm wasting my time," he ground out. "It's obvious to me a subtle form of persuasion is needed to bring you to your senses." He stared fixedly at her for several minutes, his face suddenly breaking out in a sly smile. "After a few days cooped up here I predict you'll be more than willing to comply."

Once again his eyes roamed insolently over her body, his lust pouring over her like hot lava. Instinctively, Glenna shuddered, pulling her wrapper tighter over her breasts, caring little for his avid scrutiny. She wanted him to leave, willed him to go. Once alone she knew she would find some way to escape. She was resourceful and hardly lacking in courage. Even if Duke locked the door and barred the windows she knew that somehow she would manage to escape.

What Glenna hadn't counted on was being bound and gagged and left lying helpless as a newborn kitten on the hard cot. Why had she defied him? she asked herself bleakly. Why hadn't she given him what he wanted instead of stubbornly refusing to part with her property? What she had boldly written was not the words he wanted to read, the words naming him owner of the Red Garter and Golden Promise One and Two. Defiantly she had penned a note purposely meant to goad him. She had called him a greedy coward and offered him only the saloon in return for her freedom.

Of course he had torn it up and then overpowered her with his superior strength, leaving her hopelessly bound and gagged. But how could she relinquish the one thing Da had believed in? Surely it was only a matter of time before someone would discover her missing and come to her rescue, Glenna reasoned hopefully. Her mind awhirl with possibilities, her body aching and uncomfortable, Glenna fell into a fitful sleep, warm thoughts of Kane consuming her troubled dreams.

"Are you certain you sent that telegram to Glenna, James?" Kane asked for the tenth time.

"I sent it," James insisted, "and received a reply the same day. She's returning immediately. Now stop pacing, Kane, and sit down and eat."

Having been released from jail the day before, Kane cursed the luck that placed him in Martin's room minutes after his murder and sent Glenna hurrying recklessly to Denver and Lord only knows what kind of danger. He hadn't the stomach for food. Not now. Not when Glenna might need him and he was hundreds of miles away.

"For God's sake, Kane, sit down!" James thundered a second time. "You're far too thin after your sojourn in jail, and Glenna will hardly know you when she returns."

"Perhaps I should have gone after her, James," Kane persisted. "I have this strange feeling deep in my gut."

"That feeling is called hunger," James smiled indulgently. "I'll wager that Glenna will be here before the week is out."

"And I'll be waiting at the depot with the preacher," Kane confided. "Once we're married no one will dare involve her in malicious gossip. My name will protect her and our son. If not for Judd Martin we would have been man and wife long ago. She can't return soon enough to suit me."

Duke returned to the cabin sometime the next day and released Glenna from her bindings. She cried out in agony as the circulation returned to her limbs, cursing Duke with every expletive she'd ever heard.

"I see you haven't mellowed none," grumbled Duke, hovering over her as she rubbed her bruised wrists and ankles.

"I need to go outside," were Glenna's first words once the gag was removed.

Duke laughed raucously. "Use the chamber pot over yonder," he pointed to a none-too-clean cracked jar sitting in a corner.

Glenna wrinkled her nose distastefully. "I'd rather go outside."

"So you can escape? Nothing doing."

"I promise I'll not try to run away." Could he tell she was lying? "Please, Duke, I've been tied up for hours."

"All right," grunted Duke grudgingly, "but just remember, I'm not letting you out of my sight."

Wincing from pain, Glenna hobbled out the door on wobbly legs, blinking repeatedly in the bright sunshine. Instinctively she headed in the direction of a large clump of thick shrubs, keeping a wary eye on Duke who dogged her heels. "Don't come any closer," she ordered.

"You're in no position to bargain," Duke returned, undaunted.

"You'll never get what you want if you continue to behave in a despicable manner. I'm the only one who can make you a wealthy man. Now, will you allow me a measure of privacy?"

"If you're not out of there in five minutes I'm coming after you," growled Duke, stopping just short of the brush behind which Glenna had just disappeared.

Glenna merely grunted a reply, quickly finishing her business before Duke changed his mind. Then she glanced around in all directions, getting her bearings should she be lucky enough to escape. According to her calculations she was in a no-win situation. If she refused to give in to Duke's demands that she sign over her property, he would eventually kill her and dispose of her body where it would never be found. Yet, if she complied and gave him what he wanted, he would be forced to kill her anyway in order to keep her quiet. Just like he did Wiley. Her only hope lay in stalling Duke until someone discovered her missing and linked her disappearance to Duke.

"Your time is up, Glenna. Come out or I'll come in after you."

"Another moment, Duke." Panic seized Glenna when she realized she was about to be locked in that airless shack again. What was she doing standing here when she had the ability to turn and run? Once she reached the woods she'd gain the advantage for she could hide in any small space until Duke gave up and returned to town. Suddenly her feet grew wings as she turned on her heel and made a mad dash through the underbrush, frantically dodging the long branches catching at her wrapper. So intent was she on making good her escape that she hardly felt the sharp pine needles and stones tearing at her bare feet.

But all her efforts went for naught. A painful tug on her flowing red hair brought her to an abrupt halt. Panting from his exertions, Duke lunged at her, grasping the hair that streamed behind her in one fist, yanking brutally. Glenna cried out, falling to her knees as Duke tightened his grip.

"You bitch!" he spat venomously. "Were you stupid enough to think you could escape me? Get up! It's time I taught you a lesson you won't forget. I'm going to make damn certain you stay put when I leave here. Unless, of course, you've decided to be reasonable and do as I ask."

Her face took on a mutinous expression, emerald eyes gleaming with resentment and hate. "Go to hell!"

Half-dragging, half-carrying her, Duke soon had Glenna back in the confines of the shack. "Well? What will it be? Will you deed me both claims and give me the Red Garter as well? Or do I lock you up again?"

No matter what she did her life wasn't worth a spent bullet, so why give him what he wanted? Glenna decided perversely. "You'll get nothing from me!"

Without another word Duke slammed out of the shack, returning almost immediately carrying several packages which he dumped unceremoniously on the table. "If you're careful there's enough food here to last until I return," he informed her tersely. Glaring belligerently, Glenna watched as he left again, showing up this time with a bucket of water he had drawn from the creek. "Use it sparingly," he advised. Glenna protested vigorously when he exited again, locking her inside, his chilling farewell sending her heart careening wildly inside her chest. Then she heard him outside, the pounding and banging indicating that he was nailing boards over the shuttered windows.

"I can't keep you tied all the time I'm gone so I did the next best thing," he explained when he'd completed the chores he set for himself. "There's no way out of here unless I release you. Perhaps by the time I return you will have changed your mind. If not, I might be forced to use other methods of persuasion. You're a beautiful woman, Glenna. I always did fancy you." He advanced a step, and Glenna hastily retreated.

Just the mere suggestion that Duke might lay his hands on her made her skin crawl with revulsion and she shuddered. "Don't you dare touch me!"

One long arm snaked out and caught her about the waist, pulling her against the hard wall of his chest. His head dipped and his mouth ground into hers, forcing her lips apart to accept his tongue. Regaining her wits after the suddenness of his attack, Glenna bit down hard, and tasted blood.

"You little bitch!" he cried, drawing a hand across his mouth and coming away wet with his blood. "You'll pay for that. You can rot in this prison for all I care. No one will ever find you."

His hand swung back and lashed her savagely across the face. Glenna saw his fist coming but could not avoid it. Her head snapped back from the force of the blow, bright pinpoints of light exploded before her eyes, and her vision clouded. Then he whirled and stormed from the room.

"Duke! Wait! Don't leave me like this!" Did he really intend to leave her here to die? Glenna wondered as panic rushed to her brain. Struggling through the layers of blackness threatening to engulf her, her mind shrank in horror. Was she never to see Danny again? Never again experience the magic of Kane's love? No! she screamed in silent protest. She would not allow that to happen. Nothing was worth such a sacrifice. Not even Golden Promise. "Duke!" she cried out in supplication. "You can have—!" Belatedly, she realized it was too late.

Duke had already slammed out of the shack, latched the door and began pounding boards across the opening, completely oblivious to the frantic pleas coming from within. "We'll see how brave you are when your food and water give out," he called through the door. "When I come back—if I come back—perhaps you'll be in a better frame of mind to do my bidding."

Glenna sobbed quietly against the door, the sound of retreating hoofbeats reverberating in her brain.

It might have eased Glenna's mind considerably to know that Duke had no intention of leaving her to die in the shack. Not yet, anyway. Not until he got what he wanted from her. Once she deeded him the claims and the saloon he would take his fill of her body and get rid of her for good. Dead women tell no tales. He learned that from Judd. Judd had thought to pin Paddy O'Neill's murder on Eric Carter and ordered the little Mex whore, Conchita, killed so she could not testify that Carter had spent the night with her on that particular night. Only it hadn't worked out quite the way he planned.

It wouldn't hurt Glenna to think he had abandoned her, Duke smirked to himself. Experiencing a little thirst and hunger might mellow her, rendering her more than willing to grant him whatever he asked, whether it be her property or her body. To his knowledge no one suspected that Glenna hadn't boarded the train two days ago as she had planned. Little did Duke know just how false his assumption was, for already Kane was on his way to Denver.

The morning Glenna was supposed to board the train her luggage was taken from her empty room as directed. But the chambermaid who later cleaned the room reported a strange finding to the desk clerk. Laid out neatly on a chair was Glenna's traveling dress, petticoat and bonnet. Lined up beneath the chair sat a pair of shoes. It was definitely a mystery. One that neither the clerk nor the maid could solve. Surely the lady hadn't left the hotel naked, had she? Was she so rich that she would carelessly leave an expensive outfit behind?

Later that morning the story was related to Marshal Bartow when he stopped by to ask if Glenna had made her train on time. With great relish the clerk related the chambermaid's discovery, speculating on what could have happened to make a lady leave a complete outfit of clothes behind.

Prickles of apprehension marched up and down his spine as Bartow's sixth sense warned him that something was desperately wrong. He questioned the clerk further but learned nothing else of importance, so, being the lawman he was, took matters into his own hands.

From the ticket agent he learned Glenna never purchased a ticket that fateful morning. A visit to Sal turned up the information that Glenna never showed up to bid her farewell. In fact, Sal had no idea Glenna intended to leave so soon. Once she heard the marshal's story all her instincts warned her that Glenna was in terrible danger. And she bet her bottom dollar that low-life Duke was behind it. Together they decided to wire Kane immediately. Less than twelve hours later Kane was on his way to Denver.

One day passed, then two. And panic grew like a hard knot in Glenna's breast. Was she destined to die an ignominious death in this dilapidated shack in the woods far from her loved ones? Not if she could help it, she vowed stubbornly, her bare feet slapping across the floor as she paced endlessly back and forth. The sound of her own voice was the only company she'd had for days, unless one counted the animal noises outside. Another day or two and she'd even welcome Duke's voice. Thoughts of escape became her only companion.

But to Glenn'a chargrin she learned the hard way that Duke had been thorough, effectively sealing off all avenues of escape. The shutters were nailed tightly shut emitting only thin slits of light through the cracks. Not only was the door barred from the outside but boards were hammered across the opening. She had broken countless fingernails and torn the tender skin on the palms of her hands and fingertips attempting to pry open the shutters with various kitchen utensils found inside the shack, but to no avail.

Though she had eaten sparingly of the food Duke left, consisting mostly of cheese, jerky and hardtack, and drank only when thirst drove her to it, her supplies were swiftly being depleted. It became increasingly obvious to Glenna that they would not last the week. Then what? Would she eventually die of thirst and hunger? Or would Duke arrive and kill her once he had what he wanted from her?

Glenna shivered, listening to a clap of thunder roll ominously overhead. Wind-driven rain beat against the sides of the shack, and the sun disappeared, pitching the room into an unnatural blackness. Glenna glanced at the lamp, noting with dismay that the oil was running low. What would happen when it gave out altogether and she was forced to live in darkness? Little light filtered through the cracks in the shutters and the lamplight provided her with her sole touch with reality. Once that tenuous link was snuffed out Glenna feared she'd lose her mind.

Halting beside the warped table, she stared distractedly at the puddle of water collecting on the splintered surface, forming a small stream and then spilling down a leg where it darkened the hard-packed dirt floor. Idly, Glenna glanced upward, and became instantly alert, excitement thudding through her. Above the rafters in the low ceiling was a hole as big as her fist! With a determination born of desperation, Glenna seized upon the opportunity with all the tenacity that was an inherent part of her character.

She snatched up a broom she had discovered earlier in her exploration, disappointment shuddering through her when she found that standing on her tiptoes and extending the broom upwards still placed the hole in the roof beyond her meager reach. Muttering an oath, she refused to accept defeat so easily. Though the table looked rickety at best, Glenna hoisted herself up, carefully rising to her full height. The table wobbled dangerously, but thankfully held her slight weight. Then, using the broom handle, she painstakingly hacked away at the hole in the roof, poking time and again at the rotted wood until it slowly began to widen and enlarge. Though the work was slow and tedious, Glenna toiled industriously until her arms began to ache and her legs trembled with fatigue.

Only when her legs threatened to collapse beneath her did she pause to rest, suddenly aware that the storm had unleashed its violence and moved on as abruptly as it had begun. Glenna labored for hours, through the long day and far into the night, resting only occasionally. She would accept nothing less than success, and her determination to escape spurred her to greater effort than she thought humanly possible. The thought that Duke might return and kill her was like a hard lump in her throat.

By dawn the next morning several large chunks of decayed roofing lay on the floor, and through sheer guts and determination Glenna had succeeded in enlarging the hole until it looked as if it could accommodate her slim form. But her euphoria ended in near defeat when faced with the another formidable task; one that appeared almost insurmountable.

Glancing down at her ill-clad form, Glenna grimaced at the sight of the torn and grubby gown and wrapper she had worn since her abduction. It was hardly suitable garb in which to be caught wandering through the woods. And how far could she hope to walk with no shoes? Yet what recourse did she have? Did Duke keep any old clothes in the cabin? she wondered eagerly, glancing about hopefully. If so, where would he store them?

Her eyes flitted about the room, seeking out every corner. Disheartened, she saw no dresser, no old clothes hanging on hooks, no trunk, nothing. Absently her feet took her to the corner where the cot sat against one wall. Picking up the lamp she placed it on the floor as she dropped to her knees, uttering a cry of delight as she drew forth a small, battered chest from the narrow space beneath. Eagerly fumbling with the catch, Glenna drew in her breath sharply as she opened the lid and discovered a veritable treasure trove within.

Her hands shook with excitement as she withdrew two pairs of men's trousers, two old and patched shirts, a ragged jacket and a pair of boots, badly worn but still serviceable. Several pairs of threadbare stockings and a tattered hat were included in the find. Choosing a pair of trousers that looked somewhat cleaner than the other, and the least patched of the shirts, Glenna quickly dressed. The pants proved much too large so she rolled up the legs and used the belt to her wrapper to thread through the beltloops, gathering the extra folds about her slim waist and tying it securely. The shirt was a better fit though the sleeves hung below her fingertips. Solving the problem with a few quick motions, she stuffed the tails inside the pants and then turned her attention to the footgear. Getting the boots to stay on her feet took a few minutes of thought.

Two pairs of stockings went on first. Two more were used to stuff into the toes. When she finally pulled them on she was happy to note that they stayed on her feet, and taking a few experimental steps around the shack proved they would offer sufficient protection for her tramp through the woods. Jamming the hat down over her ears, at last Glenna was ready and eager to make good her escape.

Turning her attention to the more immediate task facing her, Glenna visually measured the distance to the roof, realizing instinctively that she couldn't hope to reach it by standing on the table. Something extra was needed to give her an added boost. Her eyes fell naturally on one of the chairs and she lifted it, carefully placing it in the center of the table. Once it was in place the table did a crazy dance then stilled. Only then did Glenna gingerly hoist herself up on the table and finally climb atop the chair. Amazingly, the pyramid did little more than wobble drunkenly from side to side. Holding her breath, Glenna reached upward, stretching until she thought her arms would fall off, finding she was still precious inches short of her goal.

The agony of failure crushed the breath from her, leaving her momentarily stunned. But she staunchly refused to accept defeat. The one thing Da had drilled into her was the premise that if one looked hard enough there was a solution to every problem. As if in answer to her prayer her eyes fell on the nearly empty water bucket supplied by Duke before he left. Turned upside down the bucket would provide the extra boost needed to reach the roof. But if she dumped the last of her water and still failed to escape . . . No, she refused to dwell on failure.

Without a moment's hesitation Glenna climbed down from her precarious perch, upended the bucket and carefully balanced it in the center of the chair. To her dismay she broke out into a cold sweat when she lifted herself to the tabletop. The awkward pyramid swayed dangerously, and Glenna suddenly felt ill-equipped to undertake such a task. Until the realization struck that she had no one but herself to rely upon. Swallowing her misgivings she bravely broached the chair. It wobbled, and threatened to topple, but miraculously held her slight weight. Little did Glenna know that the worst was yet to come. The upended bucket perched atop the chair seemed a mile high and Glenna gulped in fear when she realized she could easily break her neck should she fall. Though frightening, the thought did not deter her.

Balanced precariously atop the bucket atop the chair atop the table, Glenna inhaled deeply and reached upward. The tips of her fingers touched the roof, and to her intense relief, clutched the jagged hole she had so painstakingly worked to enlarge. Inch by painful inch she hoisted upward until her head pushed through the opening into the light of day. The welcome sight of trees, sun and hills spurred her on as she kicked her feet in a concentrated effort to squeeze her arms and upper body through the opening. Splintered wood scratched deep gouges on her hands and face as she wriggled her shoulders through the space. Thank God she had donned sufficient clothing to protect the rest of her body, Glenna thought distractedly as she struggled to shove her hips through the amazingly small area.

Unbeknownst to Glenna, her struggle to free herself resulted in a bizarre turn of events. Inadvertently her thrashing legs kicked over the bucket, which in turn topped the chair and sent the table skidding across the room, accidentally overturning the lantern sitting on the floor where Glenna had left it.

Beside the lantern Glenna's discarded gown and robe soaked up the spilled oil then burst into flame. The bedding on the cot quickly ignited, shooting sparks upward and outward. The dry wood of the shack quickly succumbed to the heat, adding tinder to the blaze. Glenna felt the heat through the thin soles of her oversized boots and glanced down, horrified by the inferno licking at her heels. Scrambling frantically, she succeeded in pulling herself halfway through the opening, screaming in frustration when her hips still refused to clear the narrow space. Using her arms as levers and heaving with all her might she finally burst through, grunting in pain when the rotted wood left tiny splinters in her tender flesh.

Resting on the roof, panting to catch her breath, its near-flat pitch aided Glenna in making her escape possible without serious injury. Her one consuming fear was that should the roof fail to hold her weight she would fall through into the blazing inferno below and perish. So intense were the flames beneath her that she expected the entire roof to ignite at any moment.

Carefully sliding to the edge, Glenna estimated the drop to the ground at seven or eight feet, and was debating the best way to make her fall as painless as possible when the section of roof directly behind her burst into a solid wall of flame. Without further thought to life or limb she pushed herself off the edge, rolling into a ball as the ground came up to meet her sooner than she would have liked. Moments later the shack was totally consumed, reduced in minutes to nothing but ashes and cinders, scorching trees and shrubs unlucky enough to lie within its greedy grasp.

23

Amidst a great flurry of steam and the high-pitched squeal of metal against metal, the massive black locomotive eased to a halt before the Denver station, discharging Kane along with several other weary passengers. Glancing around distractedly he concluded that Denver had remained basically unchanged during his absence. Not that it mattered any. There were far more important things to occupy his mind. Unshaven, blurry-eyed from lack of sleep and constant worry, the trip from Philadelphia had been a nightmare. The clackety-clack of the wheels repeatedly screeched Glenna's name until he thought his brain would explode. Glenna—Glenna—

Where are you, my love? he silently entreated. Are you hurt? Or even worse—dead? If only James had succeeded in preventing her from launching herself into a potentially dangerous situation, Kane agonized. He had chastised James roundly for allowing her to leave, until he recalled Glenna's strong will, her fierce independence, her stubborn determination. And then his anger at his brother abated somewhat. Only to blaze into fury once again when he received Marshal Bartow's telegram. The news announcing Glenna's disappearance had left James devastated. He insisted on accompanying Kane to Denver but there had been no time. Kane had boarded the Union Pacific within two hours of receiving word that Glenna had dropped out of sight. And he fervently prayed that he wouldn't be too late.

"Morgan, over here!"

Kane swiveled in the direction of the voice and saw Marshal Bartow hurrying toward him. In Dodge City he had left the train long enough to wire the ex-lawman, informing him of the approximate time and date of Kane's arrival in Denver. It had been seven days and nights of pure hell.

"Has there been any word of Glenna?" were Kane's words of greeting.

"Sorry, Morgan, nothing," Bartow revealed, shaking Kane's hand. "You look terrible man, haven't you slept at all?"

Kane's clothes were rumpled, his linen soiled and a blue-black stubble darkened his chin. "It's been a hellish trip," Kane admitted grimly. "In fact, I've not had the time to wash the jail stink off me."

"Come along," Bartow said, collecting Kane's one bag. "Sal has a room reserved for you at the Red Garter. She's managing it for Glenna. You can clean up while I catch you up on all that's happened since Glenna arrived in Denver. I've taken the liberty of renting a horse for you. I hope that meets with your approval." Kane nodded and mounted the pinto gelding, anxious to begin his search for the woman he loved.

Traveling the short distance in silence, they soon arrived at the saloon where business was still somewhat slow this time of day. Kane was whisked upstairs immediately, and while he bathed, shaved and donned appropriate clothing suitable for the task that lay before him, Bartow put him abreast of all that had transpired thus far. Kane listened intently the whole time, saying nothing until Bartow paused to catch his breath.

"So Glenna fired Duke and when Sal took the reins as manager of the saloon he became angry," he repeated thoughtfully. "Didn't Glenna realize how dangerous the man could be?" he thundered. "She should have let the bastard have the place, if that's what he wanted. She needs nothing from Judd Martin. I have enough wealth to keep us both in luxury for the rest of our lives."

"I don't think it was the money," Bartow revealed. "Glenna hated Duke. She told me how he shot you and left you for dead. She couldn't stand the sight of the man."

"Do you think he's responsible for Glenna's disappearance?"

"I'd bet my life on it. And Sal agrees. That is, we did until Duke began showing up here every night. A day or two after we discovered Glenna hadn't taken the train east Duke began spending all his time either here or at the Silver Nugget where he rented a room above the saloon. If he does have her stashed away someplace he's made no effort to go to her."

"Oh God!" groaned Kane as if in pain. "Do you think that scum has . . . killed her?"

"For what purpose?" asked Bartow, still the consummate lawman. "It makes no sense to kill Glenna."

"A man like Duke needs no reason. Didn't he shoot me without provocation?"

"True," admitted Bartow, his eyes shuttered lest they convey his misgivings to Kane. When Duke first appeared at the Red Garter he and Sal had kept careful track of his comings and goings, and nothing he had done led them to believe Glenna was still alive as his prisoner.

Just then the door burst open and Sal blew in, throwing herself into Kane's arms. "Jesus, Kane, it's good to see you!" she enthused happily. "Now that you're here we can get to the bottom of this. Find Glenna, Kane. Bring her back."

"You know I will if it's humanly possible, Sal," Kane managed a parody of a smile. "My god, I couldn't bear life without her. Did she tell you about our son?"

"I heard all about Danny. Sounds like a chip off the old block."

A long poignant silence ensued as Kane struggled with the tears that lodged like stones in his throat. "Is Duke downstairs?" he finally asked when he was able to speak.

Sal shook her head. "It's a little early yet. If he runs true to form he'll be standing at the bar in about two hours."

"Does he know he's under surveillance?" Kane questioned Bartow.

"I don't think so," Bartow replied. "The cocky bastard is pretty sure of himself. We've been careful to make no mention of the fact that Glenna is missing, so he has no inkling that he is suspect."

"If he's harmed her in any way I'll kill him with my bare hands," Kane gritted out from between clenched teeth.

"We'll find her, Kane," Bartow assured him with more confidence than he felt. "I suggest you rest for a couple of hours, you look ready to collapse. I'll send Sal up if Duke shows tonight. If he does have Glenna stashed someplace he's bound to lead us to her sooner or later."

Though Kane's body ached with fatigue he could not allow himself the luxury of sleep once Bartow and Sal left. With grim determination he removed his gunbelt from his bag and loaded the cylinders of his twin colt revolvers, buckling it snugly around his slim hips. Next he packed his saddlebags with money, ammunition, shaving gear, a change of clothes and a jacket. Come what may he intended to be prepared. Then he sat down to wait.

Duke swaggered boldly into the Red Garter, greeting several acquaintances by name, nodding to the bargirls, particularly to Lil who had done him a great service. If things went well he would reward her handsomely for her part in the little deception played on Glenna, though she expected nothing, aware that he would kill her if she talked. Thus far she had given him no cause for dissatisfaction, and he seriously considered making her his mistress once the saloon was his.

It had been seven days since Duke left Glenna in the boarded-up cabin, and he figured that by now she would be ready and more than willing to do anything he wished, even spread her legs for him should he demand it. By now her meager supply of food and water should be nearly depleted and thirst and hunger her constant companions. He reckoned she'd be mighty glad by now to hear another human voice, even his.

Deciding it was time to confront his prisoner again, Duke intended to drink his fill at the bar till dark then head on out to the shack. It never was his intention to abandon Glenna to an ignominious death. She was far too important to him. He wanted her alive and well until she deeded the saloon and both claims to him. After she made him rich he would take the fill of her body and then make damn sure she disappeared forever.

For three solid hours Duke drank, and gambled, and drank some more. How he enjoyed flaunting himself before Sal, knowing that soon she would be banished to her own place and reduced to selling her body. Let her fume, Duke gloated smugly as their eyes clashed across the crowded room. It wasn't until the huge orange sun dipped below the horizon that Duke made a move to leave. Earlier he had packed his saddlebags with food, and he licked his lips in avid anticipation as he wondered just how far Glenna would go to slake her hunger and thirst.

As he strutted confidently toward the door he failed to note that the large man leaning against the stairs suddenly came alive. Marshal Bartow had seen Duke enter and from that moment on kept him constantly within sight. When Duke finally headed out the door, Bartow acted instantly. A prearranged signal sent Sal racing up the stair to alert Kane. Within seconds Kane was exchanging frantic words with Bartow.

"He left," Bartow gestured toward the door. "Just this minute. He was alone."

His saddlebags thrown over one shoulder and his gunbelt fastened firmly about his slim hips, Kane nodded curtly, his face set in grim lines. "Let's hope he leads us to Glenna," he said tersely, hastening toward the door.

"I'll go with you," Bartow offered.

"One person has a better chance of remaining undetected," Kane threw over his shoulder. Then he was gone.

Kane breathed a sigh of relief when he saw that Duke was still within sight, appearing in no particular hurry. What if he wasn't the man responsible for Glenna's disappearance? Kane wondered distractedly. What if he was just going about his business? A hundred possibilities warred inside Kane's brain as he cautiously followed Duke in a circuitous route through the city. Soon the houses began to give way to open spaces and Duke spurred his mount onto a little used track leading into the woods. Kane lagged behind until Duke gave no indication that he knew he was being trailed, then plunged into the shadows.

The trail abruptly turned and Kane momentarily lost sight of his prey though the sound of his passing echoed through the stillness. Suddenly Kane was aware of nothing but silence from all directions. Somewhere up ahead Duke had stopped! Why? Did he suspect he was being followed? Was Duke even now planning an ambush? Desperate as he was to find Glenna Kane knew he would go on, regardless of what Duke intended. For Glenna's sake he would brave anything, even death. With a determination born of desperation, Kane spurred the pinto forward.

A few minutes later, totally unprepared for the sight that met his shocked eyes as he rounded a bend in the trail, Kane unexpectedly came upon Duke who had left the path and dismounted some distance away in a clearing, staring incredulously at the burnt out hulk of what appeared to have been a small prospector's hut before the ravages of time took their toll. For what reason had Duke led him here? Kane asked himself curiously.

Suddenly a deep, abiding fear clutched at his heart and Kane felt the breath being slowly squeezed out of him. Had Duke led him to Glenna after all? To the place where Glenna had lost her life? An agonized sob was wrenched from his throat, alerting Duke to Kane's presence. Reflexively Duke reached for his weapon but Kane proved too fast, drawing on him with lightning speed, and Duke found himself facing not only Kane's deadly accurate Colt but his incredible rage.

"Where is she, Duke? What have you done with Glenna?"

Though Kane had no way of knowing, Duke was in a state of shock. Finding the shack where he had imprisoned Glenna burned to the ground had completely unsettled him, rendering him nearly speechless. How had such a thing happened? he wondered, all his dreams of vast riches disappearing in flames.

Duke's eyes shifted from Kane's Colt to the pile of charred wood and ashes that had once held a beautiful, vibrant woman. Helplessly, he gestured toward the ruins and muttered words that made little sense.

"Dammit, Duke, I'm losing patience!" Kane bit out through clenched teeth. "Where is Glenna?"

Still too stunned to communicate coherently, Duke's inane babbling served only to increase Kane's anger. Nothing Duke said made sense except for the words Glenna, cabin, and . . . oh, God! Kane prayed fervently when Duke kept repeating the word "dead."

"Was Glenna in that shack, Duke? Is that what you're trying to tell me?"

Facing Kane Morgan, a man until this moment he thought was rotting away in an eastern jail, was as great a shock to Duke as learning Glenna had perished in the fire. He could do little more than nod in answer to Kane's blunt question.

Kane went cold with shock, his body and mind numb. "No! You lie!"

"It . . . it's the truth," stuttered Duke, finally finding his tongue. "I brought her here myself." Such was his emotional state that he scarcely realized he was admitting to a charge of kidnapping and murder. He was practically signing his own death warrant.

"You contemptible bastard!" spat Kane, knocking him flat with a left hook so powerful it left him dazed and bleeding. "You abducted Glenna!"

"I never meant to harm her, Morgan," Duke insisted, rising on his elbow and wiping off the blood pouring from his nose with a dirty sleeve. "If she'd done as I asked I'd have never locked her up."

"You left her locked up in a deserted shack without food and water?" Kane raged furiously.

"No! I left her enough grub and water to last a week. I told you, I didn't want her dead."

"What did you want from her?"

"I wanted the Red Garter and her old man's claims."

"You wanted her to give up Golden Promise? You're a bigger fool than I gave you credit for, Duke. The saloon meant nothing to her, but her father's property was her inheritance."

"That's exactly why I locked her up," Duke babbled fearfully. "I thought if I left her alone for a few days she'd see the light and do as I asked."

"Then what? Did you plan to kill her like you did Judd Martin?"

"No . . . I . . . I never said I killed Judd," Duke denied vehemently. "He . . . he was my friend. Why would I kill him?"

"You paid Wiley Wilson to kill him, admit it. You're a dead man already so you may as well make a clean breast of it."

Stark and vivid fear sent a shaft of panic through Duke as Kane calmly and carefully pointed the Colt still clutched in his right hand at Duke's head, at the same time cooking the hammer. "I . . . I . . . all right, I did pay Wiley to follow Judd to Philadelphia and kill him. I never expected Glenna to return to Denver and claim Judd's estate. I wanted the Red Garter for myself. When she refused to sell it to me I decided to take matters in my own hands. Suddenly it was all within my reach, not only the saloon, but the claims as well. Why not have everything so long as it was there for the taking?"

"But you didn't count on Glenna's stubbornness, did you? When you found she wouldn't give in to your demands you set fire to the shack and killed her."

"N-no!" disavowed Duke fearfully, sensing in Kane a volcano about to erupt. "I never expected anything like this to happen when I locked Glenna up. I don't know what caused the fire."

"Glenna is resourceful," Kane stubbornly insisted, his mind refusing to accept what his eyes told him. "I'm certain she found some means of escape."

Duke shook his head in denial. "The windows were shuttered and nailed in place and the door locked and sealed with boards. There's no way, I tell you, no way at all."

White dots of rage exploded in Kane's brain as he holstered his gun and fell upon Duke with a vengeance born of shock and despair, finding far more satisfaction in killing him with his bare hands than affording him a less painful death by shooting him through the head. Duke made a feeble attempt to defend himself but was no match for an enraged Kane whose heart cried for revenge.

Though Duke was a big man, the punishment he was subjected to at Kane's hands soon rendered him senseless and beyond feeling, Kane's pounding fists like twin machines of destruction. But still Kane did not desist. His mind was numb to everything but the excruciating thought that Glenna was dead because of this man. The woman he loved, the mother of his child. Life would never be the same. Oblivious to all but his own pain, he continued inflicting punishment on the unconscious man who had been the cause of it all, callously unconcerned that he lay still as death beneath his powerful blows, offering not even the slightest resistance.

"Kane, stop! You'll kill him!" A hand grasped Kane's shoulder, and a sturdy body insinuated itself between the unconscious Duke and Kane. Exerting considerable strength, Duke's savior wrestled Kane to his feet.

"Bartow! What in the hell are you doing here?" growled Kane, fighting out of the ex-lawman's grasp. "You don't understand! Glenna is dead and this scum is responsible. He doesn't deserve to live."

Silently, Bartow nodded, his face twisted in compassion. He had already surmised as much when he came upon the burnt remains of the hut and saw Kane pounding Duke to within an inch of his life. It was for this very reason he had followed Kane. "I know, but I can't let you kill him. It's up to the law to punish him."

"Have you forgotten? The law here in Denver is on his side. What guarantee do I have that he'll get what he deserves?"

"I'll take him to Pueblo. The territorial sheriff is a close friend of mine. I promise he'll be made to pay for his crime."

Kane gave way grudgingly, moving away from Duke's prone form, and Bartow heaved a sigh of relief. He would hate to have to fight a man of Kane's superior strength, especially over a life as worthless as Duke's. But the law was the law.

"Now, tell me what happened."

"That bastard locked Glenna in that shack and left her alone for God knows how long! He denies starting the fire or having any knowledge of it. As you can see all that's left are those stones from the hearth."

Bartow sifted around in the ashes for what seemed like ages to Kane. When he returned his face was set in grim lines. "I found the remains of a lantern, a few scorched kitchen utensils, but little else. The blaze must have been intense. I . . . I found no . . . bodies—or bones. Perhaps Glenna could have escaped the fire before . . . before—"

"Not according to Duke," Kane revealed bleakly. "The bastard sealed the windows and door shut. She's dead, Bartow! Glenna is dead."

"Pull yourself together, Kane." Bartow's own composure was tottering dangerously, but for Kane's sake he forced a calm he was far from feeling. "It's possible Glenna could have escaped unscathed. Perhaps the fire burned a hole in the wall and she made it out before it was too late. Any number of things could have happened."

A long, suspenseful pause ensued. Both men finally

aware it would have been short of miraculous had Glenna escaped the fire's fury, but Kane was willing to grasp at any straw, believe anything if it meant that Glenna still lived. Until a quick and disturbing thought sent him plunging to the depths of depair.

"Judging from the ruins, the fire took place days ago. This spot isn't so remote from the city that Glenna couldn't easily find her way back. If Glenna did escape, then where is she now? Why didn't she seek shelter with one of her friends?"

Bartow wondered the same thing but refrained from giving voice to his doubts for Kane's sake. "I know it sounds far-fetched, Kane, but we have to go on the assumption that Glenna is alive, but for some obscure reason chose not to return to Denver. Perhaps she was afraid Duke would find her before she reached safety."

A tense silence invaded the stillness as Kane's silver eyes showed the tortured dullness of disbelief. From the moment he saw the gutted shack he was plunged into a kind of limbo where all decisions and actions were impossible. All his senses told him he would feel something if Glenna were dead. Yet all signs pointed inexorably in that direction despite the fact that his heart denied what his brain told him. His troubled spirits wandered far and wide, searching and finding nothing but a shadowy future stretching endlessly before him.

"Kane, did you hear what I said?" Bartow interrupted his reverie. "You can't give up hope, man. Hasn't it occurred to you that Glenna might be injured and in desperate need? Pull yourself together, she's depending on you."

Kane stared transfixed at Bartow, slowly digesting his words. Suddenly his face cleared and a broad smile split his grave features as comprehension dawned. "Of course!" he exclaimed eagerly. "Why didn't I think of it before? If Glenna was injured she couldn't possibly seek help or return to Denver. I'm positive she's still alive! I'd know if she were dead. By God, Bartow, I'll find her! I swear I will!"

Intense heat roused Glenna from her stupor. A groan of agony escaped her parched throat as she placed a trembling hand to her aching forehead. To her dismay it came away smeared with blood. My God! What happened? she asked herself groggily. Behind her raged a roaring inferno, yet she couldn't remember just how the fire had started or why she was lying injured so close to the blaze. Intuitively she knew it wasn't her father's cabin at Golden Promise that was being consumed in flames. Her head hurt, her throat felt as if she had swallowed cotton. Da! Where was Da! Suddenly her one consuming thought was to get as far away from this cursed place as possible, for she sensed evil lurking about. Staggering to her feet she was determined to find her father, for with him lay comfort and safety.

Glenna took a step, stumbled, then ventured another. But the effort proved too difficult and she collapsed in a boneless heap on the scorched ground a short distance away, unaware that she had struck her head on a rock when she leaped from the flaming roof of the burning shack and had lain unconscious for hours. Once more she was plunged into darkness while the fire continued to consume itself, leaving nothing but ashes in its wake.

When Glenna awoke next it was daylight and nothing remained of the shack but smoldering embers and a few stones. The trees growing at the edge of the clearing were scorched but luckily the rain the previous day combined with the absence of wind prevented the fire from spreading to the woods beyond the small clearing where the shack sat. If it had, Glenna would have certainly perished.

Gathering what little strength she possessed, Glenna rose unsteadily to her feet, her legs wobbling dangerously beneath her. Thinking was impossible, she could only react by instinct, her legs moving independent of her brain which was still too confused to grasp reality. Golden Promise, Glenna repeated over and over. Only at Golden Promise would she be safe from the vague shadows that pursued her. Da would know what had happened and what to do.

Instinctively her faltering steps led her in the right direction as she staggered along the trail that would eventually take her to Golden Promise. Her mind still refused to dwell on the horror she had endured the previous week or her near miraculous escape from the blazing inferno. When she allowed herself brief flashes and lucid thought, Glenna experienced an intense longing for something—or someone. But what? Or who? Later, she thought groggily. When she reached the safety of Golden Promise there would be time enough to concentrate, to puzzle out the strange circumstances that had led her here.

Given her weakened state, her hunger, her thirst, Glenna might never have reached Golden Promise if a kindly prospector hadn't happened along and offered her a ride on the pack mule that trailed behind him loaded with supplies. At first Glenna failed to hear the sound of hooves crunching over the rock and twig-strewn path. When she did she paused and stared curiously at the apparition who stared back at her just as intently.

"What are ye doing out here alone, sonny?" the prospector asked, eyeing her inquisitively. Glenna jumped at the sound of his voice.

He was clad in incredibly dirty buckskins and worn boots with scuffed toes. His face showed the ravages of time and weather and his scruffy white beard made him appear as if he had no neck. A disreputable hat, ragged and dusty, covered sparse gray hair. But his watery blue eyes exuded an innate kindness, Glenna sensed through a fog of pain.

"Can't ye talk, sonny?"

Sonny? Did he think her a boy? Curiously, Glenna glanced downward, startled to find herself dressed in ragged boy's clothing. Her brow wrinkled in concentration but her pounding head prevented her from delving too deeply into her mind.

"I . . . yes, I can talk," Glenna croaked, her parched throat working convulsively over the words.

Abruptly the prospector's sharp eyes noticed the smear of blood trickling from just below the brim of the hat she still wore jammed down over her ears. "Are ye hurt?" he asked, concern wrinkling his lined brow.

"I . . . yes," Glenna acknowledged slowly. "I . . . fell, I think."

"What be yer name, lad?"

"Glen . . . uh . . . Glen O'Neill." It was easier to maintain her disguise than to explain why she was dressed as she was, the reason even escaping Glenna.

"Where ye headed, Glen?"

"To my father's claim on Clear Creek. He's a prospector."

"Well, Glen, me name's Ben and ye look about done in. Can ye use a lift? I'm going in that direction meself. Ye look as if ye don't weigh much. What say ye climb on old Betsy's back," he motioned toward the patient mule, "and rest a spell. Being as I'm going that way yer welcome to ride along."

Glenna nodded gratefully and staggered toward old Betsy, suddenly assailed by a pervasive weakness that left her trembling. Ben's keen eyes noted the way her steps faltered and his mouth puckered in concern.

"Be ye hungry, lad? I could use a bite meself. What say we tarry long enough to fix us some grub afore we go on. Must be nigh on to noon."

Glenna licked her dry lips and nodded eagerly. For some reason she couldn't remember the last time she had eaten. Or drank, for that matter. "Do you have any water?"

"Sure, sonny," Ben said, handing her his canteen. "Drink yer fill. There's plenty of water hereabouts."

Glenna tipped the canteen and let the cool, reviving liquid run down her parched throat, gulping convulsively without stopping. Never had anything tasted so good!

"Whoa, sonny, not so fast," cautioned Ben. "Take yer time. There's plenty more where that came from."

Later they shared a meal of beans, bacon, biscuits and coffee. Glenna savored every morsel. "Ye sure were powerful hungry, lad," Ben amazed. "When did ye eat last?"

"I . . . I don't remember," Glenna admitted somewhat shamefacedly.

"Well, no matter," Ben returned easily. "If yer belly's full we'll go on. Hop on old Betsy, Glen. I'll have ye with yer father afore the day is out."

True to his word, Ben deposited Glenna within sight of Golden Promise just as the sun dipped below the horizon. The whole time she plodded along on the mule's broad rump, Glenna's head spun dizzily, snatches of something vague and disturbing wandering in and out of her muddled brain. Intuitively she realized something was amiss, but did not know what. Perhaps Da could enlighten her once she reached Golden Promise.

"This is far enough, Ben," Glenna called when they halted on a ridge overlooking the claim. "I'll be fine now."

"Ye still don't look none too good to me, sonny," Ben said skeptically. "Sure ye can make it all right?"

"Yes, thank you. I'm certain Da is there waiting

for me." Truth to tell Glenna couldn't remember if Da was waiting for her or not. "Would you like to spend the night?" she invited, sliding off the mule's back.

"Naw," dismissed Ben with a shake of his grizzled head. "Why, I wouldn't know how to act with a roof over me head. Me and old Betsy here will just mosey along. Tell yer pa he aughta take better care of ya, sonny."

"Thanks again, Ben," Glenna called to his departing back. "Drop in if you ever come by this way again."

A jaunty wave served as his reply.

After picking her way carefully down the steep incline of the ridge, Glenna gingerly approached the cabin, thinking that somehow things did not look as they should. During this murky period between dusk and dark Da would normally have a lamp burning. Dear God, her head hurt! If only she could remember the fire and why she was dressed so strangely. Whose cabin was it that burned?

Cautiously Glenna lifted the latch and pushed open the door. Enough light remained to illuminate a room devoid of human occupancy. Disappointed, she stepped inside, fumbled around for the lamp and matches kept in a jar to insure their dryness, and waited while the light flared into being.

"Da," she called. "Are you here?" No answer. Carrying the lamp aloft she explored both bedrooms, finding nothing or no one but dust and cobwebs, suggesting that the cabin hadn't been occupied in some time.

Too exhausted for coherent thought, too confused to delve too deeply into her troubled mind, Glenna stumbled to her room, vaguely aware that there was something of importance she should remember. Falling into the bed she recalled so well from her happy childhood, Glenna was asleep within minutes.

* * *

Still suffering from shock and despair, Kane returned to town, parting company with Bartow who left for Pueblo with his prisoner who had been trussed up and hustled aboard the night train before he had time to recover from the beating Kane gave him. Kane's purpose in returning to Denver was to make certain Glenna hadn't made it back to town while he was out searching for her. But after visiting Sal, Kate Jones, and even Pete at the livery, and inquiring at the Palace Hotel and the bawdy house now being managed by Pearl and Candy, Kane was satisfied that Glenna had not returned to Denver.

While there was still a modicum of daylight remaining to guide his way, Kane hastened back to the ruins of the shack and methodically began a thorough search of the immediate vicinity. An uncanny sense of foreboding caused his heart to leap from his chest when he found traces of blood on the ground, plunging him into a crazy mixture of fear and hope. Did the blood belong to Glenna? Or to some wild animal. The answer brought a stab of pain as he considered all the alternatives. Spurred on by his discovery, Kane widened his search, taking him deeper into the surrounding woods.

Then abruptly he recognized the path that led to Golden Promise, and suddenly the future looked brighter. Could it be . . . ? Could Glenna have . . . Powerful emotions surged through him as an indefinable feeling of destiny prodded him onward. Though he'd be forced to spend the night huddled in a blanket beneath the stars, tomorrow would bring him to Golden Promise. And if the Gods were kind . . . he would find Glenna.

"Sonny, are ye in there?" a voice called from the door. "I got to thinking when I left you last night there was no light in the cabin and how sickly ye looked, so I decided to double back this morning to see if everything's all right with ye and yer pa."

No answer was forthcoming.

"Glen? Can ye hear me, lad?" Cautiously he lifted the latch, and finding the door unbarred from within, stepped inside. From all appearances the cabin looked deserted.

"A stubborn old coot like me don't know enough to turn around and leave," Ben muttered to himself.

He remembered the white-faced youth he had chanced upon the day before and his conscience smote him when he thought about the callous way he had abandoned him. His kindly nature demanded he return the next morning to talk to the boy's pa and see how he was faring.

Ben's feet took him to one of the small bedrooms. One look convinced him no one had occupied the room for some time. Then he poked his grizzled head into the second small room, and nearly missed Glenna's slim form huddled atop the blankets, so slight was the bulge she made.

"Sonny? Are ye sleeping?" Ben sidled into the room, moving quietly so as not to startle the slumbering lad. He need not have worried for sometime during the night Glenna had passed beyond the state of mere slumber into unconsciousness.

Gingerly Ben reached out and gently shook Glenna's shoulder. When she did not stir a worried frown creased Ben's weathered features. "Are ye sick, lad?"

Carefully he turned her on her back, and noted instantly the slash of dried blood located just inches above her left eyebrow below the grubby hat she still wore. The bruise beneath the blood had turned an ugly purple and appeared as large as an egg. The lad must have taken some fall, Ben mused, outlining the bruise with a stubby finger. No wonder he acted so strangely, sort of confused and disoriented.

Suddenly his hand jerked back, his fingertips tingling. The heat emanating from her skin scorched him. Glenna was burning with fever. Ben acted out of instinct, his years of roaming the wilds and associating with Indians teaching him many useful things about sicknesses and their treatment.

"Don't worry, sonny," Ben muttered to no one in particular. "I won't let ye die. I don't know where yer pa is but I'll take care of ya."

Hurrying outside he fetched a bucket of water from the creek, then set about gathering clean cloths and soap. Returning to Glenna, he murmured soothingly, "Let's get yer hat off, lad, so's I can clean that nasty gash." Sweeping off her hat with one hand, his loud gasp filled the confines of the small room when tangled clouds of long red hair tumbled about her shoulders and over the pillow.

"Saints preserve us!" Ben's eyes grew round as saucers and his mouth dropped open in dismay. "Ye ain't a lad at all, yer a lassie! And a purtier one I never did see. Well, little missy, no matter. Old Ben knows what needs to be done."

The cold creek water brought a groan of protest as Ben carefully bathed Glenna's flushed face. While he was bandaging the cut on her forehead her eyes snapped open but there was no comprehension in them as they stared blankly at him. "Da? Is that you, Da?" she asked weakly.

"It's Ben, missy," Ben answered, his gruff voice gentling. "Don't rightly know where yer pa is. Do ye have a name, lass?"

Somehow Ben's question hit a spark somewhere in her drugged brain. "Glenna," she breathed raggedly, a brief flicker of comprehension bringing a moment of lucidity. "Da is dead," she revealed before she lapsed once again into incoherent babbling. Then her eyes went blank and her lids lowered, far too exhausted for conversation.

Ben worked swiftly and surely as he removed Glenna's ragged shirt and worn boots, chuckling to himself when he saw her tiny feet emerging from the oversize footgear. He marveled that she had been able to walk for they were at least three sizes too big. When it came to removing the rest of her clothing, Ben hesitated. Not that he harbored any unnatural thoughts concerning the little lassie, he was old enough to be her grandfather. Though he knew she would be embarrassed when she came to her senses and realized he had undressed her, there was no help for it. Her clothes were damp with sweat and likely to do her more harm than good. Besides, in order to bring her fever down he needed to bathe her all over with cold water.

Laboring feverishly, Ben noted absently that the girl was no girl at all, but a full-grown woman. Working steadily, Ben soon had Glenna bathed with icy creek water and gently tucked beneath the covers. She appeared to be resting comfortably, though still not conscious, and Ben turned his thoughts to food. To provide the strength necessary for full recovery she would need to be fed a nourishing broth when she awakened.

A short time later, after a successful hunting foray, Ben had a rabbit simmering on the stove. He had also found a certain herb growing on the side of a hill that Indians used to reduce fever. While the broth bubbled on the stove he fed Glenna an infusion made from the herb.

When Ben checked on Glenna later he found her thrashing around on the sweat-soaked bed, her body drenched. He could feel the heat of her reach out and engulf him and he realized that he must do something fast or her brain would fry inside her skull. Relying on Indian lore learned from his wanderings, Ben snatched up Glenna's blanket-shrouded body and carried her outside, his steps taking him to the creek's edge. Without a moment's hesitation he plunged her into the middle of the icy stream, his slight burden limp in his arms. When the cold water hit her heated flesh, she cried out, struggling to escape, but Ben's brawny arms held her captive beneath the water's sparkling surface.

"Kane! Kane!" Glenna cried out as if in agony. "What are you doing to me?" Her struggles took on a new urgency as the icy water swirled over her burning flesh.

Who in tarnation is Kane? Ben wondered curiously. Someone else from her past, he strongly suspected. Poor little missy, he clucked sympathetically. Suddenly she sighed and relaxed in his arms, and Ben judged it time to return her to her bed. Once she was dried and warmly tucked beneath the quilt taken from the other bedroom, Ben painstakingly fed her more of the herb infusion. Later he would try to spoon some broth into her.

Ben dozed fitfully in a chair beside Glenna's bed where he kept vigil throughout the long night. He left her side only to see to his needs and eat a portion of the broth after forcing a small amount down her throat.

"Ben? Are you still here?"

Ben became instantly alert, a wide grin curving his bewhiskered lips. "Where else would I be, missy?" he chuckled happily. "Ye were one sick lassie fer awhile. Ye still ain't out of the woods but old Ben will pull ye through."

"Wha-what's the matter with me?"

"Fever," replied Ben tersely. "Seen it strike many a time without warning. Ye must have suffered some kind of shock for ye were a mite muddled fer a spell. Do ye remember how ye got that nasty lump on yer head?"

Tremulously, Glenna lifted her hand and traced the

bruise marring her flawless flesh. She winced, her mind struggling to capture those elusive ghosts flitting in and out of her shadowy past. Bits and pieces that previously escaped her began to form into a picture she would rather forget.

With grave concern Ben watched the play of emotion on Glenna's pale face. "Do ye want to tell me about it?"

"Yes," nodded Glenna without enthusiasm. "But not now. I feel so . . . tired."

"Sleep, lassie," Ben urged, patting her hand comfortingly. "Best medicine in the world. There's plenty of time fer talk later. In the meantime, I'll hunt us some game and fix a nice stew. Ye'll need more than broth to put ye back on yer feet."

24

Kane halted the pinto on the ridge overlooking Golden Promise. From his lofty perch the claim appeared deserted. He started down the slope, then reined in sharply when a movement at the side of the cabin captured his attention. His senses sharpened, his body tensed, and the moment he saw the horse and mule calmly grazing side by side in a patch of grass nearby his heart surged with incredible joy, immediately concluding from the skimpy evidence that Glenna was here just as he suspected, but certainly not alone.

Spurring the pinto into motion, Kane approached the cabin, his right hand poised on his thigh within inches of his Colt. Though his appearance seemed to rouse no one, Kane maintained a state of alertness. The very atmosphere smacked of ambush, but the thought did not deter him or sway his resolve. Every instinct he possessed told him Glenna was inside and in desperate need.

The unlatched door gave way beneath Kane's hand as he boldly stepped inside, closing the door soundlessly behind him. His nose led him to the stove where a savory stew bubbled on a back burner. But the person he yearned for most in the world was nowhere in sight. And then a low moaning sound caused the hair to raise on the back of his neck. He halted in mid-step, listening intently, his keen ears noting again the distressed sound coming from the other side of the bedroom door. Fear released his feet as he immediately recognized the feminine voice. Glenna!

Racing into the bedroom, his eyes slid to a stop on Glenna's slight form thrashing and rolling around in the rumpled bed. She had thrown the covers aside and Kane was dismayed to find her completely nude, her flushed skin glistening wetly with beads of perspiration.

"Glenna! Darling!"

She appeared immune to her surroundings as well as his voice and, driven by fear and anxiety, Kane rushed to her side. Beneath the unhealthy flush of fever her skin waxed deathly pale, and he could see that precious pounds seemed to have melted off her already sparse frame. How long had she lain like this? Kane wondered distractedly as he tucked the blanket snugly about her shoulders. And who had provided the meat for the stewpot simmering on the stove?

"Glenna," Kane repeated frantically, hoping to rouse her from her stupor. "Answer me, darling. How long have you been sick? Have you been alone all this time?"

Glenna moaned and stirred, his well-loved voice coming to her as if from a great distance. A voice she recognized but seemed unable to respond to. Her eyes were heavy—so heavy. And the energy needed for coherent speech somehow eluded her. Yet she knew if she failed to answer he might disappear.

"Kane." Her voice emerged thin and reedy and Kane's heart thumped wildly in his chest. She sounded so weak, so dreadfully ill.

"What happened, my love? How did you escape the fire? How did you get here?" He knelt beside the bed, tenderly brushing damp tendrils of red hair from her fevered brow.

"Move away from her, mister, and do it real slow."

Kane swiveled in the direction of the gruff voice and froze. His agile mind registering the fact that a rifle was aimed directly at him by an apparition from out of nowhere. Though no longer young, the old-timer's hand was steady and unwavering. Kane wisely decided the man meant business and slowly stepped aside after casting a worried glance at Glenna. She needed him alive, not dead, which he was likely to end up if he disobeyed the grizzled stranger's terse order.

"Who are you?" Kane asked, eyeing the cocked rifle warily. "What are you doing here with Glenna?"

"I was about to ask you the same question. Do ye know the little missy?" Ben asked sharply.

"Of course, she's my wife." It wasn't exactly true but close enough. "We have a son."

"Be his name Danny?"

"Yes, how did you know?"

"The little missy called out his name often enough in her delirium. She also kept repeating another name," Ben said, eyeing Kane shrewdly.

"Would that name be Kane?"

Ben's lined face sagged into a mass of wrinkles as he lowered the rifle. "I take it yer Kane. Me name's Ben." A lopsided grin hung on one corner of his bewhiskered mouth as he offered Kane his hand. "Ye understand I had to make sure afore I could trust ya."

Kane nodded. All the tension drained from his body as a great surge of relief left him feeling dangerously weak. Thank God he had provided the old man with the correct answers. Anxiously his eyes returned to Glenna. "What's wrong with my wife and how did you come to be here with her?"

"One question at a time, young fella," Ben growled cantankerously. " 'Pears to me ye aughta take better care of yer woman. And her a mother. What was she doing roaming in the woods all by herself? And how did she get hurt?"

"Hurt!" Kane exclaimed anxiously. "Maybe you'd better explain first. Just where did you find Glenna?"

"I just told you," came Ben's exasperated reply. "I found her wandering in the woods dressed as a lad. Thought she was one, too. She sported a knot on her head as big as a goose egg and seemed a mite confused. She kept insisting her pa was waiting fer her out here."

"Her father is dead."

"I found that out later. When I first met the little missy she seemed so bad off I hadn't the heart to leave her so I offered her a ride on old Betsy. When we got here we said our goodbyes and I went on my way. Only later I got to thinking how deserted the cabin looked and how sick the 'lad' appeared. Got to worrying and returned the next day. Found out soon enough that the lad was a lass, and a mighty sick one at that. I been taking care of her ever since."

"Did she say how she was injured?"

"She ain't said much of anything that made sense. Do you know?"

Kane shook his head. "It could have happened during her escape from that burning shack she was locked in."

"Gawd!" exclaimed Ben, his eyes wide with dismay as well as incredible anger. "Who would do such a thing to that sweet little gal?"

"Kane."

The sound of Glenna's feeble voice caused both men to fall silent. Instantly Kane dropped to his knees as Glenna's feverish green eyes struggled to focus on him.

"I'm here, my love," Kane assured her. "I'll take care of you. You must get well, Danny needs you."

The vague shadow of a smile tilted her lips. "Danny," she sighed wistfully. Just saying the name lent her a certain strength.

"Do ye think ye can eat, missy?" Ben asked, stepping into view. "I've got a tasty rabbit stew simmering on the stove. Yer man can feed ya."

Glenna nodded weakly. She did feel hungry. Ben moved with alacrity, returning almost instantly with a steaming bowl of the savory concoction he had painstakingly prepared for her. To Kane's chagrin Glenna could eat little more than a spoonful or two, but it was a beginning. Afterwards she drifted off to sleep.

"Let her be," Ben urged, guiding a reluctant Kane from the room. "Sleep is the best healer."

"What is wrong with her?" Kane asked when they were seated at the table eating their own dinner.

"Fever," Ben replied tersely. "Seen lots of them in all my years. Only the little missy was sicker than most. That head injury weren't doing her no good neither."

"I don't know how to thank you, Ben. If it wasn't for you Glenna would probably have died."

"Hell, son," blustered Ben, embarrassed. "I'da done the same fer anyone. But that little gal in there is special to me. She's got spunk. I washed her like she were a newborn babe and carried her into the crick when her fever nearly burned her alive."

"You washed her?" Kane stiffened indignantly, suddenly recalling that Glenna lay nude beneath the quilt. "You undressed her?" He jumped to his feet, sending the chair crashing to the floor.

"Whoa, young fella," Ben cautioned, outrage bringing storm clouds to his eyes. "If yer thinking what I think yer thinking, I aughta punch you in the nose!"

The thought of the old man punching him was so ludicrous Kane's lips twisted in a parody of a smile. "That little missy could be the daughter I never had. Don't you go saying I'd do anything to harm her."

"Sorry, Ben," Kane muttered sheepishly. "For a minute there I couldn't think straight. It's just that I love Glenna so damn much I'd kill anyone who'd hurt her."

A full day passed before Glenna was coherent enough to give a full accounting of all that happened to her since Duke kidnapped her from her hotel room. Both Ben and Kane were amazed at her resourcefulness and courage.

"I nearly went mad with grief when I thought you had died in that blaze," Kane informed her, a mysterious moisture gathering in the corners of his eyes. "As for Duke, you no longer need worry about him."

"Kane! You didn't! Is he—?"

"I didn't kill him, Glenna, but I should have. Marshal Bartow took him down to Pueblo and turned him over to the law. By now I imagine he's confessed to having Judd killed and murdering Wiley Wilson as well as kidnapping you."

"You know he killed Wiley?" Glenna asked.

"I reached Denver several days ago. Bartow filled me in on all the details."

"How did you get here so soon? I expected days to pass before anyone even suspected I wasn't on the train that morning."

"You have some good friends in Denver, my love. I was on the Union Pacific the same day Duke kidnapped you. Both Sal and Bartow suspected something had happened to you only hours after your disappearance."

"I had no idea you were out of jail already. James's wire said only that you were to be released."

"Another stroke of luck. James worked tirelessly

to have me released without delay once I was proven innocent. I had barely walked through the door of Morgan Manor when Bartow's telegram arrived."

"We've so many things to be grateful for, Kane," Glenna sighed happily. "And Ben is one of them."

"Why didn't you return to Denver, darling?" Kane puzzled. "It's strange that you should come to Golden Promise."

"Truth to tell, Kane, I remember little or nothing that happened after I jumped from the burning roof. I do recall meeting Ben and for some unknown reason a strange compulsion drove me to Golden Promise."

"It was a natural instinct, darling," Kane assured her comfortingly. "But all that is over now and nothing matters but getting you well. Danny needs you. Hell, I need you!"

Under Kane's expert care, Glenna recovered rapidly. For a reason known only to Ben, the old prospector delayed his leaving, choosing to sleep in an outbuilding so as not to disturb the lovers. While Kane patiently performed the mundane chores of caring for Glenna as well as simple housekeeping, Ben provided game for the table and did the cooking. When time permitted the experienced prospector did some panning and explored upcreek from Golden Promise. One day he returned in a state of excitement. He had found a large chunk of float.

"Lookee here!" he exclaimed, showing off his treasure to Kane. "There's a rich lode around here somewhere. 'Pears to be a lot of silver in this here float."

"There is," Kane agreed knowingly. "Glenna had it assayed in Denver. Thus far no one has been able to locate the lode although plenty have tried."

"Do ye think Glenna's pa found the lode?"

"I think he found it and eventually died for it. But

it's not on Golden Promise. Paddy O'Neill staked another claim a mile or so upstream and that's where we think the lode is located. But months of searching have failed to unearth it."

"Do ye mind if I try me luck?" Ben asked. "I'd consider it a privilege to find the mother lode for the little missy."

The next day Ben moved to Promise Two. He loaded up old Betsy and left, promising to report back in a few days, before Kane and Glenna returned to Denver.

Glenna swift recovery was nothing short of miraculous. No longer was it necessary for her to rest long hours in bed. She went for short walks, performed simple household tasks, and after Ben left, prepared the meals Kane provided. But they had yet to attempt lovemaking. Kane considered her still too weak for such strenuous activity. Glenna thought otherwise. After supper one night she set out to prove just how far she had progressed in the last few days under Kane's tender care.

"Come along, darling, I'll see you to bed," Kane smiled, holding the lantern high to light her way. Since her illness he had been sleeping in the other bedroom so as not to disturb her rest.

Carefully he sat the lamp on the nightstand and turned to kiss her goodnight; that was all that he had allowed himself these past days. Glenna slid eagerly into his arms, her body melting into his. Deliberately withholding the full brunt of his passion, Kane struggled to maintain his meager control when he felt her soft roundness pressing intimately against the hard wall of his chest. It had been weeks since he and Glenna had made love and he needed her, sending his well-intentioned resolutions in desperate disarray. But he would sooner suffer the pains of hell than bring harm to her by giving full rein to his baser urges.

Carried away by her own hungry response to Kane's innocent kiss, Glenna failed to notice his lack of ardor. Her whole being was consumed with a terrible wanting and she was driven by a sense of urgency that effectively transmitted her silent entreaty to Kane. He broke off the kiss and gazed at her in avid anticipation. The question behind his probing gaze conveyed itself to Glenna as intent gray eyes traveled over her face, searching for an answer. The smoldering flames he discovered in the emerald green depths were sparked by desire so intense it startled him.

"Are you certain?" he asked hopefully. "You know I'd do nothing to hurt you. Just say the word and I'll leave you alone."

"I'd never make it through the night if you left me now," Glenna murmured in a throaty whisper. Her body ached for his magic touch. For days she'd dreamed of being crushed within his strong embrace, devoured by his special brand of ardor.

The world spun slowly, time seeming to halt as he moved unconsciously to where Glenna stood waiting, and he pulled her close. His large hand took her face and held it gently, his gaze a soft caress. His mouth covered hers hungrily, his tongue tracing the soft fullness of her lips. Knowingly he touched the pulsing hollow at the base of her throat, then seared a path over her neck and shoulders. When his mouth returned repeatedly to hers she responded with reckless abandon, stunning him with the force of her passion. He swept her, weightless, into his arms and gently eased her down onto the smooth surface of the bed.

With trembling hands he unbuttoned her blouse, his fingers icy, but his palm fiery hot. God, it had been so long! He fondled one small globe, its pink nipple marble hard. Then gently he took first one and then the other into his mouth, suckling eagerly as his hands seared a path across her silken belly. Glenna whimpered, aching to feel his bare skin against her own burning flesh. She tore at the buttons on his shirt and he chuckled, his voice low and seductive.

"Greedy little wench, aren't you?"

"Ummm," murmured Glenna, nuzzling her neck, inhaling his clean, slightly musky odor.

Kane slid her dress over her hips and down her legs, tossing it aside carelessly. Her chemise followed. Then he shifted his weight and swiftly rid himself of his own restrictive clothing, reveling in the feel of her breasts against his hair-roughened chest. He paused to kiss her again, whispering his love for each part of her body. The stroking of his fingers sent pleasurable jolts through her as his hands explored the soft lines of her waist, her hips, her inner thighs. She writhed beneath him, eager to touch his skin in order to bring him the same kind of pleasure he was giving her.

Capturing her hands, Kane led them to his hardening flesh, gasping aloud when they stroked gently in a motion he had taught her long ago. Her lips found his male nipples and she suckled gently, much in the same way he had done to her. The tiny nubs hardened against her tongue, and she reveled in her ability to bring him pleasure.

"Enough, my love," he groaned as if in agony, "else our night will end before it begins. Lay back and let me love you."

No part of her body was sacrosanct as he stroked, kissed, licked and suckled, using his hands, mouth and tongue with an expertise born of his great love for this one particular woman. He devoured her, consumed her with his passion, until it grew too hot to contain.

"Now, Kane, please!" Glenna begged raggedly. "I want to feel you inside me." But to Glenna's chagrin he was far from done with her.

Compulsively his fingers slid through the soft curls between her thighs, finding the pulsing center of her as he eased up inside her, gently, insistently bringing her to the peak of ecstasy with his stroking fingers before allowing their bodies to merge. A cry was wrenched from her throat as his erotic manipulations sent her soaring. When he felt the vibrations begin deep inside her hot core he spread her legs and thrust eagerly. She rose to meet him in a burst of unbridled passion. His hardness electrified her and she couldn't control the shriek of delight that slid past her throat. Tendrils of liquid fire radiated from the soft core of her body just before she careened to an awesome, shuddering ecstasy. His pace quickened, his breath was ragged, his own release imminent. Glenna was vaguely aware of Kane's hoarse groans and his own thunderous climax as he joined her in her sublime journey to completion.

Shortly before dawn a dazzling display of lightning blazed across the black night; then deep thunder rolled over the countryside, rattling the shutters and awakening the lovers from their contented slumber. At first Kane was inclined to ignore the approaching tempest, but it became increasingly evident that this was no mere thunderstorm destined to dump a few inches of rain on the ground and move quickly on. A wind strong enough to set the shutters banging drove Kane from the comfort of his bed as he shut and fastened them in swift order, noticing as he did how the trees bent nearly to the ground beneath the terrible onslaught of the storm.

"What is it, Kane?" Glenna asked, rousing groggily from a drugged sleep.

"Just a storm, darling. The shutters were banging and I fastened them."

"It sounds like more than just a storm," Glenna shuddered, snuggling against Kane to soak up his warmth.

No sooner had she uttered the words than the sound of falling trees crashing to the ground echoed above the howling wind, followed closely by a tattoo of pinecones on the roof. To Glenna's sleep-drugged mind it sounded as if the roof had fallen in and she clutched at Kane in horror.

"It's all right, love," Kane soothed. "The storm will soon pass. Your father built a sturdy cabin that will likely be standing a hundred years from now."

Wind-driven rain pelted the cabin, the wind rose dangerously, and all around them came the sound of trees being uprooted. Inside, cozy and warm, Glenna complained worriedly. "I can't help being scared, Kane. I don't remember a storm this severe in all my days spent at Golden Promise."

"I know of a surefire way to take your mind off the storm," Kane grinned wickedly.

Glenna's green eyes sparkled in response. "Do you think it would work? I'm very frightened, Kane. It would take a lot to distract me."

"I'm willing to try," came Kane's amused murmur. "I've had no complaints lately on my prowess in bed."

"And who besides me have you tried to impress?" Glenna asked with mock anger. "Since when have they provided women to man in jail?"

"Minx! You know damn well there's been none but you since the first day I laid eyes on you. You cast your spell on me and I haven't been the same since. I love you."

"Then prove it, Kane," Glenna urged huskily, her eyes smoldering with inner fire.

The storm continued, the wind whistled around the corners and rattled the shutters. Lightning and rain wreaked havoc on Mother Nature. But Glenna was aware of none of it as Kane wove a web of love and passion around her that kept her pleasantly distracted for hours.

* * *

"I wonder how Ben fared in the storm last night?" Glenna asked as she stood staring out the window. Except for the uprooted trees scattered amidst those left still standing and debris littering the clearing, no trace of the fierce storm remained. The morning dawned sparkling clear, all whitewashed, bright and sweet-smelling.

"Do you feel up to a short trip?" Kane asked impulsively. "We could take a ride up to Promise Two and see for ourselves how Ben weathered the storm."

"Yes, let's do!" Glenna clapped eagerly. "I know we'll be leaving in a day or two and I'd like another look around before we go. Do you think we'll ever come back here again?"

"Sooner than you think," Kane returned cryptically. Glenna slanted him a curious look which prompted him to add, "I don't intend to spend the rest of my life tied behind a desk in James's bank. I've grown to love the west. If it's agreeable to you we can return to Philadelphia, collect our son and eventually settle in Denver."

Glenna's face lit up as an enchanted smile touched her lips—then quickly faded. Kane had neglected to mention a matter dear to her heart.

"What is it, love. Aren't you happy about living in Denver?" Kane asked when he noticed her preoccupied frown. "I thought—"

"Oh, no, Kane, it's not that," Glenna was quick to explain. "It's just that I can no longer live with you. It isn't fair to Danny. People will talk about us living together and the talk is bound to hurt our son."

"What in the hell are you babbling about, Glenna? A wife belongs with her husband. And how could our living together possibly do any harm to our son?"

"Wife? But you never said—"

"Why would I need to explain something that's been understood since the day we met? We should have been man and wife months ago. I'm going to marry you the moment we get back to town. Marshal Bartow and his wife can act as witnesses. You'll not escape me so easily."

"Oh, Kane, I love you so! I don't know what I did to deserve a man like you."

"You were born, darling. Since that moment you were mine."

Riding double on the pinto's back, Kane and Glenna approached the crude cabin hastily erected on Promise Two by Judd's men. Old Betsy was tethered nearby so they knew Ben couldn't be far away. Evidence of last night's ferocious storm lay scattered about the area in the form of uprooted trees and chunks of splintered wood from the sluice and rocker Ben had put into use. Of Ben there was no sign. A quick search of the premises revealed that the old prospector had been there earlier so they took their search farther upcreek, following the stream on foot.

At the foot of a rocky ridge high above the creek, Kane chanced to glance up and saw Ben standing on the very edge, looking thunderstruck. Cupping his hands to his mouth Kane called Ben's name. Though the sound echoed and re-echoed from ridge to ridge, Ben appeared beyond hearing.

"Is he addled?" Glenna asked worriedly. "He has to have heard you."

Kane shrugged and tried again. This time Ben responded in a strange manner that strongly suggested he might have lost his mind. Jumping up and down and gesturing frantically, Ben managed to convey the message that he wanted them to join him.

"Come on, darling," Kane urged, grasping Glenna's hand. "I don't know what the old coot wants but he certainly appears excited."

Scrambling up the steep incline, it took Kane and Glenna half an hour to reach Ben's side, panting and gasping for breath.

"Saints be praised, missy, yer pa was right," Ben wheezed, his eyes sparkling with barely contained excitement. "It was here all along, right in front of everyone's noses. Only they were too stupid to see it. Almost missed it meself. But the storm last night gave up the secret that had eluded all but yer pa fer centuries."

"Whatever are you talking about, Ben?" Glenna demanded to know.

"The lode, little missy! The mother lode!"

"You found it?" A cry of incredible joy broke from her lips.

"It's here, all right, missy," nodded Ben eagerly.

"Where, Ben?" Kane bubbled excitedly.

"Look yonder at that uprooted tree," Ben pointed gleefully. The tree he designated was huge, its roots sticking out of the ground at least six feet above them, creating a deep crater. But it was not to the gaping hole that Ben called their attention. It was to the ridge upon which he had been standing a short time ago. When the tree crashed to earth a section of the rocky surface split open, revealing a startling phenomenon. Bright rays of sunlight caught the unmistakable sparkle of gold and conveyed it to their stunned eyes.

"Sink yer mineshaft on that ridge and I'll guarantee ye'll find the richest vein of silver this side of the rockies," Ben danced gleefully from one foot to another.

"Silver?" croaked Glenna, finding words difficult. "That looks like gold to me."

"Sure is, little missy," Ben nodded agreeably. "But see that dark blue color surrounding the streaks of gold? That's silver. My guess is that once a load is taken to the smelter both gold and silver will be found imbedded in the rock. And I believe the assayer will agree with me that the silver will prove of greater value to the ton than the gold."

"Your father certainly knew what he was talking about, Glenna," Kane said in an awed voice.

"I'd say he knew exactly where the lode was," Ben interjected. "When I examined the rocky surface of the ridge I found places where several large pieces had been chisled off. My guess is that he broke off those chunks to have assayed. Through the years smaller fragments broke off for one reason or another and washed into the creekbed. That explains the float you found."

"A lot of people have died because of this lode," Glenna remarked thoughtfully.

"Yer rich beyond yer wildest dreams, missy," Ben beamed widely.

"Probably," Glenna agreed, "but somehow it doesn't matter anymore. I have all I want in Kane and our son. I don't need any more riches."

Ben scratched his shaggy head in bewilderment while Kane stood with his arm curled around Glenna's tiny waist, an enigmatic smile hovering at the corner of his mouth.

"It's yer property, missy," Ben shrugged doubtfully. "I guess ye can do what pleases ya. As fer me, I'll be on me way now. Old Betsy's getting a mite anxious, what with staying in one place so long."

Kane placed a restraining hand on Ben's arm. "Not yet, old timer. We've got some settling up to do."

While Kane and Ben talked quietly, Glenna wandered over to the silver bearing rock, staring at it as if in a trance. Curiosity took her steps on a path parallel to the trunk of the fallen tree, following it aimlessly until she abruptly came to the gnarled roots which had been ripped from the ground during last night's storm. Absently, she looked up, blinked, then peered skyward again. Hundreds of twinkling stars mirrored the sun's reflection, only it was daytime and they weren't stars at all. Intermingled in the tangled roots of the tree were countless nuggets of pure gold. Everywhere she looked a golden treasure nestled and clung to the dirt and twisted vines.

Gasping in sheer incredulity, she screeched, blinked and screeched again. "Kane! Ben! Come quickly!"

A solid lump of fear rose in Kane's throat. His first thought was that Glenna had been bitten by a snake. All his senses sent danger signals to his brain as he sprinted to Glenna's side, Ben close on his heels.

"Saints preserve us!" squawked Ben, screeching to an abrupt halt. "I done died and gone to heaven." He gawked stupidly at the amazing sight that met his eyes.

Kane's mouth flopped open, adequately expressing his shock. "I never saw so many nuggets in one place in all my life."

Kane's words served to release Ben's frozen wits as he snatched off his hat and eagerly began filling it with nuggets. When his hat was full he removed his jacket, tied the sleeves together and used it as a container for more of the treasure. Then he stuffed his pockets until he could barely move from the weight. Laughing at the old prospector's antics, Kane offered his own hat, which Ben gratefully accepted. When no other container presented itself he continued gathering the golden fruit, piling it on the ground while Kane and Glenna stood back, shaking with laughter until they thought their sides would split.

Finally Ben halted out of sheer exhaustion. "Don't stop yet, Ben," Kane teased. "Everything you can load on your mule and horse belongs to you."

Ben shook his shaggy head, refusing to believe Kane's careless words. His rheumy eyes shifted from Kane to Glenna. "This belongs to yer woman. Ain't none of it mine."

"It is now, Ben," confirmed Glenna, backing

Kane's decision wholeheartedly. "It's little enough payment for saving my life. Take all you can carry with our blessing."

Ben choked back a sob as he wiped at the moisture gathering in the corners of his eyes. "It's too much, missy. I don't deserve it."

"It's not enough, Ben."

Two days later Kane rode away from Golden Promise with Glenna seated comfortably in the saddle before him, his arms encircling her in a loving embrace. They left Ben behind still filling sacks with gold nuggets and loading them on old Betsy. He promised to follow them to Denver in a day or two where he intended to bank most of his fortune and live out the rest of his days like a king, residing close enough to the little missy and her man to become a grandfather to little Danny and the children that were sure to follow.

The hour was early, the sun warm and bright, and all was right with the world. Tomorrow they would be man and wife and Glenna nurtured a secret belief that their idyll at Golden Promise had resulted in another pregnancy. Of course it was far too early to mention her premonition to Kane. He might think her foolish. But the feeling lingered nevertheless. She hoped it would be a girl this time. A sister for Danny.

"Have you decided what to do with your claims?" Kane asked, breaking into her pleasant ruminations.

"Are you certain you want it to be my decision?"

"It's yours, darling. To do with what you want. You're my Golden Promise. You're all I want or need to make my life complete."

"Then I want to sell Promise Two," Glenna startled him by revealing. "Too many sad memories are associated with it for my liking. We can sell it to one of those big eastern mining companies that are moving to Denver in droves. The money can be put into a trust fund for our children. But I couldn't bear to part with Da's original claim. I have nothing but fond recollections of the place."

"Such as?" Kane prompted.

"It was the first real home I can remember and you and I loved there for the first time. Our children were conceived in that cabin."

"Children?" questioned Kane, one eyebrow tilted in amusement.

"I know it's too early, darling, but I'm certain our loving these past few days will bear more precious fruit than mere gold or silver."

"Are you a seer?" Tender teasing colored his words.

"No, but a woman knows these things," she sniffed, undaunted.

"Do you plan on presenting me with a child every year?"

A sweet, seductive smile curved Glenna's generous lips, her answer completely entrancing Kane. "Only for the first three years. After that it will be purely for pleasure."

Kane's laughter reverberated across the lofty treetops. "My love," he quipped in a sensual whisper, "with you every time is a pleasure. And I plan on devoting the rest of my life to pleasing you."

And so he did.